Patrick Hamilton, universally known as the author of *Rope* (filmed by Alfred Hitchcock), *Gaslight* and *Hangover Square*, was one of the most gifted and admired writers of his generation. Born in Sussex during the first decade of this century, his parents moved shortly afterwards to Hove where he passed his formative years. *Craven House,* his first novel, was published in 1925 and within a few years he had established a wide readership for himself. It seemed as though his reputation was assured, but personal setbacks and an increasing preoccupation with drink overshadowed this certainty. Yet in spite of these pressures he was able to produce some of his best work, the seeds of his own despair almost feeding his vision, where an underlying sense of loss and isolation is felt beneath his tragi-comic creations. He died in 1962.

Craven House

PATRICK HAMILTON

CARDINAL

TO
MY DEAR MOTHER

A *Cardinal* Book

First published in Great Britain by Constable and Co Ltd 1926
Reissued 1943
Reprinted 1945
This edition published in Cardinal by Sphere Books Ltd 1991

Printed in Great Britain by
The Guernsey Press Co Ltd, Guernsey, Channel Islands

ISBN 0 7474 0761 4

Sphere Books Ltd
A Division of
Macdonald & Co (Publishers) Ltd
Orbit House
1 New Fetter Lane
London EC4A 1AR

A member of Maxwell Macmillan Pergamon Publishing Corporation

PREFACE TO THE NEW EDITION

I THINK that this new edition of *Craven House*, in which some alterations have been made from the original version, requires one or two remarks as preface.

In February, 1941, I had a letter from Michael Sadleir (whose firm first published the book in 1926), in which he said:

"I have been re-reading *Craven House*. It is much more congested in its earlier chapters than I had remembered. Your technique was, I suppose, a new experiment in those days, and you were tempted to overdo it. As it gets on it settles down to a more controlled method.

"Of the high spots which I remembered Mr. Spicer's Tramp did not get me as it used to, but the two maids in the kitchen impressed me much more. The little boys were still superb, the tube-journey ditto, and I laughed myself quite silly over the Russian Lady. The book is grand entertainment. If only it was simpler at the beginning! I suppose it's hopeless to ask you to go over it for a new edition. It ought to be a standard thing of its kind, but many readers must have been baffled by the involutions and parentheses of those early chapters."

With this encouragement I re-read the book, which I had not looked into for ten years. I found that less could be done about these faults of style than I had hoped. The book certainly gets better as it goes along, but throughout intermittently it shows traces of the bias I had at that time—the delight in the odd, longer word instead of the direct, simpler one—the long (and at times purely facetious) construction instead of the natural one—the "that lady" instead of "she," the "that gentleman" instead of "he," the "whereupon" instead of "then."

Nevertheless it seemed to me that any attempt to remedy this in a really thoroughgoing manner would destroy the very things which give the book its quality, its gusto, its freshness and its high spirits, which, perhaps, were only able to express themselves in this rather uncouth way. So apart from certain really outrageous passages and certain places where the congestion of style actually clouds the meaning, I have not, purely as regards style, made very many alterations for this edition.

A fault in the book which Michael Sadleir did not mention is its occasional sentimentality. I do not know that that matters much: in a book of this sort a little sentimentality is probably all to the good. What, however, is terrible is a mixture of sentimentality and archness. I imagine there are few authors who do not find things of this sort in their early work—few authors who do not, when reading such passages, slowly redden with shame to the roots of their hair. Needless to say I have tried ruthlessly to delete all such passages, though some may remain without my being aware of it.

Lastly there is the question of a book seriously "dating" after sixteen years—a thing which it might easily not do after six years or sixty. As the first part deals with a period before the last war, it is dated intentionally, and so the question does not arise; and I do not think the latter part reads too awkwardly in this respect. Slightly excited references to "bobbed hair" struck me as being the outstanding example of something about which nothing really effectual can be done in a new edition.

I have spoken of authors slowly reddening to the roots of their hair over *passages* in their early books. Sometimes they do this over their early books from start to finish. Although it was written when I was only twenty-one, I can definitely say that *Craven House* does not come into this class; and that if it can still find readers, I should still like it to be read.

P. H.

Book 1

CHAPTER I

A momentous Evening Dinner in Nineteen Hundred and Eleven: a Little Girl and a Little Boy go to Bed.

I

THE hour after lunch found Keymer Gardens in a state of grey and windless somnolescence. A pause, almost devout, and so unanimous as to have an air of being prearranged, overtook the whole neighbourhood, though there remained an abundance of petty noises. From one or two of the houses there might yet be heard the remote clatter of the washing-up, and from others, where the servants had not already had their meal, the hiss and spit of frying. A sweep was crying in a strained and inconsolable manner from some street far away; little boys and girls were making their way, less unwillingly than with vagrant buoyancy, to school; a maid dashed out to post a letter, and remained talking to a lady at the top of her basement steps. In addition to which the sound of the Southam Green High Road, a quarter of a mile distant, and the sound of all London behind it, beat faintly yet incessantly, like the roar of a waveless sea, upon the inured ears of the inhabitants. Such noises, nevertheless, were unable to disturb the lazy peace manifest in Keymer Gardens. They served, rather, to emphasise the hush.

In this state Keymer Gardens remained for two hours, under a lowering sky; so that towards the end of that time the stillness had amounted to little less than enchantment. But the postman came at last, with no nonsense about him, and he put an end to it. Little front gates shrieked open at his advance: he strode fearlessly up to front doors, played his own curt personality upon them with the knocker expressly supplied for him, and crossed the road briskly to do the same again. By the time his final *"Ta-tat-at"* was muttering at the end of the road, Keymer Gardens was wide awake and ready for tea. And while tea was yet in preparation, the lamp-lighter, a being as noiseless and insinuating as the darkening firmament itself, brought the evening.

Almost at once the atmosphere was charged with life. A motor car, like a flying particle from the mass of noise in the High Road, whirred down the main avenue that passed Keymer Gardens on its way to Kew; and above the noise of the High Road rose the agonised call of the newspaper sellers. Front doors were slammed, kindly footsteps rang through the streets, dogs were summoned by shrill voices, pink lights appeared in cosy dining-room windows, somebody beat a mat maliciously in a garden; factory hooters bewailed urgently, answering each other in vague, wakeful distances; and the District Trains, moaning home to Southam Green Station with greater frequency, brought the first silent batches of men and women from the City, hastening as it were conspiratorially to their homes.

At six o'clock, from Craven House, which was the large house at the corner of Keymer Gardens, a middle-aged woman came out, with a leather shopping bag.

II

Six o'clock was by no means the customary hour for Miss Hatt's shopping, but she had undergone an excessively arduous and dusty day within, preparing for her new guest— the Major (she was calling him the Major already!) and she had told herself that a little breath of fresh air could do her no harm. The notion of a walk for the mere sake of walking, however, though not an unthinkable notion, was a notion simply absent in Miss Hatt's bland mentality. There were such things as Sunday Walks, of course, or strictly Appetising or Digestive Walks, and there were even Lovers' Walks, but all of these could be said to have their own goal, and no other sort of irregular and unlocalised Walks was allowed.

It was, therefore, in some sort of propitiation to these axioms that Miss Hatt had remarked to her cook, Edith, that she would herself go and bring back the Fish. "Because," she said, "you can never trust these people, and I want to get a little fruit, too."

To which Edith had rejoined "Yes'm," under her breath, and without chancing an encounter with Miss Hatt's eyes; for Edith had been for several days cherishing a belief that her mistress had thought twice and better about the fish.

Fish, indeed, as a first course, was an entirely new departure, and as Miss Hatt made towards the High Road, there yet lingered some doubts as to the advisability—nay, safety—of its introduction. She was nevertheless convinced that she was a little too far compromised to withdraw now. When, two days ago, the retired Major Wildman stood taking his leave at the door of Craven House—a captured, though still verbally uncommitted and airy-gestured, paying guest—he remarked, with his winning smile, "I must warn you in time that you would find me a very hearty eater, Miss Ah—Hatt"; and Miss Hatt, already a little intoxicated by her own timid but glib reiterations of the beautiful luck and blessings falling in the course of nature upon a Major taking up residence in such a house, capped the ecstasies of hot water at all times of the day, fires in the bedrooms, hot-water bottles, and three towels changed twice in the week, with the rash and thoughtless promise, "Oh, yes? Well, we have a five-course dinner, you know. That'd be starting with fish, you know . . . and dessert. . . ."

To say that the Major's eyes lit on the utterance of this falsehood would be to put the case in a wrong light, but he murmured "Really?" in a style altogether readable as fervour, and it was only after he had left that Miss Hatt realised to the full the trying implications of her little falling-away.   In the first place there were Mrs. Nixon and her young daughter —her only other guests (as guests)—to be considered.   Mrs. Nixon had hitherto learnt to expect nothing before the joint in the evening fare, and to regard the dessert, as it lay chilly upon the table, more in its traditional and ornamental aspects than otherwise. It would most certainly not do now to let Mrs. Nixon associate the inauguration of a new first course with the appearance of Major Wildman.

Miss Hatt thought she had two weeks' grace, however, and seeing that she must prepare the way for the change at once, had a vague idea that she might cunningly break the news to Mrs. Nixon with, perhaps, a little thin soup one evening; and leading her gracefully on to small portions of, say, *Cauliflower au Gratin* on the next, bring her up through a deft Welsh Rarebit, or soft roes on toast, to Fish. This projected finesse was ruined at the outset, however, by a letter from the Major, saying that he would like to come to Craven House in two days' time. Miss Hatt was thus compelled to choose between the finer shades of her catering honour with

Mrs. Nixon, and her promise to the Major; and she plumped for the Major, as that gentleman, who was bringing his little boy with him to go to school, bid fair to be a Permanent. And though such an expression as Permanent is a very coarse and bitter expression to employ in such a connection, a Permanent was what Miss Hatt desired more than anything else in the world.

Emerging from the dark, aloof silence of the Green that gave its name to the neighbourhood, Miss Hatt came into the Southam Green High Road.

This was as bright and noisy as a fair. The trams thundered down a littered thoroughfare, and the shops glittered and hummed with humanity—humanity bustled at the grocers; deafened at the butchers; brusquely rattled at, with brown paper bags, at the fruiterers; bewildered at the post office; deferred to at the drapers; confidentially advised at the jewellers; curious and handling at the bazaars; limply appealed to from the edge of the pavement; a little sad and tense at the chemists; newly respiring and bravely conversational at the public houses, and everywhere crowded.

Miss Hatt was all at once taken with a mood of contentment verging on exultation. This was partly due to the thick sights and sounds around her, partly to a flowing, nervous relief after a hard day indoors, and partly to the two cups full of tea that she had consumed before coming out.

She felt very contented and very mellow altogether. She was contented in her life—her position—her clean and sturdy house—her new maid, Audrey (a treasure, she believed)—her glittering new pince-nez, which considerably clarified the whole quality of life itself—Major Wildman—Mrs. Nixon—and last, and perhaps least, her two Old Best Friends, Mr. and Mrs. Spicer.

For Mr. and Mrs. Spicer were, and always had been, prominent and inescapable figures in Miss Hatt's life. Indeed, even at school she had been the oldest, best friend of Mrs. Spicer, who was then merely Letty Craik; and she had known Mr. Spicer when he was merely Clifford Spicer, a very humorous young man, and they had all been immense companions and intriguers together. More, she had participated in certain sunny, rare, faded, laughing, Bicycling days, ten years later, when they had all three sped about the country on the most beautiful and lunching-out, if not picnicking, expeditions; and when Mr. Spicer had first commenced certain vague leerings, double meanings, recondite reticences, and similar astonishing mysteries culminating in the selection of a Mrs. Clifford Spicer. In fact, such a very close and intimate friend with Mr. and Mrs. Spicer was Miss Hatt, at this period, that it was almost a matter of inward doubts, from time to time, as to the exact lady in whose favour were the vague leerings, double meanings, recondite reticences, and similar astonishing mysteries.

Time, of course, cleared these doubts in its own way, and the winter following that bicycling summer witnessed the engagement of Clifford Spicer to Letty Craik; and some years later they were married. The connection with Miss Hatt was by no means dropped on this score, however, and in the seven years since that fluttering and pious day, they had happily maintained the trio. It was, indeed, the project of Mr. and Mrs. Spicer staying with her, and so helping with the expenses, that had first induced Miss Hatt to take over Craven House, which would otherwise have been a little too large both for her intentions and her personal funds. It nevertheless remained all her own, and she had furnished it entirely herself.

They had been settled here together for some five months, and it had proved still to be a house rather too large for their needs, when Mr. Spicer had been visited modestly by the idea of Miss Hatt taking paying guests. Even so delicate shirking of the issue as was conveyed in the expression Paying Guest, was distasteful to Mr. and Mrs. Spicer, and Miss Hatt, and was most tremulously dodged. Miss Hatt once went so far as to utter, "Sort of paying *guests*, you know," but it was tacitly regarded as an ill-considered utterance, and Mr. Spicer was content to allude very distantly to an Agreement, an Arrangement, or an Understanding. "Three guineas, or something like that..." murmured Miss Hatt, with shuddering timidity. . . .

It was nevertheless an exceedingly happy inspiration, judged apart from the ecstasy of fertile planning that took place in the drawing-room one night; for it bid fair to solve the Long Evening Problem, which was becoming a very acute and painful problem to Mr. and Mrs. Spicer, and Miss Hatt. For it had taken only three months' residence at Craven House to exhaust the little fund of external entertainment remaining in each other's personality. And though there was the Piano, upon which Mrs. Spicer could deliver an unimpeachable performance to her placid and respectfully alert man; and though there was the Southam Green Empire, to which they paid a weekly visit; and though they sometimes turned the lights down in the drawing-room, and sat about the glowing fire wilfully to exude middle-aged comfort and romance (with an occasional rather ghastly and aghast interlocking of hands from the mated pair), the evenings on the whole were reaching a pitch of *ennui* and amiability almost intolerable—if not positively approaching the danger mark. For one evening the Spicers took their courage into both hands and read a newspaper and a novel for an hour and a half by the clock, like perfect limpets against the bright conversational wrenches of a knitting Miss Hatt; until at last that lady, after poking the fire with an efficiency and rapidity that carried an unquestionable Hint, was driven to say, "Well, then, I'd better be going up to bed, then," to which Mrs. Spicer replied, "Very well, my dear," without raising her eyes. The first cross word between them.

The installation of Mrs. Nixon and her daughter had served to lighten this burden already, though Mrs. Nixon did not allow her little daughter to stay up to dinner, and retired herself soon afterwards. And Major Wildman came this evening, and there were two more rooms to be filled. . . .

Miss Hatt made her way to the fishmongers, where she was treated with curt deference, and where, amidst the bright, glittering dead bodies of the fish, whose morose and blood-streaked heads were even past mute criticism of the outrage done upon them, she watched her own prey, as it was sliced open, with a fascinating virtuosity, for her easier consumption. Emerging without a tremor, she went on further to buy apples and bananas; arranged the goods in her leather shopping bag, lifted her head a little to express finality, and made for home.

She crossed the Green again and passed the large Town Hall on her left. Outside this a bill was displayed, advising the Southam Green public that a free lecture on Theosophy would be delivered next Tuesday in the Houghton Room.

"This really *is* the most wonderful place," thought Miss Hatt. "Really it is. Seven minutes' walk from the High Road. Eight minutes' from the station. The Empire. Buses and trams to anywhere you want. Free Library . . . and now a free lecture. We must go to that. Theosophy . . ."

She pondered, a few moments, in a friendly and detached

way, upon the adventures awaiting her eternal soul. "Theosophy. That's reincarnation, isn't it?" she told herself. Then she wondered whether there would be a silver collection, in which case it would be necessary to fortify oneself with a sixpence.

III

The Major and his little son have arrived. A capacious winter overcoat in the hall, a silk scarf, and a small boy's bowler hat—these the foreboding centre of a little world of silence.

Faintly from the basement come sounds of the oven door slamming, and the servants calling to each other. Then Audrey, the young maid of sixteen, comes up the stairs, and softly as any conspirator, proceeds to set the scene.

She lights the gas in the drawing-room, and stirs the fire. From the little room next door, known as the Study, the parrot mutters "Ladysmith," in a feverish undertone. "What, Polly?" Audrey answers. "Ladysmith, eh?" But there is a hollow ring in her quiet voice, and no reply from the bird.

Audrey then enters the dining-room, lights the gas, and starts to lay the table. When she has finished this, she hears light footsteps running down the stairs and confronts Miss Hatt at the door.

"Oh, Audrey. You managing all right?"

"Yes. Quite all right, ma'am. Thank you, ma'am." She gazes at Miss Hatt, at once dreamy and alert.

"Have you done the table and everything in here?"

"Yes, ma'am. I think you'll find that everything is quite Shipshape," says Audrey, gravely nautical.

"Oh, very well," says Miss Hatt. "Yes. That seems all right. Yes." And then, responding, possibly, to the sailor's atmosphere introduced, she adds, "You'd best be getting down below."

Swift as her mistress's thought, for this is in nineteen hundred and eleven, Audrey runs down to the kitchen.

Miss Hatt remains for a moment to scan the table with her practised eyes, appears to be content, and goes into the drawing-room. Here she stirs the fire, lifts the cover of the piano, opens a large volume of Chopin's works, and lays it upon the stool; brings forth a calf-bound volume of Kipling's Poetry from a little book cabinet, and lays it on the little centre table; removes a dusty calendar, shifts the chairs and the sofa, and performs other homely and artistic details upon a scene guaranteed to charm the retired and widowed military gentleman now upstairs. At this moment she is joined by Mrs. Spicer. Mrs. Spicer differs as much from her old school companion in outward parts as she resembles her in all matters of inward personality. For whereas Miss Hatt is stoutish, with chubby pink cheeks, and the general bearing of a merry sparrow taking the sun, the other lady is skinny and ashen in every particular. They are both short, however, and both wear glittering pince-nez, and both do their hair the same way, and wear the same kind of beads and brooches. And they both have the same merry voice, and they share together an infinite zest and capability for brightly remarking "Oh, dear!" and "Oh, yes!" and "Oh, certainly!" and taking with suspended amiability and delight any matter on earth brought to their notice.

"Ah, Bertha," says Mrs. Spicer, and "Ah, Letty," says Miss Hatt, and there is a pause.

"Come?" risks Mrs. Spicer.

"Yes. Come," says Miss Hatt.

Mrs. Spicer now hears the scratching of her husband's key in the front door, but remains within the room.

As soon as he has closed the door behind him, Mr. Spicer is aware that he intrudes in sanctities of tense anticipation. He puts up his hat and coat with corresponding seriousness, and comes in to the ladies.

"Hullo, my dear," he says to his wife.

"Hullo, dear. So you've come back, have you?"

"Yes. Cold, isn't it? Evening, Bertha."

"Good evening, Clifford," says Miss Hatt, and goes down to the kitchen. Mr. Spicer watches her go, and then comes at once to the point.

"Major?" says Mr. Spicer.

"Oh, yes . . ."

"Little boy? . . ."

"Oh, yes . . ."

Mr. Spicer jumps away again as quickly as possible. "I'm late to-night again, aren't I, dear?"

"Oh, I don't know. Are you? Well, I must be getting up to change."

But Mr. Spicer stands gallantly in the doorway.

"Then what about a little kiss for your husband?" says

Mr. Spicer, and by the way Mr. Spicer says this, and thrusts
forth his head in quizzing defiance of any Majors or any
changings, it is plain that he is exercising one of those Little
Thoughts (possibly old-fashioned) that so enhance his
character. There ensues a moment of tragic abasement for
both. At the end, Mr. Spicer flourishes, and smiles in a very
queer and precarious manner, and Mrs. Spicer, wriggling
friendlily away, murmurs one smiling and simple "Yes" to the
Universe in general. She then goes upstairs to her room.

Mr. Spicer rubs his hands for a little in front of the fire,
stirs the fire, looks about him, handles the volume of Kipling's
Poetry, decides to go upstairs and prepare for dinner, and
does so.

On the first landing he encounters a little boy, all brushed
and washed, coming down the stairs.

"Oh," says Mr. Spicer, and then tries to hit a cheerful
note. "Is that you, then?" he asks.

"Yes," says the little boy. "Rather."

"M'm. Well," begins Mr. Spicer, "we haven't been
introduced, have we?" But he is not able to take the
conversation any further than that, and retreats, with a
courteous snigger or two, into the sanctuary of his room.

His wife is just coming out of this, and here he washes
and brushes himself with great care, and, feeling his tie
with nervous fingers, goes over to the looking-glass to study
himself. So exemplarily unobtrusive in appearance is Mr.
Spicer that to his preoccupied fellow-creatures he seldom
makes himself felt as much more than a large golden tooth,
which keeps brilliant order in this gentleman's otherwise
wearied and interdependent upper row. The looking-glass,
however (as well as sending back fire to fire from that dazzling
beauty) reveals the rest, the man behind the Tooth—a face
pale and rather cadaverous; a nose, after a magnificent bridge,
falling in so long and straight a line to the ram's-horn moustache as to achieve an almost pugilistic effect, and a weak
mouth belying that effect. "Any questions, please?" enquires
Mr. Spicer's nose, and "I think you'll find I can tackle the
greater part of them," add his large blue eyes. His thin
figure has once, with the moustache, had a shot at the 1900
military, but has now fully succumbed to the spirit-breaking
influences of bowler hat and umbrella.

While he is yet gazing at these results, Audrey smashes
at the gong in the hall.

There is a pause, weighty with the significance of the deed. Mr. Spicer draws himself erect, like an actor who hears his cue, and opens the door. But at this moment another and more purposeful door is opened, further up the stairs; so Mr. Spicer is compelled to draw in behind his own again.

The airy, high, pedantic tones of a man's voice come floating down the stairs, along with the familiar but uneasy voice of Mrs. Nixon. The Major and Mrs. Nixon pass Mr. Spicer's landing, and go down into the dining-room. Mr. Spicer again stiffens himself, and runs straight down the stairs after them, to face the music.

The dining-room is a scene of bright and bewildering animation. Miss Hatt is delivering fluttering introductions to right and left, as though it is all the most unheard-of, preposterous, yet humorous situation that could well be imagined. Mrs. Nixon is talking, and the Major is talking, and indeed they are all talking, at and through and regardless of each other—with the exception of Audrey, whose baffled and delighted smile betokens the brilliant response of her receptive soul to whatever conditions her betters originate. Then Mr. Spicer appears, and there is a silence.

"Oh," says Mrs. Spicer. "You haven't met my husband, have you?"

"Good evening, Major," says Mr. Spicer, and comes forward with a frank smile to give the Major a hand-shake which reveals the man, and is plainly unconscious of its own male strength. "Good evening," says the Major, and "No . . ." says Mrs. Spicer to the Universe. And then, "Will you sit here, Major Wildman?" says Miss Hatt. "And perhaps your son'll sit opposite you, over there. Yes. Very well, Audrey."

Audrey rushes out into the hall, whence, a moment later, the fatal fish first course may be heard distantly clinking on its way forward; Mr. Spicer asks the Major whether he has "got here all right," and the Major replies in easy tones. Master Wildman—a child at present in little less than a trance state, wrought by a large golden tooth—climbs up on to his chair, and Mrs. Nixon is about to seat herself, when her daughter makes a highly agitating proposition.

"Will I say Grace, please, mother?" she asks.

"Oh," says Mrs. Nixon. "Yes, Elsie, certainly."

Master Wildman slides off his seat, and meets the eyes of his father, who is almost as scared as himself. Elsie arranges herself primly behind her chair, and closes her eyes.

Her prayer neither includes nor alludes to the assembled company. "For what I am about to receive," she says, "may the Lord make me truly thankful. Amen." The others, nevertheless, square up to this unforeseen allusion to the Source of All, and stand erectly fervent. The little girl then takes the lead by sitting down, the others follow her, and with Mr. Spicer murmuring a hazy something about Nice Little Habits, Dinner commences.

Mr. Spicer, by way of demonstrating that all respects due to original guests are to be upheld in face of any new arrival, shoots off with his usual napkin question to Mrs. Nixon. "Been out to-day, Mrs. Nixon?"

Mrs. Nixon's eyes are resting, without expression, upon the fish. She looks up to reply, and is not surprised to find a certain distant fishiness in the glance awaiting her, but she talks it quickly away. "Yes, Mr. Spicer. I've been taking Elsie for a long walk to-day."

"Oh, good. We have some very nice walks around these parts, Major. Are you a good walker?"

"Quite good, yes. I generally manage to get in about six miles a day, some way or another."

"Really? That's a good deal."

"Yes. . . . Unless it rains, of course. In which case," says the Major with a charming smile, "I do not issue forth."

"No. Not worth it then, is it?" says Mrs. Spicer, and "No," says Mr. Spicer, and gives a little laugh in the pause that follows. "How's Elsie to-night?"

"Very well, thank you, Mr. Spicer."

"Good. Staying up to-night, then?"

"Yes," says Elsie, and fires under the slow gaze of the younger Wildman.

"Yes," says Mrs. Nixon. "She asked to stay up as a treat to-night, so I let her."

"I suppose I ought to have sent my own little boy to bed, but he put forth the same plea," says Major Wildman, and starts in upon his fish with bland and lordly innocence of its implications.

"How old is he, then?" asks Mr. Spicer.

"Only just turned eight."

"Eight? I should have thought he was rather less than that, now." Mr. Spicer puts his head on one side to smile appraisement of an interesting but not absolutely serious appendage to the military man. He then carries the little joke so far as to try it with a question.

"Going to school soon?"

"Yes. Rather."

"I expect you're not looking forward to that," says Mrs. Nixon.

"Yes. Rather," says Master Wildman, who is having a warm time from Elsie's eyes by now.

They all laugh at this. "Well, that's the spirit, isn't it?" says Miss Hatt.

"If they're Nice Chaps," adds Master Wildman, and they laugh again. (Elsie too.)

"Oh, you'll get along finely," Mr. Spicer assures him, and turns confidentially to the Major. "When's he going, then?"

"I'm taking him up to-morrow. Lyndon House, you know. I happen to know the headmaster quite well. And it's in the neighbourhood, and I don't think he can do much better than go there—for the present, anyway."

"Oh, yes. That's Mr. Staines, isn't it? Let me see now, what was it I heard about him? Didn't you tell me something, my dear? Oh, yes. He makes the boys into prefects —like a public school, you know. All responsible for each other. Very good system, I should think. I expect you'll soon be a prefect, won't you?"

"Rather."

"Not just at first, though," says Mrs. Nixon.

"No."

"A perfect prefect, eh?" suggests Mr. Spicer. "Or a prefect perfect, which is it?"

At which sally the children are immensely tickled.

"What about a Little Claret to-night, Bertha?" says Mr. Spicer, with the air of a man surpassing himself.

"Yes, that's just what *I* was thinking," returns Miss Hatt, and refuses a meeting with a pair of eyes belonging to Mrs. Nixon, who was not, on her own commencement night, accorded any such rich celebrations as these. "Do you know where it is, Audrey? Very well. Bring on the chicken first, and then go down."

Audrey lays the chicken upon the table with careless haste, for its consequence is altogether dwarfed by this new feature, leaves the room, and returns a few minutes later (to a silent and respectful company), like a flushed herald of great tidings, bottle in hand.

"Thank you, Audrey," says Miss Hatt, with a detachment which does not deceive, and "Glasses, please, Audrey," whispers Miss Hatt. "In the cupboard,"—while the Major looks on with his own style of complacence.

The bottle and glasses are laid by Audrey quietly in front of the originator of the scheme. Mr. Spicer stands up to withdraw the cork; there is an alarming moment in which a contumacious cork appears to have bettered a reddened Mr. Spicer, a lobster-like Mr. Spicer; a good pop; and Mr. Spicer is pouring the wine, a little in favour of Mrs. Nixon, but otherwise with meticulous equity.

"Let me see, you *don't* take wine, do you, Elsie?" he asks, by way of another joke.

"No, I think *not*," Mrs. Nixon replies.

"Nor you, sir?"

"No," says the Major. "I should not like to witness the results if he did."

And so the dinner goes on. Mr. Spicer tells them that he himself does not indulge himself in this way frequently, but just as he can be trusted not to exceed himself in the way of a Little Smoke, or a Little Bet, so he is not against a Little Something, on occasions. And the others fully subscribe to this doctrine of moderation, and keep the ball rolling by stretching and endorsing each other's views for an unbelievably long time. Miss Hatt, like some trim and willing little craft, veering in the lightest wind of the conversation, keeps one roving eye upon the plates, and ever and anon whispers parenthetically to Audrey, who is standing by her side, and whose hair is becoming a little loose and bedraggled, but who shares in the conversation with undaunted zest—her smile and receptive eyes flashing from one speaker to another continuously. And so the chicken goes out, and the Rice Pudding comes in.

The first definite omen of the wine having paid a call at Mr. Spicer's head would be a little difficult to hit upon, but it does so without a doubt, though at no time does it engender much more than a certain swashbuckling attitude towards the children in this middle-aged gentleman. Perhaps it really begins when, after nodding, in a rather distrait silence, to a vivid description, by the Major, of a hot Bengal night, he asks, in a bald and sudden manner, "What's your son's Christian name, then?"—a question imperfectly relevant to the foregoing description.

"Oh, he's a Henry," the Major replies.

"Henry, eh? Well, that's a very nice name. What do you think of your own name, eh, Henry?"

"Very nice," says Master Wildman.

"I'm not a Henry; I'm a William."

"Yes," says Mrs. Spicer. "You're a William Clifford, aren't you?"

"Yes. That's right. William Clifford Spicer. What do you think of that?" he says, playing up to the little boy's grin.

"Jolly nice," says Master Wildman.

"Yes. William Clifford Spicer. It's strange how one's name *comes*, isn't it, Major? Spicer, for instance. I suppose my ancestors must have been——" he pauses to deliberate the matter—"sort of—*Spicers*. Spice, you know. Must have dealt in *spice*, or something like that."

"Ah, yes. Possibly," says the Major.

"Yes, it's funny—how they Come," says Mrs. Spicer, and there is a heavy pause.

"Merchants," tries Mr. Spicer, but does no better with that. . . .

There is another pause.

Elsie comes to our rescue. "Please, mother," says Elsie, looking at her mother, who is a sort of public censoring office for her daughter's remarks, through which they have to pass, and fail or survive for the consideration of the diners, according to her decision—"please, mother, if Mr. Spicer's ancestors were Spicers, I suppose Major Wildman's—would be sort of—Wild Men—wouldn't they?"

The little boy immediately falls into a stifled but riotous spasm of amusement, and then the others laugh outright.

"Yes, I think that's more than possible," says the Major.

"And Mrs. Nixon's," offers Master Wildman, looking at that lady. "Must have been *Nixes*!"

Whereupon both children begin to splutter and redden to a dangerous extent, in an effort to control themselves at the thought of Mrs. Nixon's forbears having once been Nixes, whatever they take that to mean. There are also further indefinite spluttering noises, from which the word "Hat" does not emerge, but does very nearly do so.

"You're getting quite witty to-night," says the Major, and they all wait for the young people to pull themselves round, which the young people are as yet unable to do.

"There, that'll do," says Mrs. Nixon, and Elsie becomes immediately grave, but catches Master Wildman's eye again, and is off.

"Got the giggles," says Mrs. Spicer.

"I said that will do, Elsie," says Mrs. Nixon, and her voice and eyes are so level as to be unmistakable in their portent.

"Ah, well—boys will be boys, won't they, Major," says Mr. Spicer, and dinner is resumed. The conversation, however, lacks its first alert zest, for by the time the rice pudding is done with, the diners have stuffed down pretty well all they can, and are waiting heavily for the conclusion of the meal. But the dessert, if only to denote Miss Hatt's willingness to give, and the guests' burden to receive, their full money's worth, has to be gone through with. There is, as well, from the guests' point of view, the danger of creating a false precedent by abandoning it on the first night. It is therefore Master Wildman alone, who, with a directness denied to his elders, wriggles in his seat, and gazes around, with all the uneasiness of the overloaded.

There is a slight rally a little later, however, the conversation turning, somehow or other, into a discussion of Seasickness and its remedies. The Major claims that he has been one of five down to dinner on a liner; Miss Hatt declares that she is invariably sick upon the sea; Mrs. Nixon holds out for Mothersills; and Mr. Spicer explains that though he is a "very good Sailor as a rule," he has once succumbed, and proceeds to describe that instance in a manner escaping the lurid by a hair's breadth. There is then a long and thoughtful pause —a pause in which the children can be heard starting a smacking attack at their oranges—a pause in which Miss Hatt stares in front of her, lost to all the world—a pause in which Mrs. Nixon looks idly at her daughter, and Mrs. Spicer idly at the Major's fingers, which are idly engaged in pressing together the last crumbs of his bread for a final morsel—a pause which is broken eventually by Master Wildman who, thinking, perhaps, that it is up to him to say something to his new little friend, addresses Elsie gravely with the direct question, "Do you go to school?" To which Elsie replies, "No, but I'm going soon, aren't I, mother?" To which her mother replies, "Yes, my dear! Very soon now." Whereupon the sympathetic gentleman at the top of the table remarks, "We all have to go to school, don't we, Elsie? *Nuis*ance, isn't it?"

There is another pause after this, and then a little more conversation, and then another pause, which is again cut into by Master Wildman with another remark, over his orange, to Elsie, to whom he seems rather to have taken. "I can show you a Joke, afterwards," says Master Wildman, gravely, "if you like." "A Joke?" says Elsie. "Yes. A Joke with your Name," says Master Wildman, and the company is all ears, while the Major looks at his son with some pride and affection. "A Joke with your Name," repeats Master Wildman. "I'll do it afterwards, if you like." And there is yet another long pause.

"Well," says Miss Hatt, hinting that there is no more to be usefully eaten or said, and she rises. The others rise too, and move mechanically out and into the drawing-room. The Major, however, stops Mr. Spicer in the hall, for a soft aside. "Could I get a Bath here, in the evening?" he asks. "Yes, I think so," says Mr. Spicer, with the air of a man called upon to interpret rather dangerous forces about which he is none too certain himself. "Certainly. Ah—Bertha!" Miss Hatt immediately appears, touched to sudden seriousness by their low tones. Mr. Spicer delivers a little sentence in which the words "Major" and "Bath" are alone distinguishable, and Miss Hatt replies, "Oh, yes; you'll find the water quite hot. All times of the day, you know."

They then go into the drawing-room, and arrange themselves in chairs to consider each other's personalities afresh. Mr. Spicer starts off with gay questionings. "Comfortable, Mrs. Nixon? Good." "Will you smoke, Major? Cigar?—Good." "Couldn't we have a little more light somewhere?" "Going to stay up, to-night, then, Elsie?"

"Yes," proposes Elsie, but "No, young lady," disposes Mrs. Nixon. "You go along up to bed. You've stayed up quite long enough."

"Oh, mayn't I stay up, please, mother?"

"I said, 'Go up to your room,' Elsie," says Mrs. Nixon, and when Mrs. Nixon begins reporting her own speech in that particularly gentle way of hers, Elsie knows that it is best to obey, and makes for the door.

But Master Wildman seems to be wanting to say something. The company suspends itself amicably, and hovers over the little boy as he whispers something up to his father.

Come, come! A little boy must speak up. Say it out, boy. Say it out.

Ah! The Joke! The Joke! The little boy wants to show the little girl his Joke.

"Well, get on with it, dear boy," says the Major.

Master Wildman comes forward earnestly to Elsie.

"Have you got a bit of Paper and a Pencil?" asks Master Wildman.

"No," says Elsie. "But I think I can get it."

The house is now turned upside-down, and inside out, for a bit of Paper and a Pencil, which Miss Hatt at last obtains from the kitchen, and puts into Master Wildman's hands. Master Wildman addresses Elsie with slow seriousness.

"How do you Write Your Name," asked Master Wildman, "in Two Letters?"

"Don't know," says Elsie.

"Can't you think? It's a joke."

"Don't know," says Elsie.

("Think *I* can guess," whispers Mrs. Spicer.

"Yes. Me too," whispers Miss Hatt.)

"Can't you think?" says Master Wildman.

"Don't know," says Elsie.

"I'll Show you," says Master Wildman, and goes to the little table. Elsie comes close and leans over his shoulder. "Look," says Master Wildman, and proceeds laboriously to demonstrate—

ELSIE.   L. C.

"There," says Master Wildman. "Don't you see? Ell—Cee. Elsie. *Ell—Cee.* It Writes your Name in two letters."

"Oh, I see!" says Elsie, gleefully. "What a Good Joke! What a Good Joke!"

"Now——" says Mrs. Nixon. But, "*Can* do it another way," says Master Wildman.

"Can you?" says Elsie.

"Yes. Can do it another way. Look!" Master Wildman proceeds laboriously to demonstrate—

"In Oes," says Master Wildman. "In two Oes—two letter Oes—two letters. Do you see?"

"Oh, yes. I see," says Elsie. "That makes Two Jokes."

"Yes," says Master Wildman. "You can do it yourself

if you like." He hands her the pencil, and Elsie has the satisfaction of doing it herself.

Then Mrs. Nixon playfully objects that we can't go on writing our names in two letters all the night, and the Major takes her up on it, and both children leave the room for bed.

In silence Mr. Spicer holds a lighted match in an uncertain hand before the Major's cigar. Then: "I smoke this," he says, and produces a pipe. "Not quite for the drawing-room, perhaps. . . . Do you ever smoke a pipe, Major?"

"No. I could never get on with a pipe, somehow or other. I don't know why. I think I must have another try some day."

"Oh, there's nothing like a pipe," says Mr. Spicer. "Well, it's a Real Friend, isn't it? As a rule, you know, I smoke a poisonous sort of shag, but the ladies don't allow that sort of thing in here, do you?"

"I should think not," says Mrs. Spicer, and they laugh indulgence for the terrible manliness of men.

"Colder to-night, don't you think?" says Mr. Spicer. "What about a little Music, my dear?"

"Oh, no——"

"You haven't heard my wife play, have you, Major?"

"No. I should be most delighted."

"Yes," says Miss Hatt. "Give us that Chopin you gave us the other night. I expect you know Chopin well, don't you, Major?"

"Well, I cannot say that I am more than vaguely familiar with the body of his work. I know the odd pieces, of course."

"He was a Pole, wasn't he?"

"Yes, I believe he was."

"Yes, all these great musicians are Poles or something, aren't they?" says Mr. Spicer. "Well, my dear?"

"Oh, well . . ." says Mrs. Spicer, and goes to the piano. Mr. Spicer arranges the music for her, comes down into an armchair by the fire, and lights his pipe. Mrs. Spicer scans the score for a moment, and the music commences.

"Nice, wasn't it, Major?" says Mr. Spicer, when she has done.

"Oh, charming."

"Nice Touch, hasn't she?"

"Yes," said the Major. "Charming."

"Real Music, too, wasn't it? Give us another, dear."

Mrs. Spicer now gives them three more pieces by the same composer, including the "Marche Funebre," after which Mr. Spicer remarks that "you could sort of see the coffin going along, couldn't you?"; and she finishes with the "Rosary," which is also voted very good, if only "in its way." Mr. Spicer ventures that he could imagine "a monk in a monastery writing it." The same idea had hit Mrs. Nixon.

The Little Music thereupon being considered over, Mrs. Spicer joins the others. Mr. Spicer, with an eye upon the cards, is all for a Little Game to follow.

"Do you play Whist or anything, Major? I suppose you wouldn't like a game?"

"Thank you, no; I think not, to-night. I'd better be getting up now, as a matter of fact. I have a lot of letters to get through to-night."

"And I think I'd better be getting up, too," says Mrs. Nixon, "and see to Elsie. Good night, Major! Good night, Miss Hatt!"

"Good night, Mrs. Nixon!"

"Good night!"

Miss Hatt now turns to the Major for purely personal and private matters. "Is there any time you would like to be called in the morning, Major?"

"Let me see—what time would breakfast be, then?"

"We have it at nine, as a rule."

"Well, if I could be called at a quarter past eight . . ."

"Yes, certainly."

"Well, good night!" says the Major, and leaves the room under a shower of the same fair wishes from the trio remaining.

Miss Hatt goes to the fire, stirs it, and does not speak. Nor does anyone speak for a moment. There lies in the drawing-room a deserted atmosphere, still, as of a banquet ended.

"Nice Old Buffer," hazards Mr. Spicer, at last.

"Yes," says Miss Hatt.

"Seen the world, too."

"Yes."

There is another silence in which Miss Hatt removes chairs and newspapers swiftly from one place to another, with no apparent aim, and Mr. and Mrs. Spicer have already begun to help her in this absent pastime, when a house-bell is suddenly heard tinkling in the kitchen below.

"That's his bell!" whispers Miss Hatt, aghast, and flies out into the hall.

She has not to call for Audrey, for Audrey is there already, flushed and wide-eyed, breathlessly awaiting orders for the crisis.

"It was a bell, ma'am."

"Yes, I know; go up and see what he wants."

"Yes'm." Audrey rushes up the stairs.

"Audrey!"

"Yes'm."

"Knock at the door first."

"Yes'm."

Only the sound of Audrey's light feet upon the stairs, and the swish of Audrey's skirts, and the creaking of a highly attentive couple's shoes in the drawing-room. Then a door is heard opening from far above, and almost immediately Audrey is running down again.

"Well?"

"He wants a bath, ma'am."

"Bath? What did he say?"

"He said 'Can I have a bath, please?' ma'am."

"What did you say?"

"I said, 'Yes, sir,' ma'am."

There is a pause. Maid and mistress look blankly at each other. Then Miss Hatt gathers herself together.

"Oh, very well. Come along then, child. Go and get two towels from the cupboard and take them to the bathroom. Then turn on the hot water. When it's ready, go and knock at his door and tell him."

"Yes'm." Audrey vanishes. Miss Hatt rejoins her alert and taut companions in the drawing-room.

"He rang for a bath," she says, and "Oh, yes," says Mr. Spicer, and "Yes," says Mrs. Spicer to the Universe. They very wisely say no more about it. The Major has been Used to things.

"Well," says Miss Hatt, "I think I'd better be going up to bed."

"Yes, you must have had a tiring day of it, my dear," says Mrs. Spicer. "You might help, dear," she adds, turning to her husband, who jumps from dreams and says "Certainly."

He goes to see that the windows are locked, and out into the hall to secure his friend's property further. Then he comes back, announces all to be tight from the door, where his wife joins him, according to routine, and with cheerful "Good nights!" they go upstairs. Miss Hatt is alone in the drawing-room.

Audrey puts her head timidly round the door.

"I've done it, ma'am. He's In."

"Very good, Audrey. You must do that always when He rings. It's what He expects. That'll be all, then, to-night, Audrey. Good night, child!"

"Good night, ma'am!"

"Good night!"

Miss Hatt stretches pluckily up to the gas, draws dense darkness down upon herself with one pull, stumbles out of the room, locks the door, climbs the darkened stairs, and quietly passing the bathroom, where the Major is already making innocent splashing noises, goes into her room.

IV

When Miss Elsie Nixon reaches her room, she begins to undress in a style so extraordinarily disciplined and methodical that one might well imagine she is still under the level eyes of her mother.

She brushes her hair in front of the glass, lays her clothes exactly over a chair, washes herself extensively in exceedingly cold water, and cleans her teeth—rinsing her mouth, rattling the glass, and expectorating with whole-hearted violence. She then scrambles into a white nightdress reaching below her feet. Thus cleansed and prepared, she kneels down by the bed, closes her eyes and purses her mouth like a little girl about to receive a blow, clasps her hands, and prays. Her prayer has little esoteric significance for her. She prays that a certain hazy Kingdom may come (inwardly trusting that nothing will supersede the United Kingdom in her own life-time); she prays for this day's bread (discrepantly, for it is already granted) and to have her trespasses forgiven. (Elsie can never quite place her own Trespasses, but has a vague belief that one is Prosecuted if they aren't forgiven.) And all this to a candle-lit room with softly jocund and perfectly cynical shadows. She then jumps into her chilly bed, a little white bundle of self-chastened original sin, snuffs out the candle, and vaguely hopes for salvation in the dark.

In appearance Elsie is a little girl with miniature features, but with not very much of the perfection of a miniature. She has a freckle or two, exquisite tiny teeth, frizzy reddish hair falling on rather skinny shoulders—rather skinny arms, rather skinny legs. So much is Elsie's. Her mother encases the legs in coarse brown stockings, and the rest in a coarse brown skirt and a coarse silk blouse. Her ears her mother has personally pierced and adorned with tiny golden earrings, and in other details she has done just as she cared with this little victim of Bringing Up. For Elsie is being Brought Up—exactly wherefrom or whereunto neither of them could tell you, but they are both quite complacent in an apparently self-contained process.

Elsie does not detest her mother. She has, indeed, been given expressly to understand that she Loves her, and that is enough. But apart from this she is too well inured to her mother's behaviour to think of detesting her. Her mother, with her healthy face, her stern, level blue eyes, her eager chin, her neat, slim, authoritative figure, her measured and authoritative voice, simply represents life itself, and Elsie never has the wickedness to think that life is detestable.

In this matter of bringing up, Mrs. Nixon considers herself something more than talented. For Mrs. Nixon has been married and unmarried (by death) twice in the space of five years, and by her first husband she has a boy, Jack, and by her second (a Scotchman) the little girl Elsie; and in some period during or after her second marriage the boy Jack has come to be known as Jock. He has also taken the name of Nixon. The reason for this has never at any time been made very clear. It was said at the time, though, that his father had died in a Nursing Home, and this was, by the initiated few, taken as conveying civilly that he had died of drink. But there were few so initiated.

Mrs. Nixon herself is understood to be a Scotchwoman. At any rate, there are, and always have been, strong allusions to, and insistences upon, that nation in the whole of her rearing of her two children. The boy she has brought up in the country, and now that he is fourteen has packed him off to one of those smaller Scottish Public Schools—a hardy, open-air establishment, where the boys eat salted porridge and run to bathe at half-past five in the morning.

As a boy, Jock, strangely enough, was quite her favourite child. "His mother's blood," Mrs. Nixon would say. . . . She called him "Sunny Jim," amiably pulled his ears, encouraged him to be a "brave little man," and dressed him in a kilt. The sadder side of the Bringing Up in the country fell to Elsie.

In this process of bringing up there were various grades and fine shades of punishment suitable to the various offences. Elsie could be Sent Outside, sent to her Room, Locked in the

Bathroom, Locked in the Cupboard, Forbidden to Speak, Put
in the Corner. . . . Or, of course, she could be Sent to Bed,
in which case she was given Broth—Broth, whether for
consolation or further punishment, being absolutely indispensable. There were also Cuffs and Boxes (Fetched), Reminders,
Foretastes, Warnings, Little Lessons, Raps; or, on the spiritual
side, mere Talkings To, Scoldings, or Dressings Down. And
behind these there loomed a final horror, the supreme penalty,
as it were, known as The Stick. This was not very often
employed, but freely alluded to. Thus, "We shall see what
The Stick thinks about it in a moment, Miss," Mrs. Nixon
would say, or "If you pester me any more, child, I'll look
you over with The Stick, and where you don't want it," or
"You're asking for The Stick, my fine lady, aren't you?"
And though these threats were only seldom fulfilled, The Stick
was by no means merely an abstract figure. Elsie could tell
you exactly in which corner of her mother's chest of drawers
it lay—a dark, warped thing, under the clothes.

There was also a Strap somewhere involved in this business,
but this was a figure of speech.

In administering the minor corrections Mrs. Nixon was
sedately and carefully dramatic; but when, about thrice a
year, that Stick did come forth, her eyes would blaze in an
ardour uncontrolled, and the lady had been known to dribble.

It must not be thought that Mrs. Nixon is a cruel mother,
or that there is anything more than a light strain of sensuality
in her actions towards her daughter. And Elsie, they both
know, will "thank her from her heart," for such corrections
one day, and she invariably kisses her for them on the same
day. And the Stick itself will possibly never be seen again.
A house in the country is one thing, and Craven House is
another, and the public is capable of intervening if it hears
a little girl yelling hard enough.

Besides, Mrs. Nixon is cheerful enough, as a rule, and there
are Treats opposed to these severities. Elsie is taken to the
pantomime once a year, and is given a yearly Easter egg, and
gets a Calendar from time to time, or a beautifully bound
Prayer Book, or a School Girl's Annual, or knitting needles,
or pretty handkerchiefs—and many other gifts, quite en-
trancing, if just a bit on the useful side. And on every
birthday she is given the brightest sovereign describable, and
is able to have a good look at it before it goes into the Savings
Bank. And her mother tells her fairy tales sometimes

(Scottish ones), stirring to the romantic imagination as well as the moral. And every March the third is her mother's birthday, and for that occasion Elsie will "save up," and with much to-do present her mother with a handkerchief, which her mother wears, and Elsie watches, for three or four days afterwards. And at Christmas time Elsie is allowed to go to the Children's Parties, where she cuts a striking figure in her kilt, and arrests the evening's celebrations to perform a timid but perfectly competent Highland Reel.

She is considered a good child.

v

Master Wildman's undressing is of a very different character from Elsie's. He kicks off his shoes and wrenches off his stockings, throwing them anywhere he fancies. He washes his face, but not his neck (it is far too chilly for that), and he cleans his teeth in a rich and dispersive manner, coming out in the middle of that task to listen to the music below, and leaving frothy traces of his invasion upon the landing carpet. A cricket match follows, in which Master Wildman scores sixes so plentifully with his father's walking stick that he is not compelled to run at all. He then takes a flying leap at his bed, and the bed responding, takes seven more of the same before finally settling in it.

He is sharing this bedroom with his father, and his bed, lying in a corner of the room, can be screened at will by two curtains hoisted cleverly by Miss Hatt. He draws these.

In the little room within a room thus formed the wallpaper repeats itself around a severe portrait of Miss Hatt as a girl. The light from the gas comes in softly from the top, and the whole, until the Major arrives, is instantly transmuted into the cabin of an airship hovering over China and dropping rather cruel and senseless bombs upon the wretched inhabitants.

When the Major appears at last he treads very softly, on the dutiful assumption that his son is asleep, rings the bell, and shortly after goes down to his bath, as we have seen. During the time he is gone, his son, who has never slept with him before, decides to take this opportunity of studying a Major's habits in his natural sources, so to speak, and thrilling to the adventure of it, arranges a little aperture in the curtains for his purpose.

The Major does not keep him waiting long. He re-enters, sponge in hand, and having puddled about ("puddled" is the word) for a certain time, lights the candle, puts out the gas, climbs into bed, and begins to read.

His son watches him in this position for a little, but catches nothing of unusual interest. He sees, in the gentle candle-light, an old man with grey hair, a grey and slightly stagey moustache, and a totally hang-dog expression, which is partly cultivated and partly due to sixty years. Master Wildman soon turns over to consider his own affairs.

These are of manifold and thrilling interest, and likely (dealing largely with Love) to keep him awake for half the night. For Master Wildman is in love, being enslaved by an actress well exceeding him in the matter of years—thirty-five years ahead of him, in fact—though it must be said in extenuation of this unnatural attachment that he presumes her to be well this side of nineteen. He has seen her but once, at the pantomime last Christmas, and it is not at this point necessary to explain at any length how, when she sang the song, "If I could Sow a tiny seed of Love in the Garden of your Heart," Master Wildman had inwardly and appro-priately replied, "You *have* sown a *Big* seed of love in *my* heart"; or how, when the Major asked him if he had liked the show he had remarked, "I thought That Girl was jolly good," and blushed as the Major gave a queer little smile to himself; or how he had thought of writing her a little note, signing himself "Your humble admirer," and then thought better of it, and so on and so forth. The simple fact is that he has collapsed before her beauty, and now dreams almost incessantly of a world in which a blonde lady, at large in silk tights, governs the domestic hearth.

In the dull yellow silence, broken only by the ripple of a turning page, as the Major reads, Master Wildman falls to dreaming. By countless rivers, seas, fires, wars and bandits an ill-starred blonde lady is bothered, but is firmly saved on each occasion. Likelier alternatives follow, in which a blonde lady marries the gentleman now reading, or (abandoning the stage) appears as a teacher at Master Wildman's new school. But the incessant rescuing continues in either event, and a blonde lady, touched to gratitude at last, or reckoning, perhaps, that a permanent rescuer is indispensable in such a career, marries Master Wildman himself, and has done with it.

Then Master Wildman falls to dreaming about his life at school, to which he is going to-morrow. He defeats the school bully, leads the school football team into action against Aston Villa, founds a Secret Society, and sketches a vivid life in every possible direction, until he hears a sudden stir from his father.

He hastens to put his eye to the aperture, and there follows a sight thrilling beyond all possible anticipation—a candle-lit memory for all the years to come—a true reward for his vigilance.

The Major is saying his prayers!

A hunched, heavy back; wrinkled pyjamas, creased upwards on one leg to reveal forests of hair on an aged skin; bare, red feet—the whole attitude more limply acquiescent than suppliant. Such is the Major's gesture before the Infinite.

He soon rises, and remains standing, with his fingers picking at his signet ring, and his wide, bleared eyes upon the candle.

But there is yet another surprise to come. For almost before a little boy has time to be fast (a little too fast) asleep, the Major moves to the curtains, parts them, pauses, bends down, and puts his dry, glazed lips upon the red, wet mouth of his son.

A moment later the light goes out, and Master Wildman's eyes blaze forth in the dark. It was a kiss—there was no doubt about it—a secret kiss!

"By jove, he must like me!" decides Master Wildman.

VI

The undressing of Mr. and Mrs. Spicer bears all the naturally furtive embarrassment of two strangers compelled, as part of a compact resulting from a limited amount of words breathed over them seven years ago, to undress in the same room and in front of each other's eyes for life—an embarrassment rendered less poignant by time and its own inevitability.

Of the two, Mr. Spicer, perhaps, is the more secretive. Mr. Spicer is so far behind the times as to retain, for sleeping purposes, a lamentable night-shirt. This institution appears to be quite unalterable, having been blessed, for all time, by two words from the lips of Mr. Spicer. A little habit, in fact. Having removed his shirt and vest, Mr. Spicer would lay his night-shirt over the bed, dive, emerge with a swimmer's action—and having shaken the thing well down, would perform the ensuing phases of disrobement quietly under its flowing and voluminous cover—the trousers and socks thus shed not appearing until he stepped away.

Mrs. Spicer's sleeping apparel is much the same, with frills at the sleeves and collar.

There is little conversation between the two at this time of the evening, and what there is takes place parenthetically between the panting ardours of hurried disrobement.

"What sort of day did you have to-day, dear?" Mrs. Spicer asks.

"Oh, all right.   How did you get on?"

"Oh, all right.   Bertha a little tetchy, I thought. . . ."

"Yes, she gets like that sometimes. . . ."

"Yes. . . .   Very worried to-day, though, I expect. . . ."

"Yes. . . ."

"Major and one thing and another. . . ."

"Yes. . . ."

They are soon prepared, and resembling in their white night gear two rather bleared and long-suffering prophets—or visitants from another world—climb into bed, in the centre of which Audrey has laid a stone hot-water bottle. Mrs. Spicer goes to the right of it, and Mr. Spicer to the left, and Mrs. Spicer reaches upwards and turns out the gas.

They do battle for position in a rustling darkness. There is one absolute collision, a little more rustling and they are still—Mr. Spicer the winner by nearly a foot.

"Isn't that window open a little too far, my dear?" says Mr. Spicer, after a pause.

"Oh, I don't think so," says Mrs. Spicer, and "Yes, I think it is," says Mr. Spicer, as though she has said the opposite. He jumps out of bed and closes it as gently as possible upon his wife's sensibilities.

There follow some softly contradictory words about air in general.   Then Mr. Spicer says, "Well—good night, my dear," and turns lumpily over on his side, his wife clinging firmly to the sheets until the strain is over.

For a long while Mrs. Spicer lies awake, head over sheet, in an alert and vivid darkness, while her unconscious partner's breathing becomes heavily more regular.

She has landed a queer fish indeed! But none the less obstinate for being queer. He always manages to get his own way, somehow, doesn't he?

She dwells upon the rocks ahead in their married life, which have been growing more and more apparent of late.

She then turns over herself, with a good tug at the clothes —this jerky warfare continuing, on and off, throughout the night.

VII

And at a quarter past ten o'clock the two servants, Audrey and Edith, creep by candle-light from the bottom of the house to the top. This is done with so stealthy a tread, with such respectful whisperings, as to make the action seem almost apologetic. To the others, prone in their dark rooms, it is a vaguely necessary happening, irrelevant to the main purpose of the day.

From their little attic there issues a thud, a bump, and a word or two, and they are in bed. For sleep to Edith and Audrey is like sleep upon the high seas, limited and precious —a hasty interval rather than an appointed formality.

VIII

The day is over and the lights are out. The breeze falls with the night outside, but the sky has cleared, revealing the serene and festal coronal of the Milky Way, and the other stars glittering with a cold purpose.

Opposite Craven House a pale lamp burns, even and pitiless, and Craven House is not oblivious of its hushed and inscrutable implications. It seems, rather, to dwell at one with eternal forces, upon the queer and futile assortment of human souls that it harbours beneath the stars. After all the fuss and to-do, and plucky cheerfulness of the day within, it relapses into the dark inevitabilities of the situation.

Once or twice a late home-comer intrudes upon the silence reigning, but is soon swallowed up by another house. Sometimes a faint cry arises, as of a whole city in agony, from the plains of London behind. And through all the night, from lost distances, engines are clanking, gruffly shunting, whistling —the dim, hectic functionings of a nightmare.

Within the house the blackened landings creak in the sound of breathing without a stir.

The parrot, in its cage, is still awake. The bird flutters its wings, mutters, and remains erect, still as a stone.

CHAPTER II

*An Account of Two Servants and a Parrot. A little
Boy is Tried for Theft*

I

To Edith's alarm clock the night-long insinuations of the
powers of darkness were throughout distasteful, and taking
its cue from the first grey stealth of dawn, it shrilled im-
petuously out with a "Thank-Heavens-that's-over," a "Quite-
enough - of - that - You - jolly - well - get - up - and - no - more
of-this-kind-of-nonsense" sort of air, expressive of sheer blithe
deliverance. Then, like a creature that had abruptly done
for itself by over-exertion, it fell back upon its own inconsequent ticking, as if nothing whatever had occurred.

II

Edith and Audrey were considered a satisfactory pair by
Miss Hatt, though they both fell short of her romantic ideal
in servants.

To Miss Hatt the ideal cook was fat, Irish, faithful and
witty; prepared, at a domestic crisis, to sink into a chair with
a panted "Begorrah!" and on other general occasions to
flourish a belaying pin, harbour policemen, allude to "Ould
Oireland," dominate the kitchen with her waddling, and the
whole household, just a little, with her Irish sarcasm. The
ideal housemaid, on the other hand, would be imported from
the English countryside. She would be neat, seventeen,
almost pretty. She would arrive with an old mother and a
country bag. She would be treated very kindly indeed. She
would be called "Child"; she would give all her troubles, and
all her savings, to Miss Hatt—who would be as safe as the
Bank of England; she would flush with pleasure when re-
warded with old hats and clothes, and when taking her
afternoon off, for which occasions she might be allowed a
young man of unimpeachable character. She would remain
with Miss Hatt for life. These were the ideals, for which
Miss Hatt was compelled to substitute the human and
untheatrical realities of Miss Edith Potter and Miss Audrey
Custard.

Miss Edith Potter, the cook, was thirty-two years of age, and so out-of-drawing and blotchy in appearance, so confoundedly grotesque, in absolute fact, that the only way for Miss Hatt and the others to tolerate her presence in the household at all was to interpret her as a "Dickens' character," or, in Mr. Spicer's phrase, a "regular character study." Edith herself was not unaware of this necessity, and was therefore continuously making shrewd, queer, candid remarks, in an inflated style, to be repeated upstairs by her betters, with amused relish. For the rest, she was an energetic waddler, a caustic oven-slammer, a smasher, a rather dirty but extrinsically efficient cook. In addition she had a romantic strain, being in love with a footballer in place of the prescribed policeman.

What sanctuary and fulfilment this athlete found in Edith's raw arms, what goals he shot, for her appraisement alone, before a howling Saturday multitude, was still rather in the dark, however; for this footballer had made no definite proposals as yet, and safeguarding himself with allusions to a transfer, appeared to be leading her the devil of a life one way and another. He had been known, indeed, so to prey upon Edith's mind as to leave on more than one occasion the chilly mark of his football upon the meals, and Miss Hatt had thought more than once seriously of dismissing her.

Audrey Custard was nearer Miss Hatt's ideal, and Miss Hatt still expected to do something with her. She was almost too submissive, though, and her personality had no substance for Miss Hatt's moulding, no power of continued association to form a character. She lived from slow obedience to obedience, and the world and its people were beyond and above her comprehension, from Miss Hatt down to the butcher's boy.

To Edith Potter and Audrey Custard, Miss Hatt gave respectively £25 and £20 a year. Audrey spent most of her money to help support a paralytic mother in a hospital, while Edith gave it all over to sheer vanities and a gladiator.

The Misses Potter and Custard were on friendly terms with each other. Miss Potter called Miss Custard Ord, and Miss Custard called Miss Potter Eed.

Five minutes after the alarm clock rang Audrey put one foot out of the bed and gazed at the window with blank despair. Edith remained in bed.

III

Having dressed and washed in an unemphatic way, and crept down to the kitchen, Audrey's first duty was to scrub the front door steps. She filled a pail with water, went out into the crisp, rosy atmosphere of the early morning, and began a clanking and scrubbing process, which, with numerous other clanking and scrubbing processes taking place in the immediate neighbourhood, formed the first pale sounds in the consciousness of the warmer fortunates within.

Scrubbing the front door steps was a horrid and biting occupation, and Audrey's fingers became so numb and lifeless, and her face became so frozen and red, and she became so sick from the cold and an empty stomach, that she could scarcely be said to have breathed a sigh of relief when it was over.

She exchanged a few words with the paper boy—a boy famous for his impertinence—who thrust forth his tongue at her, discussed her face (which he referred to hostilely as "it"), and committed similar Wellerisms before having the wind taken entirely out of his sails by Audrey's slow unresponsiveness. She then went inside, murmuring a very belated "Cheek!"

Here she fetched old newspapers and raked out last night's fires—a vision of sackcloth and ashes in literal truth.

Edith was up by now and cooking their breakfast. This comprised sausages, bread and butter and tea, and was taken upon a greasy newspaper tablecloth. The sausages were ill-cooked and peppery, they rendered the tea tasteless; the bread was stale and the butter was hard. Edith and Audrey were not sorry to finish their breakfast and start the day's work, now that the weak preliminaries were accomplished.

IV

To complete the description of this household some words should be given to Mac, the parrot.

Mac, the parrot, was a parrot of doubtful gender, but masculine upon application to Miss Hatt, and sixty-eight years of age.

Its barred prison comprised a gritty sand floor, two china receptacles containing water and a parrot's nutty fare, and a wooden bar across the middle, upon which the creature spent most of the day. Once or twice in the day, as the spirit moved it, it would make a sophisticated clicking noise with a black tongue, climb the cage with greedy strides, and, spending a few moments in seeing what the world looked like upside-down, climb down again, satisfied, and consume a nut held in a quavering claw. But all other affairs were negotiated from the wooden bar.

Some of the day was spent in littering the cage with its own feathers, some of it in beautiful whistling, and some of it in exercising the talent for which it had been imprisoned. Its remarks were addressed almost invariably to its own trembling self, and were largely self-impeaching. Thus, "That's a lesson, Polly," or "You're *bad, bad, bad,* Polly!" or "Polly, you rascal!" These were uttered in suitable undertones; but when the front door was opened, or when Audrey brushed the stairs, it would shriek out: "*That's a Cat, sir! That's a Cat, sir! That's a Cat, sir!*" with all its throaty power, until the infamy was ended.

For the further entertainment of this bird a bar for swinging upon had been kindly inserted at the top of the cage, but the creature seldom took advantage of this free pleasure. Its prevailing mood was one of good-tempered caustic bitterness against its captors—a mood which its abundance of years had served to emphasise rather than soften. It occasionally obliged with a clever mimicry or a relevant saying, which would be repeated for days by the inmates of Craven House, but this was rare. So rare, indeed, that when the parrot had said absolutely nothing worth considering for a month or so on end the disappointed humans were compelled to invent—or at least to distort.

It bit you whenever it could.

V

The guests of Craven House came down to a sunlit breakfast with bright cheeks, strong "Good mornings," and an air of release. Mrs. Nixon was radiant after a night of untroubled sleep and Scottish breathing. Elsie was also very fresh, having had a cold bath; and what with her little pink nose and her blue cheeks, and her frizzy red hair, all golden in the sun, she was in a very frail and many-coloured condition. The Major's countenance bore a hint of the humorous behind the forlorn; Miss Hatt poured the tea with happy grace, as

a scintillating benediction; and the Golden Tooth itself
appeared to have had a nice sleep, and shone like anything.

Master Wildman alone was pale and pre-occupied, for he
was to be taken to School this morning.

Porridge came first, and the Nixons took it with salt. And
it should be taken like that, they all admitted. Nevertheless,
Miss Hatt still provided the pampered South with golden
syrup.

With this golden syrup Master Wildman at once began to
write his full name upon the porridge, and delayed the meal
thereby, the others slowly watching him, until Elsie giggled
and his father called him to order. Mr. Spicer was therefore
debarred from oilily shaping his own initials this morning,
which, on other mornings, he invariably did.

Bacon and eggs followed, and Mrs. Spicer asked her husband
if there was any News, and Mr. Spicer opened the paper
and announced another outrage by the Suffragettes. They
discussed the Vote. Should Women have it? Mrs. Nixon
was all against it. Women (her argument ran) had another
and sterner vocation, the home, and had other things to do
than "go trapesing round Parliament," as she put it. The
Major was questioned, and he also thought that it would
"hardly do." Mrs. Spicer concurred, but thought that
Women "might have a Say," and Mr. Spicer summed up.

"They'll never *get* it, my dear," he said. "They'll never
get it. It's not as it should be." He then made an indefinite
mumbling noise culminating in the words "Women Policemen
next," and the subject was changed with laughter.

After breakfast the guests withdrew to the drawing-room
fire. Mrs. Nixon and her daughter at once went on to a sofa
together and began knitting some article which was indeter-
minate at present, but reliable already, and of the very
best Scottish wool; and it was plain that if Satan was up
to his usual mischief, and looking about for idle hands to
express himself with, he would have a very dull time of
it anywhere in the region of Mrs. and Miss Nixon. Mrs.
Spicer saw Mr. Spicer off to his business.

With respect to Mr. Spicer's Business we may say at
once that Mr. Spicer was widely (if rather ungracefully)
known to be In Tea. How far Mr. Spicer was involved in
this comforting commodity, how far Mr. Spicer had committed himself to Tea, how far Mr. Spicer was compromised
by Tea, whether Tea was Mr. Spicer's master, or whether

Mr. Spicer was the master of Tea, were problems alike in the shadow. Mr. Spicer was In Tea. In this operation of seeing-off to Tea the woman gained her one complete ascendancy over the man. She tapped the barometer for him, jerked him into his overcoat, tugged at it, knocked his shoulders with the brush, thrust an umbrella into his hand, tugged at him all over, nudged a hat at him, and closed the door with a strident "Good-bye," upon a soundly kissed and stupefied baggage discovering itself on the road to the station.

Major Wildman did not linger in the drawing-room. He gave his son the word, and Master Wildman acknowledged it with a sickly glance, and went to put on his overcoat. They left the house without a word.

VI

Lyndon House School was an ordinary middle-sized, middle-class dwelling, but nevertheless looking like the children's prison it was, on account of the curtainless windows, frosted on the lower panes, on the ground floor, and a large board with "LYNDON HOUSE SCHOOL" written in blistered golden letters across it. It stood near the Green.

Here the Major and his child arrived at about a quarter past nine—the Major himself with certain misgivings, and the little boy in a nerveless and trotting condition, which was not improved by a carefree and tremendous sound of bawling and slamming issuing from the front room as they came to the front door steps and rang the bell—a weak and particularly unpleasant type of bell, which announced the newcomers to the back of the house with a tinkle of soft and wicked mystery, and reduced the noise in the front room to less than a quarter of its original volume.

The door was opened by Miss Staines, the headmaster's sister, who was about thirty-seven years of age, with an icy red nose and a chilly body into which she endeavoured to insinuate some comfort by rubbing her hands together, and continued wriggling motions. She gave them a bright welcome and asked them if they didn't think it was a perishing morning. She spoke in bluff tones to the child, who was fascinated as much by her plain, raw and tall appearance, as by the dragon-like hissing noise she made by drawing her breath through her teeth. She then took them upstairs to the drawing-room. Here they were soon joined by the head-master himself, and Miss Staines took her leave to hiss and perish elsewhere.

Mr. Staines was a thin man with thin rimless spectacles, clean-shaven, and thirty-nine years of age. His figure was erect to the extent of preciousness, and he entered with a soundless stride that was an almost conscious corrective to the disturbances of the atmosphere wrought by his sister. As soon as he had started to talk to the Major, the little boy was transformed into so much Goods Delivered, for which one would expect the Major to take a receipt and go on his way. They talked for some five minutes, however, and walked inadvertently down to the front door, still talking. And then the door was closed upon the Major, and the sunlight, and liberty, and Mr. Staines said, "Will you come this way?" speaking low, as though the real horrid thing began now. And two Boys were looking on, and Mr. Staines stopped to secure a pin on the hall notice board (which brought another Boy); and then they found themselves in the Study, with the door closed.

Mr. Staines lit the gas fire, and said that he thought gas fires were very useful, and went to his desk and sat in a re-volving chair, and swivelled round upon his pupil very neatly, and said, "Let me see, now." And then, after producing paper and a beautiful red fountain pen, "Let me see, how old are you, exactly?" and after a few more questions like that, "Let me see, your name's Wildman, isn't it?" He then said, "As long as you're not as wild as your name it doesn't matter, does it?" Master Wildman, of course, had heard that one once or twice before, but he laughed at it again. Then Mr. Staines, after a certain amount of careful Humming and Hawing (and revolving), said that he thought it would be best if Master Wildman began in the Fourth Form— the lowest—and he gave his reasons for it. But at that mo-ment a mob of boys in the hall outside began to make such a fiendish noise that Mr. Staines sprang up, right in the middle of a sentence, flung open the door, and asked this mob whether it would mind holding its tongue and clearing out of the hall: to which the mob made no sort of reply, but dispersed in perfect silence, various sarcastic units grasping actual tongues in actual forefingers and thumbs; but this out of sight. The next moment a Bell started clanging through the house and Mr. Staines said, "That's Prayers."

In a crowd of boys Master Wildman kept as close as he could to Mr. Staines' legs, following them into the dining-room (two rooms in one) where, on two long tables about thirty school hymn books were lying. The boys took their places, and Mr. Staines, at the top of the room, gave Master Wildman a seat next to himself.

A hymn was sung; a lesson was read by a tall boy. Then thirty chairs were made to moan and shriek into position on the wooden floor; the boys knelt, and put their elbows on them, and hid their faces while Mr. Staines read prayers. Then the thirty chairs moaned and shrieked back again, and Mr. Staines addressed the boys on School matters.

He said that it had "come to his ears" that certain persons had been seen playing football in the streets of Southam Green. Without being too explicit, Mr. Staines intimated that if such a thing occurred again he would be compelled to take measures of his own. It was a case of bringing dishonour to the School Cap.

He said that he forbade, in the future, the use of water pistols on the School premises.

He said (without lifting his eyes from his notebook) that he would be obliged if those two boys would leave off whispering at the end of the room.

He said that the boys who took Milk in the morning were to come in and take it in a decent way, remaining silent; and that they were entitled to two biscuits only with their milk. The prefects should look to this. And on this head would Ball Minor come and see him during the lunch hour?

"Very well," said Mr. Staines, and rose, which was a signal for the inner Beelzebub to let himself go in all of them. Master Wildman hated School already, and clung to his only rocks of safety, the Legs. These strode out into the hall, and appeared to have lost their protective power, supporting, as they did, a trunk that vibrated to the sailor-like orders of a Mr. Staines who seemed to have forgotten all about Master Wildman. Master Wildman was shoved by one Boy, and bumped by another, and the tall Boy who had read the lesson knocked him over the head with a Bible, saying, "Hullo, new kid!" He was very glad when Mr. Staines introduced him to a Master, who took him upstairs to the Fourth Form room.

This was already filled with chattering boys sitting, or rather wriggling, on desks for two. "You'd better sit with

Lomas," said the Master. Whereupon Lomas, who was the funniest-looking boy, with fair hair cropped like a convict's, and a staggering tweed suit, shouted, "Oh, Sir-ir-ir-ir!" as though he would never have believed it of this Master. "And you'd better share books for the present," said the master, and *"Sir-ir-ir-ir-ir!"* shrilled Lomas, something more than overcome.

Divinity was the order of the moment, and when the boys had been shouted down into a facetious imitation of silence they opened their desks and brought forth their Scripture books. Each boy, in turn, read a paragraph.

Lomas, however, remained in a very feverish state, and seemed to be in all sorts of minds about his proper attitude to Master Wildman. Just to begin with, and hit the right note, he gave Master Wildman, a sound barge to the other end of the desk, but made almost immediate amends by opening the book and showing Master Wildman the Place. After which concession the boy changed his mind again, threw his body back, pointed at Master Wildman, and pinched his own nose, to make a coarse and tittering insinuation to the onlookers in the desk behind. He then whispered something hot and unintelligible, but apparently companionable, to Master Wildman, who endured both kinds of onslaught with the same sort of complacence.

After a time, however, Lomas settled down to biting his nails and gazing out of the window, reawakening to a neglected turbulence only when the time came to turn a page of the Scripture book, on which occasions he would furiously turn over all the pages of that book, for some mad purpose of his own, leaving Master Wildman to find the Place again.

This finally irritated his Master to so great an extent that after giving the boy a single warning he turned upon him and asked him if he would very kindly oblige by leaving the room. Upon which the cruelly used young innocent again exclaimed, "Sir-ir-ir-ir!" while rising to comply; and, on receiving no reprieve, left the room in his own style—that is, by puffing out his blushing cheeks and pretending to play a trombone, and marching to the strains of that imaginary instrument.

It took Master Wildman but a moment to gather that the boys held him alone indictable for this outrage. For the door had scarcely closed upon the disgraced musician when Master Wildman became aware of a disturbance in the desk behind, and turning, observed two boys almost prostrate in an attempt to reach him with a kick. "You dirty little *sneak!*" they hissed. And "How am I a sneak? I'm not a sneak," pleaded Master Wildman, in a tone that would have softened the stoniest persons. His enemies were not in a position, however, to substantiate their charge, for at that moment the Master, who had eyes at the back of his head apparently, (for he was looking at a picture all the time), asked a picture whether Messrs. Ball and Cardley wished to join their friend outside. They had only got to tell him, he added, if they did. This suave offer was overheard by Messrs. Ball and Cardley and proved an efficient silencer. For though both would have been only too glad to escape their lessons in the way suggested, it was far from safe to be outside the door and away from the flock, particularly during this first hour, when (it was known) a wolf-like Mr. Staines, who was not yet taking a class himself, prowled.

Soon afterwards the Bell clanged again from below and the lesson was changed to Latin. This excused much desk thumping, barging, and ink-slinging (in the higher and literal sense). Also Lomas assumed that he might rejoin the class, and did so, trombone and all. He spent a large part of the ensuing hour in an attempt to pull a really satisfactory Long Nose at his Master. This activity in its simplest form involves merely an extension of the fingers of both hands and a joining of them to the nose in the direction of the enemy. But that sort of nose was not nearly long enough for Lomas, after all he had suffered; he therefore set to work on innumerable complex and collapsible arrangements, involving pens. And not content even with that extension of his hatred, enlisted the telescopic aid of a neighbour's pencil box, the whole ending in a horrible clatter and nearly another expulsion.

And then came Break. The boys made a rush for the playground.

This was a ruined enclosure, about twenty-five yards square, with little islands of mauve asphalt in a dusty ground. An extraordinary game of football was in progress here, the players not only lacking sufficient resolution to take either one side or the other, but frequently dropping their own private tennis balls and shooting their own private goals to their hearts' content.

Master Wildman kept ever so quiet as he watched this, but that seemed to call attention to himself all the more, and

there was soon a crowd of five or six boys around him, shouting at him and baiting him in every way. One Boy asked
him his name, another Boy commanded him to say "Iced Ink"
three times quickly. Another ordered him to decline the
present tense of "Iamano," another demanded his Christian
name, another (a Nice one, thought Master Wildman) advised
him not to give it, because they were only ragging him;
another said, "What's your father?"; another declared that
his father was an eel-pie maker; another (a Big one) said that
he looked like a moon-faced calf, and that he would tear
him open and make strawberry jam of him. Reinforcements
affirmed that he was a sneak and a cheat and had "got old
Lomas turned out" that very morning. But what could
you expect with an eel-pie maker's son? And perhaps he'd
learn decent manners now that he had come amongst gentlemen, and that was the bell, and old Staines was in a frightful
wax as it was.

The next Lesson was Arithmetic, and Master Wildman's
preoccupied and silent behaviour, while repudiating the
charge of "sneak," was nevertheless interpreted as a wily
cover for Cheating and Cribbing.

Then came Lunch, in the dining-room. Master Wildman
was not persecuted much here, because Mr. Staines ordered
all the boys sitting at Master Wildman's table to leave off
talking, because, he said, Lyndon House School was "not a
Baseball Match."

But after Lunch one of the boys lost his watch chain, and
it appeared that Master Wildman was a Thief as well. The
article in question was not on his person, however, as a
search established, and though one young gentleman held
that he had probably swallowed it (all thieves being gifted,
he declared, with special organs for nefarious secretions),
it was thought best and fairest to Try him, and they took
him to the boot-room for the purpose. Lomas was elected
judge on the strength of being able to say words like "Here-
tofore," "Thereby," and "Herewith" with unequalled fluency.
He also said, "Prisoner at the bar, you're hereupon accused
of impeaching the King's Royal Peace," which was a supremely
impressive way of putting things, and clinched the matter.
On coming into office he remembered an old friend and
appointed Cardley as Defence for the Council (which again
showed his power and originality), but let no one else have
much of a say. The rest remained Jurymen or Constables,

according to his decision, his whole court proving eventually
rather a Frankenstein of a court, for the Constables and
Jurymen either did not stay in their places, but went over
to the prisoner with a bald and irregular, "Look here, *did*
you do it?" and the threat of torture, or shouted "Shut
up, you asses, and let Lomas have a go. After all it's a proper
trial," or words to that effect, in such confusion, and betraying
such a lamentable bias in favour of mixing legal formula
with Football (or rather Foot-Handkerchief), that Lomas
almost wished that he had done without the honour in the
first place. Furthermore, even when some sort of order
was established, Lomas could only call upon the prisoner
to Own Up and be a sportsman, with the promise that they
would let him down lightly if he did. And the prisoner
was not accommodating in this respect, for he simply finished
a prolonged period of absolute dumbness, so uncanny and
intense to the view that it daunted even his noisiest ques-
tioners, by Blubbing outright. Whereupon Football, whose
cause had never been entirely neglected throughout, super-
seded this trial altogether.

The first half of afternoon school was devoted to History,
the general drift of the matter to Master Wildman being
that there was an Old Monk called the Venerable Bede, and
there were Romans, who made pottery, and coins, and
baths, and Old Roman Walls . . . and there was a Pope called
Gregory (like the powder) who said that they weren't angles
but angels. . . . And after this they closed their History
books and opened their Geography books to consider some
rivers in the North of England. And as absolutely no one
present could come forward to question their existence, the
lesson took a rather more interesting turn, for one of the
boys all at once asked the Master whether he thought there
would ever be a Channel Tunnel. And though this was considerably stretching the confines of a lesson called Geography,
he stretched them further still on receiving a friendly reply
by saying that he didn't think himself that there would
ever be a Channel Tunnel, because there might be an invasion
by the Germans, and then where would one be, because
his uncle had only just come back from Germany, and he
said the factories were working day and night making guns
and ammunition, and you could see the lights flaring as
you came back to England in the train. . . . Whereupon the
master said that he thought the boy's uncle was possibly

right. But he didn't call the boy's uncle an uncle, but an "Er—Avuncular Relative," which scored him a nice laugh, which he termed "these unseemly cachinnations" and got another. And this put him into an astonishingly chatty frame of mine, and there was no more Geography for the rest of the hour, after which the boys smashed their desks to, and grudged, "Not such a bad ass after all."

Master Wildman was an awful little pig at tea, being unable to eat his bread and butter at any speed or with any kind of delicacy satisfactory to his critics, who must have known the rules so well that they could afford to dispense with them, being themselves something a little more than free and easy in the matters of gobbling and swilling. After Tea the boys in the first three forms went into the front room for an hour's Prep., but the boys of the fourth form were allowed to go home and do Homework. Master Wildman was spotted by Mr. Staines and invited into the study. Here Mr. Staines gave him some stiff and beautiful new books, and almost at once began to revolve again, when it came to trying on and appraising a School Cap for Master Wildman. It took some time to do this, Mr. Staines cocking his head, drooping an eyelid, and swerving round to fresh supplies with artistic verve—and the little lay figure erect and silly in front of him. A conclusion was at last come to, however, and Master Wildman left the study very pleased with his cap—not merely because the harmony of bright green and bright red was a very touching harmony at his time of life, but because he was now a real member of the school, and had a School Cap, to wear in the street. He put it on his head and carried his bowler hat in his hand.

But the feelings of elation to be derived from the thought of such privileges were not going to bear contact with the realities of his schoolfellows and their established usages, as was soon proved when he came out into the street, where four or five of them fell upon him and snatched his cap off his head.

"Here, you jolly well give me back my cap," said Master Wildman, speaking outright for the very first time in the whole day, but not looking very formidable.

"Jolly well won't," said the holder, but even he wasn't quite sure of himself.

"You jolly well give me back my Cap," said Master Wildman, and half-suspecting a flaw somewhere in the other's courage, he advanced.

Upon this his enemy achieved the impossible by retreating and advancing at the same time, his legs looking after the fainter-hearted side of the business, and his violent expressions and charging attitude seeing to the other. Such a miracle could not be kept going for long, however, and the legs got the best of it.

A chase followed through the lamp-lit streets of Southam Green, and the fugitive, knowing his way, easily escaped.

Ten minutes later Audrey opened the door of Craven House to a little boy holding a bowler hat in his hand. She smiled upon him as one could only do on opening the door for anybody, let alone a little boy returning from School, but the little boy's eyes were lakes of unrippled and chilling gravity.

CHAPTER III

Progress in a Little Boy's Education. A Game of Cricket; and the Contents of two Drawers.

I

To Master Wildman, thinking about it all in after life, there was a colour and a certain sweet sadness supplied, perhaps, by Elsie (though she did not figure at all prominently in his imagination at the time) in the dull to-morrows of his first winter at Craven House, and the spring that followed.

In after life it would be the mornings that he would remember best—the rainy mornings, when you stood at the front door and listened to the hissing and trinkling noises, while Miss Hatt fetched Mr. Spicer's old umbrella and told you to wait a bit because it might clear, and then told you to dash—and the dashing itself—and the subsequent dank smell of your own clothes in the beetly, darkened school boot-room. The bitterly cold mornings, silver bright, with the rough feel of the Major's old Army scarf, and the pavement nearly to be slidden upon, and the absolute perishment of Miss Staines. The undecided mornings, which were dejecting, muddy, and yesterday's-wet-mackintosh mornings. The dead, snowy mornings, not nearly snowy enough, but snowballing an overestimated sport, nevertheless, owing to the acute agony experienced in, and the eventual uncompromising disappearance of, fingers encased in wet woollen gloves. The spring mornings, when you decided that nature *was* rather beautiful after all, but were still a little grudging about it. And the summer mornings at last, when you awoke to a hushed blue haze in the west, and the trees touched to stillness by it, and the summer sound of a neighbour's mowing machine, mowing away, and stopping with a clank, but soon mowing again.

The Easter term gathered pace with every week, slowed down a little when the end was in sight, and the school passages were echoing to the tune of—

> "This time next week where shall I be?
> Not in *this* academie!"

and finished, all suddenly one morning, when there was nothing whatever to do in chaotic classrooms but talk to a transformed Junior Master on new, ecstatically personal, and beautiful terms, or throw darts about, or flick cigarette cards—and old Staines wanted to see you, but it was only about if you wanted lunch at school to-day. . . .

The Easter holidays were short and rainy holidays, but none the worse for being rainy. You were taken to the Moving Pictures about once a week and once to the Theatre itself, where you saw Sherlock Holmes in person, and afterwards had a dazzling tea at Lyons' Corner House. You were taken up to town to buy a watch, and you bought a watch which was illuminated (in dial, if not in all its subsequent statements). In the evenings you played Halma or Snap with Elsie, who was being allowed an undefined sort of holiday too, on the strength of your own, and with whom you were furtively amiable.

Master Wildman was not sorry to get back to school at the end of it. He was by now well trained in the usages and idiom that had so distressed him on his first day, and was, in the habits of barging, punching, slandering or pure reviling, together with the easy interchange of such epithets as Sow, Pig, Swine, Hog, Cad, Cheat, Sneak, Cur, Fool, Liar, Ass, Cow, Beast, Insect, Worm, practically the equal of his companions.

The summer term, when given its head, flew faster than any Easter term could fly, and Master Wildman's bare knees became browner and browner, and his chatter on school matters grew quicker and quicker, and more and more "somewhat incessant" (as the Major weakly pleaded), and he began to leave more and more caps, and shoes, and cricket bats about different parts of Craven House, to the sheer amusement (and nothing else) of Miss Hatt, who put them back again; and he was given a bicycle, and straightway had an accident upon it, which sent Miss Hatt rushing for the pink lint; as well as innumerable punctures, other calamities, and speeding triumphs, concerning which Craven House was kept elaborately advised.

II

Master Wildman's general impression of the world he had come to live in, at the end of his second term at Lyndon House School, was at once shadowy and sharply defined.

The world, flattened at the bottom and top like an orange, contained two sorts of people, Englishmen and foreigners. The latter were made up of the effeminate French, who ate frogs and kissed each other; the Spanish, who had bull fights, took siestas, and were passionate; the Germans, who said "Donner und blitzen" (which meant "Thunder and lightning"), and were spies; and the Italians, who stabbed you in the back with a stiletto. There were Africans, who were natives, and there were Indians, who were also natives (unless they were Rajahs), and they did the rope trick. There were no natives in China, where they grew their nails long, shook their own hands, looked inscrutable, and tortured whoever they could. This was duplicated, with earthquakes, in Japan. There were savages, Esquimeaux, cannibals, and negroes. The Russians were mostly sent to Siberia, and were gloomy on account of it.

This world was made in two ways. It was formally and carefully laid out in a crowded and important week, according to Genesis, and simply sent whizzing off the sun, according to the junior master at Lyndon House—both versions being true, because one was religion, which could not be denied, and the other science, which was undeniable. But it was always queer like that when it came to God, whose wrath and jealousy, and everlasting mercy, and suchlike discrepancies, were very tricky matters. Anyway, a little boy's duties were made fairly clear. He knew his duty towards his neighbour, and what he desired. And he knew the Ten

Commandments, in which it was impressed upon a little boy, among other things, that he must not covet his neighbour's wife. There were further strictures concerning his neighbour's ox, and ass, which were easily observed strictures for any little boy, even in a rural district.

III

It is the first day of the summer holidays. Master Wildman has arranged overnight to go and play a cut-throat version of cricket on Southam Green with Lomas.

Lomas is Master Wildman's best friend by now, and with the ardour for sport granted only to those who are on the very first day of their summer holidays, Lomas is to be seen on the pavement outside Craven House some time before breakfast, whistling up at vague windows, loitering and disconsolate, bat and stumps in hand.

Master Wildman puts his head out of a window.

"Won't be a sec., old man. Got just to have breakfast."

"All right, man. Buck up."

After a very violent breakfast indeed, and one or two words with the Major and Miss Hatt about asking properly to be excused, Master Wildman is with him. They set off down a road flooded by the sad amber light of the late summer sun, and they are feeling very happy and very free.

"Got the ball, man?" asks Lomas.

"Yes, man," says Master Wildman, and they are quiet.

"How's that little girl staying at your home getting on?" asks Lomas.

"Oh, *her*," says Master Wildman. "Oh, she's a fool. . . ."

"Is she, man?" says Lomas, and they are quiet again.

There appears to be something on Lomas' mind.

"Does your father ever have quarrels with your mother?" he asks at last.

"Haven't got one," says Master Wildman.

"What? Mother, man?"

"Yes."

"What? Did she die, man?"

"*Rather*," says Master Wildman, disposing with that.

"Do you mind, man?"

"Not much. Bit. Never saw her. My father rather gasses about her sometimes," says Master Wildman, and they say nothing for some time.

"My father quarrels with my mother," says Lomas, ruminating.

"Does he, man?"

"R*ather.* . . ."

"Had a quarrel last night," says Lomas.

"Did they, man?"

"Yes, man. In the drawing-room. My mother said she'd go out of the house."

"Good lor', man." And they are too overcome to say anything more for a little.

Then: "My father was in the Bore War," offers Master Wildman.

"Good lor', was he, man? Have any adventures?"

"R*ather*. Bores. . . . Got wounded."

"Did he, man?"

"R*ather*. Wound still hurts him sometimes."

"Does your father ever hit you?" ask Lomas, who never keeps at one thing for long.

"Rather not. Jolly well hit him back."

"Would you really, man?"

"R*ather*."

"Good lor',. man," says Lomas, by now devout.

"Give him one in the jaw," says Master Wildman, and they laugh at that.

"Assassinate him!" says Master Wildman, and they laugh at that, too.

And both little jokes having gone so well, "Assassinate you!" says Master Wildman, and they begin to fight.

"Here, shut up," says Master Wildman. "You've hurt my eye."

"Oh, rot, man!"

"No, man, you are a swine! You've hurt it. No, man, you are a filthy hog, really!"

"I say. *Sorry*, old man."

"All right, old man. Didn't hurt."

"I say, old man," says Lomas, "I'm jolly glad I didn't live in the French Revolution, aren't you?"

"Oo, no, man. I'm not sorry. D'you know what I'd've done if I'd lived in the French Revolution?"

"No, what?"

"D'you know what I'd've done?" Master Wildman repeats, and has to pause, not being quite sure of what exact splendid thing he would have done in those unsettled days. Lomas helps him.

"Would you have been an aristocrat?"

"Ra*ther*. . . . Do you know what I'd have done?"

"What, man?"

"I'd have escaped in a tumbril."

"Would you, man?"

"Ra*ther*. . . . In a tumbril. . . . I don't expect *you* know what a tumbril is."

Lomas gently leads away from the tumbril. . . . "You'd probably've been guillotined," he says quietly.

"No, I wouldn't. And do you know why?"

"No. Why, man?"

"Because I'd've filled myself bang through with electricity. And when you do that you can't be killed because I read it."

"Kill you all the same," says Lomas, who knows his world. "Suppose you met Robespierre?" he adds, looking at it in another light. This also is a sort of counterstroke to the tumbril.

"Wouldn't mind," says Master Wildman, and thrusts back with, "Might meet Danton, too."

"Oh, rot, man. Danton was a meedeyeevle poet."

"Wasn't."

"Was."

"Wasn't."

"Anyway, man, there wasn't any electricity in those days, so Robespierre'd only got to say: 'I hereby order the commune to have you executed,' and you'd be done in."

"Wouldn't mind being guillotined," says Master Wildman.

"You'd die, man," Lomas warns him.

"Wouldn't mind."

"Oo—you would."

"Woodn't."

"Wood."

"Woodn't."

"Wood."

"Woodn't."

By this time they have reached the Green. They fix three stumps into the ground (to the detriment of the bat) for a wicket, and they fix one stump sixty-six feet, or rather little boy's boots, away from it. They toss for first innings (to the bat's further vexation) and they commence to play.

Lomas bowls. He is a fast bowler—jolly nearly as fast as Hitch, as he himself puts it. His first ball is missed by

Master Wildman, and goes through the railings and out of the ground. Subsequent balls do the same.

For two hours they play, the Southam Green public braving traffic, emerging from gutters, and flourishing and returning a ball, to receive a brisk word of thanks from a couple of cricketers who are enjoying themselves entirely.

IV

At the end of Master Wildman's summer holidays the contents of the right-hand drawer in Elsie's chest of drawers, in Elsie's room, are as follows:—

Three pairs of brown stockings rolled with the Nixon efficiency; five serviceable handkerchiefs; a snapshot of Master Wildman looking very jolly in the sun; an old hairbrush; a blouse; an old penknife that has once belonged to Master Wildman; a pink ribbon sash; a piece of paper upon which Master Wildman has written her own name in two letters in two ways; an amount of coagulated Acid Drop and Paper Bag; a picture postcard of a cow-dotted Scottish Highland on a beautiful evening, and an old exercise book that has once belonged to Master Wildman.

The contents of Master Wildman's corresponding drawer are in no way reciprocative.

There are three pairs of socks; two flannel shirts; an uncorked bottle of linseed oil; a school tie (oily therefrom); a generous sprinkling of cigarette cards; what was once a golf ball, but now the stringy-elastic outcome of an inquisitive nature; an electric battery for a hand-torch; and some lumps of milk-soaked bread for the consumption of a small white mouse which has not taken to this style of habitation at all at present.

CHAPTER IV

Sunday at Craven House.

I

SUNDAY MORNING! . . . Mrs. Nixon comes charging—and there is no other word to use but charging—into a sleeping Elsie's room, slams—and there is no other word to use but

slams—Elsie's allowance of hot water on to Elsie's washing-
stand, rattles up Elsie's Venetian blind like some stinging
fury very much enjoying her task, and lets in a flood of
blazing Sunday morning sunshine, which is a different kind
of sunshine to all other mornings' sunshine to Elsie, who
turns slowly from her sleep and knows she is in for it. For
though one is as good and retiring as one possibly can be
on all the days of the week, one has to be better and more
retiring still on Sunday, which is a holy and terrible day—a
day in which a God who has been but a gaunt, impending
threat for the six days past, now suddenly overhangs His
Universe, and you are to be rushed off in your best and tightest
clothes to pay Him your respects.

"Now then, Lazy Head," says Mrs. Nixon. "Up you get!
Five minutes behindhand already!" And she bursts out
again in the way she came.

Elsie jumps out of bed, kneels and prays what amounts
to a sort of hurried note to God that she must be quick and
dress now, but she'll be along at Church in no time, strips
herself, and begins to wash. No cold bath in the bathroom
on Sunday morning, because Mr. Spicer has a cold bath
on Sunday morning, and if you go down you encounter
Mr. Spicer in a baffling dressing-gown, and he says "Oh—ah,
you going to have a bath too?" and leers, and you have
to run up again—no cold bath on Sunday morning, and a
good thing too, because washing yourself (thoroughly, if
you please, Miss) in warm water isn't nearly so unpleasant.

But it is unpleasant enough. . . . Yes, we must wash
right under our arms (as mother has told us), and right down
our back (although we can't reach it), and all over with
the sponge, and a sloosh here, and a sloosh there, and one
more good sloosh, and we are in the towel, nearly washed
away but feeling better and better every moment. . . .

We are on to the dressing in next to no time, and prancing
into a slithering, starched, clean, white Sunday petticoat. . . .
We put on our purple, beady Sunday frock, which we are
rather proud of, actually, though we mustn't be vain, least
of all on a Sunday, and we make our own bed, being a capable
little Scotch Miss (or Lassie) and we fold our night-dress, and
by this time mother has rejoined us.

"Ah, there's a quick little girl," she says, and we run
downstairs, or rather dance downstairs, humming and waving
our hands, for a good word from mother on a Sunday morning

is a good word indeed, and perhaps we will get over the day pretty well after all. . . .

Here is breakfast, with bright new flowers in the middle of a bright new tablecloth. And here is Mr. Spicer, radiating Early Bath in his Sunday frock-coat and trousers which even his tooth cannot outdazzle. And here is Miss Hatt, rustling, rustling, rustling in her Sunday silken dress; and here is Audrey, starched from head to foot, crackling rather than rustling. And there is Master Wildman with the sun falling on to his face, and his hair falling over his brown forehead, looking even more delightful than he usually looks. But this rather depresses us somehow. We have no idea why. . . .

Breakfast is over, the Church is a quarter of a mile away, and the whole house is in a direful state of bustle and bother. "Bring my hat down while you're up there, will you, dear?" "Just a moment, dear." Thud. Thud. Thud. "If he *should* call, say I won't be back till half-past twelve, Audrey." "Yes'm." "Seen my walking-stick anywhere, boy?" "No, daddy."

We are flying about in our bedroom looking for our prayer book. Mother is calling to us. What *will* she say if we've lost it? Oh, what *will* she say? *Ah!* . . . A beautiful purple leather thing, our very own—almost a compensation for going to Church. "Are you never coming, Elsie?" "Here I am, mother." "Gracious, child, what a mess you're in. . . ."

We are wrenched away to the study by mother, and we are brushed with a hard, punching brush. "Heavens, girl (*Punch. Punch. Punch.*), what a (*Punch. Punch. Punch.*) mess! Will you *never* (*Punch. Punch. Punch.*) learn to——" (*Punch. Punch. Punch. Punch. Punch.*)

"*And* your mouth!" says Mrs. Nixon, getting hotter and hotter in the face, and thinner and thinner in the mouth. "*Oh*, you little devil! you! Egg! Come here! (Wrench.) Where's your hanky? Where *is* it? Put your face back!" We do so. Mother moistens the handkerchief with her own spittle. "Do you want a (*Dab. Dab. Dab.*) nursemaid (*Dab. Dab. Dab.*) to look after you? (*Dab. Dab. Dab.*) There! Egg!" (*Dab. Dab. Dab. Dab. Dab.*)

Three minutes later, dabbed and punched and wrenched, and shoved and white-cotton-gloved, and with our beautiful purple leather prayer book in one hand, and our other hand

painfully squashed in mother's, we find ourselves on the way
to the Church. Once we try to get our hand free, but "Don't
wriggle, girl," says mother, who is talking to Mrs. Spicer.
Mr. Spicer is on ahead with the Major. Master Wildman is
walking by our side, and we love him deeply, but he has
nothing to say to us. Indeed, he is making rude faces at
us whenever he sees mother isn't looking, the most devilish
faces and contortions, but the more faces he makes the
more we love him. . . .

At last we come to the Church door. Mother releases
our hand and the blood comes back to it again, but now
we're being squashed by the crowd. . . . Very dark in here.
. . . Here's the Verger again, with his fiery nose, and beads
for eyes, and sad expression. . . . Very dark in here. . . .
Whisper. Whisper. Whisper. . . . Rustle. Rustle. Rustle.
. . . Dim glitter of the altar. . . . We're in our pew. . . .
Smell of hassocks. . . . Mr. and Mrs. Spicer established
in the pew in front. . . . *Clatter-clatter* goes Mr. Spicer's
walking-stick on to the floor as he kneels to pray. . . . But
he goes on praying all the same. . . . We must pray, too.
Just what one likes to pray, mother has said. . . . "O
God, who art in Heaven, look upon a little girl. God bless
mother and forgive them that trespass as we forgive the
power and the glory the glory the glory make me a good
little girl make me a good little girl and bless my mother
and bless my mother for what we're about to receive may
the Lord make me truly thankful and mother's finished
praying so we needn't go on much longer make me a good
little girl, and give me my daily bread, gentle Jesus, for
Jesus Christ's sake. Amen."

"Move along a bit further, child." "Yes, mother." Deep,
deep silence. . . . Gentleman coughing somewhere. . . .
Lady blowing her nose. . . . A hundred ladies and gentlemen
coughing and blowing their noses—as though they have only
come here to cough and blow their noses. . . .

Pale moan from the choir in the vestry. Stand up! Sit
down! Stand up! Down on your knees again. . . . We're
off! . . .

II

Mr. Spicer's theory of the Universe was still largely Coper-
nican, and remained so, because there was too much Fingering
going about with all this Science and Evolution and whatnot,

as it was. He believed, mind you, that the earth was
a round object, for that was one of the first things you were
Taught at School, and he would have laughed if you denied
it; and he knew that the people in Australia weren't walking
about upside-down; because, we all knew, an apple had
tumbled on to Sir Isaac Newton's head (on behalf of gravita-
tion, which had long been waiting to explain itself) in the
seventeenth century, and made the matter clear for good.
But at the same time Mr. Spicer still believed that Heaven
was above, and Hell, though there wasn't any Hell nowadays
(except, perhaps, for Murderers), was beneath, which made
things very awkward when it came to Prayer. For there was
no doubt that, round as the world might be, and however
much Scientists might talk, one *was*, somehow, on the top
oneself. At this rate, while you prayed Up (and one was
not against a Little Prayer on occasions) the Australians were
praying Down. There were like difficulties with such peoples
as the Americans and Russians, who filled either side, as it
were, and so had to pray Out, apparently, or horizontally. . . .
The whole thing was very difficult. And this examination
of and following up of his own beliefs was very seldom
indulged in by Mr. Spicer, who held that it was best not
to Finger.

Nevertheless Mr. Spicer considered himself rather a dab
at Religion, on the quiet, and would unfailingly lower his
voice, and behave coyly, whenever he came to talk about
it. He would call himself a Firm Believer in the Bible—a
Certain Little Book, and he had evolved a certain set of
working morals of his own. He had, in fact, a Little
Philosophy.

Predominant, perhaps, in Mr. Spicer's Little Philosophy,
was to be found a Little Word. This was duty. But Mr.
Spicer became so furtive when he came to talk about this,
and so seldom got any further than "Yes, but there happens
to be a Little Word, doesn't there?" without giving any hint
of what that Little Word was, that it seems rather unfair
of us to disclose it now. This Little Word (beginning with
D, let us say, borrowing Mr. Spicer's occasional compromise)
stood for the sterner side of Mr. Spicer's Little Philosophy.
There were, on the other hand, any amount of Little Thoughts,
Little Deeds, Little Words, and Little Memories, etc., to
modify its high austerity. Without introducing a hint of

softness, for Mr. Spicer's Little Philosophy was above all things a Man's Philosophy.

A man's Philosophy had a phraseology peculiar to itself, which had varied considerably during the last twenty years of Mr. Spicer's theological advancement, taking its source from Mr. Spicer's immediate habits, circumstances, or reading of romantic fiction. Hence, as a young man of twenty-one, Mr. Spicer had found an ideal standard of conduct expressed by, and included under the simple term "White Man." As a White Man, you were opposed not to blackness, but yellowness, which disported itself in streaks; you played the Cards Straight, were expected to Keep a Clean Scroll, and Reckoned you could Face your Maker—which you were called upon to do only when your Last Trick was Played. This manner of rhetoric was of course more or less derivative from the Boy's Serial, but when, a few years later, the dying cowboy in Mr. Spicer was thwarted and smothered by the atmosphere forced upon him as a City clerk, much of this inflated style survived. Thus, after his first experiments in the art of book-keeping, Mr. Spicer was soon alluding to such things as a day when he would have to Balance the Great Ledger; Spiritual Debits, and the Final Auditor. There were many other fluctuations besides, and all according to his latest reading. Sometimes Mr. Spicer became purely naval and would image the truly righteous soul as one that Steered North and looked to the Stars, under the supervision of a Great Pilot. Sometimes he employed a military turn of speech and along came Supreme Captains, Last Roll Calls, Final Reveillés and so on and so forth. . . .

Mr. Spicer always endeavoured to concentrate upon the service. "I don't come to church to see what sort of hat the lady in the pew opposite's wearing," he would often say. There was, however, on the Sunday we are dealing with, an amount of lay concentration quite incompatible with these professions. The chief problem engaging Mr. Spicer's ingenuity at the moment was the problem of how, exactly, he was going to have three or four hours to himself after tea that day.

To the chanting of the Lesson Mr. Spicer tried over some little conversations with Mrs. Spicer.

"A little indigestion, dear. Think I'll go and walk it off. . . . No, dear. I'll go too fast for you, and I can see you're tired."

Or, "Did I tell you my old pal Shipwright came back from Celyon the other day? Lives up at Kensington. He asked if I'd go along. Think I'll go and give him a look up. . . ."

No.

A Good Tramp. . . . "Fine night, my dear. Think I'll go for a good old tramp, like I used to. . . . No, you'd never keep up with me. . . . A real Tramp. . . . Oh, all right, come if you like, but you'd never keep up with me. . . . Want a Tramp. Shake the inertia off me. . . ."

Mrs. Spicer did not look trustful. . . . Confound it all, a man must——

"The hymn will be number three hundred and seventy-eight. *'Rejoice to-day with one accord'* . . ."

Mr. Spicer jumped up to rejoice.

III

At half-past twelve the guests of Craven House took their places in the thronged and muttering aisle queue, interestedly smelt each other's clothes and hats, shuffled by slow degrees from the church, and out into the stone porch and a world blown and hissing under a brisk blue sky. The wind roared in their ears so that they could hardly hear each other speak, but they were very chatty about the sermon, in the manner of people comparing notes after a minor ordeal. They bent their bodies forward, and frowned, when the wind was facing them; and jumped lumpily along when it was ragging them from behind; and clung to their hats in either case. The wind was also revealing astonishing portions of Mrs. Nixon's red Sunday petticoat, with a malicious, flicking, "*Here-you-are-Have-a-look-at-it-I've-only-got-a-moment*" kind of gesture, which was bothering Mrs. Nixon as much as it was shocking Master Wildman. ("Too long for her," he decided.)

There was an hour before lunch, discerned as an Hour by Miss Hatt's guests, and they broke apart to spend it in their accustomed ways. Miss Hatt herself hastened back to Audrey and Edith to enquire generally why she could never rely on these girls to do anything. Elsie had to write a diffident and respectfully loving bulletin of her actions during the week to Aunt Jessica, and rule the lines faintly in pencil first, and "no blots, Miss, or you do it again." The Major read, and his son idled disconsolately about the

house. Mr. and Mrs. Spicer alone remained out of doors,
thereby observing one of their most time-sanctioned and
inviolable practices—the Sunday morning walk—and regarding themselves as in no small measure an ornament
to the neighbourhood in their capacity of a Quiet Middle-
aged Couple. For Mr. and Mrs. Spicer very much liked to
advertise themselves as a quiet middle-aged couple—as though
quietness was a fine point in their favour, and the world
couldn't keep its middle-aged couples quiet as a rule. They
were rather a loud middle-aged couple this morning, however, owing to the wind, which they had to bawl against,
like mad, in order to hear each other.

Lunch was in the dining-room in good time, and so were
the guests, but Mr. Spicer, who took the rôle both of carver
and chairman, was upstairs changing his collar; and the
guests were kept three minutes looking at the weather until
he appeared with brisk apologies and began to sharpen
the knife—every inch a stylist.

The guests were soon supplied, and, settling down to stuff
in anticipation of More, talked little. Master Wildman was
reproved for taking mustard with mutton, which Mrs. Nixon,
with a proverb ready for any child on any occasion, affirmed
to be the sign of a glutton. Whereupon Master Wildman
of course replied by asking whether, if mustard with mutton
was the sign of a glutton, was mustard with beef the sign
of a thief? The company laughed, and Mr. Spicer told
Master Wildman that he was getting quite brilliant, as he
did on nearly every occasion of dining at the same table with
Master Wildman. Master Wildman then stretched the joke
further by declaring that mustard with fish was the sign
of a bish (Op), and that mustard with eggs was the sign
(in weaker verse) that you *had legs*. And he would doubtless
have gone further still, for Elsie's benefit, had not Mr. Spicer
intervened with the question of More—just a little of which
was taken by all, all having really, no really, thought they
wouldn't, until Mr. Spicer became so very pressing.

Apple tart and custard followed, and Elsie, who was
beginning to feel quite ill, had a large plateful given her,
and dare not leave a bit of it, for "Waste not, want not,"
was another proverb only waiting to pounce upon her.

After lunch they all went into the drawing-room, offered
each other each of each other's chairs, or positions on the
sofa, settled deeply into the same, and dropped slowly off,

one by one, into a state of thick snoozing effected by a little too much More. There followed a sacred silence, as it were, presided over by the little priestess Elsie, the nick-nick-nick of whose knitting needles might have been the very working of a mystic charm. This state of affairs lasted for something like an hour and was eventually blown to pieces by the Major with an undebatable Snore, which was tacitly overlooked but not unnoticed, as an immediate series of shiftings and sighs on the part of Miss Hatt's guests plainly demonstrated. A kind of St. Martin's summer of sleep followed, but it was not the real thing, and very soon the rattle and thunder of Mr. Spicer's resumed Sunday newspaper settled the matter finally.

"Seems to be keeping quite fine, still," said Mr. Spicer.

The onus of grunting an affirmative, being everybody's business, was nobody's business, and after rather too long a silence was undertaken by the Major.

"Now what we all ought to do now," said Mr. Spicer, "is to go out and have a good long walk." A certain uncertain bluffness in Mr. Spicer's tones betokened, without at present betraying, a hidden motive.

The Major, now holding himself committed by his first grunt, answered:

"Yes, I think you're right."

Polite window-gazing ensued on the part of the others.

"Hanged if I won't take one," said Mr. Spicer.

But before there was time to see how a wife was taking all this, Mrs. Nixon cut in with a question to the Major.

"Is your little son going to be a soldier, then?" she asked.

"Well," said the Major, "I don't know whether he cares to follow in his father's footsteps. What do you think about it, eh, boy?"

The boy wobbled an embarrassed and smiling head from one side to another to express neutrality.

"Perhaps he's a little soldier already," said Mrs. Nixon, alluding to higher disciplines, and looking with severe charm at her knitting.

But the Major was unable to grapple with this lofty plane of thought.

"Oh—ah—yes. Possibly," said the Major, and the company's blushes were rescued, half in cheek, by the clanging of the gong for tea, which was followed by the appearance of an Audrey labouring under a large tray; which was followed by the appearance of a dumb waiter containing the thinnest bread and butter conceivable, swiss roll and plum cake; which was followed by much fuss and bother, uncanny feats of balancing (Mr. Spicer sidling across the floor, tea-cup in hand, as though it were an egg-and-spoon race), and the extreme little-gentlemanliness of Master Wildman, who handed things round; which was followed by more desultory conversation, which comprised another heavy remark about good long walks from Mr. Spicer, which again passed unnoticed.

After tea Mr. Spicer happened to meet Mrs. Spicer in the twilit hall.

"Think I'll go for a tramp, dear," said Mr. Spicer, and opened the front door.

"Oh, all right, dear," said Mrs. Spicer. "Shall I come along with you?"

"Oh, yes. . . . Come if you like. . . . Thought I'd take a *good long* tramp, though. Want to work off a bit of indigestion I've got. . . ."

"Well, perhaps I'd better let you go alone, then," said Mrs. Spicer.

"Oh, no. Come if you like," said Mr. Spicer.

"Well, I might then," said Mrs. Spicer.

"Well, perhaps you'd better not, though," said Mr. Spicer. "Might walk you off your feet."

"Oh, very well."

"Come if you like, though," said Mr. Spicer, who was, of course, a man attempting to eat his cake and have it too.

"Oh, very well, then," said Mrs. Spicer. "I will. I'll go and get my things."

She made for the stairs, and got half-way up them.

"You'd better not, though, dear," said Mr. Spicer. "I'll go much too fast for you."

"What? Well, dear, you might say one thing or the other."

"Sorry, my dear. Indigestion. Bit restless."

"You're going by yourself, then?"

"Yes. I'll go and have a good tramp and shake it off."

"Oh, very well. Good-bye."

"Good-bye, dear. Be back to dinner." Mr. Spicer vanished.

Mrs. Spicer encountered Miss Hatt, flying down the stairs.

"Oh, dear—these men!" said Mrs. Spicer, passing her.

"They are a bother at times, aren't they, dear?" said a flying Miss Hatt.

"Yes," laughed Mrs. Spicer.

"Never mind, they have their good points," shouted Miss Hatt, still flying.

"Oh, yes!" admitted Mrs. Spicer, and went laughing into her room.

"Something queer," said Mrs. Spicer to the Universe.

IV

That the rather restless gentleman in question was incontrovertibly up to something queer our readers will have gathered before Mrs. Spicer summed up the position by those two words in her bedroom. But of the exact nature of that queer something we can give no exact information; and we believe that Mr. Spicer himself was not quite clear on the point either.

We must therefore satisfy ourselves with simply sketching the routes taken by Mr. Spicer on this highly sinister good tramp of his, as well as some of the adventures met by the way, and make no other comment.

We must be content with saying, then, that our pedestrian's first stoppage was at "The Three Kings"—a public house—where he ordered a whiskey and soda; that he sipped the same in what appeared to be an unusually peering frame of mind, for Mr. Spicer (who peered immensely at the best of times): that he ordered another whiskey and soda from the barmaid he was principally peering at, and then peered further: that, having swung the last contents of the last-named whiskey and soda down his throat, he endeavoured in vain to nod "good evening" to the barmaid under scrutiny, and emerged from "The Three Kings," not without dropping his umbrella near the door and apologising over-fluently to the lady he dropped it on to.

That he then took a District train to Hyde Park Corner, where we lose him for five minutes or so, in another public house, but find him in the Park soon after, with another and third whiskey and soda inside him.

That while strolling up and down the main avenues of the Park, Mr. Spicer soon began to peer to the extent of downright Nosiness: that his peering was directed towards the numerous young ladies seated, with crossed legs, upon the chairs lining these avenues: that the difficulties arising from an attempt to combine (1) the intense function of peering sideways, with (2) the perfectly nonchalant function of strolling forwards, reduced Mr. Spicer's stride to something uncommonly resembling the crab's.

That darkness thickening in the Park now gently enveloped Mr. Spicer in such a way as to lead him long past the phase of mere Nosiness, and up into a higher and almost spiritual phase of Absolute and Essential Nose, wherein that gentleman *was* Nose, and nothing else: and, further, that this wraith-like entity appeared to float (rather than be carried by its human owner) like some extraordinary materialisation phenomenon, under the trees. . . .

That a Nose, at a certain point under the trees, came to a halt: that a Nose thereupon retraced 150 yards or so of its own path, or rather line in ether: that a Nose then halted again and turned back once more: that at the same time, a lady, in this manner passed while seated with crossed legs upon a chair, rose and walked away from a Nose: that a Nose pursued: that a Nose pursued not in vain, in that the lady soon came to a halt under a tree: that a Nose halted too, and did miracles in the way of looking at the weather, trees, and a lady, all at the same time, and that a Nose was now in such a highly-strung and human condition as to be recognisable as plain Mr. Spicer again.

That Mr. Spicer, summoning courage, braced himself to the extent of sidling in the direction of the lady, who remained still: that Mr. Spicer, having given a careful look to the right, and a careful look to the left, Nosed in upon the lady very suddenly. That, having given her "Good evening," Mr. Spicer asked her if she was Going Anywhere: that the lady was rather charmed than alarmed by Mr. Spicer, and gave it out that she was going nowhere: that a pause ensued in a conversation that had begun so well: that the lady was neither as young as she used to be nor as winning as she appeared at a distance: that she returned Nose for Nose, in fact, with additions: that Mr. Spicer, to restore conversation, asked how the lady was Getting On: that the lady replied she was doing all right, thanks, though there was, she affirmed as some qualification, nothing to write home to mother about: that conversation again expired: that Mr. Spicer observed, "Well, what about it?": that the lady returned, "Well, *what* about it?": that Mr. Spicer regretted having said "Well, what about it": that Mr. Spicer therefore said Well, as a matter of fact he had arranged to meet a friend along here, and he was much surprised he had not already turned up: that the lady said Well, she was waiting for a friend, really, too: that in view of the fact that both had previous appointments with suitable friends elsewhere, another state of indecision followed, and that both said "Well" at each other for some time before parting with "Good Night."

That Mr. Spicer, having plainly decided against any more conversations of this nature, now cut across the Park to Knightsbridge, and here entered another tavern.

That Mr. Spicer's first action on entering this tavern was to call for beer: that Mr. Spicer consumed it rapidly when he got it: that Mr. Spicer dropped his umbrella, picked it up again, and ordered more beer: that Mr. Spicer did not refer to it as beer, but as the Same Refreshment: that Mr. Spicer, having observed to the barmaid, by way of self-introduction, that it was a fine evening outside, proceeded to ask her if she would have one (to be named by herself) with him: that the barmaid said that she thought that was very good of Mr. Spicer, and she *would* have a port, then— thank you—thank you very much—and deferentially poured it out for herself: that a pleasant conversation ensued, during which this barmaid drew unimportant and entirely paren-thetical bitters for other customers, as well as one more for Mr. Spicer: and that the fumes of alcohol at this point entered our adventurer's brain.

That, as a direct result of this, Mr. Spicer became gallant, and having again declared that it was a fine evening outside, went on to declare that it was a fine *view* outside, which enabled him to observe that there was a still finer view inside: that, the compliment having been taken in excellent part, Mr. Spicer instantly hit upon further altogether cavalier and pot-valiant similes with respect to fine beers and finer women serving it, and so on and so forth.

That Mr. Spicer was soon so advanced with his tap-room friend that he had already asked her if she was coming out with him one of these fine (he stipulated) evenings, and was already receiving a reply of favourable doubt, when the *tête-à-tête* was interrupted by a Man.

That the Man's eyes were half-closed, that the Man held a toppling glass of whiskey and soda in a quavering hand, and informed Mr. Spicer that he looked very lonely, and he (the Man) was lonely too, and what was Mr. Spicer taking?

That Mr. Spicer was slightly in a fix at first, but rallied to say that he would have another beer.

That the Man then opened with the statement that Mr. Spicer could doubtless see that he (the man) was a Naval Man, that he had the look about him, and that Mr. Spicer must admit it, although Mr. Spicer, perhaps, was not a naval man himself: that Mr. Spicer replied No, he was not a naval man: that the Naval Man laughed very loud and long for some time, but at last consoled Mr. Spicer for such a flaw in his education with the reflection that we cannot all be naval men: that the Naval Man said that this was beside the point, however, the point being, the point being, the point being, the point being ("What *is* the point, then?" asked Mr. Spicer. "Don't interrupt me, sir!" said the Naval Man.), the point being, the point being that old England was going to the Dogs, sir!: that Mr. Spicer said he rather thought so, too: that the Naval Man said "You *do* think so, too?": that Mr. Spicer affirmed "I *do* think so, too": that the Naval Man said he *could* mention certain people's names, and Mr. Spicer allowed that certain people's names could be mentioned: that the Naval Man hinted that he *could* mention the name of Lloyd George, if he liked, but he wasn't going to, and he *could* mention the name of Winston Churchill, but he wasn't going to mention him either: that Mr. Spicer agreed that both of these names could be mentioned, but admired a naval man's reticence, and asked what a naval man was going to have now?

That the Naval Man said Mr. Spicer was the greatest sport he had ever met, and that Mr. Spicer ordered two more whiskeys and sodas: that Mr. Spicer dropped his umbrella in that act: that Mr. Spicer was now dropping his umbrella once or twice too often: that a political discussion took place: that the Naval Man suggested that the only hope for old England, that he could see, was the Boy Scout movement: that Mr. Spicer agreed: that they both wished they had been Boy Scouts: that the Naval Man swore that all *his* sons were going to be Boy Scouts: that Mr. Spicer rejoined that all *his* sons were going to be Boy Scouts: that the Naval Man asked if he had any sons, then: that Mr. Spicer replied No: that the naval man said "Then you must have some": and that Mr. Spicer replied "I certainly will," with the shrewd air of a man taking a mental note of it.

That two more whiskies and sodas were ordered for each:

that Mr. Spicer suddenly saw a clock: that Mr. Spicer's face fell: that Mr. Spicer said that he must be going, and murmured something about these wives: that Mr. Spicer left, and made for the station, where it was borne in upon Mr. Spicer that there was only three-quarters of an hour and a train journey between him and half-past eight cold supper at Craven House—and a smiling Mrs. Spicer, who would be expecting to have his tramp described.

v

The leading character of the household having smuggled himself off, the remaining guests settle down before the drawing-room fire for what that leading character, had he been present, would have described as a Little Chat, in the Gloaming.

Elsie never knows why, at all, but she is always extremely depressed at this time of day on Sunday. And it is even worse to-day. . . . For the wind is as strong as ever outside. It storms the chimney, it keeps the trees hissing and bowing to each other endlessly outside, and it causes the little leaves on the laurel bush just outside in the garden to patter urgently against the drawing-room window-pane. . . . The light grows less and less, and it is as though some very horrid and gusty consummation to the world's affairs is in preparation. Within, the red, flameless coal blazes brighter and brighter from the heavy dusk, and little licking flames, so intensely and wickedly blue as to be almost green, light the unrippled complacence of mother's face with a gentle malice of their own. And if Elsie looks away from that face, and into the fire itself, she is not made in any way more cheerful by the sight of the weirdest and cunningest little caves, and trees, and tiny men, and silent little red passages, convertible into silent insinuating monsters—to say nothing of various excessively silent mustard-pots, church spires, monks, rats, cricket bats, bishops and the like. . . .

Something over half-an-hour is spent in the gloaming, and then a walk is suggested. The Major cannot join the others, having some letters to write, but Mrs. and Miss Nixon, Mrs. Spicer and Master Wildman are soon outside the front door.

Here Elsie is no more hopeful. The air is damp, the ground is wet and glistening, the trees are tangled with all their vexation, the church bells are pealing with the weariness of

futile centuries behind them, and even the hushed and inscrutable lamp-post opposite Craven House seems to have
begun some of its pitiless implications already, at half-past
five, instead of half-past ten, when it usually sets in on such
matters.

Elsie is allowed to go ahead with Master Wildman, who
is not susceptible to the influences of the weather. She does
not venture to speak to him, however, for fear of rebuff.
For Master Wildman is an enormously sensitive young man,
these days, for a young girl, like herself, to approach; and
it generally ends in her being called a Fool for deliberating,
suggesting, or thinking anything whatsoever. This she well
knows, having made many previous attempts to enter into
Master Wildman's affairs, to achieve which would have been
a great pleasure for her.

Too much silence doesn't seem to satisfy Master Wildman
either, however. "You're not very talkative to-night," says
Master Wildman.

"I didn't mean to be," apologises Elsie.

"What? Didn't mean to be talkative?" quibbles Master
Wildman.

"No. Didn't mean to be Not."

"Oh."

A long silence follows in which Master Wildman deserts
these openings in favour of bowling several imaginary balls
down the road, accompanying each of his deliveries with the
matter-of-fact triumph, "Bowled him!" but with one "Oo!
Missed him!"; which concession adds realism, but is abruptly
rectified next ball. He then comes back to Elsie.

"If there are eleven people in a side, how many people
have got to get out before the side's out?" he asks.

"Why? What do you mean?"

"*How many people have got to get out?*"

"Why? Eleven," tries Elsie, and "Oh, you ass! Oh,
you are an ass! I knew you'd say that! Oh, you are an
ass!" says Master Wildman.

Elsie keeps perfectly quiet.

But Master Wildman is carried away by, and simply
dancing on account of the triumphant victory of his little
trap. "Oh, you are a fool!" he exclaims, and takes to cricket
again. "Bowled him! . . . Bowled him! . . . Bowled him!
. . . Hat trick! . . . Bowled him! . . . Bowled him! . . .
Bowled him! . . . Double hat trick. . . . Bowled him . . .

Bowled him. . . . BOWLED HIM! *TRIPLE HAT TRICK! . . .*"

"Keep off the road, there's a good boy!" shouts Mrs. Spicer from behind.

"Ten, you ass!" says Master Wildman, and they do not speak for some time.

"What would you do if a bomb fell in the road here, now?" asks Master Wildman, but gives Elsie not time even to think about such a crisis. "Do you know what I would do?"

"No."

"I'd pick it up in my hands and drop it in some water," says Master Wildman, and having gloomily prophesied "You'd probably run away," he does not attend to her for quite another five minutes.

When he addresses her again his voice is a little kinder and he seems to have been working something out in his mind.

"Have you ever been on the stage?" he asks.

"No," says Elsie.

"I have," says Master Wildman. "In a play."

"Have you?" says Elsie, staring at him.

"Yes. In the 'Scarlet Pimpernel.' At Bournemouth. I have."

Elsie does not reply.

"I have. What do you think happened?"

"I don't know."

"What do you think happened? The man who acted the Scarlet Pimpernel fell ill. Got Scarlet Fever. And they asked me to act his part. They did. They did! They asked me. They did!"

"Who asked you?"

Master Wildman gives Elsie a rather sullen little look before replying.

"The manager," he says, quietly.

"He did!" says Master Wildman. "He did! And I played all the part right through. I did! Don't you believe me?"

"How could you play a part like that?" says Elsie, and looks at his size in justification of her objection. "You're too young."

"Look here. Don't you believe me? Don't you believe I did?"

Elsie uses grave tact.

"I believe you think you did," says Elsie.

"Look here. Do you think I'm telling you a lie? Do you think I'm telling you a lie?"

"No. I don't think you're telling a Lie," says Elsie, quietly, and to be quite fair. "I think you're Making a Mistake."

But even this truly queenly reticence on Elsie's part is not acceptable to Master Wildman. Which is extremely ill-mannered in him; for, as the reader will have easily concluded, the child had never been chosen to play the part of the Scarlet Pimpernel during the leading actor's illness, and any other less friendly critic than the one he has might most justifiably have considered it a mightily awkward matter to make a mistake about.

"Look here, you're calling me a liar," says Master Wildman. "All right, then. You wait. You wait. You just wait!"

His threat is entirely lacking in venom, however, and he at once settles down into some more bowling, in which realism reaches a pitch of "missing him" five or six times in succession.

He then takes over the batting, which he shoulders for the rest of the walk, occasionally falling back from a droning continuity of boundaries to mutter "You just wait" to Elsie, but for the most part building century after century with "Sixer — sixer — sixer — sixer — fourer — sixer — sixer —fourer——oo! only *two*er!—oo! only *one*r!—sixer—sixer—— *three*-er!—sixer—oo! Nearly bowled-er!—sixer—sixer—sixer —nearly caughter—sixer . . ."

Thus there is little entertainment for Elsie in this walk, which, towards the end, is taken in an October mist, which lies close to the ground, or rolls over and over in the watery yellow light of the street lamps, without serving to hide various bowed wayfarers hurrying between a chilly evening service and a chilly joint and salad at home.

Sunday supper is taken late at Craven House, and the hour or so that lies before it is prearranged for Elsie, who at this time of day has to learn, and afterwards recite, what her own timid little tongue, lips and teeth are only capable of describing as a Tecks, but what her mother succeeds in naming a Text, from the Bible. Fierce hissing repetition is indulged in for the better mastery of the words contained in this Tecks, as well as noticeable weakness in the direction of eye-closing, forehead-thumping, and furtive peeping. This takes place in the drawing-room, directly under the throaty gas, where the air is very close, and where Master Wildman is still playing cricket, this time on paper, and jabbing unscrupulously in favour of Woolley, who happens to be his favourite at the moment.

This lasts until a quarter-past eight, when the appearance of Miss Hatt, in her Sunday evening-dress, denotes that supper may soon be taken, but for the fact that Mr. Spicer is not yet In—a most extraordinarily Out, inconsequent, and mystifying Mr. Spicer being the subject of some mute speculation by Miss Hatt's guests, for all their easy chatting.

Half-past eight comes, and five-and-twenty to nine, and "Please don't let's wait any longer," says Mrs. Spicer. "I expect he'll be in any minute now." So they go in to supper without Mr. Spicer, which is like a class without a master, and none the less jolly for that—in that an air of gay anarchy prevails, particularly with regard to the carving of the joint, which the Major is at last persuaded to tackle, hacking off and distributing exquisitely unfamiliar parts to eminently charmed recipients, and giving, on the whole, rather better measure than the absent expert. . . . Until a sudden and wholly violent clicking noise at the front door announces the return of the latter. "Here he is," whispers Mrs. Spicer, and a deadly silence falls upon those at table. This silence is not at first relieved by any further, or progressive sounds from outside; but is eventually succeeded by a second even more violent but (this time) successful clicking noise, which is followed by the sound of the door slamming, and no other sound whatever, for a large period in time.

The absent procedure of listening to a backward Mr. Spicer proving a little too much for the guests, the conversation is reopened. This continues for a moment or two, but is cut into by something definable as a Lurch, and the more than sudden arrival of Mr. Spicer in the dining-room.

"Hullo? Am I late?"

"Never mind. Still something left for you," says Miss Hatt.

"Oh, yes. Certainly," says Mrs. Spicer to the Universe. . . .

"Still something left for me? Good. Good. Lost all count of time."

"Been walking all this time?" asks the Major.

"Carved?" asks Mr. Spicer, surveying the joint, and there is a silence.

"Yes. The Major's carved, dear," says Mrs. Spicer.

"The Major's carved? Good. Good. Been walking all this time, Major, did you ask? Yes. Been for a grand tramp all over Richmond Park. Fine."

That Mr. Spicer is still in a fuddled condition there is no doubt. Whether, however, Mr. Spicer allows the company to detect this condition in him, is another matter. And apart from the fact that Mrs. Spicer seems to be indulging in more "Yesses," and "No's," and "Certainlies," out-of-hand to the Universe than she has ever been known to do before, it would appear that Mr. Spicer preserves his secret intact.

We are nevertheless bound to remark that Mr. Spicer's treatment of the joint is a little hazy and perplexed: that, having worked in a maladroit manner upon a problematical slice of lamb, he at last succeeds in furnishing his plate with oddments, and then sits down at short notice: that, having sat down, he immediately rises, grasps the utensils, says "More for anybody? No? No more for anybody?" and takes his time about sitting down this time: and that although conversation is maintained during the rest of supper, and Mr. Spicer gives his share to it, in the silences that do happen to fall, Mr. Spicer is to be sensed distantly, and perhaps inaudibly, hiccoughing.

The company does not stay long in the drawing-room afterwards. Mr. Spicer pleads for a little music from his wife, but instantly yawns at it when it comes, and on being brought humorously to book by the good woman, admits that he is very tired and has perhaps overdone his tramp. The others are caught in sympathetic yawnings, for which they blame the Air, in general, and think they will retire.

Therefore the usual fair wishes, door-slamming, window-closing, light-extinguishing, muttering, match-scratching, and underbreath leave-takings take place, and Miss Hatt's guests are prone and unconscious in next to no time.

In such a way was Sunday spent, in Craven House, before the Great War of nineteen hundred and fourteen.

CHAPTER V

A Winter at Craven House

I

In the long winter before the war, Craven House, within and without, submitted with its own stolidity to the depressing and normal fluctuations of the time of year. The evenings drew in upon it, leaving it as early as half-past four to the mercy of its scheming lamp opposite; rains threshed its windows, thundered on its skylight, and spat multitudinously on its front steps; half-hearted snowfalls lit its rooms with garish bright grey; a particularly shabby celestial orange succeeded occasionally in becoming a sun, and shone with a hard, dead brilliance into it at midday; fogs enveloped it, reducing it and the neighbourhood to a pea soup void vaguely conscious of existence in the distant, intermittent, grumbling alarm of the fog-signals; the fifth of November let off innumerable squibs around it; the twenty-fifth of December released innumerable bands, urchins, and choirs around it; the wild east winds blew away a large part of a chimney of it, which necessitated a call from two down-at-heel creatures known as The Men; as well as blowing sufficient soot down the remaining chimneys to warrant treatment from another (and blackened) man, who appeared before breakfast, and who was unseen by Miss Hatt's guests, but was nevertheless conceived ideally by them, and in the nature of an eternal verity, as the Sweep.

Chills were caught early in the season, Mr. Spicer being the first to announce a lowering of vitality, which he did by a series of resounding and hostile trumpetings into a handkerchief. These fierce diapasons and fanfares were soon taken up by the Major, who could also and did in imitation, trumpet, but never with quite the same overbearing verve of his model. There was little serious illness at Craven House, nevertheless, the most alarming symptoms falling to Mr. Spicer, who, having ignored a Head, pooh-poohed (against Mrs. Spicer's convictions) a Throat, and having taken no heed of a subsequent undeniable Chest, was one night taken precipitately with all the symptoms of a disease temporarily classified, for want of something better, as The Trembles.

Whereupon he was packed off to bed, conferred upon, lightly drugged, and next morning washed and put into clean pyjamas against a visit from the Doctor (another eternal verity), who diagnosed a small attack of The Flu; which, being successfully battled against by The Mixture, did not keep Mr. Spicer on his back for long.   Indeed, it took but three days' heavy trumpeting in the drawing-room, combined with a much-discussed Turn around Keymer Gardens, in the fresh air, to have him back in the City again.

In this trying period it was Master Wildman who retained his vigour the best.   This little boy developed early in the season a very deep and plotting frame of mind.   As well as harbouring unhappy obsessions regarding Secret Passages —for which, like a lunatic child, he was ever and anon to be discovered pressing, fingering, or tapping the walls both of his school and Craven House—he himself founded a Secret Society of Six (school companions), whose business it was to assemble in the evenings, under the leadership of himself, who performed dramatically upon a pea-whistle, made signs (secret ones), and sent his subordinates forth either to Scout, or to Spy (in a merely intransitive way) and return with a Report—this being the sum of the obligations borne by this society.

He also was happy in discovering, later, that the overflow pipe to the bath at Craven House was a secret telephone, connected with a branch of Secret Anarchists, conferring in a Secret Tunnel beneath Southam Green.   We are unable to account for this belief (almost certainly a false one), but we have to say on his behalf that his friend Lomas was interested to the extent of wishing to put his ear against the bath pipe under debate, and for this purpose it was considered necessary that he should spend some time, un-hampered, in the bath.   It thus happened that Miss Hatt was one evening confronted in the hall by Master Wildman, who asked her, with intrepid gravity, whether his friend Lomas might have a bath.   "Where?" asked Miss Hatt. "Here," said Master Wildman.   "He wouldn't be long about it."   Miss Hatt, here experiencing all the bewilderment a middle-aged lady might justifiably experience on being asked whether a strange little boy might have a bath on her own premises, replied that she thought they had better "see about it," but failed to allude to the matter again.   "Can my friend have that bath now, please, Miss Hatt?" asked

Master Wildman a few days later. "But why does he want a *bath*, dear?" "He just wants one," said Master Wildman. "I'll lend him *my* towels for it." But "What's all this about a *bath*, boy?" asked the Major, half-an-hour later, and "Oh, nothing," said Master Wildman, and gave in.

Master Wildman was, all the same, looked upon during this winter as a well-behaved child; which, we are afraid, cannot altogether be said of his father. In this gentleman there had now, by slow degrees, arisen a multitude of not entirely gentlemanly characteristics. A certain carpet-slippered lateness in appearing at meals, a habit of yawning during the courses, a way of replying "Possibly" when sued for an opinion, an inclination to ring bells when in a temper, an increased tendency to write letters just before music time, an almost revolting (to Miss Hatt) neglect of his own moustache, and a perverse (to Miss Hatt) bias against letting out his own bath water, now became a little too marked. And although Miss Hatt was successful for the most part in bettering her petty emotions on these scores, there was no doubt that doors, if only distant ones, had been slammed in d:rect reference to such details, and it would hardly be exaggerating to say that on more than one occasion that black and unbelievable word Notice had hung heavily in the air. This was exceptionally observable on a certain Thursday evening in December, when the Major, who had for some time taken to bathing at "unearthly" (according to Miss Hatt) hours, was to be heard plashing behind a locked door at 6.30. Now this hour, on Thursday evening, was traditionally sacred for Mrs. Nixon's plunging, and had hitherto been considered inviolable. Miss Hatt, it is understood, was present when Mrs. Nixon found herself thwarted by the locked door, and having turned extremely pale, and tried the handle herself, assumed a calm commander's air, said, "Leave this to me, Mrs. Nixon, will you?" in a terribly level voice, and flew down to the kitchen. Whence, after half-a-minute's indistinct but aggressive mumbling, the widest-eyed Audrey emerged, rushed up the stairs, and knocked (peremptorily, as instructed) upon the bathroom door. "Hullo?" said the Major. "Please, sir," said Audrey, "Miss Hatt presents her compliments and says would you mind leaving your bathroom in ten minutes' time as it is her wish that Mrs. Nixon should partake of her bath this evening as arranged." The Major paused before replying,

and then "Will you return my compliments to Miss Hatt,"
he said, "and tell her that it is my intention to take my
bath in my own time?" Whereat he splashed into the water
again, like a sea-lion, and Audrey retired in a very fuddled
condition of obedience. "Please'm, I'm to return your compliments and say that it is my intention to take my bath
in my own time." "Very well, Audrey, thank you," said
Miss Hatt, but was not defeated. She again ran upstairs,
took her stand outside the bathroom door, and shouted up
to Mrs. Nixon.

"It's all right, Mrs. Nixon. He'll be out in ten minutes!"
she shouted.

Nor did a cascade of indifferent and saucy splashes, added
to some insulting scrubbings from the caustic gentleman
within, deter her from continuing: "And I'll see that you're
not troubled in the same way again!" and rapping three
times sharply, like a school-mistress, on the bathroom door,
which might have been the Major's knuckles. The Major
turned on more hot water in a fury, decided to give notice,
and very likely would have done so, had it not been too
near Christmas—a season when satisfactory new abodes are
hard to come by.

As for the relations existing between Miss Hatt, Mrs. Spicer
and Mrs. Nixon during this winter, it would be coarsening
the most delicate shades of disagreement to say that they
were anything but cordial and open-hearted. We are nevertheless able to record that when any two of these ladies got
together, and *did* chance to hit upon the subject of the third
and absent lady, they were then often known to preface,
punctuate, or conclude their remarks concerning the third
and absent lady with the stipulation that they were
not speaking *against* the third and absent lady—which
reservation gave them a rather freer hand in the body of
the conversation. . . .

It may also be said, in regard to the relations between
these three ladies, that a certain hot-water tank on the top
floor of Craven House recorded the minor fluctuations of
their otherwise thwarted tempers in a ruthless and exact
manner we ourselves would never be able to approach—
inasmuch as all three ladies were very much given to Airing
(as one is at that time of life)—inasmuch as three ladies
cannot Air, without clashing, on three and a half yards of
string—and inasmuch as these three ladies clashed. Combine

this with the fact that certain areas covered by this string were of greater warmth than others, and you will soon see how it came about that the variations or disturbances in the mental fair weather below were sensitively and exquisitely recorded here above. For a slightly irritated Mrs. Spicer had but to move a stocking against Mrs. Nixon, to be almost Bloused off the premises by that lady—with Miss Hatt dexterously inserting petticoats to the detriment of whichever party she favoured least at the moment. . . . The battle was, of course, ultimately in the hands of Miss Hatt, who, as mistress of the house, could, and did, on any altercation or minor rupture downstairs, tersely Sheet or Blanket both her rivals; but she wisely refrained from making too much use of this prerogative. This, however (when she did let herself go), she did haughtily and with a self-assertive slam of the tank-room's door: whereas all the more considerate and delicate substitutions, insertions, or shiftings were accomplished cabalistically, and accompanied (by all three ladies) with a peculiar soft humming—of tunes not to be identified.

The parrot, during this winter season, was a fair success. Its imaginatively edited remarks were one of the principal topics at meal times. As were also, and in the same tone of amused relish, some of Audrey's and Edith's.

As for Edith, Footballer (in the light of a disease) now controlled, and threatened slowly to destroy, her mind. Indeed, a succession of Footballer breakfasts, Footballer lunches, Footballer dinners (with Footballer potatoes and greens), whole apathetic and Footballer days in fact, brought her precious near dismissal. And though Miss Hatt did her best to allow for Footballer, and even went so far as to have Footballer out with Edith, who wept, it was plain that this state of affairs could not go on much longer.

But Edith made an amazing rally for the Christmas dinner, and a happy day was spent by all. The turkey was had in the evening, along with the wine for the elders, and the tinselled crackers for the children, and afterwards there was a riot of fun. Mr. Spicer wore a cap; the Major wore a cap (put on by Elsie); even Mrs. Nixon wore a cap for a short time, and Elsie wore her kilts, and danced a Highland Reel, which was the only serious part of the evening. But this was soon done with, and they fell to Hunt the Thimble, wherein Mr. Spicer was so dense, and got so Cold, and then so much Colder, being warm enough within from certain *sub rosa* whiskies enjoyed beforehand, that the piercing squeals of the children had more than once to be complained against. After this Mr. Spicer performed some Tricks, but being unable to bring them off as he wished, and inclined to talk too much about them previously, he failed to entertain the children, who left him explaining how they *should* have gone to Mrs. Nixon. Further delight was brought about by an inspiration on the part of the Major, who left the room and returned later, smiling his own smile, in a red domino costume. Such exclamations from Elsie, who was not quite herself this evening, greeted this, that it was "Now then, Miss, any more shouting and off you go to bed" from Mrs. Nixon, who nevertheless considered it a great hit. Master Wildman was a little *blasé* and conceited, having, it transpired, "seen it before"; but Mr. Spicer said, "You look quite like an old monk, Major," with great respect, and the others joined in in giving the laurels to the Major for the triumph of the evening.

The Major himself was secretly not so sure that this wasn't the truth, too, for he took plenty of little peeps at himself in the glass long after the real fine frenzy of the thing had passed, and he relinquished his costume at last with such a modest air of having brought off a minor triumph, that Master Wildman had cause for regret, long years after, that he had been so *blasé* about it. For he then remembered exactly the unreproachful way his father had glanced at him, in his moment of success, and received nothing back.

II

There fell a curious moment upon Mr. and Mrs. Spicer shortly after the New Year.

It was in their bedroom. Mrs. Spicer, emptying the pockets of Mr. Spicer's coats preparatory to despatching them to the cleaners, produced a letter addressed to Mr. Spicer in what she afterwards summed up to herself as a Feminine Hand.

"Hullo," said Mrs. Spicer. "What's this?"

"What, dear?" said Mr. Spicer, and came across the room to her.

Mrs. Spicer gave "Yes" to the Universe, and handed it over.

"Don't know, my dear," said Mr. Spicer. "Don't know . . . at all. . . ."

"Must be a Letter," suggested Mr. Spicer, and put it into his pocket. . . .

CHAPTER VI

Elsie is Naughty

I

AND it is at the end of this winter that Elsie is Naughty.

It is promised that she shall be taken to Gamages, to choose something, and she is subsequently forbidden to go to Gamages—and she goes.

That she should ever have been promised a trip to Gamages is traceable to an almost forgotten dividend reviving and coming in to Mrs. Nixon, who one morning comes into where Elsie is sitting at her knitting, and commences tickling her.

This is the traditional way for Mrs. Nixon to show her favour and good spirits. The tickling is a bit of fun, necessarily accompanied by such exclamations as "*Oh*, you little devilt you!" and "Oo-oo-oo-oo-oo! There!" and Elsie is expected to curl up and love her frolicsome mother, which she never does with remarkable success—her poor little smile still remaining rather pale, and frightened, and wondering, and her chuckles and screwings up taking place rather half-heartedly.

"How would a little girl like to go to Gamages and choose a little something for her birthday present there, eh?" asks Mrs. Nixon.

"Oh, mother! When?"

"Oh, maybe next Thursday," says Mrs. Nixon, nodding to herself.

"Oh, mother!"

"Well, if we see a good little girl in the next few days, maybe she'll come along. No promises, mind you," Mrs. Nixon warns her.

"Oh, mother! Oh, thank you, mother!" says Elsie, and dances about the room, and looks out of windows in ecstasy, and jumps away from windows under the spur of the same emotion, and returns to windows for further delicious brooding for nearly an hour afterwards.

Master Wildman (at this time on his holidays) is at once privately informed.

"Been there, you fool," is all that Master Wildman says.

II

It becomes apparent, the next morning, however, that however much a little girl's outlook on life may have been transformed by the prospect of a visit to Gamages, there is to be no alteration in a little girl's daily behaviour, and that any signs of pestering, "worriting," "pothering," or otherwise incensing one's mother in a search for further information about the projected visit, will seriously endanger the whole notion.

It is on Wednesday (or Gamage Eve) that Elsie upsets the ink over the drawing-room table.

Miss Hatt is the first to discover her dabbing madly with the blotting-paper.

"Oh, child! What have you done! Oh, what a mess! How did you do it, girl?"

"I'm very sorry, Miss Hatt."

Miss Hatt takes over the dabbing. "Yes, but it's spoilt the cloth, hasn't it?"

"I'm very sorry."

"Yes," says Miss Hatt, "but it's rather late to think of that now, isn't it?"

"I'm very sorry."

"Well, it's no use crying over spilt——" Here Miss Hatt dabs to avoid the outcome of her sentence, and Mrs. Nixon enters. "I'm afraid your Elsie's been upsetting *ink*, Mrs. Nixon."

"And didn't I forbid you to use ink in the drawing-room, Miss?"

"Did you, mother?"

"Very well, Miss Hatt, don't you worry. Elsie'll see to it. And she knows what this means well enough."

It is a wet morning, and when a new cloth has replaced the old one ("Cloth?" remarks an amiably inquisitive Mr. Spicer the same evening), Elsie runs upstairs to fetch her knitting, and comes down and sits with her mother, without a word passing between them all the morning. "*And she*

knows what this means well enough.'' The words are all the
time in Elsie's head as she looks over her knitting at her
mother, and tries to read her face. But there is nothing to
be found there, and Elsie can hardly resist an urge to speak,
and know her fate, but she knows it will be much better
to wait until her mother has cooled down a bit. After
lunch, however, and in the long darkening afternoon, as they
sit together alone, Elsie can hold herself in no longer, and
she at last puts it as tactfully as she can.

"Will we take a bus to Gamages, mother?" asks Elsie.
"Or will we go by train?"

"There'll be no bus to Gamages for you, Miss," says
mother.

Tears shoot into Elsie's eyes, and her face goes very red.

"Little girls who are disobedient don't get taken to Gamages
for presents. They have to pay for new cloths out of that."

"Oh, mother! Please, mother!" pleads Elsie.

"Now then, child, get on with your work."

A long silence follows, in which the room darkens more,
and a red coal falls out into the hearth. . . .

"Oh, mayn't I go to Gamages, mother?"

"That's enough, Elsie."

The needles click industriously for another five minutes.

"It's no use your Sniffling, child," says Mrs. Nixon, and
silence falls again.

"Oh, no! No Gamages for disobedient little girls," says
Mrs. Nixon, and gives a very disagreeable sort of laugh.
"Oh dear me no! Heh! Heh! Heh!" laughs Mrs. Nixon,
and leaves the room.

A long silence.

A long succession of sniffs, increasing in power and frequency.

An intaking of breath amounting to a sob.

An amount of swallowing.

A whole crescendo of unashamed sniffing; a handkerchief
fumbled for in a very tense and methodical pause; and
there are tears.

"I hate her," sobs Elsie. "I hate her! I'll never forgive
her. . . . Never. . . . Never, never forgive her. . . .

"Not even when I'm Old," decides Elsie.

III

On the grey morning of an un-Gamaged day Mrs. Nixon receives a letter from her sister, Jessica, who is that day passing through London, and asks Mrs. Nixon to join her at lunch. This invitation Mrs. Nixon takes up and is away before eleven, with a promise to be back by supper time.

Shortly after lunch, Elsie is just about to settle down to an afternoon's knitting, when Master Wildman comes in to her.

He at once assumes the bantering tone which is all too common with him at this period.

"Look here, you," says Master Wildman. "Do you want to go to Gamages?"

"I'm not going," says Elsie, weakly, and wonders why he asks, since she has told him before.

"I didn't ask," says Master Wildman, "whether you're not going. I *simply asked* whether you were going to stay like a boiled potato at home all the afternoon."

"But I must stay."

"But I didn't *ask!*" shouts Master Wildman, as though this is really stretching his patience a little too far, "whether you must stay. I *simply asked* whether your mother'd *know* you'd gone, or whether she *wouldn't.*"

"No. I don't expect she'd know."

"Well, that's what I've been *asking* you, all the time. Will you *come* or will you *not?*"

"But I can't."

"Very well, then, don't! *I'm* not asking you," says Master Wildman, and is about to wash his hands of the matter.

"I should like to," says Elsie.

"I say, do you think you're being funny, because you're not."

"She couldn't know, could she?" asks Elsie.

"*Really!*" says Master Wildman. "Your brain! It really is . . . Of course she wouldn't, you Underdone Pumpkin. Come on. Buck up."

"All right," says Elsie. "I think I will. But she won't know, will she?" And five minutes later they are on the road to the station.

It is, on the whole, a very enjoyable afternoon. Master Wildman is in his usual truculent temper, of course, but

perhaps Elsie brings all her scoldings upon her own head,
for she riles him at the very beginning, and on the way to
the station, by remarking thoughtfully, after Master Wildman's adventurous statement that he is going to be a flying
man one day, that she expects it is "very difficult to learn
how to use an aeroplane"; which naturally puts him into a
towering rage. "Considering," he says, "that you know
nothing about it," and "Considering it's not difficult," and
"Considering I know a chap who's got a brother who flies
and he's going to get him to show me how, so there," and
"Considering his name's Grote, and you can look him out
in the drectry if you think I'm lying, so there," and such a
host of other "Considerings" and "So Theres,' that Elsie
decides there and then never to speak on her own account
again. This resolution she is unable to keep for any length
of time, there being far too many objects in the ensuing
train journey that call for spontaneous admiration to Master
Wildman, who meets each of her remarks with "Not up to
much," or with some instance of his having observed something very much better of the same kind elsewhere.

Nevertheless Master Wildman is by this time getting a
little appeased by his own mastery of the technique of
travelling, and (having changed into the Tube at Hammersmith with particular skill) is able, when Elsie hazards a
minor smile upon him, and puts her hands to her ears against
the roar of the train in the Tube, to smile back as though,
even if he *has* heard greater noises in Tubes before, this is
quite a good one.

Gamages is a dream of delight for Elsie, and the airman
is quite mollified under its influence; and although sundry
technical faults in the machines inspected by him stand,
on occasions, in the way of his full approval, his little companion both credits and respects the natural reservations
of an expert, and it is no blot upon their pleasure. Thus, in
the motor cycle department, when Master Wildman murmurs
such things as "H'm! Don't think much of the Exhaust,"
or "H'm! Magneto's not much good"; while another would
have more than suspected the child of talking through his
hat (as we do), the enchanted Elsie instead deferentially
enquires whether the Magneto (whatever they both believe
that to be) is more satisfactory in the next example. After
which Master Wildman abandons himself to a series of curt
and businesslike criticisms, stopping at each machine with a

monosyllabic "Good — Good — Bad — Good — Bad — Bad —
Good . . ." to the end of the department.

"Look here, I'll give you a present if you like," says
Master Wildman after this, and however much Elsie says
he shouldn't, and ought not to, and couldn't afford it, he
insists.

"You know—a shilling or something like that," he says,
rather carried away himself.

"Oh, that's too much," says Elsie. "I'll have a cheap
present."

"Well, let's go and choose it, anyhow. And buck up."

But at this point Elsie becomes rather flustered, which
makes Master Wildman angry again. At one moment perhaps
she would like one of those photograph frames, at another
moment perhaps she would like one of those purses; the next moment
she is in favour of a pencil holder (but that is one-and-three);
and the next she fancies a pen wiper. ("I say," says Master
Wildman, "Really!"). There is also a bottle of gum, which,
being marked twopence, she feels it her duty to have.

"You'd better hurry, you little ass," says Master Wildman,
"or you won't get it at all."

"Then I think I'll have a bottle of Gum," says Elsie,
"if I may, please."

"Do you *want* it?" asks Master Wildman, who, from a
purely twopenny point of view, rather admires her choice.

"Yes," says Elsie, "there are a lot of things I want to
Gum at home."

So they go up to, and hang about for the assistant, and
the gum has a piece of white paper dexterously screwed round
it; and they go out into the street with it, where it acts
as a sort of amiable third party, by whom they are both
struck rather timid.

"We'll have some tea now," says Master Wildman briskly.

It is very crowded in the small Lyons' establishment they
enter; it also takes them a great time to get served; the
waitress, who belongs to the sneering school of assistants, is
not over-civil. ("Got a good mind not to leave her tup-
pence," threatens Master Wildman.) An old gentleman with
an excessive moustache comes and sits down at their table,
and munches and spills, and munches and wipes and spills,
and leans over aggressively for the salt; an old lady comes and
asks whether the vacant seat is engaged, and the old gentleman munches at the distance without replying, so that Elsie

has to say No, she doesn't think so; the old lady soon begins to mutter "Really," and show other signs of impatience because she can't get served, but does at last succeed in being favourably sneered at, which Elsie cannot do in asking for the bill, as Master Wildman has commanded her to do. "Do you think mother'll be back by now?" asks Elsie suddenly. "Shouldn't think so," says Master Wildman. And that is pretty well all that is said. Master Wildman sits gazing at his old lady and Elsie at her old gentleman, until at last they escape.

"Got your Gum all right?" says Master Wildman.

"Yes," says Elsie, and shows it to him, and they make for the station.

"I don't think mother'll be back yet, do you?" says Elsie, and "Oh, do shut up on that," says Master Wildman. "Can't you see when you're getting on a man's nerves?"

At this point both children disappear far underground into a jostled world of roaring, clicking, and sullen banging, where, surrounded on all sides by thick, dangling bundles of overcoats, umbrella, and evening newspaper, they spend forty minutes, and emerge at last at Southam Green, and walk towards Craven House.

A long way off, Elsie descries a steady light burning behind Mrs. Nixon's blind.

IV

Our narrative at this moment becomes a trifle tense. To begin with, a silence of death lies over the whole of Craven House, as Master Wildman rings the bell, which tinkles softly below, and elicits a bump or two from the basement, but nothing else for a minute or so. But at last Audrey arrives, tying her apron strings, and with her eyes on the point of taking leave of her head.

"Your mother said she wanted to see you when you was come in, Miss Elsie," says Audrey, and at that moment Miss Hatt comes down the stairs.

"Oh, *you've* come back, have you," she says, and she speaks in a very amiable voice indeed. She goes down into the kitchen.

"I suppose I'd better go up," says Elsie, very pale.

"All right," says Master Wildman. "Nothing to be in a funk about."

Which remark does not prevent Master Wildman from

listening intently as Elsie runs up the stairs. And on hearing a door opening on the top landing, he follows her up a little way and stands still outside the bathroom door. . . .

He hears Mrs. Nixon come out and demand sharply where Elsie has been. He hears Elsie reply, "Nowhere, mother." There is a pause then, and then Mrs. Nixon is heard telling her daughter, a little louder, not to dare to "Nowhere" *her*, and she (Mrs. Nixon) will *nowhere* somebody in a minute, and where has Elsie been? There is then an almost inaudible mention of Gamages from Elsie, whereat Mrs. Nixon follows up her threat of nowhereing her daughter, with the statement that she will give her Gamages, and they will see what something Else has to say about it, and Elsie will kindly go to her room.

Master Wildman stands, like a little boy in a dream, outside the bathroom door. . . .

Half-a-minute later there are soft footsteps above, and the door closes sloftly upon Elsie's room. There is a deep silence. A bump. Some words. And then the sound of slashes and stifled deep screaming betokens the severest giving of Gamages to Elsie by her mother.

Master Wildman rushes up the stairs and bursts into his father's room. His father is apparelled in his shirt and socks alone. "My dear boy!" expostulates his father.

"*She's Hitting her, daddy!*" says Master Wildman. "She's Hitting her!"

"My dear boy, calm yourself. Who is hitting what?" But he knows quite well.

"Mrs. Nix——" But Master Wildman is almost choking. "She's hitting her in there!"

"Er—what?" says the Major, but a little limply. He then goes halfway out on to the landing and lowers his head to listen. From behind the door comes the sound of breathless long moanings and Mrs. Nixon's voice. "You thought I couldn't do that, didn't you, Miss?"

"Oh—oh—oo—oh!"

"Eh?"

"Oh—oh! . . ."

"Eh?"

Slash!

The Major springs suddenly erect, and "*Daddy!*" pleads Master Wildman. The Major looks down at himself, and knows his impotence. "My dressing-gown, boy!" thunders the Major.

The boy rushes to fetch it. The Major remains with one emergency foot in the room, but otherwise in a soldier-like attitude abroad.

"Can't find it!" moans Master Wildman from within.

But at this moment Mrs. Nixon emerges from Elsie's room, stick in hand, and the Major bounces back.

This is not because she is after him, as you might judge by his expression, but on account of the mere social exigencies which impose the strictest privacy upon Majors adorned as this one is.

v

For an hour the ignorant and usual evening sounds—the sounds of cooking, the sounds of laying the table, bathroom sounds, and the enveloping sound of the steady-breathing gas in the hall, prevail. Then, five minutes before dinner, Mrs. Nixon comes down the stairs and meets Miss Hatt in the hall.

"Oh, Miss Hatt, could I speak to you a moment?"

"Oh, yes," says Miss Hatt, looking a little mystified, but coming near to her guest and putting her head expectantly and politely askew.

"I'm afraid Elsie has been very Naughty, Miss Hatt," says Mrs. Nixon, confidentially.

"Oh yes," replies Miss Hatt, smiling vaguely.

"So I've sent her to bed for the evening. I was wondering if I could take her a little something up."

"Oh, yes. What sort of—er——?"

"Well, I don't know quite," wonders Mrs. Nixon, and with the word Broth, along with the word Gruel, making fair way to the surface of both làdies' minds, they gaze at each other. . . .

"Well, a little something," says Miss Hatt.

"I'm sorry she hasn't been Good," says Miss Hatt, giggles, and goes away.

VI

Elsie has been very Naughty! The news is down in the kitchen in a trice, and all over the house.

"Speck she got what for," Audrey surmises, and Edith, with whom Elsie is in unaccountable disfavour, slams an oven door on the proceedings and says, "Serves the little bitch right. 'Ope she got it good and hard."

"Oh, don't use such words, Eed," says Audrey, but "Bitch ain't a word," says Edith, and slams further.

"My mother knew 'ow to bring us kids up," says Edith. "Didn't she 'alf? *Oh*, no! And my brother didn't forget in an 'urry what she did to 'im once."

"Did she Flay 'im alive, Eed?" enquires Audrey.

"Did she flay 'im alive?" asks Edith. "*Ho* no!" she answers, but this is mere sarcasm.

"Did it serve 'im right?" asks Audrey, a little taken aback, in her dreamy way.

"Course it did. My mother knew 'ow to bring us up, she did."

"Couldn't 'e Sit Down for a Week?" asks Audrey, and "'E—could—Not," rejoins Edith.

"What 'ad 'e done?" asks Audrey, who rather wants to get this episode justified.

"What 'ad 'e done?"   Edith pauses a moment before replying. "Been acting indecent," she says at last. She slams another oven door.

Audrey doesn't care to follow this last rather queer statement up, so "Where's he now?" she asks.

"Oh, he's in Wales," says Edith, as though this is in some measure a natural result.

VII

Elsie has been very naughty, and above-stairs (child torture here being looked upon in a slightly less axiomatic light) there is quite as much stir about it. This, however, is only manifest in a nodding way of knitting in Mrs. Nixon, a kind of moustache-fingering reflectiveness in the Major, a large amount of affirmatives in Mrs. Spicer, and the excessive, not to say smouldering, quietude of Master Wildman, who, whenever he does look up, takes a glance at Mrs. Nixon as much as to say he knows all about *her*, and she'd better look out. But at last dinner time comes, and with the dinner, Mr. Spicer, and then the cat is out of the bag. "Where's Elsie to-night?" tries Mr. Spicer, but the conversation smothers him at first. "Elsie not here to-night?" he ventures later, but is again defeated. Nevertheless, "Anything happened to *Elsie* to-night?" he insists, and there is a heavy pause. "I think she's been——" says Miss Hatt, looking for correction at Mrs. Nixon. "Yes, I'm afraid she's been misbehaving herself, Mr. Spicer," says Mrs. Nixon. "Oh," says Mr. Spicer, and there is another pause. "In disgrace?" asks Mr. Spicer. "Yes," says Mrs. Nixon. "Sorry to hear that," says Mr. Spicer. "Well, I suppose we all get into scrapes some time or other, don't we?" "Yes," says Mrs. Spicer. "We can't all be good, can we?" "No, I suppose we can't," says Miss Hatt, and the Major fingers his moustache and looks in front of him, and matter is left.

It is, to Miss Hatt, a little inconvenient that Mrs. Nixon should have chosen to have Elsie naughty this evening, of all evenings, for this evening two personal friends of hers—Mr. and Mrs. Heaven (coupled, before the world, in a celestial way, as the Heavens) are coming into Craven House for a little Whist. And it is felt by Miss Hatt that Mrs. Nixon and her Elsie have rather endangered the carefree atmosphere of the evening. These fears are ill-founded, nevertheless, and when, after dinner, a faint double knock at the front door is heard—a knock which might have been executed by the Angel of Death, to judge from the stiffness and silence immediately falling upon all gathered in the drawing-room, Mrs. Nixon is found ready to do all honours, and even take a hand at Whist.

"Let's see now, you don't play Whist, do you, sir?" says Mr. Spicer to Master Wildman, a little sharply; for Master Wildman is gazing, a little boorishly, at Mrs. Heaven.

"No," says Master Wildman, "I think I'll go up to bed." And he leaves the room.

VIII

Outside Elsie's door Master Wildman stops to listen. Hearing nothing, he goes into his room and begins to undress.

He comes out, later, in his pyjamas, and listens again.

There is a coarse peal of laughter from downstairs, silence, the far-away shrillness of Edith's raised voice in the kitchen, more laughter. . . . Then he hears a little sob from within. . . . He goes back to his room, hastily puts on his dressing-gown, and comes out to listen again.

Elsie now seems to have given in altogether, although a succession of little labourings with, and attempts to dam the course of a real cry, show how reluctant she is. Master Wildman knocks softly on the door.

There is no answer. There is another peal of laughter from downstairs. He opens the door quietly and stands in

the doorway, letting the laughter in to Elsie, who is just
visible in the watery light given to the room from the lamp
in the street.   She is lying in her bed.

"I say," says Master Wildman, "don't worry."

Elsie makes no reply whatever, but continues to labour
with her emotions.

"I say.   Don't worry," says Master Wildman, and comes
further into the room.

Elsie makes no effort to receive him.

"Are you Sad?" asks Master Wildman, rather at a loss.

Elsie just manages "Yes," but immediately afterwards
gives way to such a flood of sobs and moans, and catches in
the breath, that no other conversation is negotiable for a
long time.

"They're playing Whist downstairs," says Master Wildman,
when things are a little better.

"Are they?" offers Elsie, and turns to look at him, in a
heart-broken way, for the first time.

Master Wildman sits at the end of the bed.

"Yes.   Two People have come in to play with them."

"Are they nice?" moans Elsie, trying to further the
conversation

"Not bad.," says Master Wildman, and a moment later,
"Don't like *her*, though."

"Don't you?" says Elsie, still very much enfeebled, but
improving rapidly.

"No," says Master Wildman, "I don't."

"Got a face like a Stewed Tomato," says Master Wildman,
and cannot help giving a little depreciatory titter at the
humour of his own image; and Elsie, too, gives a weak smile,
and brushes away certain minor and final irrigations on her
cheeks, and sits up and clasps her knees, and glances at him
as though she sees things in rather a new light now, and
then looks away, and then gazes out, with a sadness that is
more absent-minded than bitter, into the distance.

"Or a Half-Boiled Egg," adds Master Wildman, unmis-
takably tittering, and Elsie also gives a titter (if only an
absent one) at this; for such idiom, she knows, is usually
reserved for his very choicest and most intimate companions,
except when it is directed against herself; and she has never
had such kindness from him before.

Master Wildman considers the window for a moment or
two.

"Still got your Gum?" he enquires at last.

"Yes. I was going to Gum some things this evening," says Elsie, faintly, "if I hadn't been"—she makes a sad little pause here—"Interrupted."

"Well, I suppose I ought to go," says Master Wildman. "If you're not Sad any more?"

"No, I don't think I'm Sad now."

Master Wildman goes to the door, and pauses there, apparently in two minds.

"I say," he says, "I'll tell you a story if you like."

"But mother'll be up."

"No she won't; she's playing Whist. There's lots of time. Would you like me to tell you a story?"

"Yes. If you don't think it'll be too long untel mother comes up." (Elsie always pronounces "until" as "untel.")

"No. She can't really," says Master Wildman, rather taken with the new idea. He goes and opens the door, shuts it, and comes to the bed again. "Sure you want me to?"

"Yes. I do."

"All right then," says Master Wildman, sitting on the bed in very good spirits. He pauses again. "Ghost or Detective?"

"Ghost, I think," says Elsie, making up her mind at once.

"Well, as a matter of fact," says Master Wildman, "I know a better Detective one than a Ghost. Whichever you like, but I think the Detective one's better."

"I'd like a Detective one," says Elsie.

"As long as it doesn't make any difference to you?"

"No. And I expect the Ghost one would have only frightened me."

"All right then. . . . Ready?"

"Yes," says Elsie, and clasps her knees to listen better.

"Quite comfortable?" asks Master Wildman, who is now fighting for time.

"Yes. Thank you."

"Then I'll begin," says Master Wildman.

"Prob'ly bore you, but still," says Master Wildman, but Elsie only glances at him without replying, and he is really forced to begin.

"Well," begins Master Wildman in sing-song and easy tones, "there was once a *Detective*. . . . And he was sitting in his Rooms one day—quite quietly—when all at once what should happen but there should be a knock at the

door, and what should happen but In Came—a Man. . . .
And so the detective said, 'Come in and sit down,' you see,
quite calmly, but the *Man* was Mopping his Brow. . . ."

Here Elsie wants to know what the Detective's name was.

Master Wildman has to think about this for a moment.

"Keene," says Master Wildman. . . .

"Rupert Keene," he adds reflectively. "Well—where
was I?"

"Where the man came in Mopping his Brow," says Elsie.
Master Wildman continues:

"Well, he Mopped his Brow, you see, and so the Detective
could see that something was up, and so he asked the man
his Business. And so the man said: 'I'm afraid I'm very
Nervous, but I know the Preciousness of your time, and so
I'll cut a long story short and tell you what happened. I was
getting into bed last night, quite calmly, and everything was
quite quiet, and I was just going off to sleep, when *what*
should happen? What should I hear but a scratching on
the window! Well, I only thought it was the wind outside
at first, and I was going off to sleep again; but *what* should
happen then? *What* should fall on to my bed but a bit
of *paper*, and *what* should be written on it, in red ink, but:
'*If you don't return the Stolen Idol in three days' time you'll
perish by the will of Allah.*'"

Here Master Wildman stops to let his story have its fullest
effect, and it certainly appears to be already moving Elsie,
who nevertheless cannot refrain from asking what the Man's
name was.

"Stamford," says Master Wildman. . . .

"Richard Stamford," he adds, and continues:

"Well, the detective said 'H'm,' you see, and asked the
Man a few questions. And the man answered them all
right, you see, and the Detective began to Pace up and
down the room, you see, and said, 'Forgive me,'—you see—
'because I think better if I pace up and down.' So the man
said 'All right,' and the detective said: 'This is a very interesting and instructive case, and what I think we'd better
do is to Go to the Scene of Last Night's Mystery,' you see,
and so the man said 'H'm—well, *that's* on a lonely Moor.'
So the detective said 'Well, that doesn't matter, and if
you'll just wait while I Pack my Valise, we'll get off, because
this case is very interesting and instructive, and I've made a
lot of deductions already.' And so the man said 'All right,'

and the detective ran upstairs to pack his valise, and off
they went. Well, there was a trap waiting for them at
the station in the country when they got there, and they
drove in it to the House, which was situated on a lonely
moor; and the detective said 'What beautiful scenery,' on
the way, because he admired nature and wasn't frightened,
and they reached the house. . . .

"Well," continues Master Wildman, taking a fresh breath,
"they had a nice dinner, and after dinner Rupert Keene
asked to see the Old Butler, because the man had one, and
he was brought up. And directly he came Rupert Keene
began to Ply him with questions. And the Old Butler began
to quake with fear. So Rupert Keene said 'You needn't
be alarmed, my man, if you'll only tell the truth you'll be
this side of the law. And I'm sure you're not guilty, because
I'm a jolly good judge of character.' So the old butler at
last made a confession. And what do you think he confessed?" asks Master Wildman.

"I don't know," says Elsie.

"He confessed that he'd found a Secret Passage in the
house," says Master Wildman, and without stopping to
explain wherein this muddle-headed butler conceived it
illegal to fall upon secret passages on his master's premises,
continues in suave tones: "Well, Rupert Keene asked where
it was, and he got a torch and a revolver, and five minutes
later he started to go down it. And at first it didn't lead
anywhere, and he began to think he was lost, but at *last*,
what should he see but a light, and what should he hear but
voices, talking! Well, he went on a bit till at last he came
to a little hole, and he looked through it, and what do you
think he saw?"

"I don't know," says Elsie.

"He saw two Indians, all dressed in Turbans and things,
talking over the table, and on the floor there was a beautiful
girl, all bound with ropes, you see.

"Well, he was looking at this, you see, and wondering
how he was going to rescue her, when suddenly the floor gave
way beneath him, and he fell into a sort of dungeon beneath
the ground, because the Indians were working a lever. And
a merciful Bolivian came to his rescue."

Elsie wants to know what a Bolivian is.

"When you don't know anything," says Master Wildman.

"Well," says Master Wildman, "when he came to he

found himself bound hand and foot. So what do you think
he did?"

"I don't know," says Elsie.

"He got out his matches with his mouth and he lit one,
and he held it in his mouth and burnt through the rope,
and when he had done six matches he was a free man. So
he ran back along the secret passage, and met Richard Stamford, and said, 'There's not a moment to be lost.' So Richard
Stamford said, 'What are you going to do then?' So Rupert
Keene said, 'Going to India at once.' So Richard Stamford
said 'How are you going?' So Rupert Keene said "By
Aeroplane.' So Richard Stamford said 'Have you got one,
then?' So Rupert Keene said 'Yes, and if you'll lend me
your car I'll get it.' So Richard Stamford lent him his
car, and away he went."

"Did Rupert Keene know," asks Elsie, "that if he went
to India he'd find the two"—she pauses for some suitable
classification for the nefarious Easterners—"Thieves?"

"Oh yes," says Master Wildman reflectively. . . .

"I expect he knew about them before?" hazards Elsie.

"Yes," says Master Wildman, catching on to it. "Yes,
that's right. Well, anyway, he got to the aerodrome and
found his aeroplane. . . ."

"Are you comfy?" asks Master Wildman, for at this
moment Elsie gives a very slight sigh and lies back on her bed.

"Yes, thank you," says Elsie, on her back, and she shifts
a little.

"Well, he found his aeroplane and jumped into it, and
flew away. And he flew away. . . . Well, just half a tick;
I must think what happened next. . . ."

There is a long silence, in which the sound of hoarse laughter
from the Whist players below floats up to the darkened
room where the children are sitting. . . .

"Well, his aeroplane flew away, and shortly afterwards
he landed where he wanted to, and this was in a deep forest;
and in the middle of the forest there was a temple where
they worshipped idols and sacrificed human bodies to them.
Well, Rupert Keene knew that he could never do anything
because everything was so well guarded, so he had an idea.
He dressed himself up as an old lama, and went into the
temple and said that he wanted to worship the god, if they
didn't mind. And so they let him in, and after a few days
they began to trust him, and one of the priests came to him

one morning and said, 'Look here, we're going to sacrifice a girl to-morrow, and you'll be wanted there.' So Rupert Keene said 'All right,' and when the time came he was there, and who should the girl be but the very one who was in the secret passage in Richard Stamford's house! And they were putting her on the altar, you see, and she was frightfully frightened, you see, when suddenly Rupert Keene spoke out, in English, and said 'You need have no fear; I will save you.' And she was English, you see, and understood, but the others didn't know what it meant because they could only speak Indian. So they didn't mind. . . . Well, they were just about to sacrifice her when suddenly the eyes of the god they were praying to began to flash, and this was because Rupert Keene had fixed two electric torches in them, and he was working them from where he was; and suddenly the god said, 'Thou shalt not sacrifice this girl,' and it really was Rupert Keene speaking, because he was a Ventriloquist, and he could throw his voice wherever he wanted to; and so she wasn't sacrificed. . . .

"Well, she wasn't sacrificed, and Rupert Keene was getting rather fond of her now, and although he wasn't keen on girls as a rule, this one was rather beautiful, and he was getting rather fond of her. So he went into her room one day, because he was allowed to, and he spoke to her for a little, and they had a Love Scene. And Rupert Keene said, 'Will you marry me?' and the girl said, 'Yes, Rather.' And Rupert Keene said, 'Well, that'll have to come later; the problem now is how are we going to get you out of this? . . .'

"Well," says Master Wildman, "Well . . . Well . . . He . . . He . . . went back, you see. . . . Well, anyway, a Lot of Things *Happened*," declares Master Wildman. And though this treatment is, doubtless, challengeable by pedants as a rather over-drastic simplification of narrative, it serves us all well in this case, and it is not long before Master Wildman is adopting his very suavest tones for his *finale*.

"Well, they got home," concludes Master Wildman in half a chant, "and one of the first things that Rupert Keene did was to go down to Richard Stamford's house and tell him everything was all right. And Richard Stamford was terribly grateful and wanted to give Rupert Keene some money, but Rupert Keene said 'No, thank you, because I've got a greater treasure than that.' And when Richard Stamford asked him what it was, he introduced the girl, and

Richard Stamford said, 'I see you have. Jolly pretty.' And so they left a little while afterwards, and soon afterwards they were married. And they went home that evening, and they had a nice dinner, and afterwards they went into Rupert Keene's study, and there was a nice fire there, and the girl lit Rupert Keene's pipe for him, and they sat in front of the fire, and Rupert Keene said, 'Well, *Mrs. Keene, I think*—that after *all*—we shall have no *cause to regret—the—Case—*of the *Stolen Idol!*'

"And that's all," says Master Wildman to the darkness. And "Did you like it?" asks Master Wildman, and "Elsie!" says Master Wildman, using her first name for the very first time in his life. And "Elsie!" he whispers, but there is no reply at all, for Elsie is fast asleep.

Wherefore, Master Wildman, in a gentlemanly but disappointed manner, rises quietly, ties the cord of his little dressing-gown, and softly leaves the room.

END OF BOOK I

Book II

CHAPTER I

The Great War falls on Craven House.

I

AT ten o'clock on the morning of August 3rd, 1914, Audrey Custard was in the study of Craven House, giving new sand to, watering, and otherwise refreshing a sluttish and chaotic parrot. A kind of link had arisen between Audrey Custard and this caustic bird, inasmuch as it was the sole living creature she could meet on equal terms, and to any extent assert her own personality with. This, it is true, only amounted to a rather futile round of such condemnations as "You rascal, Polly," or "Oh, you bad bird, Polly," together with their dreamy reciprocal questionings, "Aren't you a rascal, Polly, eh?" and "Aren't you a bad bird, Polly?" But the bird would invariably reply, "Rats, sir!" in a very friendly and shrewd style, and a pleasant ten minutes was spent.

On the morning in question, Miss Hatt came in to her with a certain nervous cordiality, which was betrayed by her opening enquiry.

"Oh!—are you in here, Audrey?" asked Miss Hatt.

"Yes, ma'am," said Audrey, and continued to dust, while Miss Hatt went and kissed the parrot at a distance.

"Well, it looks as though there's going to be a War, Audrey," said Miss Hatt.

"A What, ma'am?"

"A War, Audrey."

"Is there, ma'am?"

"Yes, I'm afraid there is," admitted Miss Hatt, and there was a silence.

"Who'd be doin' it, ma'am?"

"The Germans, I'm afraid, Audrey," said Miss Hatt.

"Like the Boer War, ma'am?" suggested Audrey, who was busy dusting.

"Yes, but I'm afraid it's going to be larger than that."
Audrey looked at her.
"How silly, ma'am," protested Audrey.

II

How far the Great War that now ensued was to be held
attributable to the Swollen Head and other profligate
characteristics of a hell-born creature, alluded to by Miss
Hatt (against four years' steady implied correction on the
part of her guests) as the "Kayzer"; or how far purely
international and political factors entered the question, it is
not within the scope of this chronicle to discuss. Nor was
it discussed with any great earnestness or at any great length
at Craven House. For the whole affair was conceived from
the beginning as a battle between the Powers of Darkness
and the Powers of Light—and the cause of pure reason, while
existing to exonerate the Allies, was smothered by the outward demonstrations of a virtue which Miss Hatt again
tacitly challenged all comers to pronounce otherwise than
"Paytriotism." Which virtue (however pronounced) made
itself felt in the neighbourhood, in the erection of ordinary
flags, beflagged royalties, beflagged ministers, beflagged
generals, beflagged bulldogs and other beflagged popular
symbols on, outside, or in places hitherto considered exempt
from decoration. There was really little scope for more
direct participation amongst the rather elderly population of
Southam Green. The Town Hall, it is true (until now a
decaying refuge for nomadic Theosophy, Christian Science,
and local infant festivities) reassumed its command of the
neighbourhood in harbouring the Recruiting Office; and a
large body of persons in Southam Green (including Master
Wildman, at his father's instigation) offered themselves and
bicycle here for the purpose of "taking messages"—in the
existence, urgency, and multitudinousness of which they believed as a natural war time phenomenon. But there proved
at last to be a very disappointing amount of "messages"
passing between the local authorities not already arranged
for, and when all was said and done the high-intentioned
inhabitants of Southam Green had only flags and reviling to
fall back upon.

Master Wildman's Secret Passage delusions naturally at
once gave way to German Spy delusions, or occasionally, in

the wealth of his imagination, to delusions in which both German Spies and Secret Passages were confused. Nor was he wanting encouragement and example from his elders in this direction.

When the war had been going some time, Mr. Spicer, by the most gallant wanglings imaginable, was enrolled as a private.

III

Mr. Spicer had gathered for a long time that, with a little careful falsification of dates on behalf of his country, he would be taken on; but Mr. Spicer's actual decision to enlist was not come to until after a long series of dramatic inward communings, culminating in another Tramp, in which he was understood to be Fighting it Out.

This Tramp took place on a Saturday evening, and was treated with a handsome quietude and respect by the residents of Craven House, who had it hinted to them by Mrs. Spicer that some such drama was taking place, but who did not wait supper for the return of the figure in the limelight. Which was as well, for he did not return until eleven o'clock, and then in a condition inconsistent with his new character.

This Tramp commenced at Hyde Park Corner, like the previous Tramp described in this book, but it was a much more glorious Tramp. Over the first whiskey used to fortify himself on this Tramp Mr. Spicer had made his Decision (if indeed he had not made it some good time before he resolved to fight it out).

We should like to believe that there was some reasoned ideal, or true sense of sacrifice behind Mr. Spicer's decision— but in the God, King and Country—words which conveyed, ultimately, nothing whatsoever of any nature to Mr. Spicer, but which he relied upon the most—nothing of this sort could be found. And as regards sacrifice. . . . It was a little doubtful whether it was such a vast sacrifice to Mr. Spicer to risk his life in this affair. "After all," said Mr. Spicer, emerging from his second public house. "What are we but Specks in the Universe, and what does it matter either way?" And Mr. Spicer dwelt upon this aspect of the matter for some time on account of an undefinable but undeniably Large sensation resulting from the thought of being a mere speck in the Universe. In some extraordinary way it made you feel one or two feet larger in area than the Universe itself. . . .

It is also necessary to say, with respect to this Tramp that after Mr. Spicer had disappeared and emerged four or five times on his way home, the honourable main issues began to give way to sundry more detailed and less impersonal issues; wherein Mr. Spicer sketched an ideal army career for himself, which, although including promotion of a rapid nature, did not reach such heights until they had been righteously come by . . . which was accomplished in a multitude of ways.

Further, and although it is irksome for us to have to sketch this less impersonal side, it is essential, if we are to be faithful, to chronicle that Mr. Spicer—in this dream career—*was* in some way, present, as a simple private, at a certain Council of War at which both Field-Marshal French and Marshal Joffre were present: that both commanders *were* a little befogged as to the next move of the armies under their control: that Mr. Spicer *did* step respectfully forward and salute: that both commanders *were* temporarily acquiescent: that Mr. Spicer *did* illustrate his own opinions diffidently with his finger on the map, suggesting the removal of such and such a force here, the advance of such and such a battalion there, and like strategic combinations beyond our own comprehension: that Field-Marshal French *did* say, "Damn it, my man, I believe you've hit upon it!" (while Marshal Joffre testified to the equivalent in the French tongue), and that a certain Field-Marshal Spicer *did*, after a decent lapse of time, and by reason of such incidents as these, evolve.

It is absolutely necessary to admit, too, that Mr. Spicer was far from being distinguished solely as a tactician in this dream career: that he did also make himself enormously conspicuous in the way of capturing trenches single-handed, rallying his men, saving guns, rescuing tattered standards, and giving last drops of water to friends because their needs were greater than his. And these activities, combined (by the time he had reached Hammersmith) with an increasing tendency to deliver despatches, salute, and fall down dead, we can only excuse by the number of disappearances into public houses made by Mr. Spicer on this tramp, which amounted to seven in all.

Finally we are compelled to say that by the time he had reached home the whole war singularly belonged to Mr. Spicer: that his condition in front of his wife was far from suitable to so gallant and portentous a patriot: that Mr.

Spicer was fortunate in finding Mrs. Spicer alone in the drawing-room: that Mr. Spicer then had two phrases only at his command: that these were (1), "It's quite Simple, my dear," and (2) "The Brute must be crushed": that a lack of variation in the repetition of these, added to a dreamy bias in favour of going to sleep where he stood, apprised Mrs. Spicer of his condition: that Mrs. Spicer said "Yes" twenty times if once, and finally stated, between giggles that she thought he had been having "a glass too much": that Mr. Spicer retorted (happily uniting his two sources of self-expression), "No, my dear, The Brute must be Quite Simply Crushed": that Mrs. Spicer left the room with a very angry and ashen expression, and ran up the stairs, so that Mr. Spicer was left to himself, vaguely murmuring "It's quite simple," "It's quite simple," and "It's quite simple" to the furniture and crockery.

IV

The first appearance of Mr. Spicer at Craven House in his soldier's uniform was a scene of delicious palpitation indeed. The thing came upon them with such supreme unexpectedness they hardly knew where they were. . . . A blazing smile from Audrey, who announced him, a delighted and baffled cry from Mrs. Spicer, who went to greet him, and the next moment he was standing in the drawing-room, grinning sheepishly around amid a welter of acclamation! A clicking of heels and a saluting of the Major, who made a feeble attempt at returning it, and then proceeded to blush (liking the compliment, nevertheless)—a whole host of joyful appraisements—"Suits him, doesn't it!" "Yes, very smart. It *does*." "Yes, *doesn't* it?" "Think it *does*?" (Mr. Spicer) —womanly horror at the largeness and grossness of the boots —minute examinations of the beautiful bright buttons— ("Got to keep 'em clean, though, haven't I?" laughed Mr. Spicer, knowingly, to the Major)—further examinations of the puttees—("How *do* you wind those things round?" asked his wife, and "Quite easy, isn't it?" he replied, with further reference to the old war dog)—desires expressed that he should have his photograph taken—technical, if not priestly, allusions to military terms and matters between the Major and Mr. Spicer—a way of looking surreptitiously in the mirror and jerking one's coat down. . . . With all these they had a very giddy half-hour of it.

But Mr. Spicer had only one night to stay, and the next morning at dawn—a wintry dawn of dim, frosted silver and biting blue—an alarm clock rang out in the darkness of the residence; and soon after, from the Spicers' room came the sounds of hurried mutterings, half-hearted, icy ablutions, and general *sotto voce* excitement under a dreary gas lit against the bitter light outside. And soon after the door was opened and they crept down the stairs together.

And the sound of the front door closing, and footsteps retreating, was the only warning to the stirring sleepers above that Mr. Spicer had departed for the Army.

CHAPTER II

Two Children change their Environment

I

THE three years that now followed were very unhappy and bewildering years for Southam Green, years of foggy and darkening horror, in which all the activities of ordinary life were suspended, as it were, and took on an altogether temporary air; years in which the one remote strain of hope and cheer (if it could be called so) came from the mouths of the wretched citizens themselves, in the utterance of that cry from the depths, that final weary call of human tribulation, that supreme *miserere*—"Are we down-hearted? NO! . . ." Years in which (apart from the stalking affliction of Armageddon itself) a thousand local inconveniences and petty tortures were experienced—years in which the main streets grew mudded and more mudded with the wretched hue of the national uniform, and blocked with the forlorn, drab length of the food queues—years in which the act of Shopping became a sharp enterprise, a trial of wits and patience with the retailer, who was no longer the ingratiating creature of the old days, but master of the situation, and taking surly advantage of it—years in which the Servant Problem first arose in stark uncompromise, and an alarming bent in the Lower Orders towards Answering Back first became acute— potato years, corned beef, and Best Margarine (we like it almost as much as butter) years—years in which the weather itself appeared to succumb to the general depression of circumstances, having cast off (according to Miss Hatt) all previous loyalty to the arbitrary rulings of Electricity, and surrendered topically to the influence of the guns in France.

They were years of large and various changes for Craven House, too; for death itself struck the residence in the person of one of its leading figures, and a stranger came to fill the gap; and the children were growing terrifically—beyond all recognition of their former state.

Elsie was at last sent to school in the neighbourhood, which proved a very great relief to her. The temperament of the head mistress, indeed, though Jovian enough to her pupils, was not at all of the hardy Caledonian nature to be desired by her mother, eliciting from her much "Gracious me" and "When I was a little girl——"; but this was a fault very much on the right side as far as Elsie was concerned, and with one thing and another she was a changed creature. She was not at first popular in the school, being a great deal too clever and timid at her lessons, and backward in all girlish frolics. Given the chance, however, she proved a brilliant basket-baller, and though not made a "Captain" in this game (as she deserved), was invariably the first to be "picked," in so far as personal cliques and favouritism allowed. On such stepping stones she rose at last to almost complete normalcy, acquiring as many Best Friends to slip an arm into, and whisper against the world in general with, as anyone else. And after a year it is a fact that she even reached a condition of forwardness wherein she was once called by an under mistress "The Naughtiest Girl in the School." As, however, the manner of punishment at St. Cuthbert's Hall was of a pleasantly lenient order, consisting only of "Lecturing," expulsion from the class-room, or a system whereby the criminal had implicitly undesirable "Black Marks" placed against her name, Elsie did not find this a very terrifying reputation to have acquired. On the contrary, she almost appeared to foster it, and sometimes really did get out of hand. "Elsie!..Take *two* black marks!" cried an infuriated mistress on a certain hideous occasion. And she took them, we have to say, not only without a qualm, but with something resembling a smile of achievement on her features. But it is hardly necessary to say that such signs of spirit were never at any time observable in her relations with her mother, with whom it was still "Yes, mother," "Please, mother," "Thank you, mother," and all the other perfectly respectful and subservient "mothers."

In such a manner Elsie crept, or rather took diffident and spasmodic little advances, into girlhood, and it was the same with Master Wildman, who now crept into early adolescence by the customary stages.

In the space of three years he shot up into an object of five feet, nine inches in height (being reported, by Miss Hatt, to be about to reach the ceiling next), man's trousers, and a turn for the type of humour that calls Suez Canal Suet Canal, and considers it has made a joke. This object wore no expression whatever on a vaguely downy thing in no way resembling a human countenance. The habit of this object in company was to blush whenever addressed; and frequently, for private and unfathomable reasons, it could be observed gently reddening of its own accord. Its legs did not do what it wanted them to do; it was alertly and intensively polite; furtive when in any area covered by a mirror. It was generally spoken to, and had its opinion asked, in such amiable, experimental, and helpful tones as would be used towards a person on the verge of becoming sane, and it was occasionally twitted by arch reference to its legendary Best Girl. It put a large amount of oil upon its hair.

The common treatment for this phase of life being based, apparently, on a kind of homœopathic principle, it was considered right that he should now be removed to a Public School for such subjects; and accordingly, at the age of fourteen, he entered as a boarder in a venerable and royally-founded institution well known as Harringham, which existed around an Abbey of the same name a few miles outside London—the Major having strained a weakening purse to the last degree to allow of this move. At this institution Master Wildman had all the advantages of being in the midst of as many other unfortunates of the same class and in a similar critical condition, as the place would hold.

That Master Wildman should have at last emerged from these walls without any stains other than those he might easily have acquired elsewhere, may be taken either as speaking well for the homœopathic principle, or as supporting a theory that by such means he was made to exhaust, in some measure, the unaired propensities of early adolescence.

Or, again, in Master Wildman's case, it may have been due to a chastening event at the commencement of this stage of his life. For in his first term there, which was not so long before the end of the war, he was called away to witness the death of his father.

CHAPTER III

The Major has nothing further to Say.

I

THE very last words that passed between Master Wildman and his father were spoken one evening in the entrance (from Southam Green High Road) into Southam Green Station, as Master Wildman left for his new school.

It was a swift and thunderous moment. . . . The bare boards cracked, thundered under the boots of the other itinerants; from the booking-office there came the deadened and spasmodic jerking of the ticket machine, and the slap and clink of change; from the High Road, the bawling of the news sellers; and from below, the disconcerting rumble of a possibly negotiable train. The Major said: "Well, my boy, I'll be getting along then." "Right you are then, daddy," said Master Wildman. "Good-bye." And the next moment his father had gone away.

II

The next time Master Wildman saw his father, his father was a stiff, vividly conscious, and regular-breathing entity in a bed, braced and tense for a death which seemed to have taken the precaution of binding him all over first. Miss Hatt said he had had a stroke. . . .

Under the new and stark predicament he had no sign whatever to give his son.

This was at half past eight o'clock in a jostled and unfamiliar room containing white and medical things pertaining to a newly arrived, startched, and gliding nurse; and a livid green gas, sighing, sputtering, and choking over its own opinion.

At half past three the same night (morning would be a

false term to use) Master Wildman was awaked from clanging
dreams by a creaking listener outside his door, and the sound
of candle-light whispering. His teeth were chattering in a
way that almost fascinated him, and he went outside to
learn that his father was dead. He was asked if he would
like to look, and did so, in the candle-light, just as an ear-
splitting and clangorous motor lorry, containing milk cans,
crashed by outside. By the time this was clanking in the
remote distance, he was back in his own room, with his
hands in his dressing-gown pockets, again listening to his
teeth.

Soon afterwards a candle-lit Miss Hatt entered, looking
rather ridiculous (he thought) in her dressing-gown, and she
placed a candle-lit, steaming cup of tea on his table. She
said "Drink this, dear boy," and on hearing this endearment,
which was uttered with half a sob, Master Wildman made a
queer noise, more like a hiccough than anything else, and
even this was not without a certain passing interest for him.

Then Miss Hatt left the room, and he commenced panting
and gulping at the piping-hot tea, and watching his breath.
And five minutes later he was lying snuggled in the inky
darkness, listening to his teeth going "Click-click-click," and
"Click-click-click," and "Click-click-click-click-click-click-
click," until he went off into the deepest sleep òf his life.

III

In the three days preceding the funeral, Master Wildman
kept his room, taking occasional long walks in the neighbourhood, and seeing only Miss Hatt. He once encountered Elsie
on the stairs, and caught her reddened eyes with his own,
and passed in silence; and Audrey knocked at his door
every day at meal times, and murmured: "Your tray, sir,"
in the deepest tones of condolence. Edith was tenderly
struck by the idea of cooking a consolatorily irregular pan-
cake for him, which (so he learnt, through Miss Hatt) she
thought he "might like."

The rest of the household fluttered enquiringly and self-
abasingly around Miss Hatt, who now assumed a queenly
and quiet character, and entreated that they would best
help her by letting all go on as usual.

It appeared that the Major had fallen down outside the
Bank. . . .

The funeral passed off in the early phases of a wind-blown, silver-gleaming, wet, bedraggled sunset, and the stiff, black, muttering, gravel-scrunching silence peculiar to these occasions. Elsie was present with the rest, looking, for Elsie, amazingly pretty in black; and she, with her sheer, unsolicited and unostentatious wretchedness of bearing, was the chief source of comfort to Master Wildman. (He would talk about it all to Elsie one day. He would get to know Elsie well.) But there was, as well, a whole crowd of his own obscure relations and connections there, well supplied with funeral technique, and giving a certain sense of support. There was, in particular, an uncle Paul . . . who had a lot of money.

Master Wildman was sharply hurt by the depth they let his father down into the ground. He never knew they let them down as far as that. It was like a mine. And it seemed almost that his father was crying out to him, to be spared that jerky lowering into all that cold brown earthiness, so far below. He should have been nearer the surface, and the light.

IV

Only occasionally did Master Wildman give way to tears over the death of his father. His agony consisted more of sudden, tempestuous turnings of the spirit towards his father, to find nothing there—and in little inconsequent memories of a look here, and a tone there, now snapped for ever, by death, into something remote and infinitely sweet, like a tune gone. It would hardly be exaggerating to say that Master Wildman's most acute misery lay in just one of these little pictures, which came back again and again to him—a picture of the old gentleman as he came down to surprise them all in his domino costume and glanced at his little boy for a rewarding look in his triumph, and did not get it, and could not ever get it now.

CHAPTER IV

Mr. Spicer returns an Overman.   Mrs. Nixon Sums Up.

I

ARMISTICE DAY was a colourless and drab affair, in spite of
a final efflorescence of shabby flags and the sound of bells
over Southam Green; and as soon as Mr. Spicer returned,
which was shortly afterwards, all was very much as before.

Mr. Spicer's services to his country were, we are inclined
to believe, something in the nature of a burden to both
parties concerned.   In the earliest stages of his training Mr.
Spicer went down to a Throat, rallying from which he went
down under Influenza, which he had hardly pulled round
from before Shooting Pains in the Head attacked this wretched
tea merchant.   The top parts of Mr. Spicer having been now
played upon with such a variety of agonies, there was a
short lull in which Mr. Spicer was sent to guard the East
Coast of England against invasion.   Then the lower parts of
Mr. Spicer were attacked; firstly by Foot-soreness, secondly
by Rheumatism at the knee-joints, and thirdly by varicose
veins.   Another period of comparative immunity succeeding,
Mr. Spicer was at last drafted to France, where he spent
some time upon highly explosive territory and in vermin-
ridden clothes, before being gassed, and returned home prostrate.   Once in England again his miseries were practically
at an end, and he spent a peaceful time until the Armistice.

Mr. Spicer returned to domesticity with a quantity of
Little Stories (touching or otherwise); a vivid and unutterable
sense of the lurid bestiality of his short experience in France,
but no sense whatever of it being in any way other than
righteous, seemly, eternal, and cumulatively expressive of
the highest glories achievable by men.

Indeed, Mr. Spicer waxed a trifle learned on this subject,
and was capable of reasoning without the aid of his usual
patriotic stock-in-trade—(Dear Old England, Suns Never
Setting, and so forth)—and could hold forth at some length
on theories of Natural Selection and the Survival of the
Fittest; mentioning not only Darwin, but Nietzsche—which
philosopher Mr. Spicer pronounced as in Nightshirt, and
upheld without personally perusing.   The ladies, on the other

hand (soft-hearted creatures that they were), were rather in favour of something being Done, and invariably set up a "tut-tutting" noise when these mysteries were explained.

II

There were also vague questionings on these matters from below-stairs—a quarter from which very few questionings of any sort ever arose.

"Will they have another war directly this one's finished?" Audrey asked Edith, as they were washing up one day, shortly after the Armistice.

"Don't know," replied Edith, tersely. "Sincerely trust not."

"So do I," said Audrey, and was contemplative. "I Sincerely Trust not, too," she remarked a moment later, taking a note of "Sincerely Trust" for her own use—her mania for popular idiom having increased enormously with the years.

"What do you expect would have happened if there had been an invasion?" asked Audrey.

"You can't tell," said Edith, with the air of a tactician. "It wouldn't 'ave been nice, though."

"Do you expect they'd 've Pillaged the Land?" asked Audrey.

"Don't know about *thet*," rejoined Edith. "We might 've all 'ad to do the Goose Step, though."

"Oo. Do you think we would, Eed?"

"I said *Might*," returned Edith, sternly.

Audrey considered that for a moment.

"I wouldn't 've done it," she said.

"They'd 've made you," said Edith.

"Would they 've Put me to the Sword?" enquired Audrey.

"More'n likely. There's no tellin' with those."

"I expect they *would*," surmised Audrey, dreamily, "if I Refused Point Blank."

"My *brother*," said Edith, "says that if we were invaded we'd 've all been put under martial law."

"What's that, Eed?"

"Don't know rightly, myself. But *'e* ought to know."

"Why's that, Eed?"

"'E's a Scholar," affirmed Edith, which was final. "'E 'ad a real trainin', 'e 'ad."

"Did 'e, Eed? Where did 'e Learn 'is Education, then?"

"At the Colehurst Grammar School," declared Edith, with more finality still, and the subject being changed the matter was dropped.

III

The quickest reading of these enigmas, however, came from Mrs. Nixon; and inasmuch as it was a very succinct, and comprehensive, and irrefutable interpretation, and uttered in a slightly irritated tone of clinching the matter once and for all, it can well be placed at the end of these chapters of stormy interlude, and taken as a very fair summing-up.

"There needn't *always* be wars, need there, mother?" asked Elsie.

"Of course there need, you silly girl," said Mrs. Nixon. "Why, if there weren't any wars, there wouldn't be any soldiers! And what would you have then?"

Elsie did not know.

END OF BOOK II

Book III

CHAPTER I

Craven House Entertains.

I

WE must now take the reader to a period some six years after the events described in the last few chapters, and draw the curtain back upon yet another little dinner scene at Craven House, in which all its leading characters (save one, and he is replaced) appear.

It is New Year's Day, and the unshaded gas lights in an ashen way, the faces of all present in front of the chilly glitter of the holly, and dead green appearance of the mistletoe left over from the Christmas festivities. Here is Mr. Spicer at the top of the table, standing to carve; and there is Miss Hatt, at the bottom, slyly watching him as she talks; and here is Mrs. Nixon, doing the same; and there is Master Wildman, just twenty-three; and here is Elsie, only a year or so behind him; and there, lastly, is Mrs. Hoare, who has taken the Major's place. And as this character is a perfectly unfamiliar character, and as the two children are now beyond all recognition of their former state, we must ask to give some kind of description of the newcomer, and a *resumé* of any changes, spiritual or otherwise, in the others.

The transformations, evolutions and improvements that the years have brought about in Master Wildman are no less than magical. To begin with, Master Wildman has now come to some sort of contract with his legs, whereby the latter have not only agreed to concentrate, without any superfluous or wandering action, upon the business of carrying the bust of a young man from one given place to another; but to further his requests in general particulars. But there are many other seemly arrangements as well. Master Wildman now looks out upon the world without any layer of muddy water in front of his grey eyes; his hair is no longer cut upon a pudding-basin, and plastered upon a drowned rat principle; and his complexion is now clear and rough, instead of soft and smudged, as before. Master Wildman has a remarkably fine and complete set of teeth, arranged according to gradual sizes, and looking very bright and business-like in a hard, and rather well-fed face. Master Wildman is spoken of as a very handsome young man. "Like a young Apollo," *Edith* says, but this strong metaphor does not betoken any real classical discernment on Edith's part, as any reference to an illustrated "Lemprière's Dictionary," or some such volume, would have at once corrected her views on Master Wildman's type of countenance, which has none of that peach-like and rather curly serenity rife in depicted Apollos. And as, on another occasion, she has declared that he looks "rather like Napoleon," we can see how useless it is to take this predisposed cook's opinions seriously.

In addition to other advantages Nature has given Master Wildman a very exquisite talent for wearing hard white collars. To such exhaustive use is Master Wildman capable of putting this gift, wearing them, when he has the whim, at such heights and depths, and starched white dignities, and yet, withal, emerging so smiling and charming from them, and so much like the newspaper-advertised versions of ideal creatures contained in them, that he can only be called a genius in this respect.

Master Wildman is tall, without being a Height, as Miss Hatt used to call him, and he wears well-fitting tweed suits.

As regards Master Wildman's mental increase in these years, we will have to leave the reader to judge of it from the ensuing pages. It is only necessary to say that in the period since his schooldays he has conceived a strong turn for Poetry, having several sonnets, lyrical poems, dying poems, Open Road poems, Very Stately Lady Poems, and *vers libre* "*Ah, My God, the pain!*" Poems to his credit; as well as an epic (at present unfinished), and the promising commencement to a blank verse play which was to have been entitled "Vortigern" (a subject Milton dallied with), and which, from the two first lines:—

> "(*Alarum*) Vort: (Entering R.)
> Now let us breathe again, and lay our arms
> Away from savage, monstrous, bold affront. . . ."

will be readily recognisable as having been planned upon a

Shakespearean model. It is only fair to say, however, that these are by now more or less affairs of the past. Master Wildman's imagination has deserted these flights in favour of sundry prose plays and sketches in a twentieth-century setting. He has, to tell the truth, some fifteen to twenty of these sprinkled about the bottom of his trunk. One has been typed. He is likely to write a good many more, since it is his habit to sit down in the evening and get ahead with one whenever he is feeling more than usually down-trodden and beautifully sad. . . .

Master Wildman's general expression (that is, his expression in company at Craven House) is one of slight amiable smiles, born of long listening, in a knife-fingering preoccupation. He does not speak much, and then generally shifts his position a little. . . . But this preoccupation is due to other causes besides a disinclination to talk. He has left school a good long time now, and is engaged in mastering the arts of Short-hand and Typewriting, with an eye to entering a very san-guinely and jollily taken-for-granted occupation, known as Business—there being no immediate opening in Tea, to Mr. Spicer's sorrow. Now any reader familiar with this art of Shorthand will know how largely, in the early stages, it can figure in the daily imagination. Master Wildman is no exception to this, and during the conversation that follows, Master Wildman's dreamy look is almost completely attri-butable to mere mental wrestlings to express in Shorthand either such direct questions as: "May the Pope gloat on Fate?" or "Can he Cope with the Tape?"—or merely such debatable assertions as "A Pale Rope Sates Coal Boats," "A Late Moat weights the Throat," and so on. For Master Wildman is in that phase of Shorthand progress wherein the long a's and o's endanger sanity with a weltering world of Pages, Boats, Cocoa, Mates, Capes, Coaches and Cake. These are figured as governing, or being governed by, the actions of (almost exclusively) Joe Cope, Joe Page, or Job Bate—unless we mention the subsidiary exertions of Job Day. Having settled the above-mentioned problems to his satisfaction, Master Wildman goes on to his later and more difficult exercises, and starts unearthing Shorthand ore from the very outlines of his immediate surroundings. And, having interpreted the outlines of the furniture, he does not even draw himself in at converting personal properties to his own wild purpose. As in the case of a nose belonging to Mr.

Spicer, which he is rather inclined to decipher as "Checked" (∠), but for a prevailing curviness in that feature, which defies any earthly rendering whatever.

Finally it must be said of Master Wildman that, with regard to Elsie, there are no statements achievable by this young man, no domestic mistakes makeable, no smiles smileable, no humorous frowns frownable, no collars wearable, in short no human business negotiable, that is not regarded by her as being the *dernier cri* in celestial beauty and earthly fitness. Whether or no Elsie is in love with Master Wildman at present it is difficult to say, as there is no sense of contract between them, and her behaviour in his presence resembles that of a happy child in the presence of a particularly delicious uncle, more than anything else. But this is none the less transparent, and she solicits and mends his socks for him, and sews buttons on to him on the spot, and patches him in general particulars with such an air of keeping every detail of his beauty intact for her own delight; and she becomes so vague in company when she hears his key in the door, and she moves knitting from one part of the sofa to another to make room for him with such unveiled illuminations of the countenance, and such glances divided between himself and her watchful parent, that any shrewd observer may see where the land lies.

As for Elsie herself, she is getting a good deal prettier with the years, in her own miniature and reddish way, having a fresh white skin and enchanting teeth in a small mouth— though still retaining a certain early-morning-bath and self-conscious pinkness about the little nose, which has always been a rather rebellious feature in this direction. She has just a freckle or two hereabouts, also, which, on being accused of existence by Master Wildman, are rubbed by the knuckles of their owner, who weakly repudiates them, and blinks her eyes the while. "Would you Term Miss Elsie a pretty girl?" asks Audrey. "No," says Edith. "She ain't what you'd call pretty. She ain't got no style." And no wonder, since she is as much as ever under the thumb of her mother, and her blossoming prettiness is fortunate in being a gradual process, as it is already being looked upon with some dis-favour and suspicion. "Can I have my hair bobbed, mother?" asks Elsie. "No, you can not, Miss," says Mrs. Nixon. "We'll have none of these modern airs here." In fine, Elsie is still nothing more than an appendage to her mother, a human manifestation of her will, a submerged personality occasionally hazarding shy indiscretions in the way of an opinion, or becoming pretty, or Master Wildman-patching, but immediately and apologetically descending to her proper level.

But no description of Elsie at this period can be any sort of description without mention of her Fountain Pen. This was a birthday gift from Master Wildman, six months ago, and since the day of its presentation, as a Surprise (and what ecstasies there were!), it really seems to have transformed the young girl's life. She goes about with it on her person, having mysterious insertions and upright harbours for it in her clothes; she produces it with an air of getting back to the real business of her life; she shakes it, and fingers its nib, and tries it, and shakes it, and uses it, and uses it, and uses it. She is discovered in quiet corners, voraciously using it. "Shopping list, Miss Hatt?" Fountain Pen. "Washing list, Mrs. Spicer?" Fountain *Pen*. "Three times three hundred and sixty-five, Mr. Spicer?" Fountain *Pen*. "Note to leave to the piano tuner?" Why, *Fountain Pen!* She adds with it, subtracts with it, and divides with it, under a mad urge for domestic statistics, and a passion for solid premises and logical perfection that would have routed a whole company of Aristotles or John Stuart Mills. She baffles her Aunt Jessica in her letters, by pages and pages of lavish description with it; and it is, finally, a kind of link between Master Wildman and herself, and by using it she feels she is in some distant way expressing and showing her loving admiration for him.

With respect to Mrs. Spicer, Mr. Spicer, Miss Hatt and Mrs. Nixon, the years have brought no apparent changes to Mrs. Spicer, but they have battered Mr. Spicer considerably particularly in the teeth, where the Golden One still glitters, but now, we are afraid, more like hope amid the ruins than the morning glory it used to simulate. And the years have brought nothing to Miss Hatt, except another pair of pincenez, and a few more lines in her face, cut by her everlasting merriness. Mrs. Nixon is, needless to say, hale and heary, and exuding a glad confidence in complete domination of her daughter or any other rebellious event or person likely to tackle her.

And there is Mrs. Hoare. Mrs. Hoare is a slim lady, confessing to seventy years. She looks exactly the same as Mrs. Leo Hunter would have looked at the same age, and she is the type of old lady that goes into a book shop and says she wants a nice book for her *eldest* niece.

She arrived one day, at twenty-four hours' notice, on the steps of Craven House in a state of baggage-surrounded and short-sighted bewilderment, frantically endeavouring to get from her purse the sum of fourpence—which amount of money she considered the one, immutable, and eternal due payable to a Man in such circumstances and with such an amount of luggage—and having payed over which, with extremely knowing and nudging gestures, and an intimation that That was for Him, she turned to Miss Hatt and entered upon her new abode.

There is nothing out of the ordinary in this old lady except her years, which amount, in Nature's reckoning, to seventy-five. Her head nods all day about half as much as an aged flute-player's head might nod—except in haughty moments, when a flute player would have been clean outnodded. This same head is the source of much commiseration and sympathy amongst her nephews and nieces, in which she is very well stocked—being a highly disputable head, which some declare her to be Slightly Queer in, or even Not Quite All There in; which others rather weakly affirm her to be as yet Quite All Right in, and which she herself, keeping quite an open mind on the matter, sometimes confesses to feeling Rather Funny in. But as by this term she is trying to express merely certain giddiness named privately by her "The Swims," the problem continues to call for all the steady attention it continues to receive from all. The world at large, knowing nothing of the controversy, takes a sound mental state for granted, with minor reservations in Eccentricity.

Mrs. Hoare does not insult Miss Hatt much more than her other guests insult her, by implications of reduced circumstances and having come down in the world, but she does, of course, insult her. She has come, indeed, it is widely known, from the Land—as opposed not to Water, but the middle and lower orders. She herself is a little touchy on the point of getting this registered, and will repeat, when reminiscent occasions allow it, such phrases as "The Hunting, you know," or "The brother to the Duke, you know," an amount of times verging on double figures, instead of once loudly, as a less discreet person might have managed it. But then Mrs. Hoare is an excessively discreet lady. In fact, it is a certain over-discreet trait in this old lady's character that the Not Quite All There school of nephews and nieces point to, as the main proof of their theory. For Mrs. Hoare carries a sense of necessary surreptitions into the most everyday matters, and she even shirks the naked enunciation of various everyday words. She has, therefore, invented a clever system whereby such culprits, or large portions of such culprits, are, very cunningly, spelt. And although it is a pleasant and elegant softening of an opinion to have Mrs. Hoare calling a person a bit of an Eff O, when she would otherwise have dismissed him as a Fool—or rather an I Dee, when she obviously considers him an Idiot,—it is, in a small way, alarming to her nearest friends to find her declaring her intention to go O Yoo, instead of Out, or pleading a desire to stay at Aitch (Home) on the excuse that there is too much Doubleyoo I (Wind) for *her* liking, out of doors.

Mrs. Hoare's teeth are occasionally to be found in a false position making a noise like the word "Clock." Mrs. Hoare has at once joined in the airing battles at the tank upstairs, which is now the seat of a stealthy warfare not pleasant to contemplate. Mrs. Hoare is looked upon as an agreeable newcomer. Mrs. Hoare employs flattery with a trowel (as will soon be seen), but out of sheer goodness of heart, and Elsie is very fond of her. Master Wildman is fond of her too, but is inclined to make a little fun of her; at which Elsie pretends to be very ashamed, and angry with him. But Mrs. Hoare knows nothing about this. . . .

"Told them about the Picture?" asks Mr. Spicer, of his wife.

II

But what is this? What is this diamond blazing on Mrs. Nixon's finger? What is this tidy arrangement of the hair, and entirely new blue jumper upon a scintillating and scented Miss Hatt? What is this rose in Mrs. Spicer's bosom; this brighter blackness and glinting braceletedness in Mrs. Hoare; these moonstones, like lumps of blue mist, around Elsie's neck; this supreme shavedness and freshness of eye in Master Wildman; this air of an occasion?

To-night, after dinner, Craven House entertains. On a fairly large scale, too, for not only are the Heavens (in a fearful style of speech) engaged to Drop In, but a giddy falling out of events has had it that one of Elsie's old school-friends has fixed a first visit for to-night; and there is to be music, and late coffee and digestive biscuits, it is whispered, against such revelry.

But the New Year is always a rather festive time of year for Craven House, for Mr. Spicer enjoys his longest period of recuperation from Tea at this time, and numerous trips, excursions, outings; together with a visit to the Theatre, are dutifully tackled by Mr. and Mrs. Spicer before the former's return to trade. To-day they have been to the moving pictures; and having also had a musical tea out of doors, they are naturally in rather a state, and anxious to unburden themselves.

"Told them about the Picture?" asks Mr. Spicer, of his wife.

A tacit but cordial negative surges through the company present, and Mrs. Spicer at last outs with a retiring: "No, I don't think we have." But no other advance is made.

"Very Good," tries Mr. Spicer.

"Yes. Very good indeed," affirms Mrs. Spicer, and a further very cordial sound, like the ghost of a satisfied "Ah!" electrifies the air, but we are still in rather a *cul-de-sac* over the matter, until Master Wildman, who has a good heart, makes friendly noises in the throat comprising the word "About?"

"About a *Doctor*," Mrs. Spicer tells us, as though it is a slightly sad confession.

Ah! About a Doctor? Now we're getting on. That's something anyway. Master Wildman is tempted to make further noises in the throat comprising the word "Do?"

"What he *didn't* do. . . . Really . . ." says Mr. Spicer, who is poking very inquisitively at the joint.

"Couldn't get any *practice*," Mrs. Spicer admits. Another sad confession.

"Very amusing really," says Mr. Spicer, now definitely suspecting, if not accusing, the joint in front of him. . . .

"Won't you tell us?" says Elsie, and it is a great relief.

"Well, it's rather a long story really," says Mrs. Spicer.

Mrs. Hoare whispers for a little salt, please.

"Well," says Mrs. Spicer, "it's about a doctor in one of these little towns, you see, where there isn't any practice, and what did they say about it, dear?

"What was it now?" queries Mr. Spicer, looking upwards, and the company hangs urbanely in the air.

"So humorous," says Mrs. Spicer, wistfully, and the company is still hanging. . . .

"Oh, yes," says Mr. Spicer, and the company glides serenely to earth again. "Very funny. It said he thought there must have been a special law made, prohibiting illness!"

"Oh, yes! That was it!" says Mrs. Spicer, and then gets well away with the story.

We do not intend to listen to this story ourselves; but the company, of course, is compelled to do so. We ourselves will make do with saying that it deals with the Doctor; A Girl; A Man; Another Man, who gets frequently confused in Mrs. Spicer's narrative with both the first Man and Another Man Still, who is at last ticketed as The Villain. But this does not eliminate subsequent confusion in the mind of the company, for there is also an Old Man, and a Millionaire, who is old, yes, but not the Old Man; there is Another Girl; A Maid; Another Maid; a Young Girl (as opposed to the Another Girl); A Young Boy; An Attendant (No, neither of the maids. A man); and a Boy. Whenever the narrative halts, either while these confusions are unravelled or Mr. Spicer tells his wife that she has Left Out a Part, Mr. Spicer is careful to explain to the company that it "was all very humorous, really," and the company is absolutely sure that it was. Fortunately, there at last comes a time when it is allowed to rest at that.

The subject is not so easily changed, however, owing to unfortunate information given that there was, as a matter of fact, another and subsidiary film, not so good, but nevertheless about a young *lady*. . . . A young lady who was, on the strength of a single encouraging "Oh, yes,'?" from the company, Jazz (Mrs. Spicer says regretfully) Mad. . . . A young lady, who, not allowed to be known before Craven House by this single characteristic, is already showing signs of taking nightly outings to destruction (traced sketchily by Mrs. Spicer), as well as sketchily involving herself in parent-defying, motor accidents, and hotel bedroom *contretemps*, when her activities are happily cut into by the pudding.

"Terrific crowd there was in the High Road this evening," says Mr. Spicer, and Master Wildman quickly takes him up with "Yes. I expect it's the football. Always like that on a Saturday evening."

"Yes, and don't those men shout," says Mrs. Hoare.

"They do," returns Miss Hatt.

"Yes, isn't it awful," says Elsie, and endeavours to imitate the paper sellers. "'All the winners of Prizes!'"

"Of *what*?" puts in Master Wildman, smartly.

"Of what?" repeats Elsie, smiling vaguely at him, with just an inkling of a trap somewhere.

"All the winners of *what*?" says Master Wildman.

Elsie pauses.

"Prizes," ventures Elsie.

Stunning guffaws now fall upon her from all present. With the exception, perhaps, of Master Wildman, who makes do with a highly contented but rather affectionate grin. For if Master Wildman has any soft part in his heart for Elsie at all (which is an arguable point), it is possibly for certain winning idiocies of this sort in Elsie, who, since the day she first enchanted him in such a way by declaring her fountain pen to be composed of eighteen carrots, has timidly let fall innumerable similar blunders for his delight.

"No," says a recovering Mr. Spicer, philosophically. "And Prices."

The atmosphere, however, is now, cinematographically speaking, clear; and all runs smoothly through the cheese and dessert. Then they all move into the drawing-room. That is, all except Mrs. Hoare, who instead of pleading correspondence, as the Major used to, frankly excuses herself from ever staying up after dinner on the score of old age. But as she might have been expected to make an exception for such festivities as this evening will afford, she feels some slyness is warranted, and whispers to Master Wildman, as he stands at the door, that she's off to *Bee*. But she does not escape unnoticed, and ascends the stair amid a chorus of "Good nights!" This serves to drown a sardonic "Good Enn," from Master Wildman, who is nevertheless quite content to keep such quips to himself.

III

Soon a soft double knock falls upon the ears within.

Audrey, rushing to the door, murmurs "Yes, miss," as though a body is about to be taken away, and Elsie rushes out in a flutter to greet her friend.

This character does not appear at once, but goes upstairs with Elsie to remove her hat.

A period not unlike a period of silent prayer for a coming ordeal descends upon every one, suddenly breaking out into an overflow of bright and airy chatter when the two young ladies are heard conversing on the stairs, and as suddenly returning again, with redoubled intensity, as the newcomer, with Elsie as mediator, exchanges soft greetings, handshakes, and giddy expressions with all.

Now the introduction of Miss Cotterell (for that is the newcomer's name) to Craven House is not without significance, for it is the meeting of two very clearly defined, but widely opposed types of the Southam Greener, and Elsie has accomplished a rarer thing than she knows. It is a meeting between the Craven House class of persons, who have long thrown down their higher social cards, and taken to good humour, and a class of persons still steadily at the game. There is hence, if no haughtiness, a certain passive and absorbed air about Miss Cotterell, which at once and automatically reveals Craven House as a little gesticulatory, ingratiating, and jerkily ill at ease. . . .

For Miss Cotterell undoubtedly belongs to a class of persons now becoming more and more common in Southam Green— an exalted class of persons, who without having any more in actual pounds, shillings, and pence, look in a rather superior way at Craven House—being that class of persons who possess a Car, and a little dog, and a polo-playing uncle; who get free tickets for Wimbledon, or Twickenham; who are to be heard of as in a daily state of Motoring Up, and Motoring Down; who go to Rome next spring, and return from Germany, and Know people, and are at home to them with even more unbalanceable teas than Miss Hatt's.

Of this class of persons (a quite good-looking lot) Miss Cotterell is a very good-looking member.

Indeed, from the first moment, there seems little chance for Master Wildman, and no chance whatever for Elsie, if she has eyes of any description on Master Wildman. But then Elsie can hardly be said to have nourished a viper. She has invited a siren into the house, and no bones about it, and Master Wildman is the first to recognise the fact.

Miss Cotterell is now offered a sofa in a large manner by Mr. Spicer. She seats herself upon it, skilfully flicks a skirt down upon some very fine hose crossed upon it, and quietly talks, through Elsie, about the weather and the breaking-down of her car outside Richmond that afternoon. . . . Until at last a "*Rat Tat Tat!*" at the front door, and a bell, clanging through the house like the last trump, appropriately announces that the Heavens have Dropped In.

And nothing short of Pandemonium ensues.

"Oh!" shrieks Miss Hatt at the front door. "If it isn't the Dog!" And the Dog it is—a black and lashing animal, belonging to the Heavens, who didn't like to leave him alone at home, they say, and wondered whether Miss Hatt would mind.

Mind! Away with the thought. The Heavens are swept into the drawing-room to introduce the animal.

Which is something of a business. For whereas Mr. Spicer's tender but suspicious habit, on meeting any dog socially, is immediately to confront and compromise that friend of man by asking what's the matter with it, and to repeat the question with a variety of "Eh's?" while exploring its ears, Mr. Spicer does not forgo his rule now. And Elsie exclaims: "Oh, what a lovely dog!" and Mrs. Spicer says: "Yes, isn't he?"; and Master Wildman asks what make he is; and Miss Cotterell looks at him technically and says he's a sort of Retriever, isn't he? and Mr. Heaven says "Yes, he is," and Mrs. Heaven rather gazes at Miss Cotterell, while her husband explains the pedigree at greater length. There is, in fact, a great racket, which lasts for something over five minutes. Mrs. Heaven instructs Miss Hatt not to let him, Miss Hatt says he'll be all right. Mr. Spicer calls him a Good Dog, Mr. Heaven calls him a Bad Dog. Until finally the centre of controversy begins rather to justify its owner's ill opinion, not only by a swiftly increasing tendency to Retrieve various lower portions of the guests present, but by nearly smashing a vase as well; and in due course it gets terrible throat-rattlings and cannibal gestures made at it, which coerces it into taking the floor. Here, both injured and innocent, it simulates the posture of a sleeping dog, and is let lie.

We have a breather after this, but Music is soon mentioned, and Mrs. Spicer is persuaded to go to the piano. Whereupon Mr. Heaven, by request, plants himself firmly behind it, and musically testifies to the knocks of fate against the captaincy of his own soul, for which he is applauded. He then temporarily adopts a freebooter's widow's character and sings "Son of Mine." And then he sits down with the brusque air of a man having expressed himself concisely on all heads. Timidities again prevail, but Mrs. Heaven at last arises and begins to sing, with great feeling, astonishing eroticisms regarding chariot wheels and marriage months. But Mr. Heaven either takes such allusions in a domestic light, as being addressed to himself, or he is a very easy going man with respect to these irreconcilable soul-storms on the part of his married wife, for he doesn't mind a bit. After this there is some conversation, and our little tragedy begins.

For Master Wildman is now established, in a knee-grasping and questioning way, upon the remotest sofa in the room with Miss Cotterell. And although Elsie keeps on smiling at them from a distance, and they keep on smiling back; and although she goes over to them to show them the score and words of a song, and waits about while they look at it, and gets it returned with smiles; and although she sits speechlessly on the little arm-chair in their vicinity, as though she *is* one of them after all; and although she gets up and goes away upon unknown business, and returns again to have another try—it all serves her nothing if she is aiming at being treated as anything else but a pleasant aside by the two persons she has caused to meet. Eventually she gives it up and goes to fiddle with a bit of silk, with a slightly injured look she is not herself at all conscious of, amongst the others.

Here, for a long while, the severest arguments have been in progress on the subject of the Modern Young Girl. And with Elsie as a sort of lay figure for their arguments, patiently listening to their indictments, but ever and anon casting a little glance over at the two who should have been her supporters, the arguments proceed.

Mr. Heaven is all for leaving Elsie alone, and she'll "pan out" all right.

Mrs. Spicer says that she's the result of all this lack of discipline, and all this Jazz, and all this Staying Out, and all this Carrying On, and all this Going Here, and all this Going There. (Mrs. Spicer has just seen a film on the theme.)

Mrs. Heaven thinks that it must have been the war that upset Elsie.

Mrs. Nixon nods suggestively to herself, rejects the war's culpability, and hints The Stick's default.

Miss Hatt is sure she doesn't know, but things were very different at one time; and Mr. Spicer says "Now——" and proceeds to instance his own boyhood, at school, during which he never failed, no, not for one week, to write to his *Mother*. Mr. Spicer breathes this last word, like a play-actor, and having so established himself as something of a domestic rarity, he takes the lead in the discussion, and holds forth—Mr. Heaven nodding, and the ladies clicking "Tut-tut" in approval for quite half-an-hour.

But the Coffee comes at last, and we pull round from this serious talk ("I ought to have been a Preacher, oughtn't I?" says Mr. Spicer, facetiously chiding himself) in busying ourselves with the cups. Elsie takes over two cups to Miss Cotterell and Master Wildman, and succeeds in getting a conversational footing with them for the last quarter of an hour of the evening, which goes with quite a bang. Mr. Spicer makes a joke about false teeth, and the others, who are rather scared of him in his new rôle of preacher, laugh uproariously. This puts him in the humour to make another joke (which includes a banana skin). Miss Hatt begins to ask people if they're sure they won't have any port. Mr. Spicer goes out and reports the night to be starry and beautiful. Mrs. Nixon calls Elsie from Miss Cotterell and Master Wildman to see about that nightdress. . . . And finally Miss Hatt begins to tell Miss Cotterell how pleased she will be to see her again, any time. . . .

A move is made out into a hall breathed upon by the night.

The farewells begin. "Come along, Elsie," cries Mrs. Nixon from the stairs. "Time you were in bed." And Elsie, who has made an unemphasised sort of farewell to her friend already, now turns to her, and to Master Wildman, who is standing with her, and says she'll be getting up, then.

"I should think so too," says Master Wildman, in a style of humour not up to his usual style. "You ought to be fast asleep by now. Run along up." And Elsie runs along up.

The night is warm, for the time of year, and the guests linger for some time at the door, bringing their laughter out into the laughter of the stars, as though it is all a happy ending.

The little front gate shrieks once or twice, in the same mood, and the chatter continues, enforcing a pale benevolence even upon the old lamp opposite, as it casts its livid colour over all.

And in the light of the lamp, as the little gate shrieks for the last time, Master Wildman is standing right out in the street, with his easy talk to Miss Cotterell trailing up above; and in the light of the lamp, as the last "Good night" is given, a pallid Elsie is peeping out, between her bedroom curtains, on to the scene below.

CHAPTER II

A Shock.   Mr. Spicer is Modest and Natural.   Mr. Wildman enters Business.

I

ONE morning, early in the New Year, Craven House sustained a minor shock. It was not conceived as a shock, really. It was over in a moment, and only recalled a long while afterwards, when it was seen in a different light. . . .

It was at breakfast. Mrs. Nixon sliced her egg open, tasted it, looked absent.

"No . . ." said Mrs. Nixon.

"Oh," said Miss Hatt, and went to the door.

"Audrey! Audrey!"

"Yes'm."

"Will you do another egg, please. That wretched man's given us another bad one."

"Yes'm."

"That's twice, isn't it?" said Miss Hatt, sitting down.

Mrs. Hoare was now looking distant.

"Mrs. Hoare? . . ."

"Now I will not *have* you cook another," said Mrs. Hoare. "I didn't want an egg. It'll do me *good* to do without it. It'll do me good——"

"Audrey! Audrey!"

"Yes'm."

"Two eggs, please. Mrs. Hoare's is the same. I shall have it out with that man?"

"Yes'm."

Mr. Spicer was looking vague.

"Clifford? . . ."

"*Not*—absolutely," admitted Mr. Spicer.

"Audrey! Audrey! Please cook all the eggs you've got!"

"Yes'm."

"Too bad, isn't it," said Miss Hatt, sitting down. "I shall have it out with that man. I shall have it out."

"I wonder," said Mrs. Nixon, "you don't change the man altogether."

"Oh, do you?" said Miss Hatt, sharply, and then the

shock was felt. "I won't have another egg in this *house!*"
said Miss Hatt.

Her guests stared at her. Her face was white, and her
eyes were not pleasant to look upon.

"From that man," compromised Miss Hatt.

Miss Hatt had a temper, then? Her guests never knew
it. Her guests were a little far-away for the rest of the
meal.

It wasn't their fault. . . .

II

For three months more Master Wildman laboured at his
commercial shorthand, and having left a world of Cake
and Boats far away behind, and having taken a land of
tasters, coasters, feasters, ministers, and castors in his stride,
and passed swimmingly up through a domain of novels,
revels, snivels, hovels, reifers, breathers, bathers, sheriffs,
tariffs and motives (in perpetual danger of being qualified
by such adjectives as noticeable, passable, classical, blissful,
sober, sadder, or spruce)—he at last reached an almost
humane land of Pitman promise, wherein upholsterers, inco-
herence, boyhood, herbs, cohesion, hyperbole, or hemp could
mingle without any unbecoming attention to vowel sounds,
loops, or initial hooks.

At the end of it Master Wildman was given a certificate
for his performances, but at this point a dead wall seemed
to have been reached. For although Master Wildman exuded
a very nice atmosphere in Craven House of being about
to Do something, or at least See about something in the
near future, week had an undeniable way of following week
without a still amiably disposed Master Wildman having
actually looked for anything. Now as it was known that
Master Wildman had but three pounds a week, left by his
father, as income, and but three hundred pounds in the
Bank, it was clear that each of these weeks was drawing
Master Wildman nearer and nearer to facts it would one
day be unpleasant to face. At the same time, each one of
these same weeks appeared to increase, rather than decrease,
Master Wildman's light-heartedness and friendly attitude
towards the situation. . . .

This at last brought about so much concern amongst
his well-wishers at Craven House as to cause Miss Hatt

to declare that perhaps something ought to be seen about, on their own part; Mrs. Nixon to declare that somebody ought to have it out with him; Mrs. Hoare to admit that perhaps he *was* a bit of an *Eye* (Idler); and Mrs. Spicer to put forward that perhaps if her husband . . . This gentleman, on being approached, cottoned on to the idea at once, and allowed that a Little Chat, perhaps, might be of some value.

It was, therefore, only Master Wildman (for Elsie knew all about it, though she kept her own pro-Wildman musings strictly to herself) who was surprised, when he was ambushed in the hall one evening by a more golden tooth than ever, and ushered, with cabalistic gestures and a mystic request for a few words, up into the Spicers' room. Here Mr. Spicer lit the gas fire, and indicated a chair for his visitor.

"Won't you smoke, old man?" asked Mr. Spicer, who was trembling slightly. "Put on a Pipe," he added, to make the young man feel at ease.

"Cigarette, thanks," said Master Wildman.

"Oh. Good," said Mr. Spicer, and bent down to adjust the fire. "Must get this fire seen to properly. Keep on putting it off. . . .

"Still cold these evenings, too, isn't it?" said Mr. Spicer.

"Yes, it is. Still winter, though, really."

Mr. Spicer now lit a match and held it to Master Wildman's cigarette.

"Got it?" said Mr. Spicer, in seas of silence.

"Thanks."

"Now," said Mr. Spicer. "What I want to talk about is this *business* of yours."

"Oh, yes?"

"Now don't you think it's time you *got* something, old man?"

"Yes. I think perhaps it is, really."

"Now of course it's not my business to interfere. I've no doubt you know what you're up to well enough, but it's often we old ones can give you young men a hint or two, although you don't think much of us. And I've taken a sort of fatherly interest in you, old man. I've known you all this time, and seen you in all your troubles, and I feel I'm a Sort of second Father."

"That's very kind of you, Mr. Spicer," said Master Wildman.

"No," said Mr. Spicer, waving his own beauty of character away. "Not kind. Just natural. I feel I'm sort of *responsible* for you, and I want to *help* you on the right *lines*. Now

I've no doubt you think me a silly old fusser at times, who doesn't understand what it is to be young, but I've knocked about the world a bit, and I know a thing or two, and I think it's about time you really made an effort to get into business, and Get Going. Don't you agree?"

"Yes, I do," said Master Wildman.

"Now, there's nothing I hate more than Lecturing," continued Mr. Spicer, "especially from an old Gasser like me, and I don't want to bore you with my old man's talk, and I don't want to rush you, but I really think it's about time you began to think of something."

"Yes, I think it is," said Master Wildman, but the remark was passed over by Mr. Spicer, who was now getting down into his real stride.

Having again said how irksome it was for him to interfere, and having again pleaded second fatherhood in extenuation, and having again modestly belaboured his own wisdom in successively describing himself as:—

> An Old Buffer.
>   ,,   ,, Codger.
>   ,,   ,, Stick.
>   ,,   ,, Plodder.
>   ,,   ,, Geezer.

Mr. Spicer eventually wound up—through different paths indicative of how seldom he talked like this, and how few people saw this side of his character, and how he kept silent, but how it was There, and how people wouldn't have guessed, but, however—eventually wound up to the absolute matter in hand, his actual worldly advice amounting to a suggestion that Master Wildman should advertise for a job, in the *Morning Post*, and "put in about Harringham."

Having agreed, then, to advertise in the *Morning Post*, and to *put* in about Harringham, Master Wildman arose to thank Mr. Spicer for his kindness. That gentleman instantly seized his hand, ejaculated "Good *luck*, old man," with huge tenderness and vehemence, and led the way downstairs into an expectant drawing-room, where he assumed an air of shamefaced and overstressed jocularity, as though he had been fighting with the young man.

III

Master Wildman in due course corresponded with the *Morning Post*, and inserted an advertisement, and put in about Harringham (which came to six-and-six), and two days later had the pleasure of seeing himself in prmt. Two replies reached him a day or so after, on the same morning—one from Desks, in Tothill Street, Westminster; and the other from Rum, in the City. Master Wildman, on Elsie's advice and encouragement, at once went after them. Failing to make any effective impression on Desks, he returned to Elsie with Rum pretty nearly fixed at a salary of forty-five shillings, which was quite a good beginning, Mr. Spicer said.

And sure enough, one sunny and sudden morning, a week or so after, Master Wildman awoke, as it were, from a lazy dream of self-imposed labours and easy independence at Craven House, to find himself trapped in a train moaning an early city-goer's dirge—and shoved and crushed by his pale, breakfast-filled, tobacco-misted compeers. And although Master Wildman allowed no bad thoughts to cross his brain on this, his first morning, there was that in the stuffy atmosphere about him—an unconscious air of taking him for granted in the newspaper readers around—that changed Craven House into an enchanted, and well-beloved, and lost abode; and hinted at a lot of other unpleasant factors latent in Master Wildman's situation. But then Master Wildman did not allow such thoughts to get any further, and he was in a feverish enough state of mind about other matters. . . . For, in the evening of this day, he was to meet Miss Cotterell, alone, for the first time in his life. . . .

Now the thought of this gave a kind of romantic touch to Master Wildman's fever in the train—a romantic touch which was lowering to the vitality. For Master Wildman harboured remarkable sensations in regard to the person of Miss Cotterell, already. Indeed, if an astonishing lack of ability, combined with a particular effort, to express yourself on life in general whenever in the presence of Miss Cotterell; or a total loss of any desire to digest any dishes placed before you when threatened by a visit from Miss Cotterell; or the treasuring of a broken bangle given laughingly to you, from a brown warm arm belonging to Miss Cotterell; or the further treasuring of several unutterable glances given laughingly from

the dark eyes and quick mouth of Miss Cotterell; or a preposterous capacity for being haunted nightly and remorselessly
by the slim boy's shape, and the Florentine bobbed hair,
and the lissom dresses of Miss Cotterell—might all be taken
as advertising the fact that you were in love with Miss
Cotterell; why, then, Master Wildman was head over heels
in love with Miss Cotterell already.

It can therefore be easily understood that Master Wildman
came up from the Underground at the Monument in a limp
and rather chastened frame of mind, which was relieved
neither by his reaching the destined building (off Fenchurch
Street) a quarter of an hour before time, nor by a little
time-killing stroll around the plucked-bird vistas and fruity
putrefaction of the Leadenhall Market. However, at five and
twenty minutes past nine Master Wildman was climbing the
many hundreds of stone stairs that led to the office of the
Xotopol Rum Company (Ltd.), and at six and twenty past
he had entered it.

The daily responsibilities of the Xotopol Rum Company
Ltd. were shouldered by five persons, all told—Mr. Shillitoe
himself (the owner of a deadly amount of shares), who arrived
at an elevenish time of day; Mr. Casing, his general manager;
Mr. Creevy, a small and book-keeping backbone to the establishment; the shorthand typist, now Mr. Wildman; and a
more or less legendary charwoman, to whom was left two-
and-sixpences on the mantelpiece, and terse notes of reproach.

Of these, Mr. Casing was a stoutish grey gentleman of
sixty-five, dependent upon a liver, which either caused him
to retire to his room, and conduct various business irritabilities
with a yellow face from his desk, or granted him various
respites and interludes of amazing good humour. He was
not much liked by Mr. Creevy, who was, on the other hand,
about thirty-five, and Master Wildman's chief associate up
here, as he shared the same room with him. Mr. Creevy
had a clean-shaven, small face like a healthy red apple's
face, pince-nez over small grey eyes, and a diminutive in-
quisitiveness of nose. And just as Mr. Creevy's features were
on a rather miniature scale, so were Mr. Creevy's general
gestures in life accordingly thin and exact—Mr. Creevy being
a great expert in all the more Lilliputian and dapper activities
of life—an experienced and exquisite pencil-sharpener, a highly
finished umbrella-roller, a brilliant apple-peeler, a scintillating
fountain-pen-filler, a pince-nez polisher of the first order.

Any blunders made by other persons in these or similar functions caused Mr. Creevy the sharpest spiritual agonies pending actual interference. An orderly and fearfully exact citizen was Mr. Creevy, too. A man who pulled all doors he was told to Pull, and Pushed all doors he was told to Push, who went in by the Way In, and came out by the Way Out; who naturally went the longest way round, if it was the shortest way home; who Bewared of the Trains, or the Bull; who Did not Smoke, who Shopped Early, who Knocked and Rang; and *did* let you have a line from Ventnor on his holiday. . . .

Mr. Creevy's preoccupations were mainly to do with the firm, and his conversation mainly given over to discussion of the qualities of Mr. Shillitoe and Mr. Casing.

There could be no doubt of his opinion of the latter, whom he summed up directly as an old Nosy Parker of the first degree; but his attitude towards his actual employer, Mr. Shillitoe, remained more or less in the dark. Any assumptions that might be gathered from his alternating references to him either as Our Worthy Boss, Our Honoured Chief, Our Respected Employer, Our Noted Governor, Our Revered Head, Our Esteemed Director, or Our Admired Skipper, were the only guides to his inner feelings on the subject.

The first person Master Wildman encountered at the office this morning was Mr. Casing, who welcomed him, showed him a few things, and said that Mr. Creevy would show him the rest. Shortly after Mr. Creevy arrived, said "Oh— good morning," in a scared but friendly way, and quickly retired into an inner room with Mr. Casing. Hence, after three minutes' mumbling over the new typist, he emerged breezily, blew his nose, looked at the weather to see what was to be said about it, and said it was beautiful weather.

Mr. Creevy then began to "show" Mr. Wildman a few things. He was shown the filing cabinet, and the Books, and where the stamps were kept, and where the ready cash was kept, and where the stationery was kept, and where (incidentally) the Tea, and the Sugar, and the Biscuits were kept; and he was shown the press-copying apparatus, and told how to use it, and how not to get the rags too wet, for "Our Worthy Boss," said Mr. Creevy, "is very particular about his copying." Lastly he was shown the typewriter and given a shorthand notebook. He sat down looking and feeling uncommonly like the little boy who was fixed up by Mr. Staines of Lyndon House School, some fourteen years ago. . . .

And the glorious spring sun shone through the window, just as it did on that entrapped little figure long ago, and as there were no letters to do at present, he sat checking some neat figures in Mr. Creevy's hand, for about an hour, until Mr. Shillitoe arrived.

Mr. Shillitoe was a large, fair, and virile man of about forty years, brought up at Westminster and Trinity College, Cambridge, but never brought down again. Mr. Shillitoe pronounced his long i's as long a's, and failed to pronounce at all several consonants provided by the language. The strained and high-pitched effort of his voice was almost fascinating to hear.

"Ah, good mau'ing, Mis'r Wail'm'n," said Mr. Shillitoe. "You get here allraight? Mau'ing, Creevy."

"Good morning, Mr. Shillitoe," said Mr. Creevy. "I've been showing him around a bit."

"Oh, 'ess? Assraight. I expect you'll soon settle down allraight," said Mr. Shillitoe, and hovering courteously over Master Wildman for a moment or so, went and shut himself in with Mr. Casing. With Mr. Casing he soon appeared to be on the verge of quarrelling, as far as one could judge from manifold querulous dronings, culminating in as many "But my dear *Casings*" of alarming height in the musical scale. But this was all part of the daily routine, Master Wildman was soon to learn, as it was all part of the daily routine, for Mr. Shillitoe to come out in a dangerously calm condition, brush past Master Wildman with "Take few *letters*, Mis'r Wail'm'n, p'ease," and smash into his own room, with Master Wildman at his heels.

Master Wildman's shorthand was well able to keep up with Mr. Shillitoe's dictation; and with a few odd letters for Mr. Casing, and a few odd jobs for Mr. Creevy, the morning dragged on—the clock standing at the wrong side of twelve, when at Craven House it would have been well the right side of one, but at last reaching a quarter past one, when Master Wildman went out to lunch. This he took in the hot atmosphere of a Wilkinson's round the corner, and returned sharp at a quarter past two, having drearily inspected the Tower of London in the interim.

In the afternoon there was an amount of routine letters, memoranda, and minutes of the last board meeting awaiting

Master Wildman's typewriter, which lasted him over the digestive and office-deadly hour of three. And outside the glorious day declined to a mellow, full gold on the jolt and roar of the City traffic; and inside the typewriter hammered away, or abruptly ceased hammering (when Mr. Creevy, out of Master Wildman's view, fluttered a paper against the charge of sleep), and then started again with redoubled ferocity. Once in the afternoon a distant alarm bell could be heard swelling through the streets ("Fire," said Mr. Creevy, in a business-like tone), and once an old lady climbed the many hundred stone stairs on a misguided endeavour to sell an illustrated set of Dickens to the staff of the Xotopol Rum Company, Ltd. ("No. Nothing here, thank you," said Mr. Creevy, in a business-like tone.) And once Mr. Casing flung himself in to say "Where the devil's that Ledger?" immediately followed by "Oh, here it is," and to slam himself in again. ("Liver," said Mr. Creevy, in a business-like tone.) And at last, "I think a little Tea," said Mr. Creevy, and tea they had.

And such was every one of Master Wildman's days at the office of the Xotopol Rum Company, Ltd., from half-past nine in the morning to seven in the evening—the after-tea period being spent in a thick, wakeful, and electric-lit bustle over the post. Then Master Wildman would find his way down the blackened stone landings, come out into the flow of a burrowing humanity, throw his letters upon other and less fortunate shoulders, buy his evening paper, and burrow himself, for Southam Green.

To-day, however, as luck would have it (luck generally does have it, on first days at places), he was away at half past five, and at Southam Green at a quarter past six.

IV

Elsie has not been waiting about for Master Wildman. She has no idea, in the first place, that he will be back so early. But all the same she has been in an unsettled and listless state since tea, and a remark from Mrs. Hoare, with whom she has been sitting and knitting quietly for an hour or so in the drawing-room, comes out with an amazing air of conversationally continuing a long train of thought.

"Then I suppose you've known Mr. Wildman since ever such a long while ago?" asks the old lady.

"Oh, yes," says Elsie, with a quick little show of something like pride on the point. "I can remember him when he was only a little boy."

"Oh, yes. And I suppose we've always been *great* friends, haven't we?" enquires Mrs. Hoare, threatening a wink over her knitting.

"Oh, yes," says Elsie, in the same tones as before. "I can even remember the very first day he came here."

"Oh, *yes*," says Mrs. Hoare, weightily, and there is a silence.

"Oh, yes," says Elsie, who is devoted to Mrs. Hoare, and does not quite want to leave the subject where it is. "We've always been the greatest friends. I don't believe we ever had a quarrel or anything, ever. We get on frightfully well."

"I can believe it," rejoins Mrs. Hoare, and pauses momentously before speaking again.

"Perhaps we're even a little bit in *Ell* with Mr. Wildman?" hazards Mrs. Hoare, smiling and nodding fearfully to herself.

Elsie looks vague.

"*O, Vee, Ee,*" leers Mrs. Hoare measuredly, raising her voice and meeting her young companion's eyes.

"Oh, I don't know about that," says Elsie, smiling, and looks quickly into the fire.

"Not so sure," says the old lady, winking like a pandar, but an entirely engaging one.

"Not at all so sure. . . ."

"Oh, I don't know about that," says Elsie, and begins to blush.

Master Wildman's key is heard in the door.

"Talking of A's," says Mrs. Hoare, but "I think this is too early for him," says Elsie.

But Master Wildman it is, right enough, and he comes in, beaming amiably, and sits by Elsie.

"The Return of the Doubleyou," says Mrs. Hoare.

"Yes, Mrs. Hoare," says Master Wildman. "The Return of the Doubleyou."

"Did you like the City?" asks Elsie. Elsie always comes straight to the point.

"Yes. Everything went splendidly, thanks. Got away early to-day."

"Did the shorthand go all right?"

"Yes. I kept up easily. Awfully nice set of people up there, really."

"I expect," says Elsie, "you'll quite like going there when you get used to it, don't you? You'll only feel—nasty, until you get used to it."

"Wouldn't be surprised," says Master Wildman.

"Soon be a Rich Man now," declares Mrs. Hoare.

"Hope so," says Master Wildman. "Doubt it."

"Oh, no. I can see *you* mean to get on quick enough," says Mrs. Hoare.

"Un*told* wealth," prophesies Mrs. Hoare. . . .

"Hope so," says Master Wildman, and there is a long pause.

"And then," says Mrs. Hoare, "I expect we'll be thinking about a little *wife*, won't we? If I'm not mistaken."

"Ah!" says Master Wildman, facetiously, but it has cut him sharper than they know; for he has been thinking about little else daily or nightly for the last few months. This also reminds him of his appointment to-night; and he gets an extraordinary shock about the heart at the mere thought of it.

But at this moment Mrs. Nixon comes in, and tells Elsie she has not tidied up her room yet, and Elsie goes to do it.

"How did you get on at your work to-day?" asks Mrs. Nixon. "Very well, thank you, Mrs. Nixon," says Master Wildman.

A little later Miss Hatt comes in, to poke the fire. "How did you get on in the City to-day?" asks Miss Hatt. "Very well, thank you, Miss Hatt," says Master Wildman, and shortly afterwards thinks he will go and wash himself for dinner.

Audrey is on the stairs, getting the hot water for the bedrooms. "Did you Enjoy a Successful day at the City, sir?" asks Audrey. "Very Successful, thank you, Audrey," says Master Wildman. "Ah, *that* Makes Good Hearing," says Audrey, who has taken to this kind of liberties of late.

Master Wildman washes and shaves very carefully, and changes his shirt, and then comes down to the drawing-room, where Mrs. Spicer is. "How did you get on at Business to-day?" asks Mrs. Spicer. "Very well, thank you, Mrs. Spicer," says Master Wildman; and Mr. Spicer's key being heard in the front door at this moment, dinner is immediately served. "Get On all right to-day?" asks Mr. Spicer. "Very well, thank you, Mr. Spicer," says Master Wildman. "You've got two city-goers now, Bertha," says Mr. Spicer. "Yes," says Miss Hatt, and "Yes," remarks Mrs. Hoare, "I should have thought the one we've got was enough." Which is an insulting remark to make, but is not taken as such.

It is remarked that Master Wildman does not show the appetite expected of him after his labours, and he certainly does not. On the contrary, he manifests a heavy restlessness when it comes to the cheese—forgoing it himself, and besieging Miss Hatt's eyes for the sign of dismissal. This at last comes, and he goes quietly and quickly upstairs.

Elsie goes into the drawing-room, and settles herself comfortably in front of the fire with the idea of relishing her Master Wildman all the more for having been without him all the day. But he does not come, and three or four minutes later, a little click of departure at the front door notifies her that there is to be no such thing.

v

"I'll have a shot to-night," Master Wildman tells himself, as he hurries through the streets to the appointed place. "I'll have a shot."

By which Master Wildman means that he is going to try and tell Miss Cotterell how very much he is in love with her. But as Miss Cotterell, without any words on the subject at all, has already reduced Master Wildman to a state of nerveless and unconditioned feebleness never before experienced in his lifetime, Master Wildman has a notion himself that he is making this assertion in the teeth of his own intrinsic incapabilities.

By a corner near her house Master Wildman has arranged to meet her, and five and twenty minutes before the appointed time he is there. He stands in the sickly lamp-light, lights one cigarette from another, stamps his feet, waits, and peers into outer darknesses while one pair of feet after another rap their preoccupied tune towards him, pass him in a white, tense moment, and are gone. And still he stamps his feet, and still he peers into outer darknesses.

And now it is five minutes after the appointed time, and now it is ten minutes, and now it is twelve, and now it is fourteen, and now it is fourteen and a half, and now it is fifteen, which makes a quarter of an hour, and which Master Wildman reclines upon. (She was a quarter of an hour late, one says.) But now it is sixteen, and now it is seventeen, and now it is eighteen. (She was half an hour late, tries Master Wildman.) And now it is nineteen, and suddenly it is "Hullo," in a low voice behind him, and she is by his side.

She has brought her dog, and she carries a little dog-whip. She is most terribly sorry, and Not a bit of it, and So he didn't bring Elsie along with him, then?—and No, she had to stay at home—her mother and all that; and Yes, she *is* rather one of those mothers, isn't she, and Yes, she most decidedly is, and what are we going to do; and Shall we go to the movies or something, and If you like, and All right then, and I haven't been to the movies for ages, and I say, what about a walk? Glorious night, and all that, and Right you are, all the time. . . .

And so a walk it is, and they take it by the river, and Master Wildman soon gives over any idea of ever expressing himself.

To tell the truth, it is doubtful whether he has anything of himself left to express. It is doubtful whether he has any existence at all, by the time they have reached the river —any existence as anything but her dark brown eyes, and her dark hair, and the moods across her mouth. For her dark brown eyes give little angry lights back to the little tender lights on the water—and it is her dark bobbed hair, falling like a black, valiant casque, which enrages them. Her mouth is a mouth red with minor dooms for Master Wildman; and she is all the colours that Master Wildman could blend in sleep, and she is all the tunes that Master Wildman has ever yearned towards; and she is young to the last sweet point of youth, and she is as old as Asia. For she is a witch, and she is an alchemist. All she touches, all she wears, all she glances at, is changed in a trice to an object of time-defying and magic beauty from the world's beginning—the feathers in her hat have flamed in a crowd at Babylon, the little lip-stick in the bag has painted a courtesan at Cnossos, the little whip has scourged the dusty backs of the builders of the Pyramids. . . . And the ring upon her slim little finger? Why, that blazes, in one bright diamond, from the days of Charlemagne.

So Master Wildman does not express himself this evening, as can well be imagined, but he manages to keep a pretty fair flow of talk going, in which effort he is aided principally by the almost supernatural powers of melting into thin air at any and every corner, manifested by the dog. This gets called "Sir" any amount of times by its mistress, but with no noticeab.e decrease in the average number of dematerialisa-tions, and is finally put on the lead. But she lets it go, on its best honour, at the end, when it makes up for lost time by passing out into the night apparently for ever. Whereupon Master Wildman volunteers to go round numerous squares, and up numerous roads, and into various crescents, while Miss Cotterell stays right where she is.

The animal eventually rushes up to Miss Cotterell herself, however, and as they are now at the corner they started from Miss Cotterell bids Master Wildman good-bye. This she does in a manner of the remotest pertness, which, although Master Wildman has never suggested or hinted a word of his inner feelings, seems to put him in his place, just a little, as though he has.

Then Master Wildman's legs take charge of an otherwise unguided personality, and lead him back towards Craven House. And it is not until he sees that expressionless house opposite that expressionless lamp, that it comes upon him, like a cold douche, that he has to be up at half-past seven sharp to-morrow morning, for he is a city-goer now; and might have been all his life, for all the difference it makes. And the lamp is impervious alike to any lovings, and to any gettings up.

CHAPTER III

The Cat away.   A Dance.   Miss Cotterell.   Awful Character of Authors.

I

A LONG period of perfect calm, stressed enough to have a slightly threatening quality in it, now ensues. Master Wildman is up before everyone except Miss Hatt in the morning, has his breakfast against the clock, and having thundered about a close, dishevelled bedroom in a mad search for things forgotten, is suddenly out of the house for the day. He returns in the evening in a *piano* mood, and talks to Elsie in more kindly, sad, and easily intimate tones than ever. Elsie is always there to have a chat with him, and her concerned eyes follow him about the room, as though he is looking about for a rope to hang her with.

II

Mr. and Mrs. Spicer, and Miss Hatt now begin to think about taking their holiday.

As they generally set out upon this annual adventure together, and on this occasion, as on every other occasion, express a pathetic and pointed desire to "get it over early," early they take it; and a taxi thud-thud-thuds outside the front gate one morning, and they are gone.

The Cat being away, an Arcadian period of uncanny good humour and high-spirited noise prevails in Craven House for two weeks—in which as many illicit feet are put upon the sofa by Mrs. Hoare, and as much tyrannical airing is accomplished by Mrs. Nixon, and as many furniture edges are hacked by Master Wildman's shoes, as can be managed in the time.

Edith sings among her vegetables in the kitchen, and Audrey takes such shocking liberties, lumping so, out of rooms, and inventing such facetious retorts to her betters, that Mrs. Nixon really thinks she ought to be told about.

It is the spring now. Master Wildman goes out before breakfast into the garden on silver-twinkling mornings bathed in bright blue wetness, glimpses a silent-dressing Mrs. Nixon at a window above, and melts into the morning in an agonised ecstasy of yearnings for Miss Cotterell. Master Wildman returns from the City at velvet dusks, and works himself up into a slow nightly fever over her. He gets his Saturday afternoons off, and then Miss Cotterell comes round with her little dog. Elsie keeps herself more or less in the background while they hang about a bit, and chatter in the drawing-room, and all at once close the front door after them. . . . Master Wildman goes out with Miss Cotterell of an evening sometimes, too, but he has not yet expressed himself. He has got rather near it once or twice, though, when Miss Cotterell says "Good-bye" with just a degree more pertness still. . . .

Mr. and Mrs. Spicer, and Miss Hatt, duly return from their holiday, looking, after their two weeks' absence, rather like the closely resembling brother and sisters of Mr. and Mrs. Spicer, and Miss Hatt. They very callously declare that the Change from the society of the other residents at Craven House has done them all the good in the world—though they are not so brown as they might have been if it

hadn't rained most of the time.   And Mrs. Hoare no longer
puts her feet upon the sofa, and Edith sings no more.

Of late there has been another stranger at Craven House,
too, though he only comes in the week-ends, and Miss Hatt
has found him a bed outside.   This is one of Mrs. Hoare's
nephews of the As Yet Quite All Right school.   He is a
young man (two years younger than Master Wildman) and
he has been to the same school as Master Wildman.   The
latter does not remember him.

He is an anæmic young man; he is going up to Cambridge
soon, it is understood, and he has a certain amount of money
of his own, which is at present making itself felt in week-
ends in Town, and large selections of chromatic silk tie and
striped shirt.   It is against Master Wildman's minor efforts
that he is introduced to Miss Cotterell, but meet her he
does, and makes unequivocal expressions at the first meeting.
"God.   Divine," remarks Mr. Hoare to Master Wildman,
and Master Wildman agrees that perhaps she is, rather.

"Dance Mad," Mrs. Spicer calls this young man, and it
is true.   In fact it is Mr. Hoare who suggests that Miss
Cotterell and Elsie, and Master Wildman and himself shall
make a party of it, and go to the St. James Hotel, Piccadilly,
one night, for the dance and cabaret.

This, of course, throws Elsie practically into a faint, and
nights of agony are spent in going over the ways the matter
may best be broached to her mother—for without Mother's
sanction there can be no dress.   At last Mr. Hoare himself
undertakes to beard her, and after five minutes' ghastly
closeting with her, comes out with the desired leave—on
the condition (mind you) that there is none of the missing
of the last train and trapesing all over London at nights.

Elsie has no desire to trapes.   Elsie talks about nothing
else for days, asks what time we'll start, and which train
we'll take, and will we dance before supper, and when will
the cabaret come on; and she is given money for some green
material to make a dress with ("This'll be your birthday
present, Miss," says Mrs. Nixon), and she makes it in the
drawing-room under showers of feminine advice, and tries
it on, and takes it in, and lets it down, and sure enough,
lives long enough to be one of the little party of four that
meets at Southam Green Station at half-past nine on the
evening of the appointed day.

III

Mr. Hoare, Miss Cotterell, Master Wildman and Elsie (in order of night-birdly sophistication) reach the St. James Hotel, Piccadilly, at ten o'clock; enter through the wide, well-lit lounge hushed with discreet implications of near-by revelry, are crushed into a discreet lift along with a few muttering others, bent on the same enjoyments, pretend that the final lurch of the lift makes them feel ever so queer, emerge, hear music, wonder how they can get to it, and having blandly appealed, are directed towards it in a style postulating themselves as the first and last desirable arrivals of the evening. This causes (again in order of night-birdly sophistication) suitable degrees of scornful and revolted expressions to fall upon the faces of Mr. Hoare, Miss Cotterell, Master Wildman. (Elsie just stares.) Then they are shown to their table, and the evening begins.

It is on the whole a successful evening they spend at the St. James Hotel. It becomes very crowded and hot, of course, as the flow from the theatres commences, and increasingly difficult to differentiate one blaring dance from another, and increasingly easy to come back to the table and stare into eternity, rather than attend to the necessary witticisms—but then there are heaps of witticisms.

Master Wildman dances a great deal more with Miss Cotterell than with Elsie, whose lonely preparedness to smile as they come round is a rather wearied affair towards the end. Perhaps it is a little doubtful whether Elsie is enjoying herself as much as she should have been. For Master Wildman, whose moods are always pretty well her own moods, gets very nervy and crumpled about the shirt as the evening wears on, frowning away over cigarette after cigarette, glancing over at Miss Cotterell as she smiles up to Mr. Hoare in the dance, and behaving more than jaggedly when she is sitting at the table next to him.

"Enjoying yourself, Elsie?" asks Master Wildman, once, crushing his latest cigarette into the powdery remains of its blackened predecessors.

"Oh yes. Awfully," says Elsie. "And I hope you are."

"Oh, yes. Rather. . . . Got to be up early in the morning, though."

"Yes. I know," says Elsie, and is half driven out of her senses, in all that lilting noise and kaleidoscopic shuffling, with a desire to ask him to put an end to his frownings and miseries. But she ventures nothing, and at this moment Miss Cotterell and Mr. Hoare return.

"You're looking rather dissipated to-night, Mr. Wildman," says Miss Cotterell, and Master Wildman returns a gay remark about not being so young as he used to be.

"He's got to be up early in the morning," says Elsie, in defence.

"Awful," says Mr. Hoare. "Wouldn't do it, myself."

"No, it must be rather ghastly," allows Miss Cotterell, and the next moment she is carried off by Mr. Hoare to conclude the dance.

Then Mr. Hoare dances with Elsie, and Master Wildman with Miss Cotterell. And then they all have a rest, and all stare into eternity a little more, until Elsie hazards "I suppose the last train's still all right?" which comes as rather a relief, although Elsie wants to go and hide herself after saying it, having felt a great enough burden on the party all the evening.

So the bill is called for, the revolted expressions return, the lurches are again smiled at in the lift, and they come out into the night, where it has been raining for two hours. They hurry to the station.

In the train going back (the very last train), Master Wildman manages to get into a carriage apart with Miss Cotterell. He expresses himself on topics nearest to his heart.

III

It all goes very easily and light-heartedly, and it is accomplished in the thunder and roar of a last train that knows what it is after. It is Roar, Roar, Roar all the time as they talk, and Click, Slatter, Bang, and a pause in the pale, deserted tube stations (where they tactfully mutter, or wait, for there are two violin-case-carrying gentlemen just opposite): and then there is a sharp whistle, and they are roaring off again.

It is Miss Cotterell who begins it, just as the train begins to groan out of the second station—before which they have said nothing at all to each other. "Have you known Mr. Hoare long?" asks Miss Cotterell.

"No, I don't know anything about him, really," replies Master Wildman. "Why?"

"Nothing. He's rather a queer young man, isn't he?

He asked me to marry him to-night," says Miss Cotterell, and Roar, Roar, Roar goes the train.

"To What him?" enquires Master Wildman.

"To marry him," says Miss Cotterell.

"Oh," says Master Wildman. "I expect he's in love."

"Rather quick," retorts Miss Cotterell.

"You can't be too quick," says Master Wildman.

"When you're in love," adds Master Wildman. . . .

"When what?" asks Miss Cotterell, for the noise is getting a little bothersome.

"When you're in love," says Master Wildman, raising his voice.

"Oh," says Miss Cotterell.

"If it comes to that," says Master Wildman. "So am I."

"Pardon?" says Miss Cotterell, for now you really can't hear a thing.

"SO AM I!" shouts Master Wildman.

"Oh, I'm very sorry to hear that."

"What?"

"I'm sorry to hear *that*," repeats Miss Cotterell.

"Oh," says Master Wildman, half to himself.

"What?"

"OH!" reiterates Master Wildman.

"I rather guessed it was coming," says Miss Cotterell.

"You rather whatted?"

"GUESSED IT WAS COMING!" yells Miss Cotterell.

"Oh," says Master Wildman, half to himself again.

"What?"

"ONLY 'OH' AGAIN!"

"Oh."

Click. Slatter. Bang. Rumble and pause. A man's voice echoes from somewhere in the pale stone passages of the dim-lit station. One low-toned orchestral gentleman tells another low-toned orchestral gentleman that he wouldn't think of such a thing. A sharp whistle, and they're off.

"Well, what's to be done about it?" asks Master Wildman.

Miss Cotterell wants to know in what way, exactly, and she adjusts her skirts.

"Oh. In every way," says Master Wildman.

"How?" asks Miss Cotterell, and meets his eyes.

"You won't marry me, I suppose?"

"No."

"What?"

"NO!"

"WHY NOT?"

"DON'T WANT TO!"

"NOT EVEN IF I MAKE LOTS OF MONEY?" suggests Master Wildman.

"I'm afraid I've got very expensive tastes," rejoins Miss Cotterell.

"Got what?" asks Master Wildman.

"EXPENSIVE TASTES!"

"WHAT?"

"EXPENSIVE TASTES!"

"CAN'T HEAR!"

"*EXPENSIVE TASTES!*" screams Miss Cotterell.

"OH!"

Click. Slatter. Bang. Rumble and pause. One low-toned orchestral gentleman tells another low-toned orchestral gentleman that he's off to Maidenhead again next Friday. A sharp whistle, and they're off.

"Perhaps one day," ventures Master Wildman. "I'll be expensive enough to afford it."

"Not as expensive as me," says Miss Cotterell, and catches his eyes with a smile.

"You never know."

"Oh, no, you never know."

"You know I'm frightfully in earnest about it. It's not a bit of a joke to me."

"It's not a bit of a joke to me, either."

"I'm not trying to flirt or anything," says Master Wildman. "As you rather seem to think. I absolutely adore you."

Miss Cotterell bends her head politely nearer to him.

"I ADORE YOU!" thunders Master Wildman, a little out of temper.

"I'M SORRY TO HEAR IT!" returns Miss Cotterell.

"No need to be sorry," says Master Wildman.

Click. Slatter. Bang. Rumble and pause. One low-toned orchestral gentleman tells another low-toned orchestral gentleman that he hasn't seen Charley down there lately. A sharp whistle, and they're off.

"May I ask if there's any one on the same track just at present?" enquires Master Wildman.

"Yes. I suppose one might say there is."

"How many?"

"Oh—one or two."

"Who?"

"Oh, there's a man up in Scotland just at the moment. And then I sometimes get some rather touching letters from Allahabad."

"FROM WHERE?"

"ALLAHABAD."

"WHY ALLAHABAD?"

"WHY NOT?"

"WHAT'S THE IDEA?"

"THAT'S WHERE HE'S *STATIONED!*" screeches Miss Cotterell.

"OH."

Click. Slatter. Bang. Rumble and pause. One low-toned orchestral gentleman tells another low-toned orchestral gentleman that This is him, and he gets out. A sharp whistle, and they're off.

"Anyway," says Master Wildman, "I hope you won't let this make any difference between us."

"What difference should it make?"

"Oh, I don't know. . . ."

"I only wish you hadn't started it. We were getting on so well together. If you take my advice you'll go home and try and sleep it off."

"I'll never do that. But I'm glad you've taken it so decently. I don't want to pester people."

Miss Cotterell bends her head politely nearer to him.

"I DON'T WANT TO PESTER PEOPLE!"

"WHO'S PESTERING PEOPLE?"

"I DON'T WANT *TO* PESTER PEOPLE!"

"YOU'RE NOT PESTERING THIS PERSON!"

"Well, thank you very much," says Master Wildman.

Click. Slatter. Bang. Rumble and throbbing stoppage. And this is Hammersmith, and they get out to change, and walk along the platform together without a word.

And here is Elsie.

IV

The electric light blazing behind Miss Cotterell's green blind, in a still, dead neighbourhood at half-past two o'clock in the morning, had the lie given it, if it was trying to look romantic, by the Miss Cotterell within, to whom the evening's affairs, culminating in Master Wildman's proposals, were neither a new nor unexpected experience. It was true that

Miss Cotterell had never been bellowed at in quite the same way. But then the thing had generally been brought off in the reticent mauve lights of a returning taxi—and it had been so brought off, Miss Cotterell would have told you, thousands of times. By that number she would have meant to convey twenty at least, without the slightest overstatement.

From all these experiences Miss Cotterell (while polishing her technique with each adventure until she had reached a consummate mastery of manner in every crisis) had so far landed heart-whole, and self-possessed. But these experiences were never much discussed by anyone unconcerned (any more than Miss Cotterell's daily meals might have been discussed), and to all the world an unassuming Miss Cotterell, twenty-two years of age, lived a life expected of her with her mother, in the new little residence, with garage attached, at the back of Southam Green.

That is to say, Miss Cotterell alternately "But *Mother*ed," slammed doors upon, or returned to conciliate an irritable mother, to just the same extent as any other young lady, in just the same class of life, might be expected to do: she assisted haughtily with the shopping when the Wretch (as Miss Cotterell then named the general servant) failed to turn up; she got tea on Thursdays, when the Creature was out: did her own petty ironing when the Person declared herself busy; and volunteered, in a general way, to see the Man, who would murmur "Yes, Miss," in an abashed way, and become leeringly self-explanatory in her presence. These were the sum of Miss Cotterell's domesticities.

Miss Cotterell belonged to a local Amateur Dramatic Club, without performing herself; and she belonged to a Tennis Club in Kensington, where she exchanged the usual soft "My *dears?*" over tea, with her strident-voiced, supercilious, and rather more aged compeers—without playing much tennis. Miss Cotterell was also a very keen and technically forward admirer of Rugby Football, having numerous Followers (if one may transpose an expression properly applicable only to the affairs of the Creature) concerned in it, and getting from the muck and muscle and thud of it, before her eyes, a curiously exalted and half triumphant sensation.

Miss Cotterell arose each morning at ten, was out of the house by eleven, took the air with her little dog, walked along quietly by herself, returned quietly, held the front gate open for the little dog to run submissively through, and had, in short, an appearance of taking life just as it came, and finding it, on the whole, good.

For all her calm, though, it would be far from safe to say that Miss Cotterell nourished no picturesque or romantic aspirations whatever. Indeed, we have to admit that the quantity of well-groomed Austrians that loomed at intervals in Miss Cotterell's imagination, against backgrounds of Viennese violins—the worshippings accorded manifold dream Miss Cotterells by manifold dashing Crown Princes of Europe —the Big Americans who Built Bridges for, and were called "My Fool" dallyingly by Miss Cotterell—the amount of books dedicated to Very Gallant Ladies (who were all Miss Cotterells) by very famous writers—the mental pictures of fiercely beautiful and County Miss Cotterells, riding like the devil over old-world countrysides—the quantity of black squires slashed in the face with hunting-crops at the hands of magnificently proud and blazing Miss Cotterells—together with the Meredithian elopements with Sir Harrys and Anthonys following such adventures—would have shocked her most romantic admirer in the act of railing at her hard-heartedness.

The romantic aspirations sketched above, though, were perfectly irrelevant aspirations as far as Master Wildman was concerned, and as Miss Cotterell, in the light behind the green blind, got on with her undressing there was no hint of any inward perturbation whatever wrought by Master Wildman's midnight proposals.

In fact she seemed more in a hurry to get under the sheets than anything else, and the electric light was soon flicked sharply out—as much as to tell any romantically disposed neighbourhoods that that was that.

v

The extinction of this light Master Wildman missed by just about ten minutes. For though Master Wildman had returned to Craven House in good order, and said "Good night" to Elsie on the stairs, it took him but a cigarette under his own gas, to understand that the only satisfactory grappling with his problems must be undertaken in the open air.

He had, therefore, slipped on his overcoat again, crept down the stairs, clicked the door shut, and traced hypnotised footsteps to as near to Miss Cotterell as he could get—which

was on the pavement outside her house.   Here he stood, with
his fatigued eyes lit by the fiery little point of his cigarette,
as though he were waiting for someone.   Indeed, he did suffer
from a kind of delirious belief that Miss Cotterell might come
out to him, yet. . . .   And then she would come like a quick
ghost, he imagined and say "Hullo," softly by his side, and
lead him away into a very beautiful and consoling, not to
say tearful, and different scene from the affair in the train,
which was still roaring in Master Wildman's ears as if it
had happened a minute ago.

But Miss Cotterell slept on, behind a dark blind that
wasn't going to say anything, one way or the other; and it
was not until the straight, stalking tower of a policeman had
passed by twice, with pale lack of comment, that Master
Wildman moved on, and began to walk.

Master Wildman walked, and walked, and walked.   He
walked through aged and scheming slums, cried out upon
by remote infants squalling in far upper rooms, and lit by
garish lamps, to which, by comparison, the evil-doer opposite
Craven House was the frankest and most artless thing in the
world—he walked by an old Recreation Ground—he walked
by a droning, singing all-night works, and he walked through
a churchyard near by, amongst the hearkening dead.   And
he came to the river, which flowed like a thick, troubled
dream through the short black interval between day and day.
And he walked a long while by the river, but had no answer
to his questionings.

And he returned from the river in the first, grey speculations
of dawn, and came back to the nieghbourhood he had started
from.   But there was no reply from the alert and reticent
streets, and no reply from the unrustled trees, which were
bent down, as it were, in an effort of concentration in giving
back to the dawn what it expected of them.   So he tried
the High Road, where the tram-lines blazed thin mauve
phosphorescences, without a tram, and where a lonely cyclist
passed, with a pack upon his back, and an early market
cart rattled crisply by the shops, which might have been
shuttered and dead shops a century ago.

And he walked a long way along the High Road, and he
came back again by a different route, and he at last returned
to Craven House, when the eastern sky was lit with a slip
of bright daffodil.

And he had decided to write a play.

VI

Mr. and Mrs. Spicer, and Miss Hatt had little enough time for reading at the end of the day, and what with this fact, taken with their frequent confession that they "had quite enough troubles of their own without wanting to read about other people's," they got through very few books in the course of the year. And as these were chosen at random (a book being a book, and the matter ending there) from the Southam Green Public Library, and when chosen, read or skipped with the business-like purpose solely of obtaining concise information on the marital destinies of the leading characters—it was really no wonder that you found Mrs. Spicer, for instance, expressing an intense desire to Shake the Heroine, or Miss Hatt complaining of the ineptitude of the Hero in Getting Anywhere or Coming Out with it to any proper extent—in all books published since the days of Beautiful books and Helen Mathers.

Mr. and Mrs. Spicer's, and Miss Hatt's opinion of authors was a low opinion—these characters being vaguely imaged as spending eccentric and gesticulatory days, either in Tearing their Hair in search of Inspiration, Collecting Material (Mr. Spicer), Pacing Up and Down, Analysing Motives, Writing Character Studies (Mrs. Spicer), Thinking out Scenes, or Wondering how they are going to get their Heroes and Heroines out of Scrapes (Miss Hatt). Whether there was any more humane side ascribed to these characters, by Mr. and Mrs. Spicer, and Miss Hatt, we are not in a position to say, inasmuch as the idiosyncracies just mentioned are gathered solely from the different expressions used by them when they learned, two days after Master Wildman's decision, that he was going to write a play in his evenings.

The reception of this news was a mixed reception. While Mrs. Hoare at once began to address Master Wildman at meal times as "Our Famous A." (Author) and predict instant successes in the West End; and Elsie was ever so intrigued, and mad to know what it was going to be about, there were other points of view opposed to these. For where Miss Hatt expected it was quite a business to "learn play-writing," Mrs. Spicer took her up in the supposition very smartly with "Yes, it must be," and a giggle; Mrs. Nixon covertly expressed an opinion that young men in the cities doubtless knew their own business best, and Mr. Hoare exclaimed "My God!" on the spot. Also Mr. Spicer had some very trenchant, but rather chilling remarks to make on the subject.

"Of course," said Mr. Spicer. "Writing a play's quite different from writing a book. One has to write it in Scenes, doesn't one? . . ."

"Yes," said Master Wildman. "I suppose one has."

"Acts . . ." risked Mr. Spicer.

"Yes," said Master Wildman. "Acts. Rather."

"Then you have Situations, don't you?" enquired Mr. Spicer.

"Oh, rather," said Master Wildman.

"Yes," said Mr. Spicer.

"Difficult business," said Mr. Spicer, and knocked out his pipe, and left it at that.

CHAPTER IV

Audrey Answers Back.

I

WHETHER or no any signs of the terrible series of ungovernabilities, Answerings Back, and ignorances of her place, which finally dashed poor Audrey Custard to ruin in the space of a week, were to be seen coming in the distance: and whether or no it was the bobbing of her hair that began it; or the moving pictures, which taught a young girl to get above herself, Mrs. Spicer said; or the war, after which they had never been the same, Miss Hatt said; or that Young Man, who had probably put her up to it, Mrs. Nixon suggested—were matters of opinion and long discussion after the event, but Liberties Audrey had absolutely begun to take, a good while before it.

Thus, it was, that although you found your Audrey still addressing you with your "Ma'am," or "Sir," unexceptionably, you began to resent a long-standing but now distantly insolent passion for popular idiom on her part, when it came to her asking you whether you "wished to Partake of your Ablutions, Ma'am," at such and such a time, and she'd see the water was hot; or telling you it would be "necessary to Stir your Stumps, sir," to get there in time. Similarly it was dwarfing to any feudal sense remaining in you to be told you might "remain Unalarmed, Ma'am," for she would "take the matter in hand"; or that you had "Best Wrap Up carefully, sir, lest you Contract a Chill." And though these little deliveries were taken and reported quite jocularly up to a point, they had to be smartly pulled up once or twice. As when, for instance, Miss Hatt, rushing down the stairs one day, distinctly heard Audrey petitioning from above that she (Miss Hatt) would "pray not Tumble Down in her Haste." Then Miss Hatt shouted up "Audrey! Please don't forget yourself!" To which Audrey replied "No, ma'am," in a dashed way, but was soon at it again.

It may have been the moving pictures, of course, and it may have been the young man; but as the bobbed hair, which smartened Audrey up no end, in its own lank way, was probably in the first place responsible for the young man, who was in turn impeachable for the moving pictures, we are personally of the opinion that the thing was to be traced to a Delilah-like barber, who cut away all Audrey's strength and self-restraint along with her flowing and muddy coloured locks, one afternoon in a little shop just off the High Road.

But there was also a certain Christmas party which upset her.

II

Miss Custard first became acquainted with the young man in question, at a little Christmas party given by some of Edith's connections. It was an evening Audrey would never forget in all her life.

It began at about half-past six in the evening, when a scared Audrey was brought by Edith into a little gas-lit room in a superior slum at the back of Southam Green, and introduced to such a host of jolly Dads, welcoming Mums, reticent sons, staring Sisses, and slightly deaf Grannies, as would bewilder the most experienced social caller—but this was only the beginning.

For she and Edith were only the first arrivals, and there was Old Mr. Munt (who was guaranteed to make you laugh with his Ways) yet to arrive—and Ned Mumby, who was partly on the Stage (being connected with the properties up at the Empire, and known as not only having Walked on, but having said his line in his day)—and there was little Nellie Trout, who was a beautiful little thing with eyes

only for Son—and there was, lastly, Mr. Walter Cree, who
was in a Superior Galvanised Tank Making line of business,
and destined to throw in the sponge to Audrey's bright looks
and bobbed hair at the very first meeting.

And all these had to arrive, and all these had to be introduced
to the three-and-sixpenny port provided, which got on to the
giddiest terms with Audrey's head, from the preliminary sips.

Old Mr. Munt began his ways at once. "Custard?" said
he. "My word, we'll be a-drinkin' of you next! By mistake!" Which, being greeted by positive tumblings about
in jollity, he followed up with "As long as a *Trout* ain't
dropped in," which caused further tumblings about, and
which inspired him to remark that both young ladies should
go on the Halls as The Salad Dressing. Whereat Mr. Ned
Mumby could be seen smiling tolerantly but professionally to
himself, admidst the applause; for there was nothing that Mr.
Ned Mumby did not know about the Halls.

Then, after a decent interval, and some more port, but
not too much ("Or I'll be seeing those nasty purple cater-
pillars with green tails again," said Old Mr. Munt), Sis and
Son were requested to drag in the old thing from the next
room. The old thing referred to (a wondering Audrey discovered), was a harmonium; and it was to be dragged in for
the purposes of the time-honoured institution of a Sing Song.

And was there ever such a Sing Song? "Oh, I'm a regular
Robinson Caruso, I am," said Old Mr. Munt, and ran up
his scales to prove the fact so mercilessly that all accused
him of having had a couple before he came, and even Dad
said Go a bit slower, boys, because the old lady was down,
next door. But the warning was soon forgotten when the
old thing got really going, and every kind of song was sung.
Most of them were sung in chorus, but some were sung in
solo, and there were light songs, and ballads, and dance
songs, and humorous songs. ("Sing Up, Ord," whispered
Edith to her friend. "You ain't got going yet," and the
encouragement needed no repeating.)

Also a request was made that Mr. Cree should give them
"The Rosary," as he had done at a previous Sing Song, and
because Mum liked it so. This he did, and quavered suffi-
ciently over his final notes to cause Mum to reveal unmistakable symptoms of being about to Turn on the Waterworks
(as it was then put). But "You mustn't take it to heart
so, Mum," protested Old Mr. Munt. "It's only a song."

After this it was rather felt that the harmonium had reached a very fine and touching apogee to its evening duties, and would now be best cast aside in favour of further enjoyments. A little more port was taken, and someone suggested that someone ought to recite. At which suggestion all eyes were at once turned momentously upon the Stage, without any sign being given from that professional quarter, until Dad definitely asked him if he couldn't give 'em a little something. But no—Mr. Mumby didn't do anything—not amateur, you know—and after a little gentle expostulation on all sides, Dad suggested that Sis should do that piece she used to. But Sis was not to be prevailed upon, and at last Audrey herself was asked.

This did not embarrass Audrey in any way. For Audrey was now on absolutely delicious terms with the three-and-sixpenny port, and for the last ten minutes had been carrying on a succession of badinages with an entranced Tank Maker, who had been pulling her hair behind, stealing her slides, leering at her brooches, having "Don'ts" and "You silly Things" and "If you just dares" said to him, and getting threatened with smackings in a way that only increased his impishness with every minute. "Why don't *you* go and recite?" said Audrey. "I'd like to see you do it."

"Recite?" said Mr. Cree. "Me recite? All right. Don't mind if I do. What'd you like?"

They left that to him.

"Ever 'ear the Green Eye of the Yellow God?" asked Mr. Cree, and Audrey stifled a scream of hilarity in her corner.

They did believe they had heard of it ("*Oh*, yes," said Mr. Mumby), but they could well hear it again.

"Want the lights out, y'know," said Mr. Cree.

They all settled round the fire with a refill of port. The light went out. Mr. Cree stood in the middle of the room, and with a little preparatory cough, and a little preparatory warning that it would "probably give 'em the Creeps," began a stormy recital of the Green Eye of the Yellow God.

This took some time, and a tank maker could not but miss an intonation or two in the middle of it, for the cruel originator of the recital was to be observed in her corner laying back her haughty head, and going, to all outward seeming, asleep. This was either a coquettish gesture on Miss Custard's part, or it simply denoted a new arrangement come to with the three-and-sixpenny port.

The recital ended in a storm of applause, but an absence of Water Works (which Mr. Cree glanced rather wistfully over at Mum for), and Sis confessed that she got the Creeps in the middle of it, and old Mr. Munt was quiet, and allowed that they were queerish coves, they Chinese. Mr. Cree returned proudly to the side of Miss Custard, who looked at him defiantly for a little, until asked for an opinion.

"Very good," said Audrey. "You ought to go on the Stage."

Whereupon the whole company looked over with some trepidation in Mr. Mumby's direction. But that gentleman either had not heard, or would not let it be seen that he had heard, such a profane remark; and an unfortunate little case of thoughtlessness was passed over.

Favouring an atmosphere of the Creeps, they did not put the light on again, but had a little more port, with a plate of cakes, and a plate of nuts, and sat round the blazing fire "yarning," as Old Mr. Munt expressed it.

In this way they spent the last hour of the evening, which was the sweetest hour of all for Audrey. For Mr. Cree by no means dropped his attentions in the half-lights, though he pursued them in a rather lower tone, and told her how he was coming round one of these fine evenings to take her out for a spree, and insisted on the point in face of all the coyest evasions she could think of. Also Miss Custard received considerable attentions from Mr. Mumby himself, who came over in rather a drunken way, and having stared in front of him, was asked by Miss Custard what it looked like when you was behind the scenes, as she had often wondered. To this Mr. Mumby took some time before replying, but at length volunteered that it was hard to say, rightly, but it didn't look nothing like what it did from the front. To which information Miss Custard made intelligent retort, and played one gentleman off against the other, until Mr. Mumby suddenly arose, and tried another corner of the room, in the same inconsequent and mystifying way he had arrived.

It was a slightly sentimental yarning, too, for other Christmases were discussed—Christmases when Dad and Mum were younger than they were now—and at length an old photograph album was produced and passed round in the firelight. Dad was unanimously voted exceedingly handsome as a young man.

"Tell you who 'e reminds me of," said Edith. "Can't you see nothin', Ord?"

No, Ord could see nothing.

"Can't you see nothin'?" repeated Edith, and they were all attention.

"Our Mr. Wildman," said Edith, with a air of challenge.

"Oh *no*, Eed," begged Audrey. "It ain't nothin' like."

But "Yes," insisted Edith. "*Our Mister Wildman*. There's the look. And 'andsome enough to all reckonin' 'e is, too."

"What sort of folk are they up there, then?" asked Dad.

"Oh, they're all right, ain't they, Ord? Bit uppish at times. But 'e's a rare 'un—that Mr. Wildman—ain't 'e?"

"'E is that," said Audrey.

"Always civil and nice-spoken, an' ready with 'is joke. But that Elsie ain't nothin' up to 'im, is she?"

"No. She ain't the same."

"'As 'e got eyes on 'er, then?" asked Dad.

"Oh no," said Edith. "You wouldn't 'ave no eyes on 'er. She's the soft kind. She's pretty, mind you. . . ."

"Oh, she *ain't* pretty, Eed."

"Oh yes she is. For those that want that style," affirmed Edith, and then added: "Lor'. '*Er* mother knows 'ow to bring a young gel up."

In such a way they discussed the other characters at Craven House, and at last Old Mr. Munt said: Well—he was blessed if his old woman (by which he meant his land-lady) wouldn't be dancing about the streets in her night-dress or something, if he didn't get a move on soon, and this was taken as a signal for general departure. Son went off with little Nellie Trout, to see her home. Mr. Mumby vanished. Old Mr. Munt boomed away into the distance with Mr. Cree, who had not failed to bid a very particular fare-well to Miss Custard, and remind her of his intention to look in on her one of these fine evenings, and Audrey and Edith were the last to stand in the little porch and say Good-bye.

"A very Pleasant and Enjoyable Evening's Entertainment," said Audrey to Edith, as they walked home together, under the stars.

III

It was Audrey's first dose of delights undreamed of, and flowerings in social circles she had never known, and it proved a fatal dose.

Not that Audrey at once began to give any signs of it having gone to her head; though the attentions of Mr. Cree—who had swiftly run through his preliminaries in the way of Walking Out and Courting, and passed up into a state wherein he was definitely pledged to Miss Custard—were enough to make any young thing giddy. In fact, Audrey went so far as to confide in Miss Hatt, who was a little jealous at first, but rallied splendidly to give her soft advice.

"I'm very glad to hear it, Audrey," said Miss Hatt. "But you must ask him what he intends to do by you, mustn't you? Or it would never do, would it?"

"No, ma'am."

"Does he want to marry you, may I ask?"

"Yes. I think he does," returned Audrey, gaping rather. ("Ma'am," added Audrey. . . .)

"Well, you want to find that out first of all, don't you?"

"Yes, Ma'am."

"You find that out first," said Miss Hatt, and there was a pause.

"He seems very Ardent, ma'am," offered Audrey, and looked a little blanker still.

"Yes, that's all very well——" began Miss Hatt.

"He says we're Engaged, ma'am," said Audrey, as though she were a little fearful of not getting Miss Hatt's sanction for him to have said any such thing.

"I'm very glad to hear it, Audrey," said Miss Hatt. "But what's he In, may I ask?"

"Superior Galvanised Tanks, Ma'am."

"Well, I don't know whether there's any money in his—er—Superior Galvanised Tanks. But I certainly think it would be best to wait a little, and see how things Develop."

"That's what I say to him, ma'am. I say I do not wish to Prove a Stumbling Block in *his* Career, any more than he would wish to Prove a Stumbling Block——"

"In yours," capped a well-disposed Miss Hatt. "Exactly."

"And I said, ma'am, it'll be time to think of the Wedding Bells, ma'am, when he and me, ma'am, find ourselves Placed in a more fortunate Position to that in which we find ourselves Now."

"And very right, too," said Miss Hatt. "And now, Audrey, there's the top room still to be done, isn't there?"

IV

In spite of these very proper opinions, however, it is roughly from this period that Audrey first sets in upon the minor insolences sketched at the beginning of this chapter. But much as it appears from these that Miss Custard is riding for a fall, it is not until June that the actual crash comes.

It is a very dashing tank maker that calls round for Audrey at half-past eight one evening in this month, and a very flushed and light-hearted Audrey that goes out to him.

"Fine night," says Mr. Cree, suddenly, as they come to the river, for he is a sudden man.

"Ain't it just?"

"Fine gel, when it comes to that," says Mr. Cree.

"Oh, Don't Take On so," says Audrey.

"Top hole river," says Mr. Cree, with a large gesture, but is cut off from any comparisons this time by Audrey, who tells him what a "paddy" Miss Hatt has been in all the day. This makes the tank maker very indignant.

"She's a rum sort, ain't she?" says he. "Speakin' to you like that. She wants a bit of tickin' off, don't she?"

"Oh, she's always the same," says Audrey.

"She thinks she can over-ride you, don't she. If you take my advice, young girl, you'll just give 'er a bit of 'er own, one of these days."

"Oh, she's all right."

"Is she indeed? Well the next time she comes across it with you, you take my advice and let 'er 'ave it."

"Seen Mr. Grieg lately?" asks Audrey, to change the subject.

"Mr. Grieg? Oh. *'Im.* No. I ain't goin' to see 'im no more, either."

"Why not, then?"

"Oh, never mind why not. I ain't goin' to see 'im no more."

"But why, Wal?"

"I ain't goin' to see 'im no more."

"You might tell me why, then," protests Audrey.

"No. It ain't for such Ears as you to 'ear," says an enormously delicate Galvanised Tank Maker.

"Go on," says Audrey. But "No," says Mr. Cree. "It ain't for such Ears as you to 'ear."

"Go on," says Audrey.

"Well, if you must 'ave it," says Mr. Cree at last. "'E Passed a Remark."

"Did 'e?" asks Audrey, very horrified.

"Yes 'e *did*," affirms Mr. Cree. "'Bout my sister."

"Did 'e?"

"Yes, 'e *did*. 'E Passed a Remark."

"What about?"

"'Ere! Ain't that enough for you?"

"Go on."

"No."

"Go on."

"No."

There is a long pause.

"I'll give you a Kiss when we're sittin' down," tempts Audrey, "if you'll go on."

"You'd 'ave done that in any case."

"Oo, I wouldn't."

"Oh yus you would," says Mr. Cree, and there is another long pause.

"It's no use with them Griegs," says Mr. Cree, and dismisses them with his hand. "They're *common*. Dirt common."

"S'pose they are," says Audrey.

"And when they're like that it ain't no good," says Mr. Cree, by which Mr. Cree means that it *is* no good, and to which Audrey assents, "No, it ain't not no good," employing a rather roundabout route to complete accuracy. And there is another silence.

"'Ere, ain't you got a paw to give a fellow?" asks Mr. Cree, and it is given.

After which Miss Custard and Mr. Cree walk on, with a swinging and yet slightly difficult gait, and a silence which, if one silence may be said to exceed another in point of intensity, increases with every stride they take. And still they walk on, into still darker places, and still more intensely silent they become. Until Audrey says: "Don't Act so Silly," and releases her hand.

But it is soon returned, in silence, and of her own accord. And a further silence descends upon them, broken by just one little giggle from Audrey, which denotes further Actings Silly on the part of a dumb but doggish Mr. Cree.

A spot, comfortably remote from other and similar silences, is found under the trees. There they sit down, and begin,

after a pale attempt at noticing the state of the weather
by Audrey, positively to ooze silence, to exude silence, to
expound the one and final principle of silence, before the
world. . . .   Then Audrey suddenly jumps up, as though
she is putting something behind her, and Mr. Cree makes
no protest.

Then they walk home together the same way, but they
say very little to each other (for Mr. Cree is a man of very
few words after the first silence has descended upon him),
and they at last come back to the region of Craven House.

But Audrey does not go in at once, as it is quite early
yet, says Mr. Cree.   Instead they stand outside an old house
to be let, a little way down the road, where Mr. Cree at once
begins to Take On, and Act Silly, and Start It to a degree
hardly ever reached by him before—not even "stopping"
for passers by.   Until at last Audrey cheekily pulls out
his watch, and sees with dismay the time, which is five and
twenty past eleven.   She rushes away from him.

She tries the front door with her latch-key, which has
been granted on a strictly quarter past ten basis, but the
door is bolted fast.

She stands for a few moments, in a state of aghast indecision
—when suddenly the sharp rap of a bolt going back, and the
sharp rap of another, and the softer click of a chain being
slid, are heard behind the door.   The next moment Audrey
is gazing into the eyes of Miss Hatt, who is in her dressing-
gown, looking rather mad, as she always does in that garment;
and who tells her to come in and not stand gaping there.

"Sorry, ma'am——" begins Audrey, but "There's no
excuse whatever to be made, Audrey," says Miss Hatt.
"Kindly retire to your room."

v

It all comes suddenly the next day.   At one moment
Audrey is a reproved and intimidated serving maid, but none
the less practically accepted as an eternal fixture—and the
next moment she is an outcast for ever.   It has been Nag,
Nag, Nag; and Bow, Wow, Wow; and Jaw, Jaw, Jaw (as
Edith and Audrey both describe it) all the day, and in the
evening, at half-past six o'clock, the thing reaches a climax.
After a calm interlude of complete silence from below stairs,
there suddenly floats up to the guests in the bedrooms, a

guest in the bathroom, guests in the drawing-room, something very like a shriek, two slammed doors, one terribly and unchallengeably Slammed Door, and the sound of footsteps rushing up the kitchen stairs. Then comes the sound of Miss Hatt's raised voice from the top of them.

"And if I have any more of your laziness and impertinent airs, Audrey," Miss Hatt is crying, "you'll be finding yourself in Queer Street! You'll kindly come straight *to* me when I give you a call in future."

And then it is that Audrey Answers Back.

"All right," says Audrey. "All right. I can't be in two places at once, you know." And there is an interval of sickening silence.

"What did you say, Audrey?" asks Miss Hatt.

But no reply is given from below.

"*What* did you say, Audrey?" repeats Miss Hatt, raising her voice. "Will you kindly tell me what you said?"

"All right," says Audrey. "Keep your hair on. Keep your hair on."

"*What* did you say?" shrieks Miss Hatt.

"I said keep your hair on, ma'am," returns Audrey, and without another word she shuts the kitchen door.

For one moment it seems that Miss Hatt will not recover. But she gets the better of herself, stays erect for a moment, and then swings into the drawing-room with the white, tense face of a lady likely to drop any moment; and there is Mrs. Hoare, already standing, under the crisis, with her knitting in her hands.

"Did you hear that?" asks Miss Hatt.

"Yes," whispers Mrs. Hoare. "I heard it."

"She Answered Back," says Miss Hatt.

"She Answered Back," whispers Mrs. Hoare, and there is a pause.

"Keep your Hair On," quotes Mrs. Hoare, and gives a quick, fearful glance at the womanly glory thus insulted. Which rather upsets Miss Hatt, who feels she rather wants to look at it herself before replying. "Well. She must go. That's all. She must be Dismissed."

"Dee—Eye—*Ess*——" began Mrs. Hoare, measuredly, but Miss Hatt cuts in with "I'm not going to be insulted in my own house, you know."

"I should think not," says Mrs. Hoare. "Dee, Eye, Ess——"

"It's too much of a good thing," says Miss Hatt. "I've got to show that young girl that I'm not such a fool——"

"As you look," says Mrs. Hoare, fully alive to the seriousness of the situation.

"I mean to say, it's altogether too much of a good thing. Did you hear that, Lettie?" asks Miss Hatt, for Mrs. Spicer has now entered.

"Heard some of it," admits Mrs. Spicer, inclined to giggle.

"Did you hear that part about the Aitch?" whispers Mrs. Hoare, who plainly regards that as the principal crime.

"The Aitch?" queries Mrs. Spicer.

"Well never mind about the *Aitch*," says Miss Hatt, a little curtly (and very natural, too.) "The point is she Answered Back."

"Yes," says Mrs. Spicer. "I gathered that."

"And she must Go," says Miss Hatt.

"*Jee, Oh*," interjects Mrs. Hoare, decisively, and Miss Hatt is seen raising her eyes to heaven, as though calling upon God.

"Spells Go," says Mrs. Spicer, aptly.

"And that at once," says Miss Hatt. "I'll pay her her week's wages, and off she goes. Don't you think that's best, Lettie?"

"There is an Aunt, isn't there?" asks Mrs. Spicer, for Audrey's mother has been dead long ago.

"Yes. There's an Aunt."

"Well, what about waiting until my husband comes back, and seeing what *he's* got to say about it."

"Yes. That's a very good idea. Yes. That's what I'll do. I mean I'm not going to be insulted in my own house, am I?"

"I should think not."

Mr. Spicer in due course returns, is heard putting up his hat and coat, talking to the parrot, and generally fiddling about in an exasperating way, before he enters the drawing-room, when he at once appreciates the atmosphere, and enquires of a stiff row of faces whether anything is Up.

"Up?" says Mrs. Spicer. "I should think there is. Audrey has Answered Back."

"Back?" asks Mr. Spicer.

"Yes. Back. You tell him, Bertha."

Whereupon Miss Hatt relates a list of grievances against Miss Custard, from the homecoming last night to the Answering Back half an hour ago; and she repeats that she

does not, and never did, intend to be insulted in her own
house (as though such an offence might have been overlooked if perpetrated in the street). Mr. Spicer heartily con-
curring, she asks Mr. Spicer's opinion. Whereupon Mr. Spicer
hums, and Mr. Spicer haws, and Mr. Spicer says it's very
ticklish, and at last decides that the point is, What's to be
done? Whereupon Miss Hatt opines that the best thing
to do would be to wire to the Aunt, and see if she can take
her at once; which Mr. Spicer magically adopts as his own
advice, and undertakes to do the wiring. This is done
before dinner.

Audrey is very pale at dinner, and serves very quietly
and very well, putting a kind of soft propitiation into every
dish she offers; and indeed she is inclined to think that the
whole affair is going to blow over, with perhaps a talking-to:
for Miss Hatt is very quiet and dignified, and the rest murmur
their "Thank yous" very civilly and gently.

But at half-past nine in the evening, a telegram boy thuds
doubly on the door, and on to Audrey's heart as well. Miss
Hatt rushes out herself to receive it.

Yes. The Aunt will have her, to-morrow if necessary,
and Mr. Spicer advises that the matter shall be slept upon.
His advice is taken.

The next morning, at breakfast, Miss Hatt announces her
decision. "I've decided about Audrey," says Miss Hatt.

"Oh?" say the guests, who have been a little absent and
untalkative up to this moment.

"She's going," says Miss Hatt.

A courteous interrogative sways her guests.

"And to-day."

A courteous note of exclamation sways her guests.

"I know where I can get another, immediately. In fact
her mother has repeatedly asked me to have her here. And
I know she's not engaged, and I'm sure you wouldn't mind
our being without just one day."

Rather not.

"Not that it'll make any difference, really. I and Edith
can do all the work. And I'm going to show Audrey that
telegram from her aunt saying she can come, and I'm going
to give her her full wages for the week, and I'm going to
simply say to her it is neither my habit, nor my custom, to
take insolence from any one in my own house, and she will

therefore receive a week's wages and make her departure before to-night."

The guests consider th'c a very fair speech to make, and Miss Hatt changes the subject.

Sure enough, a quarter of an hour after breakfast, and after a little nervous flitting about in her own room, Miss Hatt goes to the top of the kitchen stairs and calls for Audrey, who comes up in her old impersonal and staring condition, and is led into the study.

Miss Hatt rises as tall as a goddess.

"Audrey," says Miss Hatt. "It is neither my habit, nor my custom, to receive insolence from any one in my own house. You will therefore," continues Miss Hatt, handing her the telegram and the money, "receive a week's wages, and make your departure before to-night."

"Will I, ma'am?" is all Audrey can say, and she stares, and stares, and stares.

"Yes, you *will*," says Miss Hatt, and without another word, bounces out of the room.

But Audrey cannot understand this at all. She first of all looks down at the money, and gets a certain pleasure from looking at the brightness of the coins; and then she looks at the parrot, which is engaged in eating itself, and then she goes down the kitchen stairs to Edith. "But I always been 'ere," she says to Edith. "I always *been* 'ere." "I'm regular sorry about it, Ord," says Edith, "that I am." "But I always *been* 'ere," insists Audrey, "ain't I?" "That you 'ave," says Edith. "And I'm regular upset about it." But Audrey still cannot understand, and soon she goes upstairs to see Miss Hatt about it again.

"Will I do any more work to-day, like, ma'am?" asks Audrey.

"As you wish," says Miss Hatt. "But you leave to-night."

"I always *been* 'ere, 'aven't I?" asks Audrey.

"Have you? Well, what about it? I don't have any insolence in *my* house," says Miss Hatt, and goes away.

All the morning Audrey sits in the kitchen, sometimes looking at the telegram, sometimes turning the bright silver coins in her hand, and looking so prostrate generally that at last Edith makes her a cup of tea. And all the morning it cannot be borne in upon Audrey that she has to go. Once Edith goes up to Miss Hatt, and tells her she thinks Audrey wants to apologise—but apologies or no apologies, there will be no insolence in Miss Hatt's house, as long as she lives, and Edith comes down again. And Audrey herself goes up to her again.

"Will I take the Train from here, then, ma'am?" asks Audrey.

"Take the train! Of course you'll take the train. And you'd better be looking out one, too. You know where the A.B.C. is, I trust."

But though Miss Hatt again bounces away, even now Audrey has not done with her limp questionings. For, half an hour later, she returns to Miss Hatt once more.

"Will I pack my things in my old bag, then, ma'am?"

"Oh, do not bother me with these questions, Audrey. Of course you will. And if there's not room, I'll lend you my hold-all."

Lunch comes; Edith serves it; and Audrey is still downstairs.

"Perhaps I'll hear from you, like, ma'am? When I'm gone away?"

"No—I don't think you'll hear from me. And you haven't gone away yet, have you?"

The afternoon passes—it is a dark, windy afternoon—innumerable cups of tea are made for Audrey in the feeble basement light, and a little conversation is held. "You'll be all by yourself, Eed, won't you?" says Audrey, to whom Edith is now unspeakably precious, and "That I will," returns Edith. "And won't I 'alf miss you, Ord. We've 'ad some times together, ain't we? But p'raps you're better off'n we know."

"Then I'd rather be worse off," says Audrey, after thinking about it.

Tea comes; Edith serves it; and Audrey is still downstairs.

After Tea, suddenly, Miss Hatt's voice is heard at the top of the kitchen stairs.

"You haven't gone yet, Audrey! Isn't it time you looked out your train? The book's up here."

Audrey, after a little encouragement from Edith, goes upstairs to see the book. But here such mists begin to come in front of her eyes, and such lumps begin to contract in her throat, that she cannot see or do a thing, and she comes down to ask Edith to help her.

"One from Waterloo in two hours and a half," says Edith. "Go on, Ord. You must go up an' pack. I got to get the dinner. Go on, Ord. There's a good girl. Get it over."

And so Audrey climbs up to her little room, and lights the gas, and drags out her old bag, from where it has lain, unused, ever since she has been here. And she begins to put some clothes into it, in a half-hearted way, and then she stops that, and begins to sob.

"It was that party that done it," she says. "I ought never to 'ave gone to that there party."

"I ought never to 'ave gone to that there party. . . ."

There comes a soft knock at the door, and Audrey smudges her tears away, and goes to open it. It is Miss Elsie.

"Hullo, Audrey," says Miss Elsie. "I'm so terribly sorry to hear you're going to leave. Can I come in? I've got a dress here, I thought you might like."

"Oh, thank you, Miss Elsie. I should. I'll put it in my bag."

"Audrey up there?" comes a voice from outside, and Mrs. Hoare enters, with an envelope in her hand, which she delivers to Audrey with a terrible wink, and the intimation that it contains "a little Emm to buy something pretty with," and vanishes instantly.

"It's Money, Miss Elsie," says Audrey.

"Yes," says Elsie.

"Where shall I put it, Miss Elsie?"

"Oh, I'd put it in your bag."

"Along with your dress, Miss Elsie. I'm sure I thank you very much indeed."

"Not at all, Audrey. Can I help you with it?"

"No. I can manage, Miss Elsie. We'll soon have everything Ship Shape now," says Audrey, and she almost seems quite cheerful again, in a miserable way, as she gets on with her packing.

"Oh, and by the way, Audrey. Mr. Wildman asked me to give you this."

"Another Envelope, Miss Elsie?" says Audrey.

"Yes," says Elsie.

"I'll put it in my bag, Miss Elsie," says Audrey, in a rather matter-of-fact way. And into the bag it goes.

"Well, good-bye, Audrey. I must go and dress for dinner now."

"Good-bye, Miss Elsie. And I'm sure I should be most grateful to you from the bottom of my heart."

"Good-bye, Audrey." And Miss Elsie is gone.

And now it does not take long to do the rest of her packing,

for there is really extraordinarily little to pack; and Edith
rushes up to kiss her good-bye, for she'll have to Dish any
moment now, and she wants to say good-bye proper, and not
rushed like. And Edith rushes down again, leaving Audrey
once more in tears.

But she takes hold of her bag, and reaches up to turn
out the gas, just as she has always done, when Edith was
snug in bed, every night for five thousand nights at least;
and she stumbles down the stairs, and reaches the front
door without meeting any one.

But at the front door she stops a moment, and then turns
back, and goes in to the parrot. "I'm going, you Bad
Thing," says Audrey. "I'm going!" But the creature that
has been so friendly and jolly with her, all these years, gives
no sign now in the darkness, save the black flutter of a wing,
and a distant throaty cackle. "Oh, you Naughty——!" says
Audrey, but can get no further than that.

And she shuts the front door behind her, and she drags
her bag to the station, and buys her ticket, and blindly asks
the way, and waits on the platform. And at last a train from
the distance, with one unwinking eye in front, as though it
has known all about this contingency from the very beginning, and is merely fulfilling a long-prophesied obligation,
drones into the station, waits for a little shuffling, and a little
throbbing, and a little whistling, and then is off.

And that is the end of Audrey Custard.

Who Answered Back.

CHAPTER V

*High Wind. Mr. Wildman is taken ill. A Monster.
A Bedroom Scene.*

I

IT was a grey, roaring day in late July, with the wind as
high as though the gods had come to earth, and it was, perhaps,
the most beautiful day in all the year. For anything more
beautiful than that besieging wind, brushing up the leaves
to unearthly silvers and dead bright greys, and swirling every
tree into a maddened and suffering tangle, with a whisper
and hiss and toss—or anything more lovely than those strange,

short calms, when one dead leaf against a dead sky would flutter to the ground, and an invisible rain would start patting on the ivy, and pitting the dust hurriedly against the distant but fast-returning roar—would have had to be found in a stranger and more bewailing earth than this.

"But why this fuss and infliction? Why? Why? Why?" complained the trees, but were at once swished away again into a fury beyond all questionings: an old sheet of tin on a roof somewhere banged away, with elderly resignation: distant doors slammed, as much as to say such it was, and such it must be, and no use grumbling: bicycles fell down with a clatter on to pavements: the Doctor's car rushed swiftly past: the rain suddenly began to fall, straight and experimentally, for a minute or so, on to forlorn and by now resigned trees, but it as suddenly gave it up; and the wind came back worse than ever, and there never was such a day.

A beautiful enough day for Master Wildman, too; for it was a Saturday, which was a day of liberty, and Miss Cotterell had promised to give the whole day to him. He stayed in the drawing-room for a little while after breakfast, with Elsie knitting, and Mrs. Spicer intermittently and publicly Seeing that such and such had occurred yesterday, and such and such would take place to-morrow, from her newspaper—with Mrs. Hoare as her principal Yes-woman. He watched the twinkling dull aluminium medallions on the swinging poplar in the garden behind, and prayed that it would not rain. For he was going with Miss Cotterell for a walk in Richmond Park to-day, and they were going to have their lunch out of doors.

He left Elsie with a smile that managed to convey a certain amount of penitence, and went out into the wind to the appointed meeting-place, where, as he was ten minutes too early, and Miss Cotterell was ten minutes late, he spent an agonised and buffeted twenty minutes, pleading against a lowering sky, and thinking out some things to say to Miss Cotterell, and some long-standing questions to put to her.

Miss Cotterell at last came up to him, prepared for the rain in an Asiatic mackintosh, and other Asiatic details, apologised absently for being so late, and then said: "I say, are we still going?" "Going!" said Master Wildman, to which Miss Cotterell returned: "All right, don't get alarmed." Then Master Wildman, in spite of the testimony of his own eyes, wanted to know whether she had brought that confounded animal along with her. Miss Cotterell retorted that it was not a confounded animal, and appealed charmingly to the animal itself—which, being already engaged in preliminary dematerialisations, was not there to answer.

Practically nothing was said in the train. Miss Cotterell once whispered a smiling request in Master Wildman's ear not to be stared at so, but the rest of their attention was concentrated on the dog, which, finding itself on a rushing island absolutely prohibiting the activities of the most expert vanisher going, was in a state of natural worry and concern, and could not be prevented from questioning and pawing other amiably disposed travellers on the subject—until held firmly through the collar by Miss Cotterell's strong, taut, white young hand. This Master Wildman stared vaguely and miserably at, instead of her face.

At Richmond Station it was raining slightly in a wind as high as ever, and they decided to try Kew Gardens instead of Richmond Park. The dog, they knew, would not be allowed to enter here, but Miss Cotterell had a friend in a house near by, and spent only a quarter of an hour there (Master Wildman on the pavement outside) in finding it a safe home for the day.

They came to Kew Gardens through a clinking and unpromising turnstile worked by a military-looking person in a blue uniform, and they entered a deserted world of lashed, and waving, and thunderous moaning loveliness, which was to Master Wildman, with the little left hand of Asia in his overcoat pocket, unspeakable, and he did not try to speak. At first, that is to say.

They walked through high and stormy vistas, with the sodden and petal-blown grass beneath, and the flying grey sky above. Sometimes Miss Cotterell withdrew her hand to examine a ticketed specimen, and chance sweet mispronunciations to Master Wildman's graver Latin learnedness. Sometimes she withdrew it just to touch her hair. But she generally slid it back, in a mechanical and melancholy way, and Master Wildman was very happy, and very wretched. Sometimes, too, they stopped for a whole minute, under the pattering trees. And then Master Wildman would seize and kiss her wet, cold face, in all its obliging insolence. And that would be that. . . . They would walk on again.

"Oh, God!" cried Master Wildman at last. "Can't you say anything?"

"I can't say anything. Except that I'm very sorry," said Miss Cotterell, and indeed that was all she ever did say on the matter.

They decided to have lunch in the Gardens, and went to the wind-battered Restaurant, which was quite deserted except for themselves.

After lunch they strolled again into the gardens, but the romance and consolation had gone out of the wind-tossed trees, which still waved about enough, but in an after-lunch and more earthly style; moreover, Miss Cotterell would allow of no more stoppages, and (it was objected) insisted on keeping her hand out of people's pockets, and breaking off at the most Important Part. And as time wore on Master Wildman grew weaker in body, and more daunted in spirit. For she was so much *stronger* than him, so much fitter, so much truer in her aim—like a young athlete in the passions, with that little dim smile of exquisite self-assurance, throwing him at every turn, and willing to give him any more he wanted. . . .

"Ask her if she won't look in to tea, won't you?" Miss Hatt had said. They were back at Craven House at half-past three, and spent the half hour before tea alone in the drawing-room. At ten to four Elsie came down to find them sitting on the sofa, and looking, on the whole, very Sofa together.

Whether it was the sight of Elsie's warm, watchful face, and soft movements, or merely the reviving properties of the tea that came in a little later, Master Wildman now made a slight recovery, and began a little leg-pulling at the expense of Mrs. Hoare. At these cold-hearted incivilities, Elsie, who had always said he really mustn't, because it was rude, and unkind, reproached him softly with her looks.

But this only made Master Wildman enlarge upon his wickedness, and having already asked Mrs. Hoare if she wouldn't take any Ess, and passed her the sugar; and having insisted on her having a little See A, which was a caustic abbreviation for the Cake, he leant back in his chair and remarked upon the extraordinarily windy Doubleyou for the time of Y. Whereat Mrs. Spicer gave an even vaguer "Yes," to the Universe than usual, Elsie pretended to be now very angry with him indeed, lifting a half-smiling head with unutterable scorn, and looking out of the window as though she would never speak to him again; and Mrs. Hoare, aware of no domestic *contretemps* whatever, asked how the Famous A was getting on with his Bee Oh Oh——

"My Bee Oh Oh, or my Pea Ell?" asked a mystified Master Wildman.

"Your Pea Ell," put in Elsie, a little sharply. "Your *play*."

"Oh," said Master Wildman. "My Dee Ar A Emm A?"

"Are you writing a play, then?" asked Miss Cotterell.

"Yes. Rather. Didn't I tell you. I'll be making ten thousand out of that, at least."

"A year?" asked Miss Cotterell.

"A year," replied Master Wildman.

After tea the wind roared down the chimney and round the house with a ferocity which prevented every one from wanting to venture out. Master Wildman shuffled with some cards for a bit, and then suggested a game of *Vingt-et-un*, which they played for a little. Then, at Master Wildman's instigation, they had a game of Old Maid. Mrs. Hoare joined in this, but became a trifle fractious after a time, on account of the cards never falling in such a way as to disgrace herself—which she had got into her head they must naturally do to the Oldest person present—and she first accused her friends of "playing a game" with her, and then attacked the cards themselves, for being "Fools."

At a quarter to seven Miss Cotterell had to go, and Master Wildman volunteered to see her home. He must have received the cruellest treatment on the emotional wrestling mat before returning, for when he came back it was with all the old tense expression—causing Elsie, as usual, to watch him about the room as though he were looking about for a rope to hang her with.

Mrs. Nixon was in a great flutter at dinner over a letter received from her son, Jock, who, it appeared, had taken an insult from, but had subsequently thrashed, a Coal Heaver. . . . The thrashing of this Coal Heaver was the principal topic of the evening, and Mrs. Nixon quoted gleefully from her letter, simply unable to leave the matter alone. Master Wildman, it is true, once murmured "The Coal Heaver Thrasher," ponderously, and with some irreverence, in a silence; but it was not heard, and the others—except, perhaps, Elsie, who remained silent—joined together in a perfect harmony of approval. "Scottish Way," said Mrs. Nixon.

Master Wildman made a quick dinner, asked to be excused early, and went out into the night, where the winds had allen, and the stars were a bright benediction, after stress.

He made his way to the old street corner, to take some more.

II

Two days later Master Wildman awoke in bed feeling very unwell.

His blind was up, his window was wide open at the bottom, and he looked out at the thick mist of the summer's morning in all its still, wet, pervading hush, and he mused upon the character of life. The time was eight o'clock, and it was just at this moment (Master Wildman knew) that the murderer —MacMailey—whose exploits and trial had been a sunny drama for the whole of dusty London, nay England, in the few weeks past—was being hanged by his neck. But London, thought Master Wildman as he looked out of the window, or this misty, dreaming portion of it at least, had forgotten about that final formality. . . .

Master Wildman's thought went out for a moment to that grey, lurching moment in Holloway Gaol. . . . Then he turned in his bed, to battle, too late, with all the cool and efficient answers given him last night, by Miss Cotterell.

From these he turned as well, and got slowly out of bed. But the moment he had done this, he was taken with a reeling sick giddiness that nearly made him fall; and although he staggered to the window, and giddily watched a little spider racing across the dank stone ledge thereof, he soon realised that he was in no state to go to the City this morning, and went back to bed again, with the resolution to wait till the new servant brought him up his hot water, and to give, through her, a message to Miss Hatt.

III

The servant brought in to Craven House in place of Audrey Custard was in the very deepest contrast imaginable to her forerunner. For whereas Miss Audrey Custard had always been nothing if not a rather squat little thing, Miss Bertha Yardley, who took over her office, was of a size very nearly approaching exhibition size (The Famous Tall Girl of Southam Green, Master Wildman called her), and of that dreamily stolid, pliable and silent character peculiar to the exhibit. Indeed, next to nothing in the way of conversation ever passed her lips—her chief mode of self-expression being a broad grin, combined with a slow and *crescendo* inner wheeze, which shook her frame, and left it jerking silently, in a manner intimating to you that she was in the act of laughing. That this was pretty well the only immediate reply that Miss Yardley ever gave to any requests made, questions put, or commands given to her, was perhaps to the advantage of Craven House—inasmuch as Miss Hatt (who yapped away at her from below, like the plucky little terrier she was) was not at once seized and crushed playfully to death between a Brobdingnagian forefinger and thumb, but had the gratification, after a period of patience in which the wheezing crisis could be relied upon to exhaust itself, of seeing her towering domestic glide awfully away to her duties—not unlike some terrifying monstrosity at a Nice Carnival.

It was to this figure, or rather figure-head, that Master Wildman, with some misgiving, announced his illness, and appreciating her need for something to wheeze about before retiring, let off a joke to the effect that he must have been Eating too much, which was considered quite witty enough to bring about the desired effect. Shortly afterwards Miss Hatt came in to him.

It was decided that he should have a cup of tea and piece of dry toast at breakfast time, and stay in bed for the day.

"And I must let the office know, somehow or other," said Master Wildman. "Perhaps Elsie?——"

"Yes. I'll send her up after breakfast."

Whereupon we stare at the window for half an hour, until we hear the gong, from the depths below, announcing breakfast. We then endure (1) a beastly moment before we hear our own share of it tinkling up, (2) a giddy moment when we find we can't do anything with it at all, and (3) a more or less peaceful moment when we lie back and look at the ceiling and think how very sad, and yet how very beautiful, it would be if we died. After which we experience a soft knock at the door, and Elsie is with us.

Yes. She will go out to the phone at the post-office . . . she will say Avenue 40620, probably speak to Mr. Creevy, say that Mr. Wildman is *very* unwell—(that is, not *too* very, because he expects to be back in two days at the most)—and he is *very* sorry. . . . And that is that. . . . And is there anything else we want? . . . Books? Papers, etc.?—for Elsie will be only too glad to get them for us. But no, thanks very much, we'll try and have a bit of a sleep now. Elsie has gone.

We now go off into a thick doze around a medley of thudding, sweeping, and squeaky sounds from the adjoining rooms, wherein the personal over-night chaos wrought by irresponsible guests is being put to rights. But very soon, it seems, Elsie returns.

Elsie returns and says that all went swimmingly at the phone, and what do we think? She met Miss Cotterell on the way back, and she will be looking in some time after tea, to ask about us. As Elsie leaves us we feel much better already.

Indeed, Master Wildman is almost himself again when they come to ask him if he can manage any lunch, which he certainly thinks he can manage. And Elsie comes in to him again, to ask him if he'll have a little Bovril with it, and stays to chat for ten minutes. And in this ten minutes Master Wildman asks her if she'd like to have the first two acts of his play read to her after lunch. This throws her into a state of talkative rapture, all through lunch downstairs, which rapture (apart from Mrs. Hoare), is not reflected by the company, which still is rather of the opinion that young men in Cities doubtless know their own business best. . . .

Elsie rushes up directly afterwards, spends a slightly constrained five minutes with him, until he volunteers: "Well——"; and then, for all the afternoon, with minor interruptions from Miss Hatt, who bounces in friendlily every now and then with a secret eye on the Proprieties, Master Wildman reads his play. At the mention of this play, three years later, Master Wildman would groan loudly and beg to be spared the details; but it is freshly written now, and as he reads it to Elsie in the bedroom firelight of a darkening summer's afternoon, it is quite a different affair, and they are both carried away. Indeed, Elsie can hardly say how beautiful she thinks it, at the end, on account of a voice all gone to pieces, and an unnatural brightness of eye. But the Lovely Part where he Comes Back after All Those Years, and the Part where she Turns on them, and the Part where they Leave him, and the Part where he Slowly Realises, to say nothing of the little Bit about the Old Man, and the Piece about the Maid, are all rapturously dwelt upon, and looked for again by request, and re-read in a very happy and modestly exulting tone of voice. And the unwritten last act is vaguely sketched, and gloriously approved, and there have never been such intimacies between them before.

And when the Famous Tall Girl of Southam Green brings up the tea there are two cups on the little green tray (which is a piece of Miss Hatt's sarcasm really, but Elsie takes it as a beautiful thought), and Elsie pours it out in an amber jet which chuckles into the cups, and winks back red point to the fire, and they laugh, and sit there and look at each other, and suddenly seem to have known the heart and soul of each other, all their lives.

"Enough," says Master Wildman, when Miss Hatt comes in enquiringly after tea. "For Richard is himself again." The kingly expression is fitter than he knows, too, for immediately afterwards he is holding nothing less than a Court. First of all come Mrs. Spicer and Mrs. Nixon, to pay their fire-light respects, and take polite dismissal; then comes Mrs. Hoare, who shouts high compliments and good wishes for some time, from a moral position outside the door, until she is at last persuaded to endanger her honour by entering —when she comes and sits at the end of the bed, and is quite sure she is crushing Master Wildman's toes. And then comes Mr. Hoare, himself, who is up in Town for the week-end again, with a more glorious tie than ever, and who says he "can't stand" being ill, personally.

Master Wildman's play being mentioned, Mrs. Hoare becomes exceedingly enthusiastic, and thrusts immense fortunes on everybody, all round. Her nephew says that he's got a play, too, in a drawer somewhere, and Master Wildman confesses that pretty nearly every one has.

"Then do you *write* it?" asks Mrs. Hoare, who seems a little hazy on certain points of authorship. "Or do you copy it out?"

And in the rather baffled silence that follows, Master Wildman, who has been going very gently with the old lady, for Elsie's sake, catches Elsie's eye again, but cannot resist the faintest wickedness in retort.

"Well, no," says Master Wildman. "Because, when you come to think of it—really, Mrs. Hoare—there's not really anywhere—to Copy it out from."

"But *otherwise*, of course," Master Wildman is careful to add, looking at Elsie. "I would Copy it Out."

Then comes a knock at the door, and a voice, turning Master Wildman's heart to lead, and enquiring "Is this where the wretched invalid is?" announces Miss Cotterell.

She has not long to stay, but her deadly spell is begun in a minute, and even the room grows quiet, and enchanted, and still, as she comes and sits down in the warm rosy fire-light flicking over her flesh-coloured stockings and her warm rosy mouth. She has very little to say, apart from a few mocking allusions to the Nervous Wreck, the Dying Man, the Expiring Patient, and the like. Master Wildman smiles dreamily into the fire, without replying to all these sallies, and Elsie tells her about the play. Whereupon, against Master Wildman's protests, Miss Cotterell insists upon seeing the manuscript, and seizes it, and reads bits of it in a suspended way, and at last puts it down with a little smile that withers Master Wildman through and through.

Then, with a warning that he must buck up and get well for the dance (for there is another dance for them all in a week or so), she gets up to go, and thanks Mr. Hoare for his kind offer to see her home, which he does.

Master Wildman now travels into eternity with a wide unseeing stare for a moment or so, until he catches Elsie's eyes, and comes back again with a smile, and finds himself alone with her.

"I must be going soon, now," says Elsie. "I know mother's waiting for me, and she'll be getting frightfully angry."

"Oh, Elsie," asks Master Wildman, lazily. "Why on earth do you go on hanging round that woman."

Elsie is heard protesting feebly that she is *not* a woman.

"She is a woman," insists Master Wildman. "You know she's a woman." And there is a pause.

"And what about that bobbed hair?" asks Master Wildman.

"What bobbed hair?"

"Your bobbed hair," returns Master Wildman, sulkily.

"What about my bobbed hair?" asks Elsie, but she knows perfectly well.

"'No daughter of mine shall ever make an exhibition, etc., etc., etc. . . . Bobbed Hair indeed!' That was how it went, wasn't it, Elsie?"

"No," says Elsie.

"Wasn't it, Elsie?"

"Yes," says Elsie, and there is a silence.

"Elsie," says Master Wildman. "Would you go out and get your hair bobbed for me?"

"Oh, I couldn't. You don't know."

"As a favour. To me."

"I couldn't. You don't know."

"Anything else," suggests Elsie.

"I don't want anything else. I want just that."

"I couldn't. You don't understand."

"Elsie!"

"Yes?"

Master Wildman pauses. "Only 'Elsie'—in general," he says slowly, and looks hard at her. . . .

"I couldn't. I couldn't."

"Will you think about it?"

"Yes, I'll think about it," says Elsie, and there is a long silence.

And then, with the red fire flicking over Elsie's concerned, alert little features, and all about the room behind her, as she gazes into the fire; and the dusk thickening upon a pillowed Master Wildman, as he gazes speculatively out at her, there falls a queer swift moment of confession upon them both.

"Tired, Elsie?" asks Master Wildman, at last.

"Oh, no," says Elsie, and smiling back at him, brushes away the suspicion as though it lay in her hair. Then she returns to her staring.

It is only a moment, gone in a flash of the fire-light, but in it he has known all that there is to tell of her weary love for him, and a little hint of his feeling for her.

"You'd better go," says Master Wildman. "I can hear her calling."

CHAPTER VI

*A Dangerous Hat.   No one to guide Mr. Wildman.
Something the matter with Elsie.*

I

WHEREAS the first signs of a failing brain in the average human are believed to manifest themselves in the form of odd straws, or irrelevant flowers sticking out from their persons; and whereas this is in actual fact a mainly false belief, there is no doubt whatever that, when suspicions of this sort come to centre round an old lady, the trouble first sets in around the Hat. A cherry too much, a rose too dangling, an apple too great, a bunch of grapes to the bad, and before you know where you are, you have a thick-veiled, white-booted, painted, muttering nodder, charging along the streets, mixing with the crowd, and waiting with eternal nods at street corners, to the bewildered horror of the public at large.

The concern of Craven House, then, can well be appreciated, when Mrs. Hoare came down to lunch one Saturday afternoon, in a picture hat belonging to an unknown era, and adorned with a bright blending of large water grapes and pink ribbons, guaranteed to cause the Not All There school of nephews and nieces to toss their caps into the air at the final and crushing defeat of their opponents.

Immediately she had taken her place, which she did with a mixture of slight coyness and a slight consciousness of being brazen, Bertha began to wheeze. This she continued to do before receiving a sharp glance from Miss Hatt, when she shook unsteadily, and remembered herself.

"Oh, Mrs. Hoare?" said Miss Hatt, agreeably, and in general.

"I sometimes wear it, you know," said Mrs. Hoare, and the company turned very pale. . . .

"Oh, yes," said Master Wildman.

"Yes. My Solicitor, you know," said Mrs. Hoare, with a winning smile.

"Oh, yes," said Master Wildman. "I see."

After a very tense and very silent lunch, Mrs. Hoare went into the drawing-room. Miss Hatt closed the door softly upon her, and came over to her guests, who were waiting at the other end of the hall.

"What's to be done now?" said Miss Hatt. "She can't go out in that."

"*Is* there a solicitor?" asked Master Wildman.

"Yes. At least she's said she was going to him for the last week."

"She must be spoken to," said Mrs. Spicer.

"Tactfully," said Miss Hatt.

"Very tactfully," said Master Wildman.

"But who——?" began Mrs. Spicer.

"Will bell the cat," said Master Wildman.

"It's rather awkward, isn't it?" said Miss Hatt.

"Shall I have a try," said Elsie, and Master Wildman looked at her.

"Do you dare?"

"Yes. I'll have a try," said Elsie.

"I'll come with you, Elsie," said Master Wildman.

They both went into the drawing-room.

Mrs. Hoare was gazing out of the window, with her finger on her chin.

"Oh," said Elsie. "Mrs. Hoare! What a dreadfully unfashionable hat!"

"Unfashionable, my dear?" said Mrs. Hoare. "I thought it was so nice."

"Oh, no, Mrs. Hoare. It's so unfashionable. So dreadfully un*fashionable*."

"Are you sure, my dear?" said Mrs. Hoare, looking very miserable. "I wear it sometimes, you know."

"But Grapes, Mrs. Hoare! They're so unfashionable," said Elsie, "with Ribbons."

"But it's only for my Solicitor, dear. I'll take it off after him. And he used to be quite taken with me at one time."

"I'm sure he did, Mrs. Hoare."

"Of course I'm old, now," said Mrs. Hoare, looking out of the window with what worlds of decayed passion and gaiety behind her time-reddened eyes it would be hard to say.

"Oh, you're *not* old, Mrs. Hoare. But I don't think he'd like that hat. Because it's not *fashionable*."

"I expect he'd laugh at me, then?"

"Oh, I don't know about that. But Solicitors are very fashionable these days, aren't they?" said Elsie, appealing to Master Wildman.

"Solicitors," said Master Wildman, "are incredibly fashionable."

"Are they?" said Mrs. Hoare.

"You've only got to look at Solicitors——" said Master Wildman.

"In the street——" continued Master Wildman, taking his time.

"Well?" said Elsie.

"To see how fashionable Solicitors are," said Master Wildman.

"And Grapes and Ribbons, Mrs. Hoare!" said Elsie, and turned again to Master Wildman. "They hate Grapes and Ribbons, don't they?"

"Grapes and Ribbons," said Master Wildman, "are terrible for Solicitors. Believe me."

"Then I suppose it'll have to come off. If it's so unfashionable," said Mrs. Hoare.

"And it *is* unfashionable, Mrs. Hoare."

The thing was off.

"Very well, very well," said Mrs. Hoare, looking at it wretchedly. "But it was so pleasant. So pleasant."

"Pleasant," said Master Wildman. "But unfashionable."

II

There being no worldly person in a position to indicate the futilities of a twenty-four-year-old Master Wildman besieging the West End of London with a manuscript, Master Wildman finished his play, read it to Elsie as a whole, typed it after hours on the office typewriter, and asked Elsie to send it off to Mr. Eugene Layburn, of the Empress Theatre, Charing Cross. The play in which Mr. Layburn was acting the leading part, with such success at this period, was called "Undertow." Master Wildman's play was called "Afterthought." They were that kind of play.

III

And now the year begins to fail, and with it Elsie, who has kept her spirits up all this time, and never shown a sign of inward misgiving to any one, but always preserved a modestly self-assured look in their presence, suddenly begins to fail as well. Strange moods of crying and depression sweep over her from time to time, and every night she goes early up to bed. For Master Wildman, who seems to have quite forgotten the moments of companionship that had fallen upon them at the time of the play-reading, is off after dinner, and out with Miss Cotterell, nearly every night, saying and doing God knows what in the dark.

For it is getting dark again in the evenings now, and the Cricket in the papers, which always somehow stands for summer and sunny days with Elsie, suddenly culminates in the *Champion County v. The Rest*, and is no more; and Football comes in, with its grey blotched flying heads on the back page of the newspapers; and the fire is lit again one evening in the drawing-room; and November comes in, like a betrayed lady weeping in her hair, and finds a deserted Elsie sitting before the fire after tea, in dim sounds from the kitchen below and indescribable distress, never spoken to by any one, all the day, until Master Wildman's key scratches in the lock. Then he will talk to her for a little while in the gloaming, but soon go off to dress. . . .

Sometimes of an evening Elsie goes for a walk in the High Road, to cast away her feelings; but it is so swirlingly noisy up there, and the trams thunder their brutal derision at her, for thinking of such a thing (for she knows she thinks of such a thing now), and the lights glare at her in amazement, and the butchers bellow: *"Buy, buy, buy! Come along! Watcher want! Buy, buy, buy!"* at her, with such exasperation, that she is forced to leave the turmoil of it all and take to the quieter streets; but there is the same message in the homecoming faces under the lamps, and it is the same pale, pitiless lamp she faces at last when she comes back to Craven House. And then she goes up to her dark bedroom, in the cold, and looks down at the lamp, and begins to cry. "I'm always crying," says Elsie, and so she is, and she is always in the dark, it seems.

And it seems that Master Wildman and Miss Cotterell are two ghosts now—not real characters at all, but ghosts, to slight her and fade, and leave her alone in the dark, with their voices in her ears. And every night in bed she waits, looking up at the watery reflection from the lamp on the ceiling, never believing it of love, which has always been such a proud sensation before—waits, until she hears the little gate shriek on his return, and then she covers her face, and can hardly credit the depth and power of her sobs, under the sheets. "I'm a cry baby," sobs Elsie. "I'm a cry baby! . . ." But still she cries.

CHAPTER VII

Elsie.

I

ONE day, early in December, Elsie comes quietly down to lunch in the dining-room: she takes her place amongst the others, who are already seated; she glances furtively at Master Wildman, who is not in the City, having had another small illness and stretched his convalescence as far as to-day—(in good conscience, for he is going to test his health at a dance to-night): she thanks Bertha nicely for handing the vegetables, and says no other word.

It is not till some five minutes later that Mrs. Spicer throws up her hands, shrieks "Oh!" and stares across the table.

A fit being half expected to take place, the company's attention is concentrated upon Mrs. Spicer, until the lady explains herself.

"Bobbed!" exclaims Mrs. Spicer.

"Yes, I know," says Elsie. "Do you like it?"

"Like it!" says Master Wildman. "Why, it's——"

"Who told you do to that, Elsie?" asks Mrs. Nixon, cutting in very sharply.

"Why, I did, of course," returns Master Wildman. "And I think it's——"

"Who told you——" begins Mrs. Nixon.

"And what do *you* think of it, Bertha?" asks Master Wildman to the servant.

Bertha wheezes suggestively, without committing herself. Mrs. Spicer says "Yes" has already said "Yes" five or six times to the Universe. . . .

"*Down* to the *Ground*," says Mrs. Hoare.

"Yes, it certainly does suit her," says Miss Hatt. "I must say."

"She's a Rossetti, Mrs. Nixon," says Mrs. Hoare, and becomes fervent. "A Rossetti! You've got a Rossetti!"

Master Wildman puts it friendlily to Mrs. Hoare that she's not quite as "sneery" as all that.

"No. Not as sneery. I know what you mean. But a Rossetti for all that! You're a Rossetti, my dear. I suppose you know it?"

Elsie looks as though she had never dreamed of such a thing, but pleased enough for all that.

"An undeniable R.," says Master Wildman, and insolently requests that the beet root shall be "heaved" over to him when it is done with.

"A little word with you, Elsie, please," says Mrs. Nixon, in front of the others, after lunch.

II

Master Wildman waits a long while in the little study for Elsie—for he knows she will come down to him there sooner or later—and he hums softly to himself. He had quite forgotten the little conversation he had with her at the time of the play-reading, and he had not thought she would take him at his word. . . .

When at last she comes noiselessly down the stairs, she has a very white face and she is trembling.

"Well?"

"She says I'm not going to the dance to-night," says Elsie. Master Wildman is thoughtful.

"Did you tell her what a liar she was?" says Master Wildman.

"What?" asks Elsie, but not as though she had not heard.

"Did you tell her what a liar she was?"

"Oh, don't. You know I can't. If she says not."

"Elsie, please go and tell her what a liar she was."

"Oh, don't. Please don't. I can't go on. . . ."

"Elsie. Must I go and do it myself?"

"What do you mean?"

"I'll go this second, if you don't."

Master Wildman opens the door.

"Come back!" whispers Elsie, and clutches at him. "Oh, *please* don't make me go on!"

"Either you or I go, Elsie."

"I can't go! I can't go! She's holding that Stick! She's holding that Stick! Just as she used to!"

"Elsie, if I go, I shall tear her into little pieces. Are you going?"

"What shall I say? What shall I say? She's looking just as she used to! You don't know what she used to do! You don't know *what* she used to do!"

"I say, Elsie," says Master Wildman, who is now trembling a little himself. "Be a man. You must cut out this trembling rot. Come on. We'll go straight up now, and you'll go in and open the door, and put your head in, and say: 'I may tell you I'm going,' or something like that. That's all. That's all that's needed. Then you come out to me. I'm waiting outside. It's now or never, Elsie, you know that."

"Oh, please, please, *please!*"

"Now or never, Elsie. Come along." He takes her weak little hand, and leads her gently up the stairs. But she refuses the last landing.

"But if she hits me!"

"God help her," says Master Wildman. "Run along. I'll stay here."

Elsie rushes away from him. . . . A door is heard opening

upstairs. Something is mumbled into a room. A door is quickly shut. The next moment Elsie is down with him, with an expression of absent bewilderment on her face, as she mechanically offers him her hand, which he takes.

"Elsie!" cries Mrs. Nixon, thudding out on to the landing above. "Elsie!"

Master Wildman makes terrific gestures imposing silence.

"Elsie!"

"Elsie!"

A door is slammed shut.

A door is softly opened.

There are considerable creaking noises, betokening a lady listening.

A door is slammed shut.

"The First Round," breathes Master Wildman.

III

"I did it," says Elsie. "Didn't I?" And that, combined with a silly stare, is pretty well all that she can say for the first hour.

But as time wears on, in the winter's afternoon, and Master Wildman begins to read, almost as though the skies had never fallen in at all, Elsie's dreamy and baffled expression slowly changes to something like concern, and she becomes decidedly fidgety. Mrs. Hoare is in the drawing-room now, having a nap, and so Elsie has to whisper.

"I won't *really* have to go to the dance?" whispers Elsie. "Not *now*. Will I?"

"Elsie, I shall have to speak severely to you in a moment," says Master Wildman, and there is a silence. Mrs. Hoare turns in her sleep, and they both stop to watch her doing it.

"If," whispers Elsie, and puts her hand on his. "If I promise to be nice and *rude* to her, when I see her again, may I *not* go to the dance to-night?"

"You'll be nice and rude in any case, Elsie. But you must come along to-night."

"Oh, *please*."

"Now then, Elsie. You're surely not going to spoil everything now. Please try."

Elsie looks tearful, but says no more.

Mrs. Nixon is not down to tea. "I think she's got a headache," says Elsie.

"Perhaps a little A.," says Mrs. Hoare. "About the Aitch." (Angry about the Hair.) "You'll be going to the dance, then, to-night, dear?" she adds.

"Oh, yes," says Elsie.

After tea Master Wildman is seen pantomiming largely at the door, and Elsie gets up and goes outside with him.

"I'd go on up now, Elsie, if I were you," he says, "and just barge around a bit. Maybe she'll come out and have it out with you. Then you can get it over. Because I want you to enjoy the dance to-night. And if she does come, tell her just what a fantastic old lunatic she is. Fantastic. That's the word. Explain she's in the twentieth century. . . . Go along, Elsie."

"Very well," says Elsie, and runs upstairs.

She passes her mother's door with the faintest little jump, and goes into her room.

The house is very silent up here, and there is not a sound from her mother's bedroom. She walks up and down, wondering if Master Wildman will let her come down again, if she waits five minutes. She looks at her wrist watch, notes the exact position of the large hand, listens to its imperative little ticking, and watches its glimmering dial in the dusk. Once a bump from her mother's neighbourhood stops her heart's beating, and she has a nasty sensation of being about to fall on the floor. And a door on the landing below, banging intermittently in the draught, with soft and evil suggestions, banging and pausing, pausing and softly banging, terrifies her exceedingly.

The five minutes pass, and she is just about to go down, when it suddenly occurs to her that she will have to dress. She had never thought of that. She will have to dress. The very thought makes her feel faint. She turns back into the room. Her little green dress. . . .

He would have told her to leave it out on the bed, as an impudent sign. Yes. And perhaps if she does that, he will not make her come upstairs again, into this grey, tingling, door-banging stillness. She goes to the cupboard, and opens its door.

The little green dress is there, glowing in the dusk of the cupboard. But it is no longer a little green dress when it comes out nearer the light. For it is slit down and down, with a knife, into long, fine shreds; and attached to it is a little note in her mother's hand:—

"For the dance."

IV

A minute later Elsie has flown down the stairs, and burst into the drawing-room, where Master Wildman is seated (happily) alone.

"She's tore it through!" cries Elsie. "She's tore it through!"

"Torn," says Master Wildman. "Torn."

"She's torn it through!"

"What exactly?"

"My green dress."

"Your green *what?*"

"My green dress! That I made! My green dress! It's all tore!"

"N," corrects Master Wildman.

"N," sobs Elsie, and covers her face with her hands. "Oh, how I hate her! Oh, how I hate her!"

Master Wildman rises quietly and paces importantly up and down.

"Well, I'm damned," says Master Wildman, and: "Well—I'm—damned." And he looks in front of him for a minute or so without a word.

When at last he speaks, his tones are again frightening to Elsie, and he employs a roundabout style of speech.

"I say, Elsie," says Master Wildman. "What do you think there's going to be to Pay now?"

"What?"

"The Devil," says Master Wildman. "And what would your mother be Making, Elsie, if she thought you weren't going to that dance to-night in the most beautiful dress in the entire world?"

"What?"

"A Grave Error," says Master Wildman, and continues with a raised voice: "And just When, Elsie, are you coming out with me to get it?"

"When?" asks Elsie, looking horrified.

"Now," says Master Wildman, louder still. "And what sort of humour am I in at the moment of speaking?"

"What?"

"An Awe-inspiring One," says Master Wildman. "A Smashing One. An Unbrookable One! Come along, Elsie, get your things on."

"But you can't. You can't,"

"To horse, Elsie. Ho, Varlets, there! My boots! There's only two hours before dinner, Elsie."

"I can't. I can't."

"Elsie."

"But I can't."

"Elsie."

"Can I?" says Elsie, but looks into the distance with a still tearful, but rather gleeful terror at the prospect.

"Elsie."

"And *you*. Oh, how *can* you?"

"Elsie, dear, *please*," says Master Wildman, softly by her side; and at last: "I'll come," says Elsie. "But I've never done such a thing before."

They leave the house together quietly five minutes later, and they take a train to Piccadilly. For all the shops are shut on Thursday at Southam Green, Elsie weakly tells him, and if one *must*, she rather thinks she knows the shop, as a matter of fact. Elsie is very subdued all the way going, and keeps on breaking thoughtful silences with "You *can't*. You *can't*," and fervently looking at him—but he keeps on replying "Can't I?" and punching his wallet gruesomely. "You don't know the *prices*. They're terrible," says Elsie, and "Yes I do," says Master Wildman. "But I honestly think we ought to be able to find something just wearable for fifty pounds, unless of course you're frightfully particular." "Oh, don't be so mad," says Elsie. "I don't mean don't be so mad—but don't, please. We'll be lucky if there's anything under five." "Hundred?" asks Master Wildman. "Dear, dear; then we *will* have to go back." "Oh, you are so silly," says Elsie, and looks as though she is going to cry again.

"But when," says Elsie, "I think of how she tore— torn——"

"Tore."

"Tore that dress, I do feel very *upset*," admits Elsie, and at this moment they come into Piccadilly station.

They go up in the lift, where Elsie stares forlornly at the theatre advertisements (and catches the warning against pickpockets, and protectively touches her own pockets, and meets Master Wildman's eyes in the act, and smiles at him), and they come out into the Haymarket.

Yes. Elsie knows where to go. It's just round here, really, if one still must. . . . They walk along together, and Master Wildman takes her arm. . . .

At last they come to the Shop. "So this is it?" says Master Wildman, and "Yes," says Elsie, and they look into the window. "Not much in *here*," says Master Wildman. "No," says Elsie. "I suppose one would really have to go in." "Then In, Elsie," says Master Wildman, "we go." But Elsie is looking around her in the traffic with great nervousness. "I've never done this before. Only at Barker's with mother," she says. "Shan't I look a fright?" "*In*," says Master Wildman, "we go." And he opens the door for her.

It is very hushed and thick-carpeted in here, with the sounds of the traffic beating through like sounds heard from under water, and they have to touch things and airily admire them for some time, before a brilliant, pasty woman with a nose conceived half in the Roman and half in the Bateman manner, comes out with a questioning glance.

"Well, we want an evening dress, really, don't we?" says Elsie, and appeals to Master Wildman. "Why, God bless my soul," says Master Wildman. "I believe we do!" For there is no doing anything with Master Wildman.

Whereat the brilliant, pasty woman laughs hospitably but rather haughtily through a nose conceived half in the Roman and half in the Bateman manner, and would like to know About What?

Perhaps if we could See?

Certainly.

There are all sorts, really. There is This, of course, which is very nice, isn't it? ("Yes, that's very nice," says Elsie.) And then there is This, isn't there, which is very nice as well. ("Yes. I like that," says Elsie.) And of course there is This ("Oh, that's nice," says Elsie), which is nice, and there's a nice one here. And when you come to think of it, there's This.

"I think that's very nice," says Elsie. "About how——" "That's fifteen," says the brilliant, pasty woman, and looks patient. "Very nice."

"Perhaps there are some a little——?"

"More," suggests Master Wildman, quickly.

"Oh, yes."

And some more are brought. "Oh, these are lovely," says Elsie, now absolutely swimming in them. "Do you like this?" "Very nice," says Master Wildman, and "What about this?" asks Elsie. "Very nice," says Master Wildman,

and "Oh, I love this one!" says Elsie, pouncing upon another
and holding it up in front of her. "I love this. About
how——?" "That's seventeen," says the brilliant, pasty
woman, and retires for a moment. "That's the one, Elsie,"
says Master Wildman. "Oh, you can't. You know you
can't!" whispers Elsie, and "This is the one, I think," says
Master Wildman as the lady returns.

And Elsie retires to try it on, and comes back a little later
to show it off, and "It is *short*, isn't it?" says Elsie, but in
unholy tones, and when the lady has gone for another moment
she tells him that he can't, and he mustn't, and he can't
and he can't—but he does. And they come out ten minutes
later into the traffic, which roars and honks away, as much
as to say "You've done it now!"

"Courage, Elsie," says Master Wildman, as they climb the
steps of Craven House.

v

When Elsie comes down to the drawing-room, to Mrs.
Hoare and Master Wildman, ten minutes before dinner, she
is looking remarkable, and a remarkable scene takes place.

This is begun by Master Wildman, who, at the sight of
her, shouts "My God!", clasps his head, and flings himself
behind the sofa. On being desired to account for this
behaviour, he wildly calls for "A Veil! A Veil!" and
beseeches someone to "Cover her! At all costs! Cover
her!" On being asked "What's the matter?" by Elsie herself, who is strangely bright-eyed, he is at last persuaded to
emerge, and comes up very dustily and slowly—("In your
evening dress, too," says Elsie, who is still strangely bright-
eyed)—and blinks at her dazedly for a long time.

"Do you like it, then?" asks Elsie, and he becomes himself
again.

"What do you think of that, Mrs. Hoare?" he asks, but
Mrs. Hoare is already dissolved in tears of joy.

"Oh don't ask me!" says Mrs. Hoare. "Don't ask me!
Why didn't you *tell* us about it, dear?"

"Is it nice, then?" asks Elsie.

"With the bobbed hair, too! Oh, my dear, you must be
very proud. How on earth did you get it?"

"Oh, I got it somehow," says Elsie, who is sworn to secrecy.

"But does your Emm know yet?"

"No, she doesn't know yet," says Elsie, but there is no

misgiving in the look she throws over to Master Wildman. Indeed, there is a certain queer, queenly and self-reliant little look which never deserts Elsie, as long as she is in this dress, and which is a look never seen before on Elsie's face.

"Oh, my dear," says Mrs. Hoare. "What has come over you? You look so beautiful to-day. And you always did look so *O*."

"So *O*," repeats Mrs. Hoare. . . .

By which a sadly honest Mrs. Hoare intends Ordinary, but happily does not unravel the mystery for her listeners.

"But I knew you could do it. I knew it! And now, my dear, you'll have *every* young man in love with you," says Mrs. Hoare, as though Elsie has the greater part of them under her sway already.

"Oh, I won't. You know I won't!" says the ridiculous Elsie, but dances about the room, like a little girl, and looks in the glass, with such a joyous air of being absolutely compelled to admit that perhaps she will, that Master Wildman says: "You see. She can't deny it."

"Shush!" says Mrs. Hoare, suddenly, with a Siddons gesture. "The Emm."

But the Emm goes straight into the dining-room, and the next moment the gong is beaten for dinner. They get up to go in.

"Now then, Elsie," whispers Master Wildman at the door, and "It's all right," whispers Elsie, and she is smiling up at him.

VI

Miss Hatt is the first to see it.

"Oh!" exclaims Miss Hatt.

Then it is Mrs. Spicer's turn.

"Well I nev——!" says Mrs. Spicer.

"Dress?" cries Mr. Spicer, inarticulately. . . .

And then it is that Mrs. Nixon begins to Blush.

This terrible and ever-to-be-remembered Blush begins in the neck, mounts at a furious pace to the chin, sweeps up to the cheeks, inflames the forehead, ignites the eyes with uncanny brightness, and burns, and burns, and burns. The company stares in agueish horror, Miss Hatt talks, Bertha wheezes, will not stop wheezing, behind; Mrs. Spicer says "Yes" in a delirious frenzy, time after time, to an unhinged Universe; Mrs. Hoare begins to hum an air, and Miss Hatt still talks, and still it burns. It burns until Miss Hatt has to give over talking, and it burns in the deathly silence that follows, and then, all at once, it burns itself out, into dead white ashes.

"Evening. . . ." tries Mr. Spicer, and then tries again.

"Colder this evening," says Mr. Spicer, and this time gets away with it.

"Rained down in these parts," says Master Wildman.

"What?" says Mr. Spicer. "Rained?"

"Rained," says Master Wildman.

Mrs. Nixon here makes a grisly clattering noise with her spoon and soup plate.

("Too hot?", asks Miss Hatt, smiling, and Mrs. Nixon smiles back at her, putting her serviette to her mouth.)

"Hard," says Master Wildman.

"Started about five o'clock, didn't it?" says Elsie, and that queer, queenly and self-reliant little look again comes over her, as she just glances in the direction of her mother.

"Five o'clock," says Master Wildman.

"Oh," says Mr. Spicer.

The dress is never mentioned at all, and the dinner gets along pretty fairly well. Mrs. Nixon once again seems to be about to blush, but the company at once realises that that way madness lies, and wildly plies her with questions, to which she makes decent replies. She eats very little food.

After dinner "We must buck up, Elsie," says Master Wildman publicly, "or we'll be late." "All right. I'm quite ready. I'll just get my coat," says Elsie. And the next moment she is at the front door with him. There are other guests in the hall at the time, all talking, and at the back of them is Mrs. Nixon—an ashen presence. "Come here, Elsie," she is heard saying through the noise. "Elsie, come here!" and "Courage, Elsie," whispers Master Wildman, and "It's quite all right," whispers Elsie back. "Come here!" says Mrs. Nixon, and comes forward. The door shuts softly in her face.

"When I *am* in a temper," says Elsie, as they walk towards the station. "I *am* in one."

"Never knew you had such a thing, Elsie," says Master Wildman. "I think it must be that dress."

"I think it must be," says Elsie, softly, and takes his arm.

"It makes me feel so happy," says Elsie.

VII

And it must have been the dress, for that queer, queenly and self-reliant little look never passes off all the evening. It is there as they meet Miss Cotterell and Mr. Hoare at the station, and it is there as they talk about the events of the evening in the train, and describe the Blush in all its unalleviated horrors. "And doesn't she look beautiful?" asks Master Wildman, appealing to Miss Cotterell, and "Yes. Isn't she absolutely lovely?" says Miss Cotterell, and it is just a little bit there, then. And it is a challenge to all ticket collectors, and to all waiters, and to everybody she is with, except Master Wildman, for whom it softens into an inexpressible look.

And she says "No. I'll sit this out, I think," to Mr. Hoare, when he asks for a dance out of his turn, and "Yes" to Master Wildman whenever he asks for it. And "Oh, I am so happy!" she exclaims while they dance, and "Oh, supposing I hadn't gone with you!" in exquisite agonies at the thought, and at last, "Oh, I do *like* you," confesses Elsie, beyond herself. "Why, Elsie——" says Master Wildman, and does not know what to say. "Well?" says Elsie. "Why, I like *you*," he replies. "You'll like me better now," says Elsie.

Go? At half-past twelve? Go? The last train? Is there no such thing as a taxi?

It is a gala night at the St. James' Hotel, and at one o'clock the streamers begin, and Elsie is discovered pelting unknown people, and being pelted by them, and showing her tiny white laughing teeth as she goes into action against them; and the lights go out, and the deep, whirling blue and purple lights are thrown upon the floor for the waltz; and Elsie snatches at Master Wildman before he knows where he is, and she waltzes with Master Wildman in the deep, whirling blue and purple lights.

And at last the dance comes to an end, and "God Save the King" is played, and they all go out into the star-lit night, and take a whizzing taxi home.

They drop Miss Cotterell, and drop Mr. Hoare, and Master Wildman and Elsie are left alone in the taxi, with an aloof and preoccupied back in front.

"Are you ready for the last round, Elsie?" asks Master Wildman. "She'll be up."

"Yes. I think I am," says Elsie. "I think I am." But she suddenly looks in the smallest way doubtful, and there is a silence.

"I say, Elsie," says Master Wildman, suddenly. "May I kiss you?"

"Kiss me?" says Elsie, looking into his eyes, and far away beyond them. "But why do you want to?"

"Oh, I don't know, Elsie. Because you're so beautiful, I suppose. And after all we've gone through together to-day, Elsie. It's only right, isn't it? Please, Elsie."

Nearly half a minute goes by before they speak again.

"Now I'm ready," says Elsie, "for the last round."

VIII

There is an envelope on the hall table.

"Will you read it?" says Elsie, and hands it to him.

Master Wildman tears it open and reads it to himself:

"Apparently you have thought yourself too old for what you will now receive. You will either leave this house or take off that thing and come into my room the instant you return. Your Mother."

"What does it say?"

"Only obscenities," says Master Wildman, and tears it up. "But you're to go up to her. . . ."

"You're ready for a bit of a fight, Elsie, I suppose?" asks Master Wildman mysteriously.

"Yes. I'm ready," whispers Elsie.

"Nails in good condition?" asks Master Wildman, and looks at them in his hand. "Go along then, Elsie."

"Very well," says Elsie, and goes up the stairs, Master Wildman following.

Elsie runs down again and shakes his hand.

"How do you do, Elsie."

"Good-bye," says Elsie.

"Good-bye," says Master Wildman.

Elsie goes first of all into her room, and lights the gas. Then she walks nervously up and down for a little, looking at the floor. And as she does this there comes a memory—a memory that grows upon her with every stride she takes—a memory of the little girl of long ago, who was sent by one of her mother's level glances to her room. The little girl who spent the time of waiting in walking up and down, wringing her terrified hands, and watching her scalding tears of shame coursing down, in the glass. And as Elsie casts away these memories, and looks down at her legs, shapely in silk, she can hardly credit their firmness and strength. . . . She was such a little pigmy then. . . .

And then, all at once, she sees her bobbed hair and her straight flying figure in her ardent evening dress—her evening dress! And the dark memories flash suddenly back, with all their shame, and all their hidden hatred, and all their base hypocrisy and cruelty, and there is a little catch in her breath as she knows she is an Amazon now, and her moment has come!

She goes straight out of the room, and knocks at her mother's door. "Come in," says her mother, and Elsie obeys.

Mrs. Nixon is in the dark. But her white night-dress glimmers theatrically from the armchair by the chest of drawers. And on the white cloth of the chest of drawers, lies the Stick.

"Ah, I thought we'd come to heel," says mother.

"Shut the door, please, Elsie."

Elsie obeys but makes no answer.

"Now, Elsie," says mother. "I'll hear your excuses, if you have any."

Elsie makes no answer.

"I said I'll hear your excuses, Elsie."

Elsie makes no answer at all.

"I see you've still that thing on. I told you to take that off, Elsie," says mother.

"Go and take it off, and then come back to me."

Elsie makes no answer at all.

"Did you hear what I said, Elsie?"

Elsie makes no answer at all, but there is the sound of deep breathing in the dark.

Mother continues in a hoarse voice. "You got my note, Elsie, and you didn't bargain for what I'm going to do now, did you? You thought you'd got beyond it, didn't you, Miss? But you haven't, my pretty lady, do you hear me?" Mother rises and seizes the stick. "And the whole house

shall hear it, Elsie, the whole house shall hear it! And then
you shall apologise to me, before them all!"

The deep breathing intensifies in the dark. Mrs. Nixon
goes on in softer tones again.

"Are you going to take it off, Miss? Or am I going to
flog it off your back? Come, my lady, I give you a minute
to decide."

The deep breathing subsides, and there is complete silence
by the door.

Suddenly "Take that thing off!" cries mother, and makes
a dive for it.

And then Elsie comes out with it.

"Don't you touch my dress!" shouts Elsie. "If you
touch my dress I'll kill you!"

She snatches the stick from her mother's trembling hands,
and brandishes it in front of her, until Mrs. Nixon recoils
back on to the bed.

"Give me that stick, you filthy little snake!"

"*What?*" says Elsie, and smashes the stick down on to
the counterpane with a crack like a pistol's. "*What* did
you call me?"

"Filthy little snake!"

"*What* did you call me?" cries Elsie, and smashes it down
again, already alive to its uses. "What!"

"Filthy little snake!"

Smash!

"And why am I that, please?"

There is a pause.

"Letting him buy you things."

"Oh, that," says Elsie, smiling.

"Yes. That. He only did it not to be disgraced by
your dirty looks."

"Maybe," says Elsie. "Anyway, he's just kissed me."

"Kissed *you!* Ha, ha, ha!"

"Yes. Shall I go and call him, to ask him if he did?"

"Give me that stick!"

"All right. I'll give it to you," says Elsie, and seizes it
firmly in both her Amazon's hands.

It breaks with a sound snap.

"There you are," says Elsie.

Mrs. Nixon is now making choking noises on the bed.

"It's no use your getting hysterical," says Elsie. . . . "It's
no use your getting hysterical. . . ."

There is an interval in which Mrs. Nixon becomes more hysterical still, but nevertheless succeeds in muttering certain not very clear imprecations under her breath.

"I'm tall now," says Elsie, in misty tones, and really looks it, as she stands there, for the first time in her life. "Taller than you. And I'm young. I'm young. And you're not going to make me old any more. I'm sorry if I was rude, but I'm not going to be made old any more!"

It is Elsie's moment. She wears more than a queenly and self-reliant look now. She is a queen entire. And lifting her figure even higher than a queen might have to, and wearing a little dim smile that all the more charming queens might have worn, she delivers herself of her last remark on the matter.

"And *that*," says Elsie, "will *teach* you—never to *dare*—to tear my green dress through again!"

She leaves the room, shuts the door, reaches her bed, falls upon it, and takes to tears.

CHAPTER VIII

Mr. Wildman gets better than he Deserves, and is the First to Admit it. An Eclipse.

I

THERE having been no worldly person in a position to indicate the futilities of a twenty-four-year-old Master Wildman besieging the West End of London with a manuscript, there is brought up to Master Wildman, the morning after his adventures with Elsie, a letter. Bertha, who brings it to him, says that it has been at No. 12 Keymer Gardens (it is so addressed) and the people there have only just sent it over.

It is a letter from Mr. Eugene Layburn of the Empress Theatre, and it is in Mr. Layburn's own hand. The general contents of it are that Mr. Layburn is very much interested in "Afterthought" (he calls it "Afterthought" just as though it is a real play); he was to have opened in Manchester shortly, with another play; but a hitch has arisen in that quarter, and he would be glad to see Master Wildman at once. Mr.

Layburn is still at the Empress with "Undertow," and if Mr. Wildman will look in any time during a *matinée*, or in the evening, after receiving this, Mr. Layburn will be only too glad to see him.

Master Wildman says nothing about this to Elsie—who is very white, and whose mother is staying in bed for the day—but he takes a little walk around Keymer Gardens, looking entrancedly at a stolid No. 12, sends a wire to the City, has lunch out, and goes at half-past three to The Empress Theatre, Charing Cross.

Master Wildman is not much given to nervousness, but he is nervous enough as he endeavours in vain to explain his business through glass to a photograph-surrounded and electric-lit deity at the stage-door; who at last comes surlily out to ask him what he wants; and he is nervous enough as he says he wants Mr. Layburn and his name is Wildman. He is more nervous still as he waits ten minutes in the stone passage while this request is taken up by a pale boy to Mr. Layburn, who is said to be "On" at the moment. But a message comes down at last that Mr. Wildman is to go up, and the pale boy conducts him up the stairs to a little mirrored room simply stewing in electric light and grease-paint.

Here numerous sounds from the stage filter through—the sound of spasmodic raised voices, the sound of thudding, the sound of coughing, the sound of death shrieks (apparently), and finally the low rumbling down of the curtain on the first act of "Undertow." Then comes the sound of what seems at first to be a lot of hard peas being shaken in a box, but is eventually recognised as the sound of clapping. Then Mr. Layburn's well-known voice is heard shouting gaily to a friend in the passage outside, and Mr. Layburn enters to Master Wildman.

Mr. Layburn is a large, autumnal man with a husky voice which is partly due to a pose in Mr. Layburn, but partly death shrieks. He is painted like a savage, and dressed in Victorian costume for "Undertow." He is very autumnal with Master Wildman, and comes straight to the point. He has been most surprised he has not heard from Mr. Wildman, and has indeed sent him another letter this morning, and a wire this afternoon. . . . The point, however, is that he was to have opened at Manchester with a play called "Dead Letter Office" but the thing had fallen through. Disagreements had arisen. He is very much intrigued by Mr. Wildman's play, which has been passed on to him by his reader, Mr. Yates, and he proposes putting it on instead of "Dead Letter Office." If Mr. Wildman's play had not come along, he would, of course, have done "Le Dernier Cri" as usual— (this was the play Mr. Layburn had made his larger reputation with, and almost invariably played in the provinces)—but he wanted to avoid that if possible, this time. . . . Of course, it will be a great rush to get it on in the time, but he has his usual touring cast about him, and he has the exact set (only one set, thank God), and he has practically got it into rehearsal, he admits, already. He would have written to Mr. Wildman before, only it has all been such a rush, and "One has to be kind of Napoleonic, in this wretched business," says Mr. Layburn, "or you don't get anywhere." If Master Wildman approves they can sign up to-morrow. . . .

Mr. Layburn then makes a few suggestions on the subject of the play itself; dwells upon Sympathies rather lost—Mr. Layburn thinks—in the last act, and wants to cut a large portion (in which Mr. Layburn does not appear) of the second. "These Middle Acts," says Mr. Layburn. . . . "Always the same. You read the first act and want to rush out to the nearest 'phone for the author, and then you come to the Second. . . ." And that is really all. That is a great idea of Mr. Wildman's about the Telephone at the end, and a splendid twist about the man turning round like that. . . . Gets you clean. How did he hit upon it? Mr. Wildman will be interested to hear that the Lord Chamberlain has passed his play, with the proviso that the line about the Prince of Wales is deleted, and that "the too frequent use of the word Blasted"—Mr. Layburn reads from the statement —shall be seen to.

A rather loosely dressed lady with an umbrella enters at this stage, and seems to be Mr. Layburn's wife.

"Ah, dear. This is Mr. Wildman."

"Oh, so pleased to see you, Mr. Wildman. We've been wondering why you haven't been along. We're so interested in your play."

"I suppose you've been in this business some time, then, Mr. Wildman?" asks Mr. Layburn.

"Oh, no, I haven't really?"

"Really?" says Mr. Layburn, looking hard at his visitor.

"Mr. Layburn, please!" shouts the pale boy, knocking sharply on the door.

"That's me," says Mr. Layburn. "Well, if I don't see you again, I'll forward the contract to-morrow. And if I want you for anything I suppose I can wire. You're two, not twelve, aren't you? . . . Yes. . . . Well. . . . Good-bye."

Mr. Layburn and Mr. Wildman shake hands. Mr. Layburn vanishes.

Master Wildman does not know whether he is supposed to remain chatting with Mrs. Layburn, but after a difficult silence Mrs. Layburn comes out with the rather baffling statement that she thinks "plays are very interesting things, aren't they?"

Master Wildman admits they are, in rather hysterical tones, and also admits that he is quite at a loss—Mr. Layburn taking his play like this, and so suddenly. He imagined that "Afterthought," was just one of the usual plays everybody wrote, and kept in a drawer. He never dreamed, when he sent it in . . . Such admissions as these Master Wildman does not make when he has been a little longer in the profession he has so swimmingly entered, and Mrs. Layburn stares at him a little.

"Oh, but I think it's so very good," answers Mrs. Layburn, smiling. "And things do fall out like that, don't they?"

"In this business," adds Mrs. Layburn. "It's so . . . isn't it?"

When Master Wildman at last emerges from the Empress Theatre, he carries all the natural stupefaction of a young man hearing that his play is to be produced, by one of the best-known (if most critic-scoffed) actor-managers in London, almost at once. There is a slight sense of shame, too; and a lorry driver sarcastically asks him whether he thinks he is having a whist drive, or something, in the middle of the street.

There is Craven House to tell, of course, and he does it at dinner. He lets them down as lightly as he can, for Young Men in Cities rather seem to have demonstrated that they do know their own business best, after all. . . .

Miss Hatt and Mrs. Spicer are joyful, but have a little jealous glassiness about the eye. Mrs. Nixon (down for dinner) says nothing at all, but is also glassy. Elsie is all bliss, but just a little vague in manner after dinner—which may be due to the awful and smouldering terms she is on with her mother, but which may be due to musings upon what an enriched Wildman's relations with a Cotterell will be. Mrs. Hoare is again in tears of joy, but swears she

knew it, she knew it all along, and talks of going to Manchester.
Mr. Spicer, after wishing Master Wildman all success in
the world, says: "Not in London, then?"

"No," says Master Wildman. "Though he say he'll bring
it to Town if it goes well in the North. There's Blackpool
after Manchester, and Edinburgh, Sheffield, York, and Liver-
pool, and Cardiff for sure. Of course, it's all frightfully
unfair. When you think of all the other fellows. . . ."

"Yes," admits Mr. Spicer.

"Fellows really working at it, you know. Rotten. Really,"
says Master Wildman. . . .

Injustice can be a rather exalted affair. . . .

II

And as though all these revolutionary and astonishing
incidents are not enough, as though that wrecking and disintegrating fate (which has been at work ever since Audrey
first began to Answer Back), has tasted blood, as it were,
and can never be at peace until it has undermined the whole
structure of Craven House—it now delivers a crushing blow
upon the light and mainstay of the establishment, our
Tea Merchant, and it delivers it the next day, which is a
Saturday.

It is a Saturday, and there is going to be (the newspapers
say) an Eclipse of the Sun, and Mr. Spicer is at home, all
day, in great spirits, and it is a day that Mrs. Spicer never
forgets.

It is a bright day, and the household is in a great flutter
at breakfast time over the celestial entertainment about to
be provided. Mrs. Hoare is at first a trifle doubtful as to
whether They'll Do it, when it comes to the point, but her
suspicions are immediately crushed by Miss Hatt, who points
out that an Eclipse is Science, after all, when you come to
think about it—with which everyone agrees, and most of the
morning is spent in preparations.

Mr. Spicer quietly and at an early stage appoints himself
Eclipse Master, and is very soon seen fixing a managerial eye
upon the sun, as though it is all a private theatrical arrangement between it and himself, and he commands that a bucket
of water shall be brought, and put in the middle of the
garden. This he readjusts himself, to his own liking, and
he gazes technically at it, as though it is a work of art, for a

long while. He then goes down to the kitchen, looks about
for bits of broken glass, finds various dangerous edges, which
he draws a little blood with, in a casual way, and commences
to smoke, upon a candle. He is then bandaged by his wife,
who tells him she can't bear to see him going on Sucking
at it. Then Miss Hatt rushes in gleefully with a bit of yellow
gelatine, and a bit of green gelatine, and Mr. Spicer accepts
the green gelatine, but banishes the yellow gelatine, and says
that what we really want is a bit of blue gelatine. Then
Mrs. Hoare says she's got the very thing. and rushes mysteriously upstairs, to return ten minutes later with a telescope,
which Mr. Spicer at first rejects politely, but begins to look
wistfully in the direction of the candle. Whereupon Mrs.
Spicer says she hopes he doesn't think he's going to start
Burning People's Telescopes; to which Mr. Spicer replies he
never had any idea of Burning People's Telescopes, but does,
when the ladies are out of the room, immediately proceed
severely to Burn Mrs. Hoare's Telescope; stating, in a curious
voice on the return of the ladies, that he thought he might
give it a Bit of a Smoking. Then there is a long argument
as to whether he shall Buy Mrs. Hoare Another Telescope, and
Mrs. Spicer says he shall, and Mrs. Hoare says he shan't, and
calls Mrs. Spicer a Fool. Mrs. Spicer says Well, it is very
nice of her to take it like that, and Mr. Spicer puts in a
pathetic plea that he thinks he remembers noticing That
Mark on it Before, and the matter is settled. Mrs. Spicer
asks if he's going to Go Burning Anything Else this morning,
and Mrs. Hoare asks when he'll let them see it, and Mr. Spicer
tells them "Not till 1.25," and comparative calm prevails.

A light lunch is taken early, and after lunch they all go
out into the garden, stare at the bucket, blink at the sun,
and talk gaily, until the manager, who holds the telescope,
suddenly announces that it is nearly due.

The deathly edges are handed tensely round. (Master
Wildman offers one to Mrs. Nixon, but the offer is ignored,
and she goes very silently over to a corner of the garden
by herself, without an edge at all. Master Wildman offers
it to Elsie instead, and stays by her.) The servants are
called, and told to be quick; they arrive, apron-wiping, and
a deep silence falls. . . .

A deep silence falls, and nobody speaks.

"It's late," whispers Mrs. Hoare. "It's late."

"No. Be patient," says Mr. Spicer.

"It's late!" insists Mrs. Hoare, and there does seem to be some sort of hitch somewhere. . . .

There is a long silence, in which Bertha begins to wheeze madly for shame. But the others are forgivingly silent; and the centre of the Universe, rather red in the face (metaphorically speaking), makes a very great effort indeed to fulfil the programme according to schedule.

Mrs. Hoare mutters that this is a fine state of affairs. . . .

"H'm," says Mr. Spicer, and removes the telescope from his eye, rather inclined to shout up and ask what's the matter. When "Here we go," says Master Wildman. . . .

And sure enough, a slightly apologetic sun, having looked as though it was going to make a bit of a fool of itself, after all its promises, gracefully begins to perform, as if it knew quite well that it could, if it hadn't been bothered in the first place.

"Where?" shouts Mrs. Hoare. "I can't see it!"

"Look," says Mr. Spicer.

"I can't see it! *I* can't see it!"

"Look through mine," says Elsie.

"Oh!" cries Mrs. Hoare. "I don't call that an Eclipse!"

"Look, ma'am," says Edith. "It ain't 'alf at it."

"Oh, I don't call that an Eclipse," says Mrs. Hoare.

Edith intimates that Eclipses ain't never much, not to look at, and Mrs. Hoare, looking rather unhappy, supposes that it's all Electricity, then.

"Moon," says Mr. Spicer, learnedly, under his telescope.

"Who's last from school?" asks Miss Hatt, under her green gelatine.

"Quite simple, really," says Mr. Spicer, and gives an explanation. The moon, it transpires, goes around the earth, and the earth goes around the sun, and what is going to happen when that ha pens? Why, when the moon is in a certain position, and the sun is in a certain position, the moon, obviously, is going to Get In Between, and you'll have an Eclipse.

Mrs. Hoare wants to know what the Moon thinks about it all.

"It prob'ly don't think nothin', ma'am," says Edith, who knows the way of heavenly bodies.

And after this the interest begins to fall away a little. The earth is no darker as yet, and does not show much promise of becoming so, and Miss Hatt suggests to the servants that

that will be all, and they retire satisfied. Master Wildman says that he thinks it "quite a good Eclipse," and is the only one inclined to linger; but Miss Cotterell calls round for him in her car, as has been arranged. Elsie goes back to her knitting.

Mrs. Spicer says she wants to do some cleaning, and tells Mr. Spicer that if he will give her those coats of his, she will see what she can do with them. "Yes, my dear," he says, in a jolly tone, and they go to their room together. Mr. Spicer takes manifold old garments from the cupboard, taps them easily to see there are no moth, or letters or anything, secreted therein, and says he thinks he will be getting off. "Where are you going, then?" "Oh, just for a little stroll. If I'm not in to tea, don't wait." "Very well," says Mrs. Spicer, and she is left to herself.

The earth, by this time, has taken on a mellow, sweet, bright golden colour, and the sparrows are screeching, screeching somewhere, far away; and there is a strange, excited sense of the sad beauty of all things upon Mrs. Spicer, as she fetches the petrol, and chooses a rag, and considers the work in front of her. "Start on the worst," says Mrs. Spicer, and picks up the oldest coat of all, which reminds her of sunny bicycling days, years before the war, when Mr. Spicer was newly married to her. He has worn it occasionally since, but not often, and the talk, and dust, and laughter of those days echo dimly in Mrs. Spicer's brain, as she picks it up and shakes it, to see that there are no moth, or letters or anything, secreted therein.

And now the earth is taking on a deeper, more truly golden colour, with the threat of doom in its slanting light. And the sparrows are screeching, creeching, screeching, somewhere far away, in wild protests at it. "It *is* coming over," says Mrs. Spicer, and rustles the coat again.

A faint crackling responds from its dark satin lining.

"What's this?" says Mrs. Spicer, humming, and she puts her hand into the lining.

She withdraws an old, grease-shiny envelope, inscribed, in a slow but sincerely hard-working hand:—

> "Mr. Spiser Esquire,
>   5 Penny Lane,
>   London, E.C.4."

Mrs. Spicer hums as she opens it. Mrs. Spicer glances at the beginning of the letter, and glances at the end of the letter, and at the beginning of the letter she reads: "Dear Mr. Spiser," and at the end of the letter she reads:

> "From your little companion,
> "CATHERINE TILLOTSON."

Mrs. Spicer leaves off humming, and all at once the birds leave off their screeching. The earth lies with breathless expectancy under the light of a reddening sun that is like the last sun on the last day of the earth. Mrs. Hoare comes out into the garden, laughing up at the darkness, with Elsie.

Mrs. Spicer closes her eyes for a moment, and draws in her breath. Then she begins to read.

> "596 Delancey Street,
> Camden Town.
> Wednesday evening

"DEAR MR. SPISER

"I was much pleased to Receive your letter of the 12th ins but I have shown to my friend and she says I must write and ask what you mean as at present it leaves in doubt as it does not explain My friend says I must write and ask what you mean by me. . . ."

Mrs. Spicer closes her eyes again, and puts the letter down. Mrs. Hoare's footsteps are scrunching the gravel in the garden, as she walks up and down with Elsie. Miss Hatt is humming at a cupboard, just outside the door. . . . Mrs. Spicer continues.

"I do not wish to go hard with noone but I must not make myself cheap can I and I am a doctor's daughter as you know though I am only eighteen and my friend says I am a lady and must see I am treated as a lady or I will Be made to look cheap And I am a good girl realy and all the other girls in the park know it, as they said only last night they wonder a girl like me goes in there when she might Be somewhere else as she is a doctor's daughter and there is no need for *her* to go in there, and my friend says the same as she knows And she says that if you wish me to go into rooms where we can Be quiet with each other you must give me

something regular as a lady cannot manage to subcist on a
little preasant now and again when she is a lady and not like
others And Mr. Kelly has said again he will take me to
New York only last night soon if he gets his deal through
as he expects and that will Be nice So if you will write me
please to above address by the return and say what you
intend by me And if you can aford something weakly like
it will Be nice, as we could have very pleasant times together
and it would Be pleaseant and I will for the present sign
myself

> "Your little companion,
> "Catherine Tillotson."

"P.S. After I saw you last night I met two boys who
took me out to Richmond in their car it was so nice I am a
little bloto tonight as I write as they have all been giveing
me more than is good."

Mrs. Spicer closes her eyes and keeps them closed. Miss
Hatt is still humming at the cupboard outside. . . .

Miss Hatt knocks at the door, and thrusts her head round
it. She carries towels over her arm.

"*There's* an Eclipse for you—if you like!" says Miss Hatt,
and goes as suddenly as she came.

III

All such vain and unprofitable questioning as to Where
he Picked her Up, or What on Earth Induced him, or How
Ever he Could, or If he had Always, or How far he had Gone,
being sad questionings and problems gone over by Mrs.
Spicer for years after the event, without any satisfactory
answers ever coming to light, we will confine ourselves to
relating the mere incident of our involved Tea merchant's
downfall before his wife, and the confrontation with his
sin.

Mr. Spicer does not return to tea in the afternoon, but
Mrs. Spicer is perfectly and smilingly calm when she comes
down to it herself.

After tea she goes out for a long walk, as far as Hammersmith, and back again.

When she returns her husband has returned as well. He
himself is in immense spirits, and very garrulous. Mrs. Spicer

makes no attempt whatever to damp his mood, dealing out affirmatives equally to him and the Universe, and smiling just as usual.

After dinner Mr. Spicer soon begins to stretch himself, and "Oh-ah-ah!" and blink from the depths of his arm-chair, and asks his wife if she is friendly to the idea of retiring early. Mrs. Spicer is agreeable to that idea, and is told by Miss Hatt that she is looking rather white.

"Am I?"

"Yes, she is white, isn't she?"

"Oh, well, I've had a tiring day. Let's come along."

They both go to their room.

Here Mr. Spicer at once becomes garrulous again. Mrs. Spicer says not a word. Mr. Spicer ignores her silence.

Mr. Spicer performs all his undressing actions in a perfectly usual way. That is to say, Mr. Spicer removes his shirt and vest, lays his nightshirt carefully over the bed, dives, and emerges with a swimmer's action, and having shaken the thing well down, performs the ensuing phases of disrobe-ment quietly under its flowing and voluminous cover—the trousers and socks thus shed not appearing until he steps away. Mr. Spicer talks all the time he is doing this; and his appearance at the end of it is, as usual, that of a slightly soiled and long-suffering prophet—but for a certain default in dignity occasioned by a certain blue Cricket Cap, which Mr. Spicer these days wears as a protection from the chills of night, and which is a sharply undignified characteristic.

Mrs. Spicer, who is doing her hair in the glass, comes out with it quite suddenly. She asks him how Miss Catherine Tillotson is getting along.

"Catherine Tillotson, my dear?" says Mr. Spicer, in all innocence, five years having elapsed since his dealings with Catherine Tillotson.

"Oh, don't you know?" Mrs. Spicer is tugging away at her hair.

Mr. Spicer loses his colour.

"Who's Catherine Tillotson?" asks Mr. Spicer. . . .

"Catherine Tillotson?" pursues Mr. Spicer.

Mrs. Spicer leaves her hair, jumps up, and punches him in the face.

They look at each other.

Mrs. Spicer again punches him in the face.

Mr. Spicer limply requests not to be punched in the face.

Mrs. Spicer again punches him in the face, and looks at him in another silence.

"My dear," protests Mr. Spicer. "I think you're Upset."

Mrs. Spicer hysterically asks him if he thinks he is Playing a Cricket Match, and commands him to take that thing off his head, or she will knock it off.

Mr. Spicer stares at her as a rabbit is said to stare at a snake. The cricket cap is knocked off, flying.

"I can *see* you're upset, my dear," says Mr. Spicer.

Mrs. Spicer repeats the words "Upset, indeed!" five or six times with increasing savagery, and drives her man, feebly protesting that he "only took her to a cinema," before her.

Mrs. Spicer repeats the word "Cinema!" five or six times with increasing savagery.

Mr. Spicer makes a soft parenthetical plea on the subject of Spitting; but he is over-ridden by a torrent of abuse. Among other things, Mrs. Spicer calls him a low crawler, a slimy snail, a snarling insect unworthy of tying her (Mrs. Spicer's) "latches," a slinking cur, and a French libertine. She ends up on a top note by calling him a Brothel. Mr. Spicer weakly demurs that he is not a Brothel, and Mrs. Spicer shouts that he *is* a Brothel in a manner no gentleman would like to contradict.

"You don't know the meaning of the word Brothel," murmurs Mr. Spicer. Mrs. Spicer pauses, rather dashed, and weakens her position by asking what a Brothel is, then.

"It's a Place, my dear."

"Then you're all the *more* a Brothel!" shouts Mrs. Spicer.

"Very well, then, my dear. I *am* a Brothel, if you say I am." ("You *are*," says Mrs. Spicer.)

Mr. Spicer is heard muttering the word Dictionary.

"I'll give you all the dictionaries you want in a minute! Personally, I never use such filthy words. I'm not a low snarker like you!"

At this moment a knock falls on the door, and Mrs. Spicer flings it open. Miss Hatt is standing outside with a letter in her hand. "I've had a most funny letter to-night, dear," says Miss Hatt, and looks vaguely through Mrs. Spicer at a wretched Tea merchant sitting on the bed.

"Oh—what's that?" says Mrs. Spicer, protecting her husband from the caller's eyes with her body.

"A Russian coming here, my dear. To-morrow evening."

"Oh?"

"It's all in this letter. She was to have gone to Miss Creed, but she can't put her up, and so I'm having to do it."

"Oh, that's very interesting. We'll have to talk about her." Mrs. Spicer puts a stop to further vaguenesses on Miss Hatt's part, by softly smiling, and closing the door in her face.

"Russian, my dear?" says Mr. Spicer, in great astonishment.

"Don't you try and Russian *me!*" says Mrs. Spicer. "If you're so keen on Russians, perhaps you can Russian yourself out of Catherine Tillotson!"

"I'm not Russianing myself out of anybody, my dear. It's you that's doing all the Russianing. I only took her to a Cinema after all."

Mrs. Spicer now says that it is no use his Cinemaing her, and Mr. Spicer returns that if she would only listen . . .

Mrs. Spicer bellows that she has done enough listening to him, and what she is going to do now is to Divorce him. She immediately flings herself into bed with him, to emphasise her decision, and orders him to put out the light. Mr. Spicer resumes his blue cricket cap, by slow and apologetic stages, and with a watchful eye upon the lady who has taken such a dislike to it. The light goes out.

And now that the light is out there is little more to be said—or little more to clarify the situation in any way.

We will confine ourselves to noticing that Mr. Spicer touches Mrs. Spicer, in the darkness, without result: that Mr. Spicer again touches Mrs. Spicer, and thinks she must be upset: that Mrs. Spicer wriggles away so sharply as to fall half out of bed; that there is a very grappling and suspended moment in the darkness: and that Mrs. Spicer, apparently saved, says that perhaps he is trying to drive her out of her own bed now, is he?

That Mr. Spicer says: "No, my dear, but I think you must be upset," and that Mrs. Spicer does not reply.

That Mr. Spicer says that if she would only listen. . . .

That Mr. Spicer swears that he only took her to the cinema, because she was a poor girl, and that it was all a mistake on her part, writing letters and so on. . . .

That Mrs. Spicer says that she is not listening to One Word he is saying, and that he can Poor Girl her until he is Blue in the Face, if he likes, but she is not listening, and perhaps he will allow her a little sleep.

That Mr. Spicer says that Mrs. Spicer must be out of her head.

That Mrs. Spicer says she is too much in it for a French libertine's liking.

That Mrs. Spicer adds that if Mr. Spicer was half a man he would go out and shoot himself, with a gun.

That Mr. Spicer, after a thoughtful silence in which he seems to be contemplating the suggestion, nullifies that impression by asking if a man isn't going to be allowed any bed-clothes. That Mrs. Spicer intimates that possibly Miss Catherine Tillotson will give him some bed-clothes, and that Mrs. Spicer suddenly flings all the bed-clothes at Mr. Spicer, submerging that protesting personality, and as suddenly gathers them in again, Mr. Spicer managing to retain a square foot or so.

That there is a long, dark silence.

That Mrs. Spicer begins to cry.

That Mr. Spicer says she will have to go on crying, if she will not listen to reason.

That Mrs. Spicer cries for half an hour without a word from her man, and at last gives a long sigh, and goes off to sleep; and that Mr. Spicer after looking up at the ceiling, chin over sheet, in a blue cricket cap, for another half hour, drops off into a heavy sleep himself.

CHAPTER IX

A Russian. The Dark Hour before Dinner.

I

AND now, on the shoulders of all this—with Mrs. Nixon on smouldering and deadly silent terms with a now rather terrified Elsie, who has burnt her ships—with Master Wildman in a fever over his play in regard to its effects upon Miss Cotterell, though he has not, for some reason absolutely unknown, yet told her about it—with Mr. Spicer pathetically touching Mrs. Spicer at every private moment of the day, only to get his head bitten off—and with Miss Hatt in a state of nerves at which we have hardly yet hinted (she has kept them down so well hitherto)—on the shoulders of all this, and as though that wrecking and disintegrating fate is not content with its wicked work alone, but must put out its tongue to mock at them—comes the Russian, and she comes the next evening.

She is simply there, when they come down to dinner. She is dark, and she is about thirty, and she is very shy, and willing to smile at you and say Please, she does not understand. She reduces half-a-dozen living creatures to frozen inarticulation. Miss Hatt says her name is Miss Strarley F. "Miss Strarley F," says Miss Hatt. "Mrs. Spicer." Miss Strarley F. bows—Mrs. Spicer bows. "Miss Strarley F—Mr. Spicer." Miss Strarley F. bows—Mr. Spicer bows. Miss Hatt does this to every one of them, and all bow. Then Miss Hatt bows herself, like an opera singer, and the company as a whole is inclined to bow again, in general, until Miss Hatt adjusts her chair with a sweet smile, and a delicate (but operatic) sweep, and sits down in it—her example being taken by the others. A silence falls.

"Colder to-night," says Mr. Spicer.

We smile blushingly, and glance over at the Russian lady, as much as to ask her what she can do with that. The Russian lady gives a charming smile all round, and goes on with her soup.

"Colder, I expect," suggests Miss Hatt, "in Russia?"

"Please?"

"Colder," says Miss Hatt, raising her voice a little. "Colder in Russia. You are Cold in Russia."

"No, I am Varm. I am Varm."

"But you are Cold," insists Miss Hatt. "In Russia."

"In Russia," explains Mr. Spicer. "Cold."

"No, no! Russia is Varm. Very Varm. Very Varm. I am Varm in Russia!"

"Ah, I always thought Russia was Cold."

"No, no. Russia Varm. Russia Varm. Cold in weenter, but Russia Varm."

"Oh, I see."

"Please?"

"I see."

There is a silence of recuperation.

"Do you have Meals—?" asks Miss Hatt—"Meals. Meals. *Meals*——" and "Please?" asks the Russian lady.

"*Meals* like this—*This*," continues Miss Hatt. "In Russia?"

"I have meals, yes, I have meals."

There is another silence.

"I have meals," repeats a rather obtuse Russian lady, in the silence.

"Steppes," says Master Wildman, *a propos* of nothing. . . .

"Oh, yes. Steppes," says Mr. Spicer. "What are Steppes? Hanged if I know. Ask her, Bertha."

"In Russia," commences Miss Hatt, leaning over.

"Yes, please?"

"In Russia you have Steppes," announced Miss Hatt. "Steppes. Steppes. Steppes!"

"I have no Steppes."

"She has no Steppes," says Master Wildman, and there is another recuperative pause.

Mrs. Hoare wants to know if that isn't where they have Siberia.

"Ah! Siberia! Siberia! Yess?"

"In Russia," says Miss Hatt. "Russia. Russia. Russia, they send them to Siberia, do they Not?"

"Please?"

"It's difficult, isn't it?"

"Let me try, Bertha," says Mr. Spicer.

Mr. Spicer pauses.

"Siberia," says Mr. Spicer, as a general principle.

"Yess?"

"You. Siberia. Russia," says Mr. Spicer, as another sound basis for argument.

"Yess?"

"*You,*" says Mr. Spicer, pointing at her, "are sent to Siberia."

"Oh, yess! Ha, ha, ha!"

"Ha, ha, ha!" laughs Master Wildman.

"Quite easy if you go slow," says Mr. Spicer.

"Please?"

"You — have — not — been — sent — to — Siberia — though," says Mrs. Spicer, by way of a joke.

"Please. I do not understan'."

"In—Russia—you—are sent—to Siberia. But you—you, *you*—are *not* sent to Siberia."

"No, I have not bee sent to Siberia."

"She's learning," says Mrs. Hoare.

"But you *would,*" says Mr. Spicer. "If you were——"

"Please?"

"But you *would* be sent to Siberia," repeats Mr. Spicer, "if you were——"

"Impertinent to the Czar," offers Master Wildman. . . .

"Please?"

"If," says Mr. Spicer, "you were Impertinent—Rude—to the Czar, you would have been Sent to Siberia."

"But I am not rude to Czar," protests a Russian lady, seeing light at rather an awkward moment.

"No, you *are* not rude to Czar," says Mr. Spicer. "But If!"

"But zere is no Czar, please."

"No, no, zere *is* no Czar, but if zere *was* a Czar!" complains a tortured Mr. Spicer.

"I do not understan', please."

"Perhaps she speaks French," says Miss Hatt.

The time comes for Mr. Spicer to ask us if we will have any more meat.

"Will you have some more, Miss Strarley F?" asks Miss Hatt.

"Please?"

"Have? More?" says Mr. Spicer.

"Please?"

"More? Have?" explains Mr. Spicer, waving his arms about this time, as though that would help matters.

"Oh, ye-e-e-ess! Ha! Ha! Ha!

"You *will?*"

"Oh, ye-e-e-ess! Ha, ha, ha! Ha, ha, ha!" laughs a Russian lady, who can see a joke when it is put to her.

The guests look at each other. No. She doesn't understand. Let's have another try, shall we? Softly this time. . . .

"*Will*," says Miss Hatt indomitably.

"Yess," returns the Russian lady, with all solemnity.

"*You*," says Miss Hatt, throwing an infinity of significance into the word.

"Yess."

"*Have*."

"Yess," whispers a breathless Russian lady, when Mr. Spicer cuts in and spoils it all.

"*Meat! More! Have! You!*" shouts Mr. Spicer, as though inspired; but since Mr. Spicer is merely turning the required statement upside down, which is necessarily confusing to a foreign mentality, we are back to where we started from.

"Give her some more, Clifford," says Miss Hatt.

The Russian lady is not spoken to during the remainder of the meal, except when she is passed things operatically and bowingly by her beaming neighbours, who are all at once the most continental dogs on earth. Mrs. Hoare, also, being too far to pass things, is to be seen bowing at her from time to time, to be in the movement, and a very polite atmosphere is kept up, in spite of the silence.

But when Miss Hatt arises, and the others rise with her, a Russian lady keeps her seat and looks rather lost. The others realise that all will be well if she is left alone to follow, but Miss Hatt foolishly goes over to her, so giving the impression that something more serious (and, maybe, peculiarly English) is afoot.

"We go," says Miss Hatt, "into the drawing-room after we have had our dinner."

"Please?"

"We go——" begins Miss Hatt, but Mr. Spicer takes it up.

"Room. Drawing. Go. We!" says Mr. Spicer. "Drawing."

"It is our Habit," interprets Mrs. Nixon.

"Habit. Custom. We go. Sit. Talk. Habit," says Mr. Spicer. "Little Custom. English."

"Please?"

"Habit. English. Go. Not in Russia—perhaps. English. We go. Come."

"Perhaps she's mad," whispers Mrs. Hoare.

"She won't come, will she now?" says Miss Hatt. "I don't think you understand, Miss Strarley F. We go In."

"In," says Mr. Spicer. "In."

"She won't come, will she?" says Miss Hatt.

But at this moment Elsie comes forward, smiles at a smiling and misted Russian lady, takes her softly by the hand, waits for her to rise, and leads her quietly into the drawing-room, and seats her before the fire.

A laboured evening is spent.

II

We have given the last little dinner scene in some detail so as to demonstrate the nature of the nerve-tearing labours imposed upon Craven House at a moment when its whole structure is hanging by a thread; and to extenuate, if such a thing is possible, the disgraceful public explosion that is to follow. And we should recall, once more and as further extenuation, the relations existing between guest and guest, and Miss Hatt at this critical conjuncture.

Mrs. Nixon, then, is on smouldering and deadly silent terms with Elsie, who is now rather terrified, having burnt her ships.

Master Wildman is in a fever over his play, in regard to its effects upon Miss Cotterell; though he has not, for reasons absolutely unknown, yet told her about it. On Saturday night there has been a mention of his play in the *Evening Standard*, headed "Young Author" and reading—"'*Afterthought'—a new play by Mr. Henry Wildman, a new young author, will be produced at Manchester by Eugene Layburn on Monday. Miss Gladys Busbridge will be of the cast.*" This Mr. Spicer knowledgeably calls "only a Puff," and it causes a little more gaiety and glassiness of eye amongst the other elders—which is not improved by a wire, arriving late on Monday night, and announcing enormous success on the first night at Manchester and great booking for the rest of the week. And Master Wildman clears no eyes, save Elsie's and Mrs. Hoare's, by hazarding amounts on royalties at five per cent accruing to him. For it is not entirely pleasant to have a young man who was in the City (and not knowing his own business best, at that) sitting in front of them at mealtimes with anything from £40 a week rolling in upon him without the expenditure of any energy whatever.

Mr. Spicer is still pathetically touching Mrs. Spicer at every private moment of the day, only to get his head bitten off; but they are both at one in rather suspecting Miss Hatt of having wilfully overheard a little of the argument on Saturday night.

Mrs. Hoare is at her maddest, and the Russian lady is more obtuse than ever.

As for Miss Hatt herself, she is in a state of nerves at which we have hardly yet hinted; and to Miss Hatt, since she at last gives way to an even more shocking degree than the rest, we must now give some attention.

For Miss Hatt, who has kept up a gallant show for something like fifteen years against the sprawling and lazy insults of the intruders she has contracted to warm, shelter, clean, tidy, and feed in her own house, is no longer the same Miss Hatt. For the sum of three and a half guineas—a wistfully ideal sum, each guest being on very secret and very Special Terms—the sum of three guineas and a half, coyly demanded, and received weekly with furtive and apologetic compliments from each guest in turn, has proved a very untidy sum with respect to that Tidy Little Sum she once looked forward to as a result of her labours; and Miss Hatt is suddenly brought up against the fact that she has been slaving her middle life out in mothering a brood of secretly allied and hostile human beings, who break up her house, and demand replacements, and give out an air of conferring a benefit with every week they remain with her. Which is a black fact to come up against when those fifteen years have been spent in an unending series of fifteen-hour days (6.30 a.m.–9.30 p.m.) in which you have worked on and on and on, and been merry and merry and merrier, until you are giddy and sick with fatigue, and fall upon your bed, at last, with the one long sigh you are allowed to express, to fall asleep.

The only little hour of rest that Miss Hatt gets from her endless labours during the day, is the hour before dinner. And then Miss Hatt runs into her bedroom, slams the door, flings herself on to her bed in the inky darkness, and lies still, listening to the beating of her heart. And the darkness is alive, with grimacing images, and cries, and sounds, and flashes from all the rush of the day behind her. . . . And the most fantastic half-awake dreams assail Miss Hatt, as somebody commences to use her bath outside, and footsteps carry humming bodies past her door, and laughter peals from downstairs . . . Fantastic dreams in which she gives her guests a little of her own mind. . . . "I'm tired of working myself to death for all of you, and now you shall listen to me! . . ."

"You, yes, you, Clifford! You're nothing but a Low Dirty Drunkard, and if your wife wasn't the sloppy little fool she is—yes, sloppy Lazy little fool—she'd see it, but she's such a Sloppy Lazy little fool I ought to pity her! . . . And you, Mrs. Nixon, hanging your filthy clothes on my line and smiling at my remarks as though you're so superior . . . your filthy, filthy, filthy clothes! You filthy, filthy people, all of you! Treating my bathroom as though it's a pig sty! You *filthy*, *filthy* pigs! I loathe all of you, and *out* of my house you shall go! Get out! Get out! Get out! . . ."

And Miss Hatt suddenly finds herself sitting up, with her brain whirring madly in the inky darkness, and the water falling with a steady splashing flow into the bath outside, as much as to say "Come along then. Let's have it. We're ready."

CHAPTER X

The Storm bursts. Prodigious Conduct of Miss Hatt and Mrs. Nixon.

I

THAT little sketch of the trend of Miss Hatt's thoughts, in the dark hour before dinner, covers but one instance among many less stormy instances; but it serves to show the state of Miss Hatt's mind in these last days left to Craven House, and to excuse, more than anything else, her prodigious behaviour at dinner, three days after the downfall of Mr. Spicer.

And as this is the last dinner she ever presides at, and is therefore the last dinner, as a Dinner, of all the gas-lit dinners lost in the mists of time; perhaps we should make one last survey of our characters, as they sit around the table, in all their weary jollity, before passing out into nothing.

Miss Hatt sits at the top of the table, with no expression at all coming through glittering pince-nez, and her still face carved with the deep lines of fifteen years' merriness. She is fingering her bread. On her immediate left is the Russian lady, who has a quiet, tentative air of apologising for everything she eats, and keeps on looking round with a full mouth to see whether she has been caught. On the left of the Russian lady is Master Wildman, looking very nice indeed, in one of his happiest collars, and fingering his knife, in the pauses, with a kind of strong thoughtfulness which one would not attempt to interrupt. On his left is Mrs. Spicer, very pale, and metaphorically wriggling away from a Mr. Spicer, who, at the bottom of the table, is metaphorically touching her. On Mr. Spicer's left (and going up the other side) is Mrs. Hoare, nodding and smiling optimistically over the whole world, as usual. On Mrs. Hoare's left is Mrs. Nixon, level-eyed, very calm. On her left is Elsie, at her very prettiest, and her very quietest. And on Elsie's left, between herself and Miss Hatt, is another stranger, whose name is Jock Nixon, and who is Mrs. Nixon's son and Elsie Nixon's half-brother; and only Mrs. Nixon, and Elsie, and Master Wildman know why he is here.

(For "They're going to take me away," Elsie whispered to Master Wildman, last night on the stairs.

"Take you away? Who is? Where?"

"I don't know. But she's telegraphed for my brother, and they're going to talk about me, and send me away somewhere. She's just told me so."

"What's your brother going to think about all this, then?" Mr. Jock Nixon's visits to Craven House having all occurred during the war, Master Wildman has never met him.

"Jock? Oh, he hates me. He always did hate me. They're going to talk about me."

"I've a notion I shan't like your brother, Elsie."

"Yes. But what am I going to do if they send me away?"

"I expect I'll see your brother, Elsie."

"Oh, but you mustn't be rude to him!"

"Coal Heavers?"

"No, not coal heavers. But you mustn't be rude to him."

"Oh, we'll see then," said Master Wildman, and left her.)

Mr. Jock Nixon is a bonny, round-faced young man with a fresh, glowing skin, and fair, curly hair; wearing a white soft collar and an oldish blue suit, and standing about five feet ten, as opposed to Master Wildman's five feet eleven—which fact had an air of being demonstrated when they were introduced by Elsie, and gave each other a rather curt nod and "Howdyoudo." He speaks with a faint Scottish accent which Mrs. Nixon has always insisted upon in a true son of hers; and he is, to her, a bonny, sunny, clean, canny, open, healthy Scottish Lad—a breath off the moors, and a credit to her upbringing and his country.

Almost as if there is some far-hidden prognostication of the scene to come and the mood in which they will rise, there is a long, weighty silence after the guests have taken their places and are awaiting the fish. They look placidly at the table-cloth, and wait for Mr. Spicer to Open Dinner, as it were, according to his custom, with a critical appreciation of their latest buffetings at the hands of the sky. This, Mr. Spicer, after staring open-mouthed at the stranger, whom he has never met before, and to whom he has not yet been introduced, at last does.

"Colder to-night," says Mr. Spicer.

The company shivers a polite affirmative.

"Ay," says Mr. Jock Nixon. "And ye don't call this weather cold now, do ye?"

Well, the company did, on the whole—but open to Caledonian correction on the matter—feel it a trifle nippy.

But, of course, "You," says Miss Hatt, "probably don't feel it at all, because you're so——"

"Scotch," says Master Wildman, who has taken a very great dislike to Mr. Jock Nixon already. Mrs. Nixon glances sharply over at him, but he is picking bones out of his fish.

"Yes," says Mr. Spicer. "You get it cold enough up there, don't you?"

"Ay," says Mr. Jock Nixon. "That we do. I don't call the little breezes you have down here weather, now." There is a long silence.

"Your son?" asks Mr. Spicer.

"Yes," says Mrs. Nixon. "I haven't introduced you, have I? Mr. Spicer—Mr. Jock!"

Both gentlemen half-rise, both gentlemen sit down, both gentlemen half-rise again, both gentlemen remain uneasily bobbing, and then come across the room and shake hands— both gentlemen being very violent and strong in this respect. There is then another long silence.

"He—is—Scotch," says Miss Hatt, pointing at Mr. Nixon, and speaking to the Russian lady.

"Please?"

"Scotch. Scotch. Scotch. *He*. He is Scotch. From Scot Land."

"Oh yes. He is Scotch."

"She's getting on well, isn't she?" says Miss Hatt, cheerfully, and turns confidentially to Mr. Jock Nixon. "She is Russian. Russian. Russian."

"Oh, ay. She's Russian, then."

Russia and Scotland smile, as though at a kind of coincidence in the situation, across the table, and there is another long silence. There is no getting ahead with things to-night.

"And how do you like our English food?" asks Miss Hatt.

"Please?"

"No. I spoke to him. To *him*. Who is *Scotch*."

"Ay, and ye do us well enough down here, but it's all the fancy stuff. Now ye don't get the fancy stuff up there, but ye do get the wholesome."

"Oh," says Miss Hatt, vaguely looking at his fish.

"Haggis?" suggests Master Wildman. "In a manner of speaking?" And the silence that follows is the silence of distant thunders gathering.

"Now I expect you've travelled about a lot, Mr. Wildman?" says Mr. Nixon, at last.

"I can't claim much in that line," says Master Wildman. "But I once went to Stratford-on-Avon."

"Oh," says Mr. Nixon.

"And saw Anne Hathaway's Cottage," says Master Wildman, picking his fish.

"Oh," says Mr. Nixon. "And would ye have been over the border at all?"

"Isn't that what Bonny Leslie did?"

"Would ye have been over the border at all, Mr. Wildman?"

"No," says Master Wildman. "Unfortunately I wouldn't."

"Ah, well. That's a pity, Mr. Wildman. If ye had, ye'd know that the Scots don't go carrying around a haggis all the day, as your London newspapers seem to think they do. You should travel a wee bit, Mr. Wildman."

"Heh, heh, heh!" laughs Mrs. Nixon, and the others laugh.

"In that case," says Master Wildman slowly, "I withdraw my Haggis."

And the silence that follows is the silence of distant thunders gathering.

"I don't like Scotch food, very much, myself," says Elsie, by way of conversation.

"Ay, and that's because ye don't know what's good for ye, Miss Elsie," says Mr. Nixon, smiling. "If you refuse good Scotch food, meleddy, what you want is a good dose of that castor oil."

"Oh, don't talk about Castor Oil!" says Miss Hatt, and puts her hand to her mouth.

"Like the Fascists give the Bolsheviks," says Mr. Nixon.

"Good Punishment, that," says Mr. Spicer. "Does no harm, and just Teaches them. Always think that's a very good punishment."

"Ay. That it is," says Mr. Nixon. "Did I ever tell ye, mother, what we did to the Bolshie up our way?"

"No. What's that, Jock?"

"There was one of they Socialists, ye see," says Mr. Nixon, looking round at every one except Master Wildman to whom he is obviously addressing this story. "Holdin' meetings with a few of his associates in his rooms of a night."

"Oh, yes?" says Miss Hatt.

"So we watched him a few nights, ye see, and then we got a few boys together and went round there one night. And we waited till the others was out, and then we broke in at the door, and went up to his rooms, where he was standin' looking wild."

"Oh!" exclaims Miss Hatt.

"So we got his books first, all that low Socialist stuff, ye know, and we burnt them over the fire, an' he was screeching out the Red Flag in defiance all the while, and we just let him do it. But he up and hit one of our chaps at last, and then we started in. An' we gave it him where he wasn't lookin' for it."

"Where was that?" asks Master Wildman, and there is a pause, in which both young gentlemen's eyes meet across the table.

"And when we'd finished wi' that," continues Mr. Nixon, "We set in wi' the Castor Oil, and we got near half a pint down him before we'd done. And then we told him we weren't havin' any of that Remsey *Macdonald* (Mr. Nixon brings forth the word Remsey as though it is the very worst epithet to apply to the very vilest substantive, Macdonald), Remsey Macdonald stuff in our parts, and then we left him to look after himself. Bit in the papers about it, and all. . . ."

"Expect he Deserved it," says Mr. Spicer.

"Ay, he did that. But there was another trouble with *that* young man. He'd been interferin' with one af our chap's sisters up there. Carryin' on with her against her people's wishes. . . ."

Mr. Nixon again meets Master Wildman's eyes across the table, which is not a difficult thing for Mr. Nixon to do, inasmuch as Master Wildman has forsaken his fish, and has been gazing steadily at Mr. Nixon, during the whole course of his little narration.

"Oh, that's bad," says Mr. Spicer.

"Ay, it was," says Mr. Nixon, laughing, and the others laugh.

"For him," says Mr. Nixon. . . .

Mrs. Hoare wants to know if it wasn't a little cruel.

"Oh, I don't know. They deserve it, these chaps," says Mr. Spicer.

"Yes," says Mrs. Spicer, to the Universe.

"Scottish way," says Mrs. Nixon. "We take care of our bairns up there."

"Ay, Scottish way," says Mr. Nixon, again looking over at Master Wildman. "An' we're always ready with it."

"Scotch Way," says Master Wildman, contemplatively.

He looks at the table-cloth, and the air shudders in the first spasm of the thunders long gathering.

"That being the Scotch way, Mr. Nixon," says Master Wildman, quietly looking up. "What would be *your* way, now, of dealing with young fellows who start interfering with chaps' sisters?"

There is a tingling pause in which both young gentlemen look straight into each other's eyes.

"Hadn't we better Stop?" asks Miss Hatt, giggling. "I think we'd better Stop." But all eyes are now glued madly upon the antagonists, and her remark goes by unnoticed.

"My way, Mr. Wildman?" says Mr. Nixon. "Why, I guess it would be the same way. I'm a Scottish lad."

("I think we'd better Stop," says Miss Hatt. "Hadn't we?")

"I believe that to be a mistake, Mr. Nixon," says Master Wildman.

"I think I should know my own birth and upbringing, Mr. Wildman; seeing I've had a very much better one than some I can mention."

"Nevertheless, I believe that to be a mistake, Mr. Nixon," says Master Wildman.

("Don't want any Antagonism, you know," says Mr. Spicer.)

"Perhaps, then, you know all about it, my friend," says Mr. Nixon, speaking low. "Mebbe you've been looking out my pedigree at Somerset House?"

"That," says Master Wildman, lazily slapping his breast pocket, "is exactly what I have done." He leans back in his chair.

("Don't want any Antagonism, you know," murmurs Mr. Spicer.)

"What do you mean by that, Mr. Wildman?"

"Why, do you want me to make myself any clearer?"

"What do you mean by that, Mr. Wildman? Where've you got it, then? . . . Where have you got it, then, Mr. Wildman? . . . Perhaps you'll oblige by producing this highly interesting information, Mr. Wildman."

"That might be unkind and rude, Mr. Nixon."

"I'll thank you to make good your assertion, Mr. Wildman, or acknowledge yourself the liar you are!"

"You are too pressing," says Master Wildman, and moves one hand slowly into his breast pocket.

"What's that ye've got there, Mr. Wildman?"

"A Genealogical Tree," returns Master Wildman, and produces a pocket-book. "Do you care to hear it?"

("Is the Scotch gentleman angry, please?" asks a Russian lady softly of Miss Hatt. "Please? Please?"

"I really think we'd better Stop, hadn't we?" says Miss Hatt.)

"Read me what you've got there, Mr. Wildman, please."

"Here we are," says Master Wildman, and commences to read. (That Master Wildman has actually paid a visit to Somerset House, and so obtained his Genealogical Tree, as he professes to have done, we, ourselves, do not believe. But it seems that he is reading from real words and figures in his pocket-book; and we can only conclude that he must at some time or another been elaborately into the question of Elsie's parentage, with Elsie herself. Anyway, Elsie is glancing at his pocket-book in a mightily guilty way all the time.)

"Here we are," says Master Wildman, speaking in a slow, steady voice. "There's a Mary Elizabeth Pearce, isn't there? She was born Burgess Hill, Sussex. Eighteen—something or other—never mind. That'll be you, Mrs. Nixon, won't it? Daughter of John Edward Pearce, of Avonmouth, and Elizabeth Willis, of Bootle. Nothing Scotch in that. But then you never actually said that you were Scotch, did you, Mrs. Nixon?"

"I have not said that I was," says Mrs. Nixon, very calm. "Please read on. I should like to hear it."

"Must I?"

"Read on, please, Mr. Wildman!" says Mr. Nixon.

"It's you that say you're Scotch, isn't it? But listen," says Master Wildman, and turns to another page. "Married. Eighteen ninety-nine. John Llewellyn Price. Of Merthyr. Has a Welsh sound, hasn't it? Son. John. That'll be you, Mr. Nixon."

"Will you put those notes away, Mr. Wildman? Or will you take something you won't like from me?"

"Let him read on," says Mrs. Nixon, as white as ashes. "*Please* let him read on! That can come after."

"Am I to read on?"

"Read on, please!"

"Nineteen two, we come to now. Married again. James Stewart Nixon. Didn't know Nixon was a Scotch name, but he's a Scotchman without any doubt at all. Scotch through and through. Here you are. Born Inverness. Died nineteen five. Daughter. Elsie Nixon. That'll be you, Elsie. Always knew you were half Scotch, didn't you?"

Master Wildman lazily flicks the pages, and closes the book, and flicks the pages again.

"Glad of that, Elsie," he says, ruminating. "Half Scotch myself. Got a mother buried with heaps of grandmothers and grandfathers at St. Cuthbert's, Princes Street. That's Edinburgh, isn't it, Mr. Nixon?"

"Is the Scotch gentleman angry, please?" asks a terrified and urgent Russian lady. "Please! He is angry!"

"The gentleman is angry, I believe," says Master Wildman. "But he is not a Scotch gentleman."

There is a very long and very deep silence.

"Do you know what I'm going to do now, Mr. Wildman?" says Mr. Nixon, speaking low again.

"I gather that you have thrashed Coal Heavers," says Master Wildman, "for Less."

And this reply is a difficult reply to handle.

"Now this must really Stop, mustn't it? I say it must *Stop*," says Miss Hatt, firmly.

"I may have thrashed Coal Heavers, or I may not have thrashed Coal Heavers——" begins Mr. Nixon.

"And I put it to you that you thrash an almost hourly Coal Heaver?" says Master Wildman.

"But whether I've thrashed Coal Heavers——"

"Or whether you have not thrashed Coal Heavers——"

"I'm going to thrash you, Mr. Wildman."

"Who am not a Coal Heaver," says Master Wildman.

"Oh, please, don't go on! Please! Please! Please!" says Elsie.

"Please!" says a Russian lady.

"Go on, Jock, please," says Mrs. Nixon.

"Now this must stop, please," says Miss Hatt, very firmly.

"Oh, yes," says Mrs. Spicer, ever so gaily, to the Universe.

"And first I'm going to give you a bit of my mind, Mr. Wildman."

"Good," says Master Wildman.

"And first I'm going to give you a bit of my mind, Mr. Wildman! And I'm goin' to tell you what a dirty low little skunk you are! And I may tell you, Mr. Wildman, that

I've had my eye upon you, ever since my mother first began to write to me about you, and I'm now goin' to tell the ladies present what I think of a little cad that buys my sister dresses, when she's forbid to go out."

"Now this must really Stop," says Miss Hatt, and brings her tumbler down with a little bang.

"Go on, Jock."

"But I said it must Stop, didn't I, Mrs. Nixon?"

"Go on, Jock."

"But did you hear me say it must stop, Mrs. Nixon?"

"Go on, Jock."

"An' I'm goin' to say right in front of the ladies——"

"Mrs. Nixon! Will you please Stop him?"

"Go on, Jock," says Mrs. Nixon, very calm. "Don't mind her."

"Right in front of the ladies——" says Mr. Nixon, and on these words, the whole of Craven House, united with the great labourings of fifteen years, crashes and smatters into ruin.

"You won't stop him!" screams Miss Hatt, rising and grasping the table-cloth in both hands. "Then *I!* . . . *I!* . . . *I!* . . . *I will stop him!*"

And with these words Miss Hatt gives a long, screeching and theatrical pull at the table-cloth (like a person summoning infernal spirits), which causes plates and knives and forks and spoons to fly off singing and clanking both sides of the table, and the evening Leg of Mutton to slide swiftly from a crestfallen Mr. Spicer at the bottom to the horrified lady magician at the top. "Please!" exclaims the Russian lady.

"*I!* . . . *I!* . . . *I!* . . ." yells Miss Hatt, and gets the leg of mutton a bit nearer to her. "*Now who will stop him!*"

Mr. Spicer has now half-fallen upon the floor. Mrs. Spicer is dabbing madly at the water from the spilt vase, with her serviette. The Russian lady is saying "Please!" Master Wildman is picking up plates and spoons, and placing them thoughtfully upon the table. Miss Hatt is screaming "I! I! I!" Mrs. Nixon is standing with a blazing red face with her son.

"Now," says Miss Hatt, in a low tone, and at bay.

"Hadn't we better call the servant?" says Mrs. Spicer. "I think we'd better call the servant. Oh dear, it's gone all over your dress, hasn't it, Mrs. Hoare. Oh, dear, what a Peculiar Spill. What a Peculiar Spill! . . ."

"Now!" says Miss Hatt, a little louder, and still at bay.

"Go on, Jock!" says Mrs. Nixon.

"Hold your filthy tongue!" shouts Miss Hatt.   "Or I'll come and hold it for you."

"Who called my tongue filthy?"

"I called your tongue filthy!"

"Who called my tongue filthy?" asks Mrs. Nixon, making a growling noise.   "Jock, who called my tongue filthy?"

"*I* called it filthy!   I! . . .   I! . . .   I!" yells Miss Hatt. "And it is filthy!   It's as filthy as the filthy filth that's been filthing through my house all these filthy years!   You filth! You Mud!"

"Who's calling me mud?   Jock?   Who's calling me Mud?

"Am I right in thinking that somebody's calling me Mud, Jock?   I think I heard somebody calling me Mud!"

"Mud, I called you and Mud you are!   You're a Mud Pie!   A Mud Pie!   A Children's Mud Pie!"

"A Children's Mud Pie!" yells Miss Hatt, as though the infancy of the imagined creators of Mrs. Nixon is a very expressive touch.   "*A Children's Mud Pie!*   That's you!"

"Am I right in saying, Jock," says Mrs. Nixon, speaking to her son, and looking straight at Miss Hatt, "that a certain person of our acquaintance is alluding to me as a Mud Pie? Am I right in saying, I only want to know if I am right in saying, and if I'm wrong I shall be the first to admit it," continues Mrs. Nixon, who is still quite open on the matter——

"Oh, yes, quite the first to admit it; but am I right in saying that a certain low filth of my acquaintance, a certain low filth from the gutter, who's been cheating and poisoning us with filthy food that only filthy workhouses would eat (yes, you see, I can filthy as well) and charging us three guineas, three filthy guineas for it, am I right in remarking that this person of our acquaintance referred to me as a Mud Pie?"

"*Mud——!*" says Miss Hatt, taking the leg of mutton in her right hand, and arranging herself like a discus-thrower. "Pie!" screams Miss Hatt, and hurls the leg of mutton at Mrs. Nixon.

It goes over her head, and lands in the fireplace.

Master Wildman goes round and picks it up.

"Please, please, *please*, is this English habit, please?" asks a Russian lady.

"Yes.   Yes," says Master Wildman.   "English.   English. English habit.   Purely.   Our Way.   Temperament.   Pas-

sionate People. Roast Beef. Meat eaters. No alarm.
Every day. We all do it. No alarm. Please."

"I think I go," says the Russian lady, but does not go.

"Hold me back, there!" shouts Mrs. Nixon, dragging
at the table-cloth. "Hold me back someone! Hold me!
Hold me!"

Mr. Spicer and Mrs. Hoare approach her in a feeble attempt
at obedience, but do not come in too near.

"Hold me! Hold me!" cries Mrs. Nixon. But no one
will hold Mrs. Nixon.

"By Heaven and by Hell, Miss Hatt!" hisses Mrs. Nixon.
"That is the last leg of mutton you shall ever throw at me!
Hold me! Hold me! Hold me!"

But still no one will come forward to Hold Mrs. Nixon.

"Hold me, I say!" shouts Mrs. Nixon.

"Hold her!" shouts Master Wildman, dramatically, for
which Mrs. Nixon suddenly throws a plate at Master Wildman.

"Ah," says Master Wildman. "Plate."

Mrs. Nixon then throws another plate at Master Wildman,
and a plate at Miss Hatt. And on a minor objection (on
the score of Antagonism), from Mr. Spicer, she throws a plate
at him. Whereupon Mrs. Spicer screams, and Mrs Nixon
throws a plate at her. She then throws two plates, one
after another, on to the centre of the table, as a general
principle; and a dish at the Russian lady, for saying "Please."
There now being no more crockery to hand, she asks: "*Now*
will you hold me?" But still no one of the company present
will come forth to hold her.

There is a long silence.

"I think *somebody* ought to be held down," says Mrs.
Spicer.

"Hold *yourself* down, then," says Miss Hatt.

"Really, Bertha——"

"Hold *yourself* down!" says Miss Hatt, and "Well!" says
Mrs. Spicer.

"Perhaps if we had a little chat about it?" suggests Mrs.
Hoare.

"Hold your tongue."

"But what have I done!"

"Hold your tongue!"

"Please?"

"Hold your Russian tongue."

"Please. I go."

"Go."

But the Russian lady does not go.

"It's all quite Simple," says Mr. Spicer. "We're all upset. Now don't let's have any more of this. We're all upset." Mr. Spicer catches Miss Hatt's level eye. "May I go on, Bertha?"

"If you want the leg of mutton in your face. Yes."

"I don't want that, Bertha, but mayn't I go on?"

"If you *desire* the leg of mutton in your face, you may certainly go on."

"But I don't desire the leg of mutton in my face, Bertha."

"Then don't go on. Or you'll *get* the leg of mutton in your face. Does anybody else, by the way," says Miss Hatt, looking at Mrs. Nixon, "want the leg of mutton in their face?"

No. No one in the company can actually say they do.

Mrs. Nixon speaks. "There's such a thing, Miss Hatt, as throwing legs of mutton in other people's faces."

"Go on."

"Oh, that's all."

"Repeat that!"

"Oh, no. Heh, heh, heh! That's all and that's quite enough."

"Will you repeat that?"

"Oh, no! Heh, heh, heh!"

"And there is such a thing, Mrs. Nixon, as other people throwing legs of mutton *back* at other people—with interest. However this is not a discussion of legs of mutton, it is a discussion of certain people who have been filthing my house."

"Repeat that, Miss Hatt!"

"Certain people who have been filthing my house!"

"And who does that include, Miss Hatt?"

"All of you!"

There is a silence.

"You're all upset, Bertha," says Mr. Spicer. "You're all upset."

"*I* think she's dotty," says Mrs. Spicer.

"Oh, so you think I'm dotty, do you. You think I'm dotty?"

"Yes, I do!"

"Oh, so you think I'm dotty, do you. Good. And what do you think, Mister Spicer?"

"I think you're very funny, Bertha."

"Oh, so you think I'm dotty, do you?" says Miss Hatt, raising her voice. "Then perhaps you both think Catherine Tillotson's dotty, do you! Ha, ha, ha!"

"Who's Catherine Tillotson?" asks Mr. Spicer, becoming white.

"Who's Catherine Tillotson," says Miss Hatt, "I don't know. How should I know? Catherine Tillotson? Never heard the name. Oh, no, I don't know who Catherine Tillotson is. Oh, no! Ha, ha, ha! Oh, dear me, no! Oh, dear! How funny. How very funny! Catherine Tillotson. Oh, what a name and a half! Oh, dear! Ha, ha, ha! So amusing! Oh, dear me! What a name. Catherine Tillotson!"

"Then I shouldn't speak about people until you know who they are, Bertha," says Mrs. Spicer.

"Oh, my God! Supposing *I* had married him! Oh, dear! How funny that would have been!"

"Oh, so that's it, is it? You wanted to marry him badly enough at the beginning," says Mrs. Spicer, now getting angry herself.

"Did I? I suppose I did! I suppose I did. I suppose I *haven't* spent every moment of the day all these years upon my knees thanking God I didn't marry him—when he practically asked me, before you, only I wouldn't fall so low. I suppose he didn't! If you say he didn't! I suppose he *didn't* kiss me at Chiselhurst when you were outside chaining up the bicycles. Oh, no! Dear me, no! I suppose he *didn't* say you didn't mean anything much to him, and that I was the one he wanted? Oh, no! I suppose he *didn't* call round for me in the evenings when you knew nothing about it! And I suppose I haven't had to slave my life out while you've lazed about—you Sloppy Lazy Little Fool—while you've lazed about simply because I myself wouldn't fall so low as to take him myself. I suppose I couldn't have had him! You know best! You know best!"

"Don't know what you mean by Catherine Tillotson, Bertha," says Mr. Spicer, wildly.

"Oh, then I suppose that's another mistake! I'm making a lot of mistakes, aren't I? But do you know what I'm going to do now. I'm going to drive you all out of my house! Every one of you! No more of this for me. I'm going to drive you out of it! You wait!"

Miss Hatt charges out of the door, is heard spilling the

umbrella stand in the hall outside, and returns with her
own umbrella in her hand.

"Now then!" shouts Miss Hatt. "Are you going? Or
who am I going to start on? I'm not afraid of you."

"Miss Hatt, please," says Master Wildman, coming forward.

"Please. We only want to help you," says Elsie, and comes
forward too.

"All right, then, I'll start on you!" cries Miss Hatt, to
Master Wildman. "I always thought you were a gentleman,
but I hate you now, as I hate the rest. Get out! Get out!"

Miss Hatt strikes Master Wildman twice across the chest,
and Master Wildman looks at her gravely.

"Get out!" cries Miss Hatt, and keeps time with this
command upon Master Wildman's chest. "Get out! Get
out! Get out! . . ."

"Oh, *will* you get out?" says Miss Hatt, appealingly. . . .

"I'll hit you out," says Miss Hatt, still feebly striking.
"I will. No more of this for me! I'll hit you out. There!
. . . There! . . . There! . . ." Miss Hatt pauses. "Oh,
dear. I'm afraid I'm going. . . . I'm going, I'm afraid. . . .
I'm going. . . ."

Master Wildman and Elsie are standing each side of her,
with their arms apart.

Miss Hatt closes her eyes, reels, and chooses Master Wildman.

II

At ten o'clock the same evening a quiet and chastened
little band of guests is discussing the events of the evening
in the drawing-room. The fire is out, and they sit around
the grey and brown dreariness of the ashes, with the door
open, in case of alarming sounds from upstairs, and they
talk. Miss Hatt is in her bedroom, and Elsie, who has been
comforting her, and putting her to bed (sobbing and sobbing,
and sobbing, and crying "Oh, what a Fuss!" for the benefit
of the listeners on the stairs), now reports her to be asleep.
Mr. Nixon has gone away. (He is lodging temporarily in
Kensington.) Mrs. Nixon has gone to bed, after remarking
that if people will do these things, they can only expect
Nervous Breakdowns—which is mistaking cause for effect.
Mrs. Hoare has been prevailed upon to retire to her room,
and after repeatedly coming out to enquire whether Miss
Hatt is Dead (which this old lady is unalterably convinced

she is, only they're trying to keep it from her, because she (Mrs. Hoare) is Old) stays there. The Russian lady has packed up and gone, presumably back to Russia, no other hint of her destination ever coming forth. And Bertha and Edith, having asked Master Wildman whether they are to clear away, are clearing away, but have got no further than the carpet.

"What an end," says Mrs. Spicer. "What an end."

"I mean, she got mad at one time, didn't she?" says Mr. Spicer. "Absolutely raving mad at one time. Didn't she? What was that she was saying? That was the maddest part. Catherine Willet, was it?"

"Tillotson?" says Elsie. "Yes. That was silly, wasn't it?"

"Oh, *Tillotson*, was it?" says Mr. Spicer. . . .

"And then all that Marriage part," says Mrs. Spicer.

"Absurd," says Elsie.

"Of course it was all my fault, really," says Master Wildman. "I should never have set in on that brother of yours, Elsie."

"He *started* being rude," says Elsie. . . .

"Yes. But I made him."

"And then those Plates," says Mrs. Spicer.

"I never knew my mother could throw plates about like that," says Elsie. "I do hope it didn't go too near you, Mrs. Spicer."

"Well, it did come rather close, didn't it? But fortunately I saw it coming. She did throw them about, didn't she?"

"I'm very sorry, Mrs. Spicer."

"Not a question of a Plate here and there, so much," says Mr. Spicer. "It's the Madness that worries me. . . ."

"But Plates are quite enough," says Elsie.

"Yes," says Mrs. Spicer. "But that didn't worry me so much. . . ."

"I suppose we shall all have to go off immediately," says Mrs. Spicer. "It's so funny. I've known her all these years. Where shall we go, I wonder?"

"Yes, we'll have to go," says Master Wildman, looking at the desolate old fire, and finding Elsie's eyes for a second. "There's no doubt about that."

"Oh, we can find somewhere to go," says Mr. Spicer. "That doesn't worry me so much. . . ."

"I don't think I'll be sorry to leave this house," says Elsie.

"No," says Master Wildman, and meets her eyes quickly again.

"I'll be glad to get out of it," says Mrs. Spicer. "I wonder if she'll stay on."

"Shouldn't think so," says Mr. Spicer. "Too ill. . . .   I mean, I don't mind a Nervous Breakdown, but she went mad, didn't she? . . ."

"Yes," says Elsie. "All that part about the leg of mutton. It was mad."

"Yes. But I don't worry about the leg of mutton part so much," says Mr. Spicer. . . .

"That Catherine Tillotson Business that got me," says this ass. . . .

CHAPTER XI

Ernie, George, and Mr. Ewart. A Train Journey.
Mr. Wildman sleeps badly.

I

MISS HATT does not appear at any of the meals next day, but before dinner a little note is quietly passed round to all, by Elsie. If her guests will kindly be in the drawing-room at nine o'clock, she will have a little chat with them. There is much restlessness before that hour, as they sit around the fire, but Miss Hatt is sharp upon her time.

"You'll excuse my dressing-gown, won't you?" says Miss Hatt.

Silence murmurs "Not at all."

"There was rather a catastrophe last night, wasn't there?" says Miss Hatt.

Silence thinks, perhaps, that that is overstating the case, but does remember a little trouble.

"Well, I think I must be the first to apologise, mustn't I?"
Silence takes that as great magnanimity.

"I'm afraid I was a little Hasty."

Silence does recall a leg of mutton, but thinks this is too much.

"At the same time, there were others, weren't there?"
Certainly. Certainly.

"My fault," says Master Wildman.

"I'm afraid that I'm on the verge of a Nervous Breakdown."

The Verge, perhaps.

"Now I don't want to put you to any inconvenience, but I'm afraid I'm moving out of here, as I don't think I can stand it a moment longer."

Quite. Quite.

"I've been to the removal man this morning, and he says he'll start on the Tenth."

The Tenth? Ah——

"That would be Thursday, wouldn't it?"

It strikes silence as though it would be Thursday.

"But he would not finish till the next Monday, or possibly Tuesday. So that would leave you till Saturday at least, wouldn't it. I can leave your rooms untouched till then, if you wish; though the meals would have to be taken in the Study. How does that strike you?"

Mr. Spicer murmurs the word "Others," and the word "Us," and the words "All right"—which is just what silence is trying to murmur.

"I will not charge you after Thursday, I may say."

That is more than magnanimous.

"Then I can expect you out by Sunday evening at the very latest?"

Mr. Spicer murmurs "Us," which is just what silence is trying to murmur.

There is a pause.

"I am going to Margate," says Miss Hatt, pronouncing every word carefully. "I shall sell the furniture, and I shall sell the house, and I shall go to Margate. To my Cousins. I have Cousins at Margate."

Mrs. Nixon makes an unfortunate utterance under her breath with respect to Sea Air.

"Did I hear any one mention Sea Air?" asks Miss Hatt.

Silence thinks not, apparently.

"Did I hear anyone mention the name of Sea Air?" repeats Miss Hatt, and a distantly leg of mutton look returns momentarily to her eyes.

"I don't think this is the time to start arguing about Sea Air," says Mrs. Nixon calmly, but not without a certain counter-look reminiscent of Plates.

"No, I think Not," says Miss Hatt. "We will let Sea Air apply to the boot it fits."

Silence is acquiescent.

"Well,", continues Miss Hatt. "As there is nothing more to be said, I will only apologise once more for circumstances that were out of my control at the time—and saying that—make bold to retire."

There is a little pause.

"Thank you," says Miss Hatt, bows distantly, and with these two words expressing finally all the good, and all the ills, of her fifteen years' association with them, leaves the room.

Miss Hatt keeps to her room, and never speaks to any of them again.

II

And then, on Thursday morning, at ten o'clock, the thing begins.

It is all over very quickly. There are about six despoilers altogether, but three principal despoilers, who are known as George, Ernie, and Mr. Ewart, who is the foreman: and they all three possess the bow legs and obedient expressions of the professional side-board carrier, and they get down to their work with good-will and humour.

They are shown over the house, as a preliminary, by Miss Hatt, who knocks at the doors, opens the doors, and ushers them in with "Here we are, you see." They stand respectful, hat in hand, roving of eye, and quiet of voice, as though half aware of the sanctities in memory they have come to destroy, and then go into the next room and do the same. They will start on the upstairs carpet, if the lady is willing.

Then the hammering noises begin, and it is at first experimental hammering, on deadened surfaces; but it soon becomes hollower and louder, and the old house shakes, and holds, as though it is having its teeth drawn, and the lady guests begin to lift their skirts and say "Oh, dear," when they go upstairs to fetch anything. And it goes on all the morning and all the afternoon.

They are brimful of quips, are Ernie, and George, and Mr. Ewart; but George is the fullest of them, being a tall man, packed with wit which he exercises on every possible occasion. "What's this 'ere?" asks George. "A Antimacassar?" and goes off into fits at the thought; and "What's this 'ere picture?" asks George, "Souls Awakenin'?" and again explodes. "In the Nood," says George, contemplating a little green statuette of a nymph, unearthed from somewhere. "Come on, 'eave up your end, chum," says Mr. Ewart, and down they go. Mr. Ewart shouts up to Ernie that he wants a foot, and Ernie tells Mr. Ewart that he can't give it him, not anyhow, not this way, but can manage six yard if he'll wedge her up a bit, and so on, all the day. The furniture is all of the feminine gender, and treated with appropriate tenderness. "Let 'er down slow, matey." "Give 'er way, boy." "Mind 'er legs, chum, she's a bit on the weak side."

The boys are very gay and dirty as they trundle down the stairs, at Edith's invitation, for a bite of tea, and there is a very festive air in the kitchen. Edith, indeed, is having the flirtation of her life, and engages in humorous duels with them more like a lady in a salon, than the raw-armed oven-door slammer that she is: and Bertha also stands wheezing at her friend's witticisms, offering the sheer beauty of Tallness (even if she cannot undertake any pointed badinage herself) to assist the general gay effect. "D'you never win no prizes for that there overwhelming 'Ieght of yours?" asks George, and Bertha wheezes. "Reg'lar Amazon," says Mr. Ewart. "Shou'dn't like to come on 'er on a dark night on the Cross Roads." "Ah," says Edith," but then we don't know what *you* might be doin' at the Cross Roads of a night. I suspects strongly." "You suspects strongly, does you?" says Mr. Ewart. "You suspect away, my girl. I'm a reglar Lothario, I am." "Well, you don't look it," says Edith. "Looks is notoriously deceptive," says Mr. Ewart, and catches Bertha's eye with worlds of meaning in his glance. "They call me Big Bertha, at home," says Bertha, who is more interested in that side of the question.

It is all over very quickly. . . . The next day the wind is high, and there is a lot of rain. Miss Hatt is a tearful presence in the hall, from time to time, and these masters, these dusty, knotted, hairy, final masters of the whole situation, with their careless jokes and light curiosities, and studded boots, and requests for inches, set in upon the drawing-room. The carpet is up before you know about it, and the rain is threshing, and the little laurel bush is pattering, in fervent torment, against a window that seems begrimed and out of use already. There is a draught everywhere. . . . And if you can bring off a journey from the stairs to the study, without quarrelling with little tables turned acrobatically upside down on each other, or armchairs in affecting embrace with armchairs, or squat vases taking advantage of these absurd circumstances to play hide and seek round the legs of sneering Chippendale, you are both clever and lucky.

But these are at last cleared away, and the dining-room is attacked in the afternoon. The boys again have tea down in the kitchen, in the same dusty state, and the same give-and-take is begun. Elsie is casually mentioned, by Ernie, as a "Nice, soft-spoken little bit, up there—pretty too," and the boys heartily concur. And indeed we are afraid that Elsie is rather more of an attraction than the kitchen by now, for she is always somewhere about in the centre of the hustle, looking forlornly out of windows; at least Master Wildman (who is doing the same sort of thing himself) is always finding her at it, and having little conversations with her, to the wind and the rain, and leaving her to it. . . . And the boys often stop their work to speak to her. George asks her if this would have been a "paying guest do-out, like?" and Elsie says "Yes, it was": and Elsie says how strong she thinks Mr. Ewart is, and wonders however he can, which causes Mr. Ewart to become coy, and do more in the way of large glass book-case lifting than a single-handed professional should be allowed by law to do: and Ernie confides in her that he is going to sing in a Concert to-night. Elsie thinks that it must be very nice to have a voice, and Ernie goes on to sketch one or two of his larger victories on the platform, and tells her what Mr. Craddock, up at the Empire, had said about his Future. That Ernie has a Future, Elsie is as much convinced as Mr. Craddock is.

But all at once the second day is over, and the boys are gone. The dusk gathers, the winds fall. The house (which all the afternoon has shaken, and held, as though it was having its teeth drawn) suddenly begins to express itself in creeping terms it has been waiting to express itself in, for fifteen years. It is like a thing edging nearer, and closing in. . . . The echoes of footsteps on its bare boards disturb its mood in no way at all. Rather do they add to the unruffled, emptied hush that is always there. . . .

Darkness falls, and some fool lights the gas in the drawing-room. This intensifies the drear, expectant, stillness of everything to twice its original power, as its livid light shines upon nothing but the piano, and a few wisps of straw, and little nails lying in torn shreds of felt. The laurel bush still patters its misery against the window. The window reflects the bleak desolation of the room.

All the evening solitary footsteps go Clock, Clock, Clock, Clock on the bare boards in the emptied hall. These footsteps are whispering-silent on the stairs (which are still carpeted), but at once take it up again, Clock, Clock, Clock, Clock on the landings up above. . . . And it is Clock, Clock, Clock, Clock, into the night, until the last door is closed. . . .

The wind is as high as ever when the boys return next day, but they are in great wrecking spirits, and very pleased to see Elsie again. Ernie describes, by her request, the reception of his voice at the concert last night, which was a very successful reception, it seems: Mr. Ewart comes over to her in an interval, and shows her his bare arms with the simple and smiling comment "Knotty 'ands!"—so infatuated is this bowlegged man with the praise bestowed by the magnanimous beauty yesterday. ("That's because they're so Strong," says Elsie. "Oh, don't know about *thet*," says the enraptured mover. "Very ugly, any'ow.") And George also comes over to her and surmises (amazingly) that it was a "kind of Victorian 'ouse, wasn't it?" Elsie supposes that it was. Also George gets into hot water with his companions, for picking up the rather disgraceful green nymph and muttering some shocking witticism about Wishing she was Real. "You mustn't 'ear 'im, Miss," says Mr. Ewart, and Elsie says she didn't hear.

But by eleven o'clock there are two large trunks, marked C.S., in the hall, as well as two suit-cases, and two hold-alls, bristling umbrellas. Mrs. Spicer is bustling about in a large, nervous hat, and very white cotton gloves. She is waiting for Mr. Crewe, the grocer, who is going to carry their luggage to the station in his cart. Mr. Spicer is sending a wandering eye over the dismantled rooms in the background.

"Here it is! Here it is!" cries Mrs. Spicer. "Ah, there you are, Mr. Crewe. Thought you were never coming. Seven pieces in all. That's right. Help him, Clifford!"

She watches them go in, one after another. Mr. Spicer stares miserably and unhelpfully at the air.

"Well, that's all. Good-bye!" "Good-bye," "Good-bye," "Good luck!" "Same to you. Good-bye!" "Good-bye!" "Good-bye!" "Good-bye!"

"Thought that man was never coming," says Mrs. Spicer to her husband, as she runs down the steps with him, and with these words, and a lot of other apparently argumentative

ones, our Quiet Middle-aged Couple goes clanging out of our
story, and away into the wind-swept distance.

The moment they have gone Craven House is taken with a
sudden tranquillity—which may be for memories, but which
may not—dispassionate in either case; but it wakes from it
instantly with a knock upon its door, which announces the
Men to help with the Piano, and from this moment the boys
get really under way. And with Elsie upstairs, packing for
to-morrow, they never look back.

They have the piano out in next to no time, and it is
followed by the dining-room side-board, and they then start
clattering up in the Spicers' bedroom, which is easy work,
and two wicker chairs follow a sofa down the stairs as a
mere preliminary.

It cannot be said that a cold lunch is eaten in the Study
by the remaining guests; but it is spread in a sickly way
over the plates; and directly after there is a prodigious racket
over the departure of Mrs. Hoare, who seems to regard it
all as a savage and unwarranted attack upon herself, and
whose trunk and baggages (labelled, MRS. HOARE, in defiant
capitals) are already littering the hall. Master Wildman
frantically goes out to 'phone up the taxi people for her, to
ask why they haven't come, and returns to find the much-
discussed machine throbbing outside the front-gate. But
Mrs. Hoare is on the verge of swooning. This is on account
of a certain Fourpence, which she swears she must give the
Man at the Other End, having been mislaid. Sixpences and
shillings are gallantly proffered on all sides, but they are of
no use at all. The Man is to have Fourpence. ("*Eff. Oh.
You. Ar. Pea!*") This sum being at last secured by general
loan and several rushings upstairs, she puts it carefully into
her purse, and enters the taxi, only to jump out again to
declare to the neighbourhood that she has forgotten her
Kettle: and will the taxi man, perhaps, go upstairs and fetch
it (it's on the ring)? This Master Wildman, after listening to
the man's reticent mumblings about the Lady's Kettle, does
himself, and returns brandishing it like a standard. Whereupon Mrs. Hoare thanks him from the bottom of her heart,
and declares, in Imperial tones, that he has Saved her Evening
Cocoa—which is her Life. She is then inclined to assume
dangerous positions through the taxi-window, until the man
starts his engine, and slams her in with a curt bang. By

this time a small crowd has collected at the gate. The taxi moves off, and the last thing seen of Mrs. Hoare is an old lady leaning sadly out of an open window, and dreamily waving a large, bright kettle, in farewell.

Craven House is absolutely oblivious of the loss of Mrs. Hoare. The despoilers are up in her room before she has gone, and one thing follows another out of the front door, as Craven House gives up its dead.

A soft rain sets in again at about four o'clock, and it is Clock, Clock, Clock, Clock, wherever you go now, and Clack, Clack, Clack on the stairs—for their carpeting is now removed. Elsie is in an overcoat now, looking very chilly about the nose, and still gazing forlornly out of dirty windows; and Master Wildman (who is doing the same sort of thing himself) is always catching her at it.

"Know where you're going yet, Elsie?" asks Master Wildman.

"Yes. We're going to North London. Holloway. To my aunt."

"Oh, yes," says Master Wildman. . . .

"Have you fixed yet?"

"No, not yet, Elsie. I rather fancy I'll get a room in the West Kensington line; just for the present. Don't know what I'm going to do. I'll look for it to-morrow."

"Sunday," Elsie warns him.

"Yes, but I'll fix somewhere. I'll manage somewhere. I say, when will we say Good-bye, Elsie?"

"I don't know," says Elsie, looking at him.

"Want to do it properly, you know," says Master Wildman. . . .

"Perhaps you'll be coming up on the same train as me, part of the way?" suggests Elsie.

"Perhaps. But I don't want to say Good-bye in a train, Elsie."

"Let's say it to-night, then."

"Right you are. Before we go to bed. And then I'll avoid you. All I can."

"Very well," says Elsie. "That's right."

"Going out now, I think," says Master Wildman.

"Are you going to Barbara Cotterell?" asks Elsie.

"Cotterellish," admits Master Wildman. "Why?"

"You might tell her all that's happened, and give her my address. It'll be Six Bath Road, Holloway. We must write."

"Very good," says Master Wildman, and begins to go. But at this moment, the boys, who were thought to have gone away, are heard gently arguing with each other in the dusk outside. They enter.

"You 'ere, Miss?" says Mr. Ewart.

"Yes," says Elsie smiling.

"Seeing we wouldn't see you on Monday, like, Miss, we thought we might come in and say Good-bye."

"Oh that *is* nice of you," says Elsie. "Good-bye."

"Good-bye, Miss." The foreman is nudged lumpily by Ernie, from behind. "'Ere, leave 'old, you! That wouldn't be quite all, Miss."

"Oh no?"

"Seein' what interest you took in our Ernie's voice, Miss, us three made bold to purchase you a ticket for 'is go at the Charity Concert at the Town 'All, Miss. Monday, Miss, thinkin' you might be able to get over from 'Olloway where I believe you was goin', and 'ear it."

"Oh, that *is* kind!" says Elsie. "But surely you didn't go and——"

But Ernie will have none of that, and he comes forward. "Now you'll be able to 'ear me proper, Miss, and judge fer yourself," says Ernie.

"Oh, thank you!"

"Not at all, Miss," says Mr. Ewart. "*We* ain't a-goin', mind you, not George and me. But you'll like to see Ernie."

"If you's fond of Catterwauling," says George, knowingly, and the scene breaks up in laughter. "I'll be there," says Elsie. "Good-bye, Miss." "Good-bye." "Good-bye, sir." "Good-bye." "Good-bye."

The boys trundle heavily away, putting on their caps.

"Unhappy victims," says Master Wildman. "In George, Ernie, and Mr. Ewart."

He goes out.

III

It is raining softly in the dusk as Master Wildman goes along to Miss Cotterell's house. He has not yet breathed a word to Miss Cotterell about his play—he still knows not why, unless it has been a dim, dramatic desire to let her read about it herself, in print—but she has not done that, and he has decided to tell her to-night, directly he sees her. She does not know, either, that he left the City on Monday.

He rings the bell at Miss Cotterell's house, and there is no reply from within. He rings again, stamps his feet, and waits. He comes out into the crazy-paved front garden, and looks up at the windows.

The door is opened.

A new Creature. The latest Creature, doubtless.

"Miss Cotterell in?" asks Master Wildman, coming to the door.

"Well, she wouldn't be in like, not now, sir," says the Creature, looking a little mystified.

"Oh? Are you sure? She said she'd be in at this time to-day for certain."

"No. I don't know, I'm sure. Maybe you'd come in like. If you was"—the Creature pauses—"a Known Gentleman, like. Mrs. Cotterell ain't in neither."

"Right you are. I'll come in and wait. She's bound to be back."

"Don't fancy she'll be back myself, I don't. But there's a fire in 'ere, and if you'll sit down, maybe I'll be wrong."

"Well, no harm in waiting a bit. And she certainly said she'd be here." Master Wildman takes a large armchair. "Thanks."

The Creature goes away. Master Wildman withdraws a slip of blue note-paper from his pocket, and casts his eyes over it.

"It is afraid it has been most dreadfully unreliable in its appointments in the last three days—but it is most awfully contrite, and if he will call round at half-past five to-morrow—it will be there to receive him and make amends.

"B. C."

Master Wildman puts this away into his pocket, and gazes in front of him. The firelight flicks across a warm, flowered, silver-glittering drawing-room, in which it is extremely pleasant to have an armchair, after the echoes and bare dustiness of a dismantled Craven House; and he thinks of Elsie. She stands, chilly in her overcoat, looking out of dusty windows. . . .

The Creature begins to sing from the kitchen. A thicker rain begins to fall outside. It falls softly at first, and then a little louder, as though in frenzied appeal. And then softly again, as though confident of calm victory in its pleading. A drain trinkles somewhere. . . .

Half-an-hour passes like this, and then the Creature returns.

"You still 'ere, sir?"

"Yes, but I think I'll be going," says Master Wildman, rising, and the Creature is inclined to stare.

"I'se thinking, sir," she says at last, "that it might be that there Alla'erbad Gentleman."

"Allahabad Gentleman?"

"Yes. Alla'erbad Gentleman, sir."

"Which Allahabad Gentleman would that be, exactly?" asks Master Wildman.

"Gentleman come back from Alla'erbad, sir."

"Oh, yes?"

"She's been out with 'im all these three days, sir. Three days ago it was, 'e came."

"Three days, eh?"

"Yes, sir."

"Oh, I see. . . . Well, I suppose I must be going. She opens the door for him. "Good evening."

"Good evening, sir."

Master Wildman takes a long walk. Such a long walk he takes that he is not in for supper, which is taken by Elsie and her mother alone, in the Study.

"Allahabad Gentleman," says Master Wildman, towards the end of his walk. . . .

IV

It is half-past nine at night. There is no light in the house, save the little blue-and-yellow flare, quivering like a little blue-and-yellow flag, from the little bracket on the draughty top landing.

It is half-past nine at night. The front door is slammed.

Clock, Clock, Clock, in the hollow hall.

A door on the top landing faintly slams to, like a delayed, vague echo from the front door. . . .

Clock, Clock, Clock. . . . Clock. . . .

Clack, Clack, Clack, Clack—we're on the first flight—*Clack, Clack, Clack, Clack, Clack, Clack, Clack.* . . . The first landing. Clock, Clock, Clock—*Clack, Clack, Clack, Clack, Clack, Clack, Clack.* . . .

Master Wildman meets Elsie on the draughty top landing.

"Elsie!" whispers Master Wildman.

"Good-bye," whispers Elsie, and he has her hand. There is a pause.

"But I can't say good-bye now, Elsie. I simply can't. I'll be seeing you to-morrow. It'd be silly."

"Yes. I suppose it would."

"I can't help seeing you to-morrow, can I?"

"No. I suppose not. Good-bye." She releases her hand, and is in her room, with the door closed, before he can speak.

V

Master Wildman does not put in an appearance at breakfast the next morning—which is taken by Elsie and her mother alone. It is a bright, still Sabbath, and the sun glares into the dirty, dismantled rooms, in a dazzling way it never seems to have used before. Master Wildman is away all the morning, and returns with a bedroom and sitting-room in West Kensington, which will do for the time being. He does not know what he is going to do after that.

At three o'clock the rain sets in again, along with great gusts of wind.

"She says if you're coming with us," says Elsie, at six o'clock, "she'll go earlier. She says she won't speak to you, and she'll go earlier."

"Then she'll have to be quick," says Master Wildman. "I'm starting in half-an-hour."

And half-an-hour later Master Wildman and Elsie are on the way to the station together. Master Wildman holds Elsie's bag as well as his own. They have not a word to say to each other. It is quite dark by now.

They get into the train, the doors are rumbled to, and the journey is begun. There is a nun opposite, in spectacles, and a woman, and a little boy, who wants to know if he is going to be taken to see Charlie Chaplin. He spends his time between rushing to the door, crushing his nose against it, spectacled-nun-staring-at, and asking if he is going to be taken to see Charlie Chaplin. He must be still, like a good little boy.

Elsie throws her head back, crosses her hands over her bag, and looks at the advertisements. Master Wildman looks at her, and then looks in front of him. The train thunders on. Elsie looks at the advertisements, and Master Wildman looks

in front of him. Once he leans over and says: "All over,
Elsie," and Elsie doesn't quite hear.

"All over."

"Pardon?"

"All over. O, Vee, Ee, Ar!"

"Oh—yes."

"Like Mrs. Hoare. . . ."

"Yes."

Elsie throws back her head and looks at the advertisements.
Master Wildman looks in front of him. The little boy will
certainly not be taken to see Charlie Chaplin unless he is
still. The little boy is still. The train thunders on.

At Baron's Court, which is the last station before Kensington,
Master Wildman takes her hand. It is leathery and small
and soft in a brown kid glove. Elsie sits up a little, and looks
at him shyly, and then looks at the floor. Master Wildman
looks at the floor as well. The train thunders on. The
little boy stares at them. "Write, you know," says Master
Wildman. "Yes," says Elsie. The train flies in at West
Kensington station.

"Good-bye, Elsie," says Master Wildman, releases her hand,
and gets out. He stands on the platform, and looks through
the window. Elsie has her back to him and does not turn.
The little boy will *not* be taken to see Charlie Chaplin now.
The little boy screams. The train starts. Master Wildman
still stands on the platform. The train gathers speed, has
left Master Wildman in a flash, and the next moment is
thundering and crashing away to Charing Cross.

Master Wildman goes up the stairs to West Kensington.

VI

Master Wildman reaches his rooms—and his landlady, Mrs.
Madden, says she wouldn't have got much ready, like (it being
so sudden and the other gentleman only just out), that there
wouldn't be anything much In, owing to Sunday, and all shut,
excepting for a little bread and cheese, and that she's sure
he wouldn't mind giving her the Advance, like, which she
wouldn't ask for but for she's short this week, and she's
always made it a Point since one of her gentlemen ran off,
after being nigh five years with her.

Master Wildman's sitting-room wallpaper reiterates several

thousand glazed blue sailing ships in the light of a gas that roars and sputters away, like a long-winded giant with hay fever, breathing everlastingly through his nose; and his gas fire pops beautifully, but does not otherwise function. He refers this to Mrs. Madden, who blossoms out, after several more experienced popping manœuvres, with the announcement that it will have to be seen to, and her other gentleman had the same trouble. She then brings him his bread and cheese.

He can do very little with this, and after a long period spent in attempting to read "The Last of the Barons," which he has found on the sideboard, he goes up to his bedroom on the top floor. The bunches of violets that bend themselves over to him eternally and multitudinously on the wallpaper up here, give him no more—rather less—pleasure than the everlasting sailing fixtures downstairs. He puts out the light, thinking he may get to sleep early, and forget about them, but soon finds that this is not to be the case.

And the first hour he does not mind so much, for he is used to tossing about in the first hour ever since he has known Miss Cotterell. But it is not Miss Cotterell that turns him from one side of the pillow to another, to-night.

It is not Miss Cotterell to-night. It is not in fact any one or anything in particular, but simply a whirring selection of ridiculous dreams woven wildly from the material of his past. Sometimes it is his father, calling from illimitable distances. Sometimes it is Miss Cotterell's dog, which is lost in Gamages. Sometimes it is Mrs. Nixon, laughing "Heh, heh, heh!" Sometimes it is Elsie, in tears, saying "Thank you," and "Thank you," and "Thank you." Sometimes it is a pale lamp, burning steadily. Sometimes it is the Major again, wiping his moustache over his tea, and sitting down in a stormy sunset to play chess; and sometimes it is Mrs. Madden, on the sea front, railing at Miss Cotterell, with a brush in her hand; and it is all absurd sorts of things.

The second hour is even a little more absurd, though there is a main thread running through the second hour—a main thread—which is Elsie. And Elsie, it seems, is for ever in a train, which is for ever thundering and crashing away to Charing Cross—shrieking along the lines out into the night. Or Elsie is playing cards with him, at Craven House, and he suddenly rises and throws the whole pack in her face. And she looks so hurt. . . .

Or the English Channel is all frozen over, and he is a little
boy again, in his overcoat. . . . And the sun is setting on
serene mile after mile of even, frozen sea, and he is with his
school companions. He cries to them to come out on the
sea. "You can! You can!" he cries, but only a few of
them listen and he soon leaves them behind as he scuds out
at a flying pace. . . . And when he looks behind, the shore
is gone, and he stays still, and looks around at mile after
mist-lost mile of even, frozen sea, and knows he is lost. . . .
And all at once he hears a far, weak voice calling, and Elsie
is rushing out to him from the distance—a little girl in brown
stockings, waving an umbrella. . . . "You *would* come out
to me, you fool," he says. The next moment they are both
back at Craven House, in the drawing-room; and they are
both grown up again, and they are quarrelling. And suddenly
he turns upon her, spilling a vase. "All right, I'll marry
you, if I must!" he shouts. And she looks so very hurt.
And he entreats her not to look so hurt. "What have I
done?" she says. "What have I done? The vase is all
broke!" And she picks up the pieces, and he begs her not
to look so hurt, but he cannot marry her. . . .

And then he jumps out of bed, and sluices his face in the
water from the jug, and gets back again.

And so the third hour, which is the hour of two, begins.
And first of all it is a telegram he has sent to Elsie, and Mrs.
Nixon has got hold of it. Elsie knows nothing about it, and
Mrs. Nixon is showing it to Aunt Jessica, and tightening
her lips, and tearing it up, and throwing it into the fire with
"Heh, heh, heh!" Then it is another telegram, and then
it is another, and Mrs. Nixon treats them all the same way.
Then he sends a letter to Elsie, which Mrs. Nixon also gets,
and reads carefully, and stores away in the pocket of a red,
red petticoat. . . . And he sends twenty other letters, and
they are all stored away in the pocket of a red, red petticoat.
. . . And then he takes the train and asks the way to 6, Bath
Road, Holloway, and rings the bell. And Aunt Jessica comes
to the door, and directly she sees him, slams the door in
his face. He calls up at the windows for Elsie, but there is
no reply. . . . And he has lost Elsie for ever, and he writes
to Elsie, and waits for Elsie in Bath Road, Holloway, and
he looks for Elsie in the streets, but he never meets Elsie
again, in all his life. . . .

He advertises for Elsie. . . .

"Oh, do cut it out!" Master Wildman moans to himself, as he turns to the other side.

But there is only a red, red petticoat to taunt him the other side, and Master Wildman jumps up, and gives himself another sluicing, and makes a fresh start.

And now, out of the night, and the deadly hour of three, there comes another vision to Master Wildman, who lies very still. And it s a vision of Elsie. But it is not a speaking Elsie, or a piteous Elsie, or even a joyful Elsie, but simply Elsie with her brave, red head thrown back in the train, after all the stress of all the years at Craven House, and her weary but unregretting eyes upon the advertisements. And it grows and grows upon Master Wildman in the dark, and stays and stays; and "I *can't* marry you, Elsie," says Master Wildman, and it is there; and "I'll give you everything, Elsie, but *need* I marry you, please?" says Master Wildman, and it is still there, in all its unasking sorrow.

CHAPTER XII

The Lamp

I

WHAT it is that brings Master Wildman, on the very next day of his life, to Southam Green (of all places in the world), he has no manner of idea himself: but here he is, at the hour of five on a winter's afternoon, leaving the High Road for the quiet streets, in the direction of Craven House. He passes his old school, where a few little boys in red and green school caps are shrilly debating upon the ownership of cigarette cards; and he passes the Town Hall, and he takes to the streets that are quieter still, where the stark trees, newly clipped, stand against the evening sky like trees that are involved in an argument with each other, and are madly desirous of making so many points—each stumpy, naked branch being an irrefutable point. The whole of Southam Green is glistening, blue and dusky grey, in the rains that have never ceased to drizzle upon it since Craven House has fallen. Master Wildman has a vague sense of being thwarted

as he looks upon these quiet streets he knows so well. He
seeks some comment from the still houses, and the glistening
slates, and the wet, arguing trees—some comment which is
not forthcoming from those dispassionate immutabilities.

There is no sign of life about Craven House, and the lamp
opposite is already lit. It shines with livid tranquillity on
to windows that are already thickly begrimed—shines on,
suspendedly, as though some impenetrable and malevolent
forces have been caught unawares, and stay their silent
functioning as he goes by. The house itself has taken on
the abrupt repose of an ill thing—an ill thing that has dis-
gorged its contents. Master Wildman passes it by hurriedly
and with a sideways look.

By this time five has crept on to half-past five. All the
lamps are lit, and shine diminishingly along the twilit vistas
of the evening streets. Master Wildman still walks around,
and all at once stops, as it comes over him in a flash that
he still has his key, in his waistcoat pocket. He first of all
thinks the door will be bolted, and then he wonders how a
door is going to be bolted with no one inside, and then he
remembers that people generally go out of back doors on
such occasions. Then he wonders whether they have done
so on this occasion, and thinks he'll go and have a try. He
turns back and makes for Craven House.

With a soft, burning excitement upon him, that he cannot
understand, and tries to quell, he runs up the steps and
tries the key in the door.

For a moment Craven House looms in angry defiance over
him, expostulating through its front door lock at this outrage
of its final fastness: then the door gives, swings back, and
Master Wildman steps inside.

He closes the door, as an afterthought. . . .

He stands in the hall, in the mauve, palpable dusk, and
waits breathlessly for some reply. "And what now?"
whispers the first flight of stairs. "And what now?"

Master Wildman begins to whistle. But that is no reply
to the first flight of stairs, and it tells him as much.

Clock, Clock, Clock, suggests Master Wildman, and pauses.

The upper landings, door-quivering in a light gust of wind,
think nothing of that.

"Well, well," says Master Wildman, implying that two can
play at this game, and Clock, Clock, Clock, Clock, goes Master
Wildman, insolently.

But Craven House only echoes, under protest, and does not commit itself.

"Well, we'd better give you a look over," says Master Wildman.

He commences on the drawing-room, which is very dark, being at the back of the house and away from the lamp. By the window in here there is a little three-legged stool, which he has never seen before, and he wonders how on earth it got there. . . . The laurel bush outside is still pattering on; but it is grievously resigned now, and no more distressed over the new circumstances than it was over the old—though it always was an afflicted thing. He leaves this and goes into the dining-room. This still holds the last light of the day, struggling with the insinuations of the watery lamp, and he does not stay a moment there.

He comes out into the hall, and decides upon the kitchen, which he has never been into since he was a very little boy. He goes as quietly as possible down the basement stairs.

Here is the servant's sitting-room, with nothing in it but a fireplace. . . .

Here is the cellar, with nothing in it but shelves. . . .

Here is the Kitchen, with the oven (he had forgotten there would be an oven)—the cold, black, ash-sprinkled over, with dampers communicating mysteriously with the tank and bath upstairs. . . .

The larder—this was all Edith's realm, wasn't it—the larder, with nothing in it but a splodge of cold gravy grease, and a tin grating for a window, and a vague smell of cheese. . . .

And here is the scullery, the desolate scullery, with one potato peeling in the sink, and a piece of blue, and—what is this?—an old medicine bottle labelled "The Mixture." To be taken three times daily, before meals. Master Wildman holds this and looks at it for some time, and then puts it very quietly down. He goes upstairs.

It is quite dark now in the hall, and he climbs the stairs and tries the Spicers' door, which is, strangely, locked. So he tries Miss Hatt's door, which is locked as well.

He looks into the bathroom, and at the bath, which is monstrous and stagnant, under a dirty white sheet.

He cannot leave without going upstairs, and he takes the second landing, whistling courageously against something that

is falling upon him in spite of himself, falling in and in upon
him with the night outside. And he goes into Mrs. Hoare's
room, which was once his father's room, and where there is
nothing but a large sack, which alarms him at first, but which,
he discovers, contains nothing but wood shavings. "Where
on earth have *they* come from?" says Master Wildman, and
starts whistling again, and goes out. He goes out, and he
enters Elsie's room.

And at the sight of Elsie's room, which is the quietest,
smallest, and most unasking of them all (like her own self),
and with the lamp-light shining up upon the wall and ceiling,
like a frail, silver ghost of her; and at the memory of Elsie, as
she moved about in it, warming it with her own thoughts,
and her own senseless and serious little pre-occupations,
Master Wildman knows himself for a fool in ever having
started to walk this gallery of shades, and he needs Elsie
more than he ever dreamed he could need her, more than
he dares allow that he needs her—Elsie, who knows about
it all,

For all at once he knows the whole emptied house for what
it is. He knows the desolate message of the resigned laurel
pattering in upon the drawing-room downstairs, where once
coarse laughter pealed up to him (with Elsie) from the ladies
and gentlemen at their cards; he knows the desolate message
of the kitchen below, with its dark, iron oven, for ever closed
to the hands that opened and slammed it, in the resounding
days gone by. And he knows how the sack lies in the room
where his father died, and how the sheet lies on the bath,
where the ladies and gentlemen sang songs of cleanliness for
dinner at eight o'clock. And he knows, above all, how each
and every hollow apartment has waited for this issue, com-
muning with the lamp outside, which now shines in with
level, silver, and irretrievable triumph. And "Elsie!" he
says, and can stand up against it no longer, and makes his
way quietly and quickly down the blackened landings, and
goes (he doesn't know why at all), into the drawing-room.
And "Elsie!" he cries, for she is there.

She is sitting on the stool—she has not heard him—her
hat is off, and her face is in her hands. She looks up in the
dark, and it is wet with tears. He knows her face is wet
with tears.

"Elsie!" says Master Wildman. "Elsie!"

"Yes?"

"Elsie, dear! I knew you'd come. I knew you must come."

Elsie makes no reply at all, but begins to cry again.

"Oh, Elsie. Thank God you've come. Don't cry. I've been looking it over. Elsie. . . ."

"I had the key," says Elsie, in between her sobs; and "Oh, I am glad. I am glad," says Master Wildman.

"I've been looking it over," says Master Wildman. "You haven't seen it, have you? Have you seen it, Elsie, dear?"

"I know," sobs Elsie. "I know."

"But don't cry, Elsie. It doesn't matter now, does it?"

"Does it, Elsie?"

"No."

There is a silence.

Elsie is heard pronouncing the word "Reminds" between her sobs. . . .

"Reminds? Reminds what?"

"When you told me—the story," says Elsie. "In the dark."

"Story? Why, yes. So I did. So I did."

"Yes," says Elsie.

There is a long silence.

"Elsie, dear," says Master Wildman softly, but there is no reply.

"Elsie, dear," says Master Wildman, urgently. "Elsie!"

"Elsie!" whispers Master Wildman, and kneels down by her stool. "Elsie, dear—Elsie! I've got another story now!

"I've got another story, Elsie. Would you care to hear it?"

"What?"

"Ghost or Detective, Elsie?"

"Oh, please . . ." says Elsie.

"Or another kind of story, Elsie?"

"Whichever you like," moans Elsie.

"Shall I begin, Elsie?" says Master Wildman, and takes her small gloved hand. "Shall I begin?"

"Yes."

"Elsie, I do hope it won't bore you, but there was once a Young Man."

"Was there?"

"Yes. There was. And what do you think happened, Elsie?"

"I don't know," says Elsie, and attends to her face with the palm of her hand.

"What do you think happened, Elsie? . . . Well, I don't quite know what happened. But anyway, there was a Young Girl in it somehow, Elsie. And what do you think she looked like?"

"I don't know," says Elsie.

"Unspeakably beautiful, Elsie. Like a dawn—or a twilight —or like all the dawns or all the twilights that ever were. And why was she so like a dawn, Elsie?"

"I don't know."

"Because her hair was red, Elsie."

"Was it?"

"Yes. It was. Very red. But that's not in the story, Elsie," says Master Wildman, but contradicts that assertion by putting up his hand and slowly passing it over the red hair of his very audience. "Very red," says Master Wildman. "But that's not in the story. What do you think happened next, Elsie?"

"I don't know."

"Can't you guess?"

"No."

"Try."

"I don't know."

"Why, they had a Love Scene, Elsie."

"Did they?"

"Yes. They had a Love Scene. They *did*. Because they could. Because they were alone in an empty house, and they had a Love Scene."

Elsie is heard weakly protesting that they didn't.

"But am I telling this story, or are you, Elsie?" protests Master Wildman. "I ought to know, didn't I?"

But Elsie is heard weakly protesting that they didn't.

"But they did, Elsie, they did, I tell you!" exclaims Master Wildman, and then he moves much closer to Elsie, and begins to whisper. "Elsie, dear, need I go on? I needn't go on, need I?"

"Elsie," says Master Wildman. . . . An immense silence falls upon them.

When Master Wildman speaks again, his voice comes through like a voice in a dream.

"Oh, Elsie," says Master Wildman, "I do love you so!"

Elsie is heard feebly, very feebly, and very distantly, protesting that he doesn't.

"Oh, Elsie, will you marry me, please? I know I don't deserve it, but will you marry me, please?"

"I can't. I can't," says Elsie.

"Oh, Elsie, don't, please, say that. Why can't you?"

Elsie does not reply.

"Why can't you, Elsie?"

Elsie takes a long time before she can utter her objection, but at last comes out with it.

"I don't think you would Like it," says Elsie.

"She doesn't think he'd like it!" echoes Master Wildman, in ecstasies. "She doesn't think he'd like it! She doesn't think he'd like it! Oh, Elsie. Please."

"But you wouldn't," says Elsie. "Would you?"

"Oh, Elsie, dear, I *would* Like it. I *would* Like it. How can I prove to you how much I'd Like it?"

There is a pause in which Elsie looks miserably at the floor.

"You like Her," says Elsie, softly, and turns quickly away.

"Like her, Elsie?" says Master Wildman, again in a dream. "I may have once thought I did. Even till lately. But I don't now. And I never liked her—as I like you. I love you, Elsie. Please."

But Elsie will not be touched now.

"Well, we've proved we would Like it, Elsie. Are there any more objections?"

There is no reply.

"Any more objections, please?"

There is no reply.

"Perhaps my Fortune's not enough for you, Elsie. But I'm really getting on, and so you must be awfully mercenary. I've had a letter from Layburn only this morning, and he's fixed for Town in March, and there's six more dates before that, Birmingham and five more others, and there's a Mr. Harlan who wants it for America. . . ."

"Oh, you are silly. . . ."

"Ah, but you can't answer Birmingham and Mr. Harlan, Elsie. You *must* be schemer, after all.

"Any more objections, Elsie?"

Elsie again pauses for some time before delivering herself of her next objection.

"I think you would be making a Mistake," says Elsie.

Which throws Master Wildman into more dazzled ecstasies. "A Mistake! She thinks he would be Making a Mistake! A Mistake! A Mistake!'

"A Mistake, Elsie," says Master Wildman, in humorous appeal, and Elsie herself cannot help smiling a little, but still under protest.

"A Mistake, Elsie," says Master Wildman, as though this is the last straw, and Elsie smiles weakly again.

"Of course, it's very Complimentary," says Elsie.

"Complimentary!" groans Master Wildman. "Complimentary! It's very Complimentary! Oh, Elsie! that's the best of the lot, isn't it?"

And now Elsie is altogether smiling, but she is altogether crying, as well, and the mixture is an engaging one.

"And Thoughtful," says Elsie, and "Thoughtful! Thoughtful! Thoughtful!" moans Master Wildman.

And in the next ten minutes Elsie makes many other comments on the situation, and each one is greeted with such moanings of ecstatic applause, and it seems to please him so much, that she goes on making them, with a smiling and swimming air of surpassing herself in ridiculousness. And Elsie admits that (if one must argue on such silly lines) she has quite a nice little bit of money of her own, now she's twenty-one, about two hundred a year, which her mother's never told her about, and Aunt Jessica let it out last night. And at last Elsie can contain herself no longer, and "Oh, I do like you! I do like you!" she bursts out, and "Quiet, Elsie," whispers Master Wildman. "Or you'll wake the dead."

"The dead?" asks Elsie, and rises, and takes his hand.

"Yes. The dead," says Master Wildman. "I'll show you. You haven't been over here as I have."

He leads her to the door.

"I wonder what this place is really and truly trying to say, Elsie? There's something there, but I can't get clean at it. I don't think it's anything about us."

"*I* think it's smiling," says Elsie.

"No. It's not smiling. Or it may be smiling at us. But I don't believe it's thinking of us. It hasn't caught us. It's the others, Elsie, it's the others. It hasn't cottoned on to us."

"No, perhaps it hasn't," says Elsie.

"No. It's the others. I thought it was a comedy, Elsie. I thought it was a silly comedy. I thought it was all so funny. . . . But it's not now, Elsie, now it's over—now they've all gone away. . . .

"Fifteen years," says Master Wildman. "That's getting on for a quarter century. . . . And after all that noise, and all that silly laughter, and all that aching politeness and cheerfulness, they've gone away and left it to itself. Drawing-room. . . . What happened here. What on earth didn't happen here?"

"Lots of things," says Elsie, not quite able, perhaps, to cope with these solemnities.

"Do you remember when I Showed you the Joke?" says Master Wildman. "On the first night of all? Years and years ago? When we all came into the fire in here, and I Showed you the Joke? L. C. for Elsie. That was a great joke, wasn't it, Elsie?"

"I remember," says Elsie. "And that makes me think of something."

"What's that, Elsie?"

"If you do—" says Elsie, "If you do"—but she cannot quite bring the word out—"if you do what you say to me," she achieves at last. "My name wouldn't be Nixon any more, would it?"

"So it wouldn't, Elsie. And I hope it won't be by the time the week's out."

"But it will be so nice, won't it! It'll be so nice, being together. I've thought about it such a lot!"

"I hardly dare think how Nice it'll be, Elsie. And just supposing that one of us had been walking this place alone, Elsie. Just think of it!"

"Yes," says Elsie. "And I wonder something."

"What do you wonder, Elsie?" says Master Wildman, taking hold of her again.

"If you——" Elsie is again in difficulties—"if you *feel* things towards me——"

"And I do feel things towards you, Elsie. Very strong things."

"If you feel things towards me," says Elsie, struggling with her question. "When did you *first* begin to feel them?"

"That's difficult. But do you know when I think it was?"

"When?"

"Weird moment, but I believe it was when you first came forward when Mrs. Hoare was in that mad hat, and you said 'I'll have a try.'"

"Why then?"

"Because it was so like you, Elsie, so like you, to say you would have a try, quietly like that. It was Elsie from beginning to end."

"Was it?"

"Oh, I do love you, Elsie!"

"But do you feel——"

"Love. Adore. Worship. Idolise."

"Love then——" Elsie grants him—"Me—because I was Nice, like that, in that way—or because I was, am, was, a little *prettier*, than I used to be?"

"I love you, Elsie, a good deal because you were Nice like that—but principally, principally because you are so perfectly pretty."

Which seems to give Elsie by far the greater satisfaction of the two, for her eyes are suddenly bright, like jewels in the dark, and she leans up and kisses him on the mouth.

"Talking of being reliable," says Elsie, after an interval, "I remember now that I came over here to see Ernie."

"Ernie? Ernie? What is this?"

"I promised I would go to his concert, didn't I?"

"Ernie? Ernie? Fiend! Coquette! Tormentor! Ernie! In my arms, and to remind me of Ernie! Elsie, you're cruel, you're too cruel!"

"Oh, I'm not. You know I'm not!"

"Yes. I know you're not, Elsie. I know you're not. And I don't grudge it of Ernie. Poor, unblessed Ernie. You must hear Ernie's voice, miserable victim that he is. And then we'll go and have dinner together, shall we, Elsie? We'll wire your mother, and have dinner together, shall we?"

"Yes. Yes."

"And as the time's getting on, we'd better not stand here any longer, but get along," says Master Wildman, and he again embraces Elsie.

They go out into the hall.

"Listen," says Master Wildman, and "Listen. Just to think that we laughed. Listen!"

They stand in the hall for a moment or two, in the last dead immobility of Craven House. And out of the silence neither a gust nor a quiver, nor even the sound of the laurel pattering at the drawing-room window, gives answer to their mute enquiry. And yet this silence is not a silence; for it is a cry, an ultimate, distant, echoing cry from all the quelled voices that have laughed in it, and all the poor gay scenes that have been staged in it, and all the tears and crying that have never shaken it, in its dark, stumbling quest in eternity.

"Open the door, Elsie," says Master Wildman.

Elsie goes softly to the door, and opens it. A faint, blurred sound from the street is wafted in.

"Wider, Elsie," says Master Wildman, and the quiet evening sounds come more clearly through.

Master Wildman goes to the door. "You close it, Elsie," says Master Wildman. "I think that's your job, some-how. . . ."

"Very well," says Elsie. "I will."

Master Wildman runs down the steps, and stays by the gate, where the yellow lamp-light falls, soft as velvet upon the thickening night. He looks up to Elsie to close the door.

Elsie pauses. She looks down at him, looks up at the first-floor window, looks quickly into the hall. Then she takes the knob, and pulls it slowly to. There is a little click, and it is over.

"Settles you," whispers Elsie.

She stops for just a moment to fasten her little brown glove in the light of the lamp. She fixes it to her liking; and then, lifting her head very high and without ever a look back, joins Master Wildman at the gate.

THE END